LIBERTY FARM

Dean Biddulph

Liberty Farm
libertyfarmbook.com
@libertyfarmbook

written by Dean Biddulph
©2020

edited by Alex James
alexjameseditor.co.uk

graphics by Kim Ho
@kimho.art

part of The Happy Caterpillar community
thehappycaterpillar.com
@rawsomethc

To Kimbo,
You make my dreams come true.

This book is a work of fiction.
Let us wake up before it becomes a reality.

1

It was the first time that Christopher had finished work before seven in as long as he could remember, though he was hardly pleased. He was far too confused by what he had seen and concerned at what it meant.

Senior Override—the words had flashed red over his liberscreen, as he was locked out from the system.

"Christopher 165-189-198," a calm robotic voice spoke directly into the audio receiver in his ear, so that no one else around could hear. "A senior systems monitor has overridden your observations. You are relieved of your duties for the day and free to leave your workstation. Christopher 165-189-198. A senior systems monitor has overridden your observations. You are relieved of your duties for the day and free to leave your workstation ..."

Now, heading for the exit port on the way out of the Systems Monitoring Department, he felt alone and uneasy. Was it his mistake, he wondered? Should he have reacted quicker?

There was just a single liberbot guarding the port at this time. The tall white android seemed to stare at him as he approached, though it had no eyes on its faceless head. Christopher felt a flush of blood warm his cheeks. Such an extreme show of emotion, he thought, would be hidden from any human eyes by the liberskin that enveloped him head to foot, though the liberbot could surely easily detect such things as a fluctuating body temperature and Christopher's elevated heart rate. Still, the light at the top of the tall triangular archway that marked the entrance to the port platform flashed blue as he passed underneath and he was allowed to travel freely.

He stepped through the translucent shimmering surface of the front of the liberport and took a solitary seat inside the cylindrical space within, which he was used to seeing crammed with co-workers. The front wall appeared to thicken and shimmer more, sparks of color flickering until the Systems Monitoring

Department he had just departed completely disappeared. A slow low whirring sound began then built in circles with an increasing rhythm, then a high pitched frequency that threatened every time to pierce his eardrums. And then silence, simultaneous to a bright white light that shattered the whole surrounding reality before the world outside slowly reappeared. *Hospitality Department,* a voice announced.

The Hospitality Department was an area designated for drinking and eating, where Christopher chose to spend most of his evenings. It was filled with an array of bars and restaurants, of various styles and price ranges, ready to cater to anyone's needs. It was usually beginning to be busy by the time he arrived, with fellow dorms on their way to unwind after work, but today it seemed eerily empty. His footsteps echoed off the shining streets beneath him. He looked up to see that the libersphere high above, the protective dome of nanobots that enclosed the entirety of the West, still glowed a clear blue. In the liberscreens that warped and curled themselves around the skyline of tall buildings, he saw the face of the Writer, the creator of Liberty Farm and savior of its many millions of residents. Chiseled, stern and now becoming wrinkled, he seemed to stare down at the lonely Christopher walking below.

He arrived at his favorite bar. Its name—Body—curled in large dark blue italic letters against a clean pale blue wall; the *B* leaning backward and shaped in such a way as to subtly resemble a curvaceous female form. As he approached the entrance, he heard the calming melody of the bar's own audioprogramming begin in his receiver.

"Good evening, Christopher," an alluring female voice said. There was no one physically there to greet him; the bar was entirely automated. "Come inside and make yourself comfortable."

He always did feel comfortable here; never too busy, but just enough people to allow him to blend in to the background. It would be empty now, as the first dorm to finish work and arrive at the bar that day, but not for long. He walked through the dim blue-lit hallway, lined with voluptuous sculptures and hourglass-shaped urns and vases, and turned right toward the main seating area.

He stopped suddenly, heat rising in his face once again, seeing that he was not alone as he had expected. There sat at a round table in the middle of the room were three troubleshooters, each strapped tightly into their navy uniforms, crimson capes hung over their broad shoulders and matching caps on their heads, their six eyes staring back at him.

He had done nothing wrong—as far as he knew—other than to walk in and inadvertently interrupt their conversation. But he could not help but feel gripped by fear in their presence, such was their ruthless reputation. Troubleshooters were the elite security force in the farm, tasked to track down hackers or any other potential threat to the Program, equipped with all the same sorts of scanners as liberbots and who-knew-what other mind-reading capabilities. Christopher couldn't calculate whether it would be more conspicuous to stay and sit down or turn around and walk away.

He had never seen troubleshooters in Body before, but more shocking still was the appearance of the middle one of the three. *A black troubleshooter?* He asked the question in his own head so suddenly he worried he might have spilled it out loud. The black troubleshooter stared back through dark eyes, his face worn yet striking, towering several inches over his two white colleagues sat either side of him.

"Sit," a deep voice sounded in Christopher's head. It was not a robotic voice like at work or the liberport, nor the female voice of Body's virtual hostess. It was certainly a man's voice, but none of the troubleshooters' lips moved. Still, he felt compelled to move to a small table at the side of the room.

"How can I be of service?" the virtual hostess said. Up from Christopher's table sprung a holographic menu for his perusal. Normally he would simply speak his choice out loud, but today he thought it best to stay silent and avoid disrupting the troubleshooters any further. He flicked through options with his fingertips, his liberskin stimulating his nerve endings to give a tactile impression. He selected his favorite dish at Body—spaghetti libernara—and watched as its digital image was gradually replaced by its physical form, printed directly to his table in a matter of seconds. He glanced toward the troubleshooters to see that they were now back in conversation and paying him little attention, then began to eat.

Curling the creamy spaghetti around his fork and into his mouth, he soon began to lose himself in the audioprogramming running through his receiver—a sultry sounding singer moaning meaninglessly over a calming melody—until it suddenly stopped, midway through his meal. And he could hear the conversation of the troubleshooters.

"So do you think it's true?" one of them asked. Christopher could see from the corner of his eye that it was one of the white men. He appeared the older of the two, his face masked by a thick but sharply groomed brown beard. "Do you think they could come up with something as sophisticated as this?"

Christopher slapped the side of his own head, as if his audio receiver had fallen loose—though it never had before—hoping to restore its function.

"It is not my job," the black man said, "to think about the hypothetical sophistication of hackers as spoken of in rumor. It is my job to base my ongoing investigations of the hacker enemy on actual evidence."

There was no use. Christopher couldn't help but overhear. He continued to eat so as not to make it too obvious.

"Be that as it may," said the other white man. He was blond and appeared younger than his two colleagues. "You must have some thought as to whether they are capable of this, particularly as the threat we are describing is by its very nature almost impossible to evidence."

"The threat that you are describing," the black man said, "may be impossible to evidence given that it is based on rumor. And should actual evidence of such a threat resembling the rumor become apparent, I am sure we will uncover whatever threat there is and exterminate it."

There was a pause in which all that Christopher heard was his own awkward slurp of spaghetti, before the bearded man eventually spoke again.

"Ok, look, now we of course are always confident in our power to eliminate whatever threat the hacker enemy may come up with. It has been our power to do so since the Program was first established and since the first technological attempts to jeopardize it were conceived. But the threat that is being spoken of is a kind of which we have never heard of before. This kind of collective hacking of BRAINs in hibernation makes it untraceable yet potentially so contagious. It is a threat that would create who-knows-what kind of problems for the Program and for the farm if it spread, perhaps even as much as dyspheria itself—"

"Dyspheria is," the black man said, "always was and always will be the single greatest threat against the farm and against humanity, until the day we eliminate it once and for all. And until that day that alone will remain our highest goal."

Christopher swallowed a heavy mouthful that seemed to stick in his throat for a moment on the way down. *Dyspheria is, always was and always will be the greatest threat to humanity.* It didn't need a troubleshooter to know that, nor even a systems monitor like him. It was not only known throughout the farm but lived to this day by all its residents, still affected by the disease more than a century after the Outbreak. Just as the devastation of the Last War of Nations was coming to an end, it was unleashed by an unknown enemy and plunged the remaining population into the deepest deadliest fear: First delusions, hallucinations and paranoia, then the psychogenic pain that turned the victims completely insane. They became violent without control and then, worst of all, they began to eat one another's flesh.

He stared at what was left of his spaghetti, losing his appetite as the familiar images of life before the farm flicked through his head. *Zombies*, he shuddered.

"Come now," the bearded troubleshooter said to the others. "It's nearly seven. We'd better leave before any more dorms arrive."

The three cloaked figures stood in unison and headed toward the exit, the two white men leading the way. The third, black troubleshooter, walked a little slower and paused directly in front of Christopher as he passed, turning his head to look down at him. He sat frozen in the man's huge shadow, jaw hanging helplessly, gripped by the fear of what deep dark intention—unknown even to him—the troubleshooter might detect. He could see now that the troubleshooter's otherwise perfectly chiseled face was spoiled only by a deep old scar carved across his left eye, from his forehead to his cheek. Christopher stared at the scar, and the troubleshooter stared at him. But after a moment, he followed his colleagues out the hallway, and the audioprogramming returned once again to Christopher's receiver.

"Are you satisfied?" the virtual hostess asked.

"Y-yes," he said, still confused as to what had just happened.

The top of the table opened up and what was left of Christopher's dinner disappeared down the chute for libercycling.

"Something to wash your dinner down?"

"Yes," he said. "Libeer."

He watched as a tall bottle materialized from bottom to top on the coaster at the edge of the table. Midway up on its face was printed the same logo that he had seen a million times, today and every other day, on every street he ever walked and every product he ever bought: A red *L,* a blue *F,* and two correspondingly colored halves of a triangle that dared never touch to complete.

He barely heard the muttering of more customers, over his own audioprogramming, as they came into the bar: two men who looked like senior systems monitors, two older well-dressed women, then another man who appeared to be on his own. They made their way to their respective tables without paying him the slightest notice. He gripped the ice-cold libeer bottle and raised it to his lips.

He took a hefty tasteless swig and swallowed, and sure enough soon followed the familiar flow of liberhol working its way around his system. However many millions of libertons—the fundamental particle, the elixir of life—let loose in his body, transported quickly to his BRAINs (biotechnological reproductive artificially intelligent nanobots), triggering a domino-like ripple of reward responses and subtle delirium that he had become all too accustomed to and left him unfortunately unimpressed.

More dorms continued to come, slowly filling the bar.

What were the troubleshooters doing there, and what was this new threat—this new hack against the Program—that they discussed? He continued to drink, as his mind began to wander.

He had heard that there were all kinds of malevolent hacking going on around the farm, either to disrupt the BRAINs to produce some kind of altered state or experience, or otherwise steal another's liberos, but he assumed those hacks were only used by or against one person at a time. What was this collective hacking that the troubleshooters spoke about? Was it a means to steal from or hack into the BRAINs of many people at once? Or a means for a group of hackers to experience some shared altered state collectively? He had no idea what that could even mean.

And what about hacking into BRAINs in hibernation? Why would anyone want to do such a thing? He thought that hackers were either interested in some sensory pleasure or libernomic gain and there were surely neither to be gained during hibernation—when residents docked overnight, unconsciously uploading their daily data to, and downloading updates from, the mainframe. It seemed pointless to him that anyone would want to hack or tamper with such a mundane and forgettable process. But the way the troubleshooters spoke about it, and in particular how even the black man seemed so reluctant to discuss it, stirred in him some sense of trepidation.

His thoughts were suddenly interrupted, along with Body's audioprogramming, by a familiar fanfare. It sounded like a cross between an action movie soundtrack and a liberwedding march. He saw his fellow customers all stop their meals and conversations to watch as the wall at the far-end of the room transformed into a large holographic liberscreen. He quickly finished what was left of his bottle, placed it on the coaster and tapped twice for a refill.

"A lifetime of struggle ... " an unnamed male announcer said. Images of a cold grey cityscape covered by clouds of pollution; dark-skinned men doing manual labor outdoors; riots in streets filled with sirens and smashed windows.

"A history of horrors ... " Women and children crying; soldiers firing round after round at rampaging zombies; a nuclear mushroom cloud erupting over a dark landscape.

"Almost a hundred years ago humanity stood on the brink of extinction ... " Ferocious fires; blood on the ground; body after body after body.

"But we were saved by the genius of the Writer... " The stern but reassuring face of the Writer filled the screen, cold eyes piercing through everyone in the room, appearing not as the young man he was at the time of the Outbreak, but the elder paternal figure he had since become.

"Saved by advanced technology that would supersede our primitive instincts and guarantee our safety ... " Close-up images of the microscopic BRAINs managing the movement of molecules inside someone's mind; a circle of suited men smiling and shaking hands in front of a shower of camera flashes, laborbots building homes and roads at rapid pace.

"Together now and forever we look toward a brighter future ... " Images of immaculate emune residents eating in lavish restaurants and laid relaxing in luxurious locations; their tall towers floating over the farm. Then more elaborate lighting effects synchronized to the soundtrack culminating in the red and blue halves of the same logo on Christopher's libeer: The libertree— the symbol of the red bloodshed of life before the farm, and the

cool blue control of the Program—coming together from opposite sides almost to meet in the middle of the liberscreen. Letters appearing below as the announcer finished with the familiar slogan.

"Liberty Farm: Working For Your Future."

The music faded out as the libertree made way for the appearance of another face that resembled a younger, smiling version of the Writer. Indeed it was his clone and intended successor, leader of the blue party and incumbent Prime Resident, Dean Perish.

"Good evening residents," said Perish.

"Good evening," said the customers of Body. They all echoed Perish, except Christopher.

"I hope you don't mind me dropping in on your dinner, but I thought I should just remind you—though I'm sure you already know—that the liberlection assessments are just around the corner, so if you haven't already decided your favorite—guess what—you're looking at him right now!" Perish laughed, along with everyone else, except Christopher. The picture on the liberscreen zoomed out to reveal Perish in his full length, looking sharp as ever with neat dark hair, suit and blue tie. "But joking aside, the serious truth is that I, Dean Perish, alongside the Writer, am the one that has kept you safe these past years and the only one that can guarantee your safety for years to come—with a final solution to destroy dyspheria, which will be just around the corner when I'm re-elected. So remember, if you want to stay sane …"

"It's got to be Dean!" Christopher completed the last line he had heard every night for the past few weeks, though much less enthusiastically than everyone else in the bar. He watched as the other customers raised their thumbs on their right hands, directing a shower of likes toward the Prime Resident, reflected in a flurry of blue upward pointing triangles floating up the screen, sent from residents all over the farm.

"Dean to destroy dyspheria!" A crowd of residents appeared behind Perish on the liberscreen, chanting his slogan, with the customers of Body joining in. "Dean to destroy dyspheria! Dean to destroy dyspheria ..."

Then another face appeared on screen, of a mousy middle-aged man, as the chants in the bar fell into low grumbles at the appearance of the red party leader Morty Caine. They pointed their thumbs down, adding to the shower of red downward pointing triangles on screen.

"Good evening," said Caine. He received no further audible response in Christopher's vicinity. "This is Morty Caine, leader of the red party. I'm speaking to you today to remind you that I am a viable alternative to the rule of Perish and that change is in our power." A couple of boos rung around the bar. "I urge the dormant residents especially to recognize this opportunity and support me, as the symps are already doing. Perish has continued to look after the interests of the well-off, but he has done little—"

The screen switched back suddenly, cutting Caine off mid-speech, to the scenes of Perish and his crowd of chanting supporters. "Dean to destroy dyspheria. Dean to destroy dyspheria ..." The customers in Body joined in once again; except Christopher, all seemingly oblivious to the sudden cutting off of the red party leader, or even that he had appeared on screen at all.

"Liberty Farm: Working For Your Future." The red and blue libertree logo appeared once more before the liberscreen closed down, and the customers returned to their drinks and dinners.

Christopher downed a large portion of his second libeer. He could hardly care less about the liberlections; the same old political back and forth between the red party and the blue party that he could barely tell apart that seemed to fight for libervision coverage more than anything that actually mattered, and had been won—one way or another—by the same man for so many years now. But he did feel a certain loathing for Dean Perish, after all these years seeing his face plastered all over the place.

It was his entitlement—that was the word—to a life and a role he had never had to work for, but had been groomed and provided the perfect upbringing to reach, that Christopher didn't like. It was the struggle to survive before Liberty Farm ever existed, the horrors of life before the Unification, that understanding of the depths as well as the heights of humanity that inspired the Writer to create and continue to maintain the Program, which Perish knew little about. It was the struggle for rehabilitation, *Working For Your Future,* that a modern dorm like Christopher experienced every day and that he felt put him at polar opposite to the most privileged Perish.

Only now, nearing the end of his second drink, did he recollect and reflect on the day's work and how he had ended up at the bar so early that evening.

Today, like many days recently, he had mostly been assigned to observing service symps around the mine—where materials collected from the outside world by drones were gathered, cleansed and deconstructed by the massive particle liberator into pure, uncontaminated libertons; where the building blocks of life were disassembled to be stored and put to optimal use in the farm. He had watched on screen from his workstation in the Systems Monitoring Department, observing the behavior and psychological stability of symps in the area, making minor adjustments to their antivirus—AV—levels as needed.

It was following one such delivery that chaos suddenly broke out, as a number of service symps abandoned their work to watch—and he watched on screen to see the cause of the commotion—as a small white thing jumped out from the load on the conveyor belt, just before it could be liberated, scuttled around the floor for a moment and then straight out through the libersphere; the only entrance and exit to the farm, normally crossed only by drones and machines.

He had never seen such a thing, and neither had the symps working around the mine. It must have been less than a minute, but perhaps not quick enough for him to realize what was happening and send quick boosts of AV directly to the symps' BRAINs, before a bunch of liberbots burst into the area to restore order. But he could also detect his own elevated excitation, and so too could whoever was observing him. *Senior Override*—the words flashed red over his liberscreen, and in his head now once again. Had he been too slow to react? What on earth was that thing that scuttled around the mine? And what might it mean?

He tapped his bottle for two more refills before losing count.

2

"Eight-point-five," the virtual hostess said in his receiver. "The time is eight-point-five. Residents are politely asked to finish their drinks and return to their homes by nine for hibernation. Return to your home by nine for hibernation."

He sat up straight in his chair, not realizing he had been slumping over his table. He had lost track of time as well as the number of libeers he had drunk. His BRAINs felt fuzzy. The bar was nearly empty, and so too was his bottle.

And then his eyes fell across her—a woman sat alone at a small table across the room. She wasn't the most attractive woman he had seen that night, by conventional standards, but there was something striking about her. She had long curly red hair, which itself was rare to be seen; most women opted for more desirable colors. He thought for a moment that he might have liked to reproduce with her, as she displayed some positive genetic characteristics: She was slim; although who wasn't these days; reasonably tall for a woman, and indeed quite pretty. Of course he wasn't interested in approaching her; he had no interest in reproducing any time soon and besides, when he did, he would hope it would be with a certified positive libergenic match.

No, it was something else about her that drew his attention, and as she took a slow sip from her glass he realized, it was her drink. No not her drink itself—her red wine looked much like anyone else's—but the color that seemed to float around outside of it. A hue that enveloped her hand and her chest and her face; it was a shade so unusual he could barely think to give it a name. It looked a little bit like the pale blue vapor that emitted from a liberette, except it wasn't that color, and she wasn't vaping at all. It was a color that was so strange compared to the reds and blues he had seen all day that seemed to somehow unify the two and all the feelings that both invigorated in him.

He wasn't sure he had even seen the color at all before and yet it felt so familiar, and from somewhere the word popped into his head—violet. And just as soon as the word came to him, her eyes fell on his—two deep brown pools in a forest of curls. The strange color seemed to radiate over her entire being. Like a halogenic glow it seemed to breathe its way across the walls behind her and over their surroundings, until all that he knew was that he was staring across the room at this woman who was staring back at him through a haze of—yes—violet. What was that she was drinking? And how many libeers had he drunk to see such a thing that evening?

But just as quickly as the moment arrived, she rose from her seat and rushed for the exit, leaving a trail of color floating behind her. In a rush of curiosity, Christopher gulped down the last of his libeer and followed in the hope that he could continue to savor this sweet color sensation. Almost toppling a sculpture as he stumbled through the hallway, he fumbled its hard breasts to straighten it back on its stand, before heading for the door.

Stepping outside he turned first to the right to see no sign of her, then turned to the left just quickly enough to see her turning a corner. He took after her, not knowing why or what he would say if he were to catch up. His footsteps echoed off the deserted streets. He looked up to see that the center of the libersphere was now red, spreading quickly outwards across the entirety of the West. He should get home soon, but first he had to see her.

He turned down the passage he had seen her enter and stopped as he saw her remarkable appearance ahead of him. Her shape silhouetted against the scarlet backdrop of the glow from the libersphere, but around her still was that mysterious violet mist. Her left arm extended away from her body, she held in her hand a small rectangular object—indistinguishable at this distance and darkness—dropping it deliberately for him to see, then turning and walking away.

"Wait!" he said. He started to walk after her again. But before he had taken two more steps he stopped, as the scarlet night was split by two white figures. Liberbots—two of them appeared from opposite sides of another passage that bisected the one on which Christopher stood, surrounding the woman. They picked her up from her feet swiftly and silently carried her out of view, the violet color disappearing along with her.

Christopher froze, trying, failing, to work out what had just happened. Eventually he plucked up the courage to walk toward the spot where the woman had stood. She and the two liberbots were gone and all that remained was the small object on the floor that she had dropped. He could only make out its dark outline, as he bent down to pick it up, only becoming clearer as he stood and lifted it toward the red glow of the sphere. It was a book.

Without thinking, he shoved the object inside his jacket and under his armpit, and started a lopsided jog toward the liberport.

"Eight-point-eight." A liberbot called as he approached the port. "Last port at eight-point-nine. Move it, dorm!"

He skipped under the triangular archway, flashing blue despite the object he had in his possession, and into the port. The Hospitality Department disappeared behind a shower of sparkling colors. A whirring of circles before a high pitched frequency and bright white light. "Dormant Residence Block 3."

He ran from the port and into the libervator opposite, pressing the red downward pointing triangle to head to his floor. Finally, stumbling back into his familiar, comfortable apartment, he ran through his bedroom and flung his jacket and its contents to the floor, continuing to the bathroom, only just catching himself on the sink. Only now did he realize the severity of his actions and their likely consequences.

The woman—whoever she was—was a criminal, and by collecting the book from her, an object that was strictly forbidden for anyone but a troubleshooter to use, he too would be implicated and most likely meet the same fate. Advanced Rehabilitation, or AR, would mean an end to a life shared with other residents in the farm. It would mean a life limited to unknown experiments, deep in the Libermid where unresponsive residents were housed indefinitely, where the most brilliant and ruthless programmers worked toward their *final solution* to eradicate dyspheria from its mindless hosts. And ultimately as they would fail, as Christopher assumed they always did—given the virus' ongoing infection among the population, he would be permanently shut shown. And though they didn't call it death, it would surely mean an end to life as he knew it.

As he glared at the libermirror, the face of Dean Perish popped into his mind. He thought how they actually looked quite alike: Fairly tall, slim, with neat dark brown hair and blue eyes. Only Perish had a much healthier, darker complexion; Christopher looked pale and comparatively under nourished. He thought again how their lives careered in opposite directions: One would step into the Writer's shoes and be able to create a version of Liberty Farm for his own choosing while the other's life would soon be ending. He gave a drunken growl through gritted teeth, as angry at himself as he was at anyone else for his foolish behavior, and the libermirror quickly scanned and automatically bleeped on screen: *teeth: clean.*

He trampled into the bedroom, gripped by liberhol and fear . He clasped his hands on the window to catch himself from falling. As far as he could see, he was at the mid level of a sprawling metropolis, surrounded by row upon row of apartment buildings, inhabited by how many hundreds of dorms—dormant residents— that were, up until today, much like him. Below, in the darker parts of the farm, were the lower levels occupied by the symps— the symptomatic residents—whose BRAINs and behaviors he was employed to observe. Above, in the beautiful unique tall towers and floating castles, were the emune—whose idyllic lifestyle he had once hoped himself to live—separated from the struggles of rehabilitation and the inward facing fear of a despicable disease called dyspheria.

And all around, always, was the face of the Writer; the creator of it all, the genius who had saved humanity from sinking into complete and bloody ruin, who had given the residents a future to work for. His clear blue eyes pierced the scarlet night knowingly. Whether it was a video loop or a live feed of the Writer that Christopher was watching he did not know, for the Writer's exact state of consciousness was always a mystery—he merely showed whatever face he wanted to the residents of the farm at any time. Through the silver, inverted triangular helmet that covered the top of his bald round head, with a deep indigo light glowing at its bottom in the middle of his forehead, he remained connected, interfacing with the Program—his Program. Christopher didn't know whether his crime today had already come to the Writer's attention, amid the millions of data streams pouring in from residents across the farm, but knew that as soon as he laid his head to dock for the night, his sin would make its way tellingly to the mainframe. And he would face his consequence.

In the center of the great circular city toward which he now gazed, he could see the top of the Libermid. Not the tallest building in the farm, but by far the broadest and biggest by volume, the Libermid was a huge pyramidal building—two red sides, two blue—that housed the most cutting edge research and development in dyspheria control that was happening anywhere in the farm; as well the farm's directors, the Emortal Council, the Prime Resident and at its peak, the home of the Writer, who spent the majority of his time in silent solitude, interfacing with the Program.

His eyes drifted up past the peak of the Libermid, where the BRAINs began to drip and flow upward into a huge, nebulous, inverted pyramid that reflected above the building and the entire farm below: The mainframe, where the multitude of nanobots that comprised the all-powerful Program returned, recycled and rejuvenated continuously, with increasing activity overnight as the residents went into hibernation. From the flat top of its shape, flowed an upside down ocean of the BRAINs themselves as they cascaded down around the entire region in a shimmering, impervious dome: the libersphere, which was now almost completely red.

He sat down on his liberbed—a quite uncomfortable thing, for what use was comfort when one was unconscious—and bent down to pick up the forbidden object from under his jacket.

He took his first proper look at the little red notebook he now had in his possession. It was like nothing he had ever seen before; old and shabby, yet strong in the way its cover held the book of pages within. As he ran his fingertips around the outside, it struck him how it felt somehow alive, like it was made from the skin of some long lost animal from the old times before the farm. How could he explain such a thing in his possession? What use would anyone have for writing hidden notes for oneself, when one could type or speak or simply scan their thoughts into any dynamic technological device that could be found in any corner of the farm, through which content could instantaneously be stored and observed by the Program?

But it was too late. He had already committed a crime by picking up the book in the street as the woman with a violet glow disappeared into the night. He had committed it twice and a hundred times over by carrying it home. Now it made little difference whether he opened it or not. He decided he would look and find out the words he had lost his life for. His heart pounding, he turned the cover.

All things may not be as they seem.
And so tonight I lucid dream.

He stopped, confounded, infuriated by the words he had just read. This was all there was, in the middle of the brown paper page. Handwritten in black ink: Coarse, curly and confusing. He read the words again.

All things may not be as they seem.
And so tonight I lucid dream.

What was it supposed to mean? Its words sounded like incomprehensible gibberish at his first and second glance, though he felt that the rhythm of the two lines across the page possessed a certain bounce that reminded of some of the more bearable audioprogramming tunes on the liberadio. He ruffled through the remaining pages of the book, hoping there would be something else within, but there was not. He returned to the two lines of text, trying to decipher them.

All things may not be as they seem.

How could any thing not be as it seems, let alone all things? Is a thing not exactly what it seems, given that what it seems is inherently what it is? What else could a thing be except what it seems? To think that any thing could be anything other than what it seems, and thus what anyone would have thought it was, would seem to question the essence of reality. Surely, everything here, in Liberty Farm, was as it appeared to be.

And so tonight I lucid dream.

The first four words of the second line made sense to him as they were, but the last two were utterly unfamiliar. *Lucid* elicited in him an association with liquid and clarity, some form of clear, fluid thing that flowed and maybe cleaned, but this was a guess based purely on the sounds of the word that were somewhat familiar, but the actual meaning was entirely alien.

And what was meant by *dream*? He was sure he had never seen or heard the word before.

What did it all mean? For what reason would this strange woman write these words, if they were indeed hers, in this tatty old notebook? And why did she drop the book like that right before she was arrested? If she was trying to leave him some kind of message, she had done so in the most unintelligible way he could imagine.

All things may not be as they seem.
And so tonight I lucid dream.

The words echoed in his head, reverberated by liberhol, as he placed the book on the floor beside his liberbed. He laid his head down within the red domed cover that would allow him to hibernate, as he drifted away for what he feared might be the last time.

All things may not be as they seem.
And so tonight I lucid dream.

Christopher woke with a single deep gasp of air, as if emerging from a deep and silent lake. He had not expected to experience such a breath again.

For a moment the image of a woman flitted in his mind; not the violet woman from last night, but another that was just as mysterious to him. Rather than silhouette against the scarlet night as the first stranger had before, she resembled a pale figure cast against a background darker than any Christopher had ever seen. A small and feeble looking woman, she bowed down in agony over her own round stomach. Zombie, he thought.

And like that, she was gone. And Christopher's mind returned to his apartment bedroom. Where had she come from? Perhaps a random memory of a movie randomly aroused by a last drop of liberhol lapping around his BRAINs.

He sat up slowly upon his liberbed, counting the fingers on his hands to see that he was in one piece, as he came to the realization that he had not been plucked away by liberbots to Advanced Rehabilitation in the night.

He looked across to the window opposite and saw the peaceful blue light of the libersphere surround the apartments and towers across the farm. He had lived to see another day.

Down by his feet, there it was. The little red notebook; the bringer of his doom that had not yet arrived but surely would soon. He knew last night's foolish deeds had already been observed by the Program, and by the Writer. It would only be a matter of time before his destiny would meet him. Still, it seemed sensible to hide the thing from plain view in the event of any unexpected guests to his apartment, and so he stowed it in the gap beneath his bed. He should probably find a safer place to put it.

He made his way to the bathroom and stood in front of the libermirror. Here he was, a young man, not yet in his prime. Though it was useless to put a number on it, for first he couldn't remember one and second it had become almost meaningless these days. He was sure he looked as young as most dorms and younger even than many emune, and that was without any of the augmentations that would be affordably available to him as he progressed in his rehabilitation. Yet today he felt like an old man. The face of Dean Perish once again appeared in his mind; the man who was leading the charge, in announcing it to the residents if not in scientific practice, toward a *final solution* to dyspheria, to destroy the kind of disobedience Christopher had demonstrated toward the Program—and rightly so. Christopher knew that he had been a fool, and for what—a riddle?

All things may not be as they seem.
And so tonight I lucid dream.

The words echoed within him again.

He crossed the room toward the libershower, a floor-to-ceiling device with a shimmering blue holographic surface. He removed his clothes and dropped them on to the floor for libercycling, then stepped inside. From within, his bathroom blurred as if beneath water, as he peered through the misty pool of nanobots. A second later began the familiar low hum as his liberskin began to float away and be replaced from toe to top, clearing with it any contamination that may have been picked up in the farm the previous day and providing optimal protection for the day to come. He emerged a minute later, physically refreshed but still bearing the weight of heavy thoughts.

What could he do? The deed was already done. He had no plan nor motive to do anything now other than to proceed with his day as he must, as he had every day of his adult life. He pulled on a new suit from the liberdrobe, filled himself with liberflakes in the kitchen and headed out to work.

The way to work was most like any other. He passed by a number of vaguely familiar dorms in the quiet corridors of the apartment building. He was the first of four coinciding at one of the libervators. He pressed the blue upward pointing triangle and stepped inside, with the others silently following.

Outside the apartment building, larger numbers of people came together on the streets, brightly lit with the glow of the various libermarketing screens, but it was not especially busy. The time was only around one-point-seven and the residents had until two to get to work. Christopher was surrounded mostly by other dorms. The only symps around were those assisting laborbots in street servicing and maintenance tasks, dressed in red so that they could be easily identified and avoided.

As Christopher filed into the queue for the port to the Systems Monitoring Department, he felt his anxiety build as he wondered when the liberbots would pounce. Shuffling toward one of the tall triangular archways peeking out above the crowds, he saw the light at the top flashing blue as it scanned the residents making their way onto the platform, validating their LDs—liberdentifications—and access to the port's destination. Surely, as soon as he passed below, the liberbots would be alerted to the presence of a dangerously disobedient dorm and escort him to Acute Assessment if not directly to Advanced Rehabilitation. He walked through as competently as he could.

"Red light" spoke the metallic voice of a liberbot close by. Christopher shot his head toward it, terrified, but the bot was facing in another direction, darting away. He watched as the bot and two others quickly arrived at another platform nearby with a red light beaming from the top of its entrance archway, surrounding a disturbed and shouting symp, having apparently tried to gain access to a part of the farm that he shouldn't have. The other residents in the vicinity assembled themselves quietly and orderly as the symp was escorted away, the archway behind them closed temporarily by a red liberscreen. They were scanned again and the light above the archway turned blue, allowing them to enter the port safely.

"You, dorm," said another voice behind Christopher. "Are you entering the port or not?" Christopher turned and saw another bot looking toward him. Realizing he was the only resident still on his own platform, he saw the archway he had passed under was lit blue and no threat had been detected in him. He brought himself back to his senses and walked through the triangular entrance to the port.

The port itself was half full; twenty or so dorms and two bots, stood interspersed. The walls began to shimmer and sparkle. The sound of the street fell silent and was slowly replaced by a whirring that built in circles into an increasing rhythm, then a high pitched frequency for a second, then silence. Then a bright white light before the world outside slowly reappeared. *Systems Monitoring Department,* a voice announced.

Christopher's workstation consisted of a comfortably adjustable, swiveling seat opposite a semicircular holographic touchscreen—about as big as a libercar front window—that enclosed one-hundred-and-eighty degrees of his vision, through which his daily assignments were administered and addressed, in a large, tall room of similar workstations all filled with other systems monitors silently tapping away. Christopher didn't know exactly which symps his co-workers were assigned to observe and report upon on a daily basis, but could at least see their general performance ratings on libergram—the farm's primary social network platform—should he wish to. There was no practical requirement for any of them to speak, nor indeed for them to share the same workspace. Anyone could easily carry out their duties via a screen at home should the farm require it, but Christopher had learned—indeed it was common knowledge—that residents were most performative in their various lines of work, and generally better aligned to the Program, when sharing an environment where peers could reflect optimal behavior.

Through his screen, Christopher was fed his action items through the day: Observations of individuals and groups of symps; their responsiveness generally and to specific operations of the Program as well as all the means to complete them; live video feeds and Program performance data of his subjects; essential updates on libernomic trends; and even targeted audioprogramming to optimize his individual work performance. He slid and tapped his fingertips around to navigate information as needed and input his observations and any suggested adjustment of AV levels among his assigned symps.

Once again, he was assigned to observing service symps working around the mine. It was an area he had been intrigued by for some time, at the very edge of Liberty Farm; the factory and source of everything that existed around him and simultaneously the place where the darkness and death of the world outside stood so vividly in mind behind just a single wall of floating nanobots. Only now, having been distracted by the distress and the book from last night, was he reminded of the incident at the end of his working day yesterday. He saw now that there had been a massive turnover of staff around the mine today, with twenty-five of the forty symps having been replaced. It was normal for perhaps a handful or so symps to be replaced on a daily basis—their symptoms becoming more acute, making them incapable of work and requiring Acute Assessment or Advanced Rehabilitation—but not this many. Whatever happened yesterday—whatever that small white thing was scuttling out from the mouth of the liberator—it must have provoked significant disturbance.

Before he could think on the matter for too long, a libergram notification popped up on screen and a calm robotic voice spoke into his ears. "Christopher 165-189-198, please report for internal assessment immediately. Christopher 165-189-198, please report for internal assessment immediately ..."

It was quite normal for Christopher to report for internal assessment, as a more thorough evaluation of his rehabilitation and performance than observation alone, perhaps every few weeks or so, but the timing of this particular request felt concerning. Was it something to do with the incident in the mine that had seemingly led to the removal of a high number of symps that he had also witnessed over live video and admittedly been alarmed by? Or was it to do with his actions last night, which had surely by now been detected by the Program? Could this be his last assessment?

He rode the libervator up one floor to the internal assessment ward. As he walked under the archway that marked its entrance the light above flashed blue and a voice spoke in his ears, "Christopher 165-189-198, please enter examination room six." He walked past five triangular doorways, all sealed shut and marked with a red light above, before the sixth, marked blue, which slid open automatically at his arrival.

"Christopher 165-189-198," he said, entering the tall white room. "Reporting for assessment."

"Yes." The woman at the opposite end of the room croaked from behind her desk. "Enter. Have a seat."

As Christopher approached he immediately recognized the woman who had examined him many times before, though he didn't know her name. She was an unattractive and rather old-looking woman with scraped back black hair and a large mole on her forehead. It was something that could have easily been removed, Christopher thought, and an almost obnoxious decision to keep—staring at people like a third eye.

"Christopher 165-189-198," she said. "Rehabilitation status: Dormant. Freedom level: Three. Is that correct?"

"Yes," Christopher said. He sat in the tall chair opposite. The examiner was looking down at information on the liberscreen on her desk surface, but the mole continued to watch.

"Program-designed … no parents … and you've been a systems monitor for twenty-seven years? Good for you."

"Yes," he said. *And how many times has she said that,* he thought.

The examiner looked up at him, knowingly. "Lean back," she said, tapping a button on her desk.

He put his head back, though there was little need for any intentional leaning, as the tall chair reclined to a horizontal position automatically, so that he was staring at the white ceiling, as wires emerged from the arms of the chair and wrapped themselves around his wrists. How any of this technically worked, he didn't know, but the physical discomfort it provoked seemed to be conducive to the state of honesty the assessment demanded.

"Do you enjoy your work?" the examiner asked.

"Yes," he said. There was a pleasant chime and the ceiling above his head changed momentarily from white to blue.

And so began the DST-3, the Dyspheria Standard Test for level three dorms.

"Do you find your work boring or repetitive?"

"No." And again the ceiling flashed blue.

"Do you find it difficult to follow instructions?"

"No." Another blue flash.

"Do you always try to do the best job you can?"

"Yes." And again.

"Do you hope to progress to a higher role?"

"Yes." And another.

There were four versions of the DST, tailored to examining specific aspects of dyspheria relevant to each of the four levels of residents affected by the virus: Symptomatic level one experiencing the most acute symptoms, followed by symptomatic level two, dormant level three and dormant level four.

"Do you enjoy your time away from work?"

He considered for a moment before answering. "Yes." Another blue flash.

"Do you find it difficult to relax?"

"Yes." There was a dull buzzing sound and the ceiling flashed red.

"Do you find your enjoyment of pleasures such as food and shopping decreased?"

"Yes." Another red flash.

"Do you experience mood swings, sometimes feeling quite high, other times low?"

"No." A blue flash.

"Do you feel stuck in life?"

"Yes." Red.

31

The third and upper class of residents—the emune—had no requirement for any assessment like the DST, as they were no longer affected by the virus, although they still enjoyed the antivirus—more for a liking of its performative benefits than any physical requirement.

"Do you find it hard to express yourself?"

"No." Blue.

"Do others find it difficult to understand you?"

"No." Blue.

"Do you find it hard to concentrate on what other people are saying?"

"No." Blue.

"Do you struggle to take care of your basic needs such as food and hygiene?"

"No." Blue.

The emune—like the symps and dorms—were also divided into two further sub-classes: Level five being those who had earned their emunity through their successful rehabilitation, purchase or a prize, and level six being those who had inherited emunity from their parents—considered the elites of the farm. Though that didn't mean that they were actually physically freed from the virus; it was simply that their BRAINs were in such accord with the Program that they no longer had any risk of symptoms resurfacing.

"Do you find it difficult to stay organized?"

"No." Blue.

"Do you struggle to complete your daily activities?"

"No." Blue.

"Do you find it difficult to sit still?"

"No." Blue.

"Do you misplace or have difficulty finding things?"

"No." Blue.

"Do you feel you have things in common with your peers?"

He paused for a moment. "Yes." But the answer was met with a dull buzz and a red flash.

"Do you drink too much liberhol?"

"No." Another red flash.

"Do you find it difficult to dock at night?"

"No." And again.

"Do you feel well rested when you wake in the morning?"

"Yes." And again.

He shuffled in his seat. Four red lights in a row. It was as if the Program could detect inner truths that he hadn't even realized himself.

"Do you find it hard to concentrate on one thing for a long time?"

"No." A blue flash.

"Do you find yourself easily distracted?"

"No." And another.

"Do you make decisions quickly without thinking of the consequences?"

An image flickered in Christopher's mind of the book as he picked it up from the ground last night.

"No," he said. A red flash.

"Do you believe things that others don't?"

"No." Blue.

"Do you have any abilities that others don't?"

"No." Blue.

"Do you believe you are in any way special?"

"No." Blue.

"Do you believe that you can read other people's minds or that they can read yours?"

Except troubleshooters, he thought. "No." A blue flash.

"Do you see patterns or connections between things that others don't?"

He paused before answering. "Yes." A red flash.

"Do you know what's going to happen before it does?"

"No." Blue.

"Do you experience memory loss or gaps in time?"

"No." A red flash.

"Do you ever find yourself somewhere and not know how you got there?"

"No." And another.

"Do you see or hear things that others don't?"

"No." Blue.

The DST assessed the alignment of residents' thoughts, speech, behavior, perceptions and sensations with the Program, and the extent of the virus' influence over each.

"Do you feel in control of your own behavior, thoughts and feelings?"

"Yes." Blue.

"Do you trust your own thoughts and feelings?"

"Yes." Blue.

"Do you trust other people?"

"Yes." Blue.

"Do you feel that you are being watched specifically?"

"No." Blue.

"Do you feel that anyone wants to cause you harm?"

"No." Blue.

Just a few more questions.

"Do you feel safe?"

"Yes." Red.

"Do you suffer from any physical pain?"

"No." Blue.

"Do you ever feel like causing physical harm to others?"

"No." Blue

"Do you ever feel like causing physical harm to yourself?"

"No." Blue.

"Do you feel valued by the farm?"

"Yes." Blue.

"Do you trust the Program?"

"Yes." Blue.

"Do you trust the Prime Resident?"

"Yes." Red.

Christopher's seat began to rise slowly back to its upright position. He felt dazed from the lights flashing in front of him, from the interrogation and the self-doubt it seemed to provoke. He wondered what he had given away, and what the consequences would be.

"Well Christopher," the examiner said. She tapped on her desk screen, her mole staring across at him. "It seems like everything is within satisfactory parameters, just about."

He breathed a sigh of relief.

"But we'll continue to closely monitor you," she said, "and I'd recommend you try a little retail therapy, give yourself a little boost, help you to relax and enjoy yourself in the evening."

"Yes," Christopher said. He started to get up from his seat. "Thank you."

But the old woman raised her hand.

"There's just one more thing," she said. "Another test, for the liberlection."

Christopher sat back down. "Yes."

The examiner tapped a blue triangle on the desk and its screen immediately transformed to reveal a series of nine white dots against a black background. They were arranged in three lines of three, equally spaced, to form an invisible square.

. . .
. . .
. . .

"Please pay close attention to the instructions I am about to give," the examiner said. "You must attempt to connect all of the dots with your finger, drawing four straight, continuous lines to pass through each of the nine dots, without lifting your finger from the screen."

Christopher stared down at the screen, before glancing back up to the examiner.

"Remember that the test is not to test you specifically," she said, "but to test the suitability of particular and potential courses of the Program, and that there are no right or wrong answers—only what's best for you and the farm."

Christopher had heard those words many times, issued alongside a variety of tests over the years, mostly before the liberlections. Whether or not there were really any right or wrong answers, he knew that his responses would be used to calculate which course of the Program would be suited to him, and which prime residential candidate, although he didn't understand exactly how. He paused for a moment, ensuring that he had understood the instructions properly and then considered what to do.

See, four straight lines would most obviously form a square around eight of the nine dots in the arrangement, but then he wouldn't be able to pass through the center. He decided to start in one corner, the bottom right, and go up to the top-left; that way he could go straight through the tricky center spot and bisect the square with his first line. From here there were only two, equally obvious and equally effective lines that he could make; he chose to go down to bottom-left—five of nine dots connected with two lines done and two more to make. But as he approached the bottom he started to puzzle over his next move, and as his mind wandered his finger almost wandered past the corner. Oh what a silly mistake that would have been, to go outside the square and end the test with two lines left. He turned right and went back to the bottom right corner—six dots connected with one line to complete. He went up to the top right, connecting two more as he went. One spare—the top-middle he never touched.

The desk surface gave a pleasant chime and changed from black to blue. Christopher was confused as he felt a certain dissatisfaction at having failed to complete the task as instructed. Still, as the examiner had said, with these tests there wasn't a right or wrong answer, only what's best for you and for the liberlection.

"Christopher 165-189-198", she said. "You are free to go."

She raised her right thumb and Christopher received a momentary mood boost, direct to his BRAINs. He raised his own thumb back at the examiner, returning the social gesture, before leaving the room.

4

It certainly was a curious test. More curious still was that it had distracted him entirely from the stress he had been feeling beforehand. Only when he returned to his workstation did it occur to him that he had made it successfully through the assessment and back out again without being taken away to Advanced Rehabilitation, despite his misdeeds of the previous evening.

After work he decided to follow the examiner's instruction to go for some retail therapy. It was true he did have some liberos to spare and hadn't been shopping for a while.

The Retail Department was a multi-story mall within the farm, with a multitude of stores selling every kind of product and service, from fashion to food, household and personal physical upgrades, liberdays and libergenic matching. Christopher wandered the middle floors along with mostly other dorms, the lower levels were more densely packed with shopping symps while high above the emune arrived directly at their desired destinations via their self-flying libercars—rather than sharing liberports with lower level residents. Each class of residents, and each individual, could access only a certain range of stores according to their libernomic status; it would be undesirable for example for a wealthy emune's retail experience to be disrupted by some symp shopping nearby who couldn't possibly afford the same levels of luxury. Of course there was some overlap between symps and dorms, between dorms and emune—some stretch in showing residents things that they couldn't afford currently but might be able to one day—as it was beneficial to provide lower level residents with some sense of aspiration to work toward, and a reminder by comparison to the more rehabilitated residents of how fortunate they were.

Certainly there was little practical requirement for shopping in person for most products—he could purchase most things he ever wanted much quicker on the libernet and have them delivered directly to his apartment at any time—but there was some psychological benefit to the physical retail experience; the BRAINs released small doses of reward chemicals during the shopping experience itself as well as larger amounts after purchases, corresponding to their size, though of course a resident would ultimately lose liberos as a result of their expenditure.

The Retail Department provided a highly personalized and interactive experience. Every liberscreen-fronted shop window responded automatically to show examples that were most attractive and suited to those residents walking past at the time. Targeted advertising sent personalized messages directly to residents' own audio receivers; no two would hear the same. *Hi Christopher, we haven't seen you for a while, still enjoying that suit you bought last month? Perhaps you could use some new shoes, yours are looking a little dated ... How about some trendy new evening wear to help attract that perfect match ... Are you seeing clearly Christopher? Maybe you could use a vision upgrade ...*

He walked past the large open shop front of Liberty Farm's most popular life extension and physical augmentation provider, *Live Forever. Live Forever* provided everything from dental and facial reconstruction, visual and hearing upgrades that improved the senses far beyond "natural" human limits, muscle molding, to organ replacement and age-reversal. Whether they could actually guarantee anyone would really *live forever* was uncertain, although there were plenty of emune who lived for a very long time and often with little evidence of deterioration. He was already subscribed to their *Stream of Salubrity* service, which provided basic injury cover, annual check-ups and capped his genetic aging at eighty percent of natural rate. He hoped one day to upgrade to their *River of Life* or *Fountain of Youth* services, but for now these were far beyond his libernomic means.

Continuing his walk, Christopher was surprised to see what seemed to be a familiar face behind the next store's liberscreen. Curly red hair, deep brown eyes, relatively tall and slim. It was her, the woman from last night—but no. It was merely a hologram in the shop front of *Liberfect Match*, a leading provider of genetic matching and partnership services.

"Hey Christopher, like what you see?" said the artificial voice, straight into his audio receiver. "Come inside and let us find your Liberfect Match to reproduce with. Maybe she could look like me."

He stopped and stared for a moment into the hollow eyes of the hologram, which, despite its flirtatious expressions, was in no way sentient. He didn't know how close the resemblance was to the woman from last night—it had only seemed a brief moment that he had seen her, a blur as he followed her out of the bar and saw her whisked away by two liberbots—but it was close enough to remind him of her, and to cause his pulse to raise in alarm. He didn't think he had felt particularly attracted to the woman; although he could agree she had some positive attributes, he had never imagined matching with a redhead. It was probably just his thoughts of her and the events of last night, lingering in his BRAINs, that the interactive software had detected and attempted to reflect. Regardless, he had no interest in matching or reproducing with anyone any time soon, and didn't want to linger on the hologram of the woman any longer, lest he attract undue attention. And so he scurried away.

"You look like you could use a liberday!" said a male voice. Christopher walked by the next store front. Its liberscreen molded into a luxurious scene of lavish lights and furnishing, with Christopher himself shown sat relaxing by a pool and dining on some highly decorative dish. "Live like the emune for as little as a thousand Ls a day in liberality."

Liberality was a virtual reality holiday service, providing simulated getaways for residents from their everyday reality; a window of respite from their working responsibilities and a taste of luxury—fed directly, immersively to their BRAINs—that they couldn't actually physically afford. Christopher had experienced a number of liberdays in his life and, though they could be enjoyable, he found them to provide only brief and hollow relief from his regular reality, which always seemed to be worse by comparison upon his return.

Finally he arrived at his favorite shopping destination—probably because it most resembled his home. Indeed *Libernsraum* provided an exact replica of his apartment, also using virtual reality technology, with options to view, alter and purchase options for the various items he might have there. *Libernsraum* was the leading household technology and furniture retailer, which produced and sold all the latest home comforts. He entered and walked into one of the available rooms, which simply scanned his BRAINs as he passed under the triangular sliding doors, and within a fraction of a second produced a fully lifelike three-dimensional reproduction of his home—with added text not normally visible in his actual apartment detailing the name, price and expected lifespan of his various household items as he glanced over them. A red halo would appear around the older items, with the boldness of the color corresponding to how out-dated they were. He could then simply select by pointing and switch with a flick of his fingers to see the latest and greatest models before his own eyes and exactly how they would look in his apartment. Here, he could visualize his home with an infinite combination of items he would probably never purchase as well as rearrange his furniture without lifting a finger.

Standing in the holographic reproduction of his tidy blue apartment, he remembered the thing he had so foolishly seen fit to bring back to his real home last night. He had simply stuffed the book under his liberbed this morning and he needed somewhere safer to put it.

He flicked through the storage options and came across a small libersafe, a secure storage device with a holographic surface on its front that would scan the user's hand as it approached, granting access only to its rightful owner. He decided to buy one for 399Ls and place it in his bedroom on the wall next to his liberdrobe. Not wanting to appear too suspicious by buying just this item, he bought a new rug for his living room for 175Ls.

He continued to be bombarded by libermarketing messages as he meandered the mall of the Retail Department, though he could feel the pleasure of his purchases rolling around his BRAINs. He looked up toward the libersphere, slowly starting its nightly transition from blue to red. He saw the stern but reassuring face of the Writer staring back from one of the tall liberscreens high above and silently thanked him, as he often did, for saving humanity, for creating this world of opportunity and, most of all, for keeping him safe.

But the pleasure of retail therapy was replaced by dread as he returned home to find that the rug and libersafe—already installed automatically as expected—were not the only changes in his apartment. The red notebook, which he had brought home with him just last night, was now mysteriously missing.

5

Christopher proceeded to work despite the conflict of panic and pretense that persisted within him; panic that someone knew about the notebook and had entered his apartment to steal it, and pretense that despite this, he was still just another resident with a single Program to follow—*Working For Your Future.*

Who could have entered his apartment while he was gone? The rug and libersafe must have been installed automatically—like every other piece of furniture he had ever purchased—by way of the nanobots that connected his home with the rest of the farm. Only a liberbot or a troubleshooter was able to bypass normal liberdentification to enter another's accommodation without invitation. Unless, some hackers had found a way to do likewise.

And what if it was a liberbot or a troubleshooter that had retrieved the notebook? The biggest mystery in that case, once again, was why they hadn't yet taken him away to Advanced Rehabilitation. But his only motive, his only action—today like every other day—was to proceed with his daily duties as normal.

Performance in the mine was a little slow, which was to be expected following yesterday's turnover of symps, but there had been no further disruption. At lunchtime, he made his way to the department cafeteria and went and put both hands through the front of the nearest liberwave. In a second the machine scanned him to calculate a suitable meal—he didn't have any particular craving in mind right now—and he retrieved a tray containing a long large sandwich, a bag of liberitos and a bottle of libercola. He took a seat alone in a corner. He took a cold sip from the bottle and felt its sweet bubbles slide down his throat, followed by the familiar flow of libertons released by his BRAINs. Not intoxicating like liberhol, the libercola provided a simple stimulant that was more conducive with his daily duties in the farm.

He took a hefty bite of his sandwich; two hunks of white bread wrapped around a patchwork pile of Program-produced protein, made to imitate the meat people ate in the past. It struck

Christopher as strange that the farm would seek to imitate such a thing. The depths of the descent of the dyspheria Outbreak had of course led to cannibalism. It seemed almost as disturbing to Christopher that humans had at one point regularly eaten the flesh of other creatures, let alone one another. He wondered if people would still be eating animals today, if there were any left.

His thoughts were interrupted as the large holographic liberscreen that dominated the middle of the cafeteria sprung to life with a flood of blue and red flowing lights, in unison with a familiar fanfare and the veracious voice of an unnamed announcer.

"Calling all residents, we interrupt your routine for a special broadcast. Please stop what you are doing and listen."

The voice echoed around the cafeteria, ushering dorms making their way around the room to sit at their nearest seats, before the libernews musical introduction rang around.

"A lifetime of struggle ..." The same images of life before Liberty Farm, repeated every day. *"A history of horrors ..."* Despair, dyspheria, death.

"Almost a hundred years ago humanity stood on the brink of extinction. But we were saved by the genius of the Writer ..." The savior's face filled the screen. *"Saved by advanced technology that would supersede our primitive instincts and guarantee our safety. Together now and forever we look toward a brighter future."* The soundtrack reached its crescendo as the red and blue halves of the libertee logo came together from opposite sides of the liberscreen, letters appearing below.

"Liberty Farm: Working For Your Future."

It was the introduction to the libernews that Christopher had seen and heard maybe a million times before; a regular reminder of the horrific history of humanity and how fortunate we were to find ourselves saved by the farm; by the Writer.

The music faded out as the libertree made way for the appearance of two exquisite emune residents, one male, one female, both blond, blue-eyed and beautiful, the top libervision presenter pairing.

"A beautiful blue day to all you residents across the farm, we hope you don't mind us interrupting your lunch for a special announcement. I'm Leo," said the man, through a bright beaming smile.

"And I'm Fiona," said the woman, through luscious silvery lipsticked lips. "We're coming to you live today with an important update ahead of the upcoming liberlection."

"That's right," Leo said. "As you know the liberlection results were due very soon, and early analysis had suggested that this would be one of the most closely contested for some time."

"However, news just in is that the challenging candidate Morty Caine has just this morning been taken to Advanced Rehabilitation and is now out of the running for the liberlection," Fiona said.

Christopher almost choked on a large chunk of sandwich he swallowed too fast.

"This comes as a result of the discovery that Mr. Caine has been found guilty of using prostitutes, fraternizing with certain undesirable symps and indeed involvement in what we've been told are counter-Program activities," Leo continued. "This has resulted not only in the breakdown of his marriage, but ultimately his arrest and transfer to AR."

Christopher watched, mouth agape, as the liberscreen showed footage of Caine, the red party leader, walking the streets of the lower levels of the farm, talking to some shady looking symps; walking around the Scarlet Sector, the area known for its prostitution; then shots of his devastated wife, and Caine himself being carried away from his home by a group of liberbots, begging and shouting as he went. A flurry of blue likes already began on screen, from Christopher's colleagues in the cafeteria as well as residents across the farm.

It was no surprise to Christopher to hear that Caine might have used a prostitute—he was pretty sure most emune men did—more so that he had been so foolish as to be spotted in the Scarlet Sector, when he could have afforded a much more discreet high-end option. Christopher suspected that it was Caine's fraternizing with undesirable symps that had been more problematic. And what exactly was this counter-Program activity he was involved in? He had always seemed to Christopher like a decent enough candidate—a good one in fact. He was certainly less vociferous than the Prime Resident Perish when it came to a *final solution* to dyspheria. Caine seemed to think that there might not be such a thing; that dyspheria was an inevitable condition that required more subtle management. It was perhaps an unusual perspective, but Christopher could see the logic. He also seemed to be much more interested in improving the freedoms and welfare of the symps than Perish—who seemed to be more protective of the rewards for more rehabilitated residents.

I always knew Caine was a pervert! The libergam ticker at the bottom of the screen began to scroll through residents' live comments. *At last that loser goes to AR where he belongs ...* Christopher watched as many of his colleagues tapped on the holographic keyboard displays integrated on top of their left hands. *#NoMoreMorty ...*

"This means that current Prime Resident Dean Perish now has a virtually clear path to retaining his position." The beautiful Fiona returned to the screen. "Of course assuming that that is approved by the Emortal Council."

#DeanToDestroyDyspheria ...   #PerishForPrimeResident ... #ItsGotToBeDean ...

"Yes," said Leo, "and we've been told that all members of the Council will be liberporting from their respective regions of the farm this evening—two each from the North, East, South and the Island regions—to join with our two representatives in the West, to discuss in person before confirming the liberlection results."

The liberscreen showed brief clips of each of the council members, all dressed in black; one man and woman, original representatives—or replacements thereof—from each of the old continents, tasked to protect the interests of their people in the formation and continuation of Liberty Farm. No one knew whether they were actually immortal—though they certainly seemed to have lived longer than almost anyone else—but the Council itself was guaranteed to be a continuing body throughout the future.

And so Christopher realized that it was practically a forgone conclusion now that Perish would remain the prime resident, as he had done for so many years now, as there was little chance that the Council—the same people who had basically molded the young politician—would reject that inevitable course. He finished off his sandwich and liberitos with little enjoyment.

Shortly after lunch, he received a libergram at his workstation to attend another internal assessment. It was certainly unusual to require two such meetings on consecutive days, but he suspected it must have something to do with Caine's removal from contention for the liberlection, and a need to subsequently re-evaluate residents' alignment with Perish. Thoughts of the notebook and the events of two nights ago had all but left his BRAINs, at least for now. He caught the libervator up to the next floor and walked through to internal assessment—examination room three this time. But as he entered, he was caught in his tracks, as it was not the familiar face and mole of the old examiner that stared back at him, but another more foreboding figure—the troubleshooter.

Christopher felt a flood of fear pour through him, fortunate perhaps that he did not faint; he simply stood paralyzed as the dark eyes of the man behind the desk at the opposite end of the room pierced through him. This was it.

"Good day, Christopher."

He sparked back to life, surprised by the apparent pleasantness of the greeting.

"Sit," the troubleshooter said, his deep voice reverberating around the room.

Christopher continued to stare, transfixed by the troubleshooter. He wore a small round crimson cap tightly over what seemed to be an otherwise bald head, along with a crimson cloak over the back of his navy uniform that hugged his muscular physique. His skin was dark but his features more chiseled than any Southern specimen Christopher had ever seen—though admittedly most of those had been in the midst of brutal combat in the Genelympics. He stared back at Christopher, unblinking. Here it comes, he thought, as he moved slowly to the seat at the desk opposite the troubleshooter.

"My name is Canaan," he said, "and I've been watching you."

He appeared to be at least a foot taller than Christopher and probably two feet wider. He looked like he could have competed well in the Genelympics himself; perhaps that was the source of the long scar over his left eye. Christopher wondered whether he would tear his mind apart or just his body limb from limb.

"You're a very capable systems monitor," Canaan said. "You have high potential. I'd expect you should be in line for promotion to senior systems monitor within the next couple of years. Twenty more and who knows, maybe you could even become a troubleshooter."

Christopher sat speechless. He had considered the appeal of becoming a troubleshooter before; what it would be like to go on mysterious adventures, from the darkest gutters to the tops of the tallest towers in the fight to eliminate dyspheria, building evidence against the hacker enemy to solve the case, recording secret notes and then …

Canaan let out a short but hearty laugh.

"But that isn't going to happen." His face snapped back to its previous stillness. "I assume you noticed the high turnover of service symps around the mine yesterday?"

Yes, Christopher thought.

"Do you know what that thing was in the mine that they saw—that you saw?"

No.

"It was an animal."

There was a pause, as Canaan seemed more determined to wait for an actual verbal response from Christopher.

"An—an animal? But—but I thought all the animals were extinct?"

"Not quite," said Canaan. "Some—rodents mainly—survived by living underground. It seems that this one—a rabbit—was unfortunately gathered within a load taken back to the mine for liberation. As you saw, it caused quite a disturbance in the performance of the symps who witnessed it, all of whom have since been transferred to AR."

"But—why?"

"Because—like you—it was just about the last thing a symp would expect to see. And most are not ready to see things that they do not expect. It leads to questions. And it would be counterproductive to the Program for residents to question such things as the presence of animal life outside the farm. Which brings us to you." The hulking troubleshooter hunched over the desk closer to Christopher. "You were the only systems monitor to witness the incident. And if it wasn't for my intervention you would already be in Advanced Rehabilitation as well."

Christopher swallowed hard.

"See I believe you can serve a higher function," Canaan said. "I know that you've been contacted by a certain individual. An individual of some interest to me."

The violet woman flashed in his mind.

"I know that you retrieved from her an object." He reached around to the rear of his uniform, and returned in his gloved hand the red notebook, slapping it purposefully onto the desk. "An illegal object."

His heart pounded in his chest.

"And I want you to use it," Canaan said, "to find out what you can about this woman and her activities."

Christopher's heart leapt as if it was surprised to be still beating at all. Canaan leaned in closer still.

"This woman is part of a group. A group that has the potential to bring an end to Liberty Farm as we know it."

A memory made its way into Christopher's mind. Was this something to do with the collective hacking that he had heard Canaan and the other two troubleshooters discussing?

"It is true," said Canaan, "that the farm faces a threat the likes of which it has never seen before. And that is why we need your help. I want you to follow this woman. I want you to find out all you can. And I want you to continue your observations around the mine—you will find answers there. I'm going to be adjusting your freedoms in order to assist with our investigations. I'm going to keep a close eye on you. And I don't want you to mention any of this to anyone besides me. Not even any other troubleshooters, do you understand?"

Christopher managed to muster a nod.

"Good," said Canaan, reaching around his back once more. "And you'll be needing this." He returned a thin cylindrical metallic object about twice the length of a liberette, shiny silver with what appeared to be a small red triangular button on one end, and placed it on the desk in front of Christopher.

Christopher stared down blankly at the object on the desk. Was it a weapon? Some kind of tracking device? Christopher carefully picked it up in his right hand and looked at the red button on the end. Perhaps it was a bomb or some kind of suicide button, and the whole conversation a charade, a form of twisted torture before watching Christopher end his own life. He closed his eyes, took a deep breath and pressed the button with his thumb. *Click.* He opened his eyes and saw that a narrow point had emerged from the opposite end to the button, with what appeared to be a sharp nib at the tip.

"It's—it's a pen. But—I thought it was against the Program for anyone except a troubleshooter to use a pen?"

"It is." Canaan smirked. "But now you have a pen, remember, don't let anyone but me know anything about this."

Christopher sat still, staring at the device, not knowing what he was meant to do with it, or understanding much at all of the conversation he had just experienced. The troubleshooter started to get up from his seat, towering over him.

"And one more thing," he said. "Think outside the box."

And with that he strode briskly to the exit, his crimson cloak sweeping after him, leaving Christopher alone in the room.

6

The rest of the afternoon seemed to pass by in a blur. Christopher was sure he had returned to his workstation to continue his observations for the rest of the workday but he couldn't remember a second of it. The next thing he knew, he was sitting in Body, sipping a bottle of libeer. He felt like he'd had a few.

What was he doing here? Drowning his sorrows again, it seemed. But he was alive—the incident of two nights ago had yet to lead to his demise. What had happened to the rest of the day? The last thing he knew he was in internal assessment. That's right … Canaan … the troubleshooter had asked for his help … to find out about that woman … that's why he was here.

He looked around the bar at all the well-dressed dorms there to wash away their dull days and watch one another, heard the mutterings of mindless conversations from a few small groups scattered around the place. He felt disgusted by them and by himself. His BRAINs felt like a mess. The usually soothing audioprogramming seemed to thump in his head.

Then she walked in. Tall and slim with long curly red hair and a burgundy dress, she walked swiftly to the bar and downloaded a glass of wine that matched her outfit. She leaned casually against the bar and cast her eyes across the room before landing on Christopher. She smiled slightly to herself and took a sip of her drink, before walking over to his table.

He fumbled in his chair, attempting to straighten up as she sat down in front of him.

"Hey Christopher', she said, her voice slightly husky for a woman.

"How do you know my name?" he said, trying to pull himself together.

"Oh, I know a lot about you Christopher." She laughed. "The question is how much do you know about me?"

"I know you dropped that book for me the other night. I know I saw you get taken away by two liberbots, but now you're back."

"Oh you're going to want to know more than that Christopher."

She took a slow deep sip of her red wine before peering into his eyes. Christopher felt like he was falling into those deep brown eyes of hers. The room seemed to become quieter, the audioprogramming too. He saw the glow from her drink begin to radiate that mysterious visual effect he had seen last time, not red but something darker. And then it dawned on him what was happening, and what had happened two nights ago. What else could explain the most peculiar visual sensation, but some malevolent intervention in his BRAINs?

"I'm being hacked, aren't I?" he said, as the violet haze seemed to grow between him and the woman.

"Oh you've already been hacked," she said. "Don't you see? These BRAINs, these robots inside of you—you're already controlled. You don't even know what's you and what's the Program. You don't even know if you really exist."

She reached over the table and pinched the skin on Christopher's hand between her long red fingernails for a moment before he pulled away, but he felt no pain.

She spoke in riddles just as she wrote, assuming it was indeed her that wrote the note that Christopher had found inside the book.

All things may not be as they seem.
And so tonight I lucid dream.

"I know you've been asked to follow me," she said, "but I don't think you've got what it takes. You're too afraid."

She swallowed the rest of her drink and stood up, the violet haze seeming to merge with and follow her, leaving a trail behind as she headed for the exit before he could even process what she was saying. He took a large gulp of his libeer before staggering after her.

He emerged on the scarlet street, quiet except for her footsteps moving away to his left. She was already way ahead of him. He looked up to the libersphere, which was nearly red—almost time for bed—before giving chase.

"Wait," he called as she turned a corner, "who are you?"

He jogged after her down another street as she skipped through a passage between a couple of late night liberhol stores.

He followed through the dark passage and emerged to his surprise at the liberportation station. He hadn't known this way. The place was oddly deserted, not even any liberbots around, as far as he could see. Turning all around, he eventually saw her running through the triangular entrance to a port platform at the other end of the station. He ran after her only for the entrance to close as he arrived.

"I'm the rabbit!" he heard her shout from inside the whirring port just before she disappeared from view.

Without knowing where she had gone, he saw the next port platform along open and ready to depart. He passed under the triangular archway, its blue light flashing, and stood inside the port, alone, drunk, frantic. He didn't know where he wanted to go. His only intention was to follow her. The sound of the street was replaced by the slow whirring that built in circles to an increasing rhythm; a high pitched frequency for a second and then silence, a bright light before the world outside slowly reappeared. *Mining Department,* a voice announced.

Christopher had never been to the Mining Department, but it was an area that fascinated him, and never more so than now. The voice of Canaan, the troubleshooter, echoed inside him. "You will find answers there," he had said.

He found himself in an unfamiliar corridor with walls that were now red. It was getting late. He hoped he could find his way back and catch a port in time to dock before nine. But where was she? He heard her footsteps behind him, and her laughing.

He turned around to follow her but she couldn't be seen, except for that color—it hung in the air like a smell. He ran to the end of the corridor and reached the top of a staircase. He couldn't remember the last time he had used stairs, he seemed to use libervators to get everywhere, but ran down regardless. His feet clattered on the metal steps as he clasped the cold railings for support.

He emerged in a vast space overlooked by many storys of windows. Around the walls below were all manner of advanced technologies; cranes, robotics, drones, aircraft. And in the middle of the space there stood a huge magnificent tunnel shaped machine with what appeared to be a conveyor belt leading toward its entrance. It lay dormant, inactive now, but Christopher could sense its power; the particle liberator at the heart of the mine.

A loud siren erupted through the night and red lights began to flash all around. Christopher was not supposed to be here; he had passed the point that any resident was allowed to cross into the mine; he was in the area occupied only by those robotic life forms that crossed the perimeter of the farm to retrieve materials from the outside world.

"Christopher!" the woman called from his left. He saw her again, her curly red hair, and behind her a huge archway that glowed red with nanobots—the edge of the libersphere, the edge of the world as he knew it.

Suddenly, there were footsteps thundering down the stairs, and emerging around him were half a dozen liberbots that poured into the mine, straight past him and toward the woman. He was surprised they hadn't shot the both of them down already. Just as they reached her, something inside Christopher called out.

"Stop!"

Why? What was he hoping for? Did he care that the woman be taken away to AR? Surely he would be next. But what would they listen to his scream anyway?

But somehow the liberbots froze in their tracks before they reached her. And Christopher too stood frozen. The sirens stopped, the flashing stopped, time itself seemed to come to a halt—except the violet woman. She laughed and waved her hand, the strangest hand Christopher had ever seen, with—could it be—six fingers.

And stranger still, the woman did something Christopher had been certain he would never see any resident do, as she ran straight under the huge archway, straight through the red wall of nanobots and straight out of Liberty Farm.

Christopher's head was spinning. This couldn't be real. He looked down at his hands: One, two, three, four, five, six fingers on his right hand. His head and chest pounded as the liberhol and chaos of the night overflowed inside him, and he fell to the ground.

7

Christopher was struck with the sudden awareness of his own body, as if falling back into life from a great height. He felt disoriented, but without any immediately obvious injury. He blinked his eyes open to find himself in his calming blue apartment bedroom—or so it seemed. Perhaps this was Advanced Rehabilitation, he thought; a replica of his room designed to analyze then deconstruct the resident. What BRAIN malfunction had led him one night to pick up an illegal object left by a strange and apparently dangerous woman, and then another to follow her into the mine, and watch as she passed through the perimeter of Liberty Farm itself?

He slowly sat up on his liberbed, head stooped, and saw the silver cylindrical object lay on the floor, given to him by the troubleshooter. That's right—he had been told to follow her. But surely not this far, he thought. Canaan had told him he would be adjusting his freedoms—to help with his investigation—but surely not to grant access to the heart of the mine. And the way those liberbots had seemingly stopped in their pursuit of the woman at his command—a simple systems monitor—was unbelievable.

He picked up the pen and placed his thumb over the red button at the end. He wondered again—or was it hope—that it might be some kind of secret suicide device, but no, the nib protruded as normal as he clicked.

Why had Canaan given him such an object? It was the last thing Christopher remembered of the working day before finding himself in the bar last night. "I want you to follow this woman. I want you to find out all you can. And I want you to continue your observations around the mine." Canaan's booming voice echoed in Christopher's mind.

He decided to take a chance. He had taken at least two too many already and was still alive, what worse could another do? He went to the libersafe beside his liberdrobe—the secure storage device that instantaneously scanned his hand to identify him as the owner and simultaneously ascertained the object he desired—and retrieved from within the little red notebook he had stumbled upon three nights previous. He had hidden it away there last night, he remembered. He didn't understand why the troubleshooter had taken it yesterday, only to give it back, nor why he hadn't been arrested, but he knew it was best now to store the thing out from plain sight in the event of any other unexpected visitors. Stroking its shabby surface with his fingertips suspiciously, it felt to him ancient and yet still somehow alive. He carried it slowly to the living room sofa, before carefully opening the cover.

All things may not be as they seem.
And so tonight I lucid dream.

There they were: The two lines of nonsense that epitomized two nights of nonsensical behavior. He understood them no more now than the first time he saw them, but found them less offensive—more farcical than fearful—perhaps in comparison to the further confusion that had happened since. He turned the page, holding the book against his lap with his left hand and the pen in his right. He took the nib to the paper and slowly began to write.

My name is Christopher ...

He hovered the pen over the page. His handwriting was even more crooked than that already in the book. It was the first time he had written, or handled something like a pen, for many years. For most of his life any notation he had needed to make had simply been tapped on screen, or the holographic keyboard integrated in his left hand, if not transcribed directly from his thoughts. He recalled briefly a memory of himself as a young child drawing a picture in libergarten, an infantile illustration of the Libermid looming over the landscape of Liberty Farm, in pens of different shades of blue and red. There would be little use for such creative tasks in his libercation, but it was conducive to the Program to channel such impulses positively in the early years before eradicating them.

Christopher was probably one of the first things he learnt to write, he now reflected. Although he would typically be identified throughout life in the farm via a variety of scanning technology, it was useful to write physically at first to embed his name in his mind and learn the characters of the alphabet by motor memory. Here he was now writing his name once again. He continued.

My name is Christopher 165-189-198.

As an entirely artificially designed resident, Christopher had no surname and no parents from whom to inherit one. Instead he had a unique liberdentification number. Like most residents, his characteristics had simply been calculated and created by the Program to fulfill whatever role the farm required, to facilitate its balance and progress. However, he was in the minority among other dorms, and certainly among other systems monitors—most of whom were at least partially designed by relatively privileged parents; designed and paid for that is, and grown in artificial wombs, as women had all been made infertile by the Outbreak of dyspheria. It was symps who were typically artificially designed, or "factory farmed", to maintain a constant population on which to test the Program against dyspheria, although these too did often invest what little libernomic savings they had gathered to reproduce—such was the misguided maternal instinct that still persisted. With his relative success as a systems monitor he had at times wondered if he had surpassed expectations, though he had no idea what those expectations were. He had always been quite intelligent but he had certainly felt some struggle adapting to the Program in the past; it always felt to him more like an intellectual challenge than automatic integration.

He looked around the room. It would certainly have to be an accurate replica if not the real thing. The familiar blue of morning in the farm flooded into his apartment through the windows. He glanced at the doorway, wondering how quickly liberbots would come rampaging through to take him away to Advanced Rehabilitation, before continuing to write.

Last night I saw a woman walk out of Liberty Farm.
Last night the walls of my world opened up.

It was true. He had seen probably the last thing he could ever have expected to see, the last thing he could possibly imagine; a resident leaving the farm. To where? Surely, only dyspheria and death lay there in the deserted wilderness. Why then would she leave?

He sat for a minute more, remembering the face of the woman, laughing as she left her world behind; waving at him with—was it really—her six-fingered hand. He looked down now at his own, five fingers on each. Whatever had happened last night he was now certainly back in his own apartment, with another day in the farm to face, and like every other day of his adult life there was nothing else to do but get himself together and head to work. He felt surprisingly comforted having confided his secret to a book; certainly he would not be able to share it with anyone he knew. He hopped in the libershower, got dressed and headed on his way.

The way to work was most like any other; slightly busier due to his slight delay in getting ready, reflecting on and writing in the book last night's events. He caught the libervator out of his apartment building and caught the port to the Systems Monitoring Department, scanning blue on his way with no threat discovered within him, no indication of any excess attention from any liberbots.

It was only as he approached his workstation that it occurred to him he had the opportunity to watch back last night's events—his arrival into the mine, the liberbots, the woman walking out through the libersphere—as part of his role of monitoring the mine. It would do no good, but then it would do little harm either. What had happened had already happened and would be known to the Program, to the liberbots, to the Writer; but he wanted to see it back for himself—it was so hard to believe.

He completed his usual morning tasks and reviewed updates on yesterday's observations and key data first of all, to avoid arousing unnecessary attention. There were no reports of any unusual activity around the mine, though of course his report items were focused on symps working there—not on dorms such as him wandering around late at night. After completing his initial tasks and peering around to check that no one was watching—just a bunch of other systems monitors as usual, silently engrossed in their own screens around the room—he began searching for the video footage of last night in the mine.

It was certainly well after eight that he had been down there— the sphere was almost red when he had been chasing after the woman. He held his breath as he watched the footage from the last hour of the day from the main camera overlooking the heart of the mine. He sped through until nine, but there was nothing—no mysterious woman, no flashing lights, no sirens and no Christopher.

He rewound and rewatched again more slowly to check he had not missed anything. He watched from all the available cameras. He observed the resident mapping of the whole area surrounding the mine from six onward; the drones returned with their final loads, the particle liberator shut down and all service symps in the area departed as always by seven, with no sign of anyone else entering before nine. Then at one the liberator and various robotics began to power up, before the symps came in to work at two today. It was as if all trace of him, the woman and the liberbots down in the mine last night had been completely erased and replaced with empty footage—by Canaan perhaps. Unless they had been down there after nine—but that was impossible; all residents had to be docked and in hibernation by then. There was no video footage between nine and one, the whole of Liberty Farm was practically shut down.

He decided to track his own movements after work yesterday. He didn't expect to have access to footage of the internal assessment ward—he had never needed it, and his observations focused on symps of lesser rehabilitation rather than his own peers—but it worked. Perhaps another freedom adjusted by Canaan, he thought. He pulled up the stream from the camera overlooking his workstation and saw himself reflected on his own screen, looking confused, anxious. He clicked on himself on screen, selected to track and went back one day to see himself sat in the same position, working on his observations as usual. At four he went to lunch, at four-point-five he returned, at five he went to the libervator up to the internal assessment ward. He was unable to access footage inside the examination room, and he saw no sign of Canaan entering or exiting—troubleshooters may well be removed from video footage altogether. But at five-point-five, he saw, he left internal assessment, headed back to his own desk and completed the rest of his working day as normal.

Christopher watched himself, yesterday, finish work at seven and make his way to Body. He watched himself eat his spaghetti libernara. He watched individuals and small groups of residents come and go as he sat there still. He watched as he refilled his libeer again and again, appearing progressively more sad and lonely as the evening rolled on. He watched himself stagger out of Body, alone still.

He rewound and rewatched again. There was no sign of the mysterious woman; no violet haze and no chase in the night. He watched as he left the bar at eight and went back home to his apartment. He watched himself emerge again at one-point-seven this morning and head to work again. He watched himself right up to the present moment, staring back at himself in his screen. He had had the strangest night of his life, he was sure, yet perhaps stranger still was to find that there was no record of it on the video system whatsoever. It was as if the whole thing had somehow been in his imagination, yet still remained as vivid as any real memory. *All things may not be as they seem.* The now familiar riddle flitted through his mind.

He felt slightly faint. It was not just the confusion of the moment, but the forgetting to eat his morning liberflakes that now caught up with him. He decided to head for a slightly early lunch.

In the cafeteria, Christopher's lunch was interrupted by the familiar fanfare of the libernews.

"A lifetime of struggle ... A history of horrors ... Almost a hundred years ago humanity stood on the brink of extinction ... But we were saved by the genius of the Writer ... Saved by advanced technology that would supersede our primitive instincts and guarantee our safety ... Together now and forever we look toward a brighter future ... Liberty Farm: Working For Your Future."

The same old montage of images; our horrible history, the protected present, the promise of a brighter future and the same perfect pair of presenters.

"A beautiful blue day to all you residents across the farm, we hope you don't mind us interrupting your lunch for an extra special broadcast. I'm Leo," said the man, blue eyes beaming below his blond hair.

"And I'm Fiona," said the woman, through luscious silvery lipsticked lips. "We're coming to you live today from inside the Libermid where the results of the liberlection have just been calculated and confirmed."

"That's right," said Leo, "We've been told that the Emortal Council gathered yesterday and have approved the future course for the Program, and I'm sure you are eagerly anticipating the announcement to find out who will be the new—or will that be continuing—prime resident."

#PerishForPrimeResident ... #DeanToDestroyDyspheria ... The libergram ticker began to scroll as Christopher's colleagues tapped their comments on their left hands.

Leo and Fiona stood on stage smartly dressed in the finest farm fashion alongside a posse of political persons: The ten dark-cloaked members of the Emortal Council, a group of unhappy looking red party members stood to the left without their former lead representative Morty Caine, and confident looking blue party members to the right led by the incumbent Prime Resident Dean Perish. Christopher stifled a scoff as he swallowed another chunk of his sandwich; it would be no surprise to anyone, he was sure, who the victor of the latest liberlection would be.

"So without further ado," said Fiona, "the winner of the latest liberlection and the prime resident of Liberty Farm is …"

Despite declaring an intention to deliver the results *without further ado,* Fiona delayed the announcement for at least twenty seconds. Whether it was to create genuine suspense, or to intentionally give the audience an extra window to leer over her fantastic physique, it was certainly Christopher's favorite few seconds of the show.

"Dean Perish!" she said, throwing her arms in the air, her perfect breasts bouncing in her tight dress as she jumped in celebration. The spectacle was at least some consolation to Christopher for the inevitable liberlection result. Fiona bounced all the way, through shimmering blue confetti falling from the ceiling, to kiss Perish on the cheek and squeeze her bosom against his chest as he stood smiling and waving, feigned relief and humility professionally etched upon his face. Dorms cheered and chatted around the cafeteria in celebration, thumbs raised high, a flood of blue likes appearing on screen.

"Dean Perish." Fiona repeated through her broad grin. "It's my absolute pleasure to announce you as prime resident for the ninth time, please tell us how you feel right now."

"Oh the pleasure is all mine Fiona," said Perish. "Honestly, I'm delighted, as I'm sure you can imagine, to remain prime resident and continue to lead the wonderful residents of Liberty Farm toward a brighter future. It is my purpose and my passion to do so; it is what I was born and raised for and what I will continue to do for as long as I possibly can."

Hooray for Perish! The libegram comments continued. *Perish is my hero ... OMG he's so handsome ...*

"And I'm sure I speak for the whole of the farm when I say I hope that will be a long, long time," said Leo, making his way across the stage toward Perish. "Before we talk about your plans for your latest term as prime resident, there's one question I'd like to ask, and that's how in the world anyone is supposed to solve that latest test we were given, with all those dots and lines."

Christopher thought back to the test he was administered a couple of days ago, where he was asked to draw through nine dots with just four lines, where he had almost accidentally ran outside their perimeter but instead completed the lines only to leave one dot spare at the top. He was sure he had failed the test according to its brief, but the screen had turned blue which was usually a positive and probably pointed toward the re-election of Perish.

"Well I couldn't possibly tell you that." Perish laughed. "Honestly because I don't know. Thankfully I don't come up with these tests myself. There are a fantastic team of examiners working inside the Libermid who create these kinds of puzzles to test different aspects of the Program and its interaction with residents, and I'm just pleased that on this occasion, once again, it's been determined that I'm the right man to lead the farm forward."

"You certainly are," Leo said, "and I know your wider team are very busy with a lot of important work in the Libermid. You've said repeatedly in your latest campaign for liberlection that they and you are working hard toward a final solution to dyspheria, one that could eliminate the disease once and for all. Could you give us any more details at this point as to when and how exactly that might be achieved?"

"Well I can't tell you too much," said Perish, taking on a more serious look, "for reasons I'm sure you can understand. But what I can tell you is that it does have something to do with what has previously been referred to as the blind spot, a part of the mind that the BRAIN system has so far failed to fully control, believed to be a primary source of dyspheria. I can tell you that this part of the mind is no longer a blind spot, as we have come to understand its workings, and that we are on the brink of a final solution that will completely control this part of the mind and eliminate dyspheria once and for all."

Applause erupted around the crowds on stage and around the dorms in the cafeteria, another burst of blue triangles appearing on screen. Christopher felt his own right hand twist, thumb up, as if of its own accord.

"And finally," said Leo, pausing for the noise to settle, "there is one more question which is probably the most pressing that the residents of the farm would like to know. This is of course your ninth term as prime resident; you've demonstrated your continued excellence in leading the farm in this position. Can you tell us, as perhaps many have wondered, as and when our great Writer, savior of humanity and founder of Liberty Farm, moves aside, is it your ambition to take his place at the helm in driving the Program?"

Perish paused, peering over his shoulders at the directors and other elites of the farm. Leo stood transfixed, smiling still. Fiona bit her lip nervously. The whole cafeteria in which Christopher sat was still and silent. It was something that he, like all the other residents in the farm, had speculated. But he was sure he had never heard the question asked so overtly. To hear the suggestion of the Writer *moving aside* filled him with discomfort. The Writer, the savior of humanity and founder of Liberty Farm, was approaching a hundred and fifty years of age. Apparently he spent most of his time in suspended animation, preserving his physical body while maintaining continuous connection and communication with the Program—overseeing its interaction with the residents. To hint that his life might be coming to an end, as Leo the libervision presenter did, hinted at an end to the Program as he knew it, to the beginning of a new phase for Liberty Farm created no longer in the image of the Writer, but Perish. The thought filled Christopher with fear.

"That is the big question isn't it," said Perish, "and it is a question I have considered for some time. It is not an easy question, as it necessitates the imagination of a world we have never seen, but I have imagined it. The Writer is our savior, undoubtedly, and we will remain grateful to him for eternity. But his time will one day come to an end. And when it does, I will be ready."

The liberscreen was filled with blue likes flooding in from across the farm. The cafeteria erupted into cheers and applause around Christopher. He was surprised by the reaction, more so by his own that followed suit. His hands clapped along almost involuntarily. He did not feel happy that the Writer's time might be ending, even less that Perish would be the one to assume his mantle, but still he clapped along. Was it the Program that made him do so, or the social pressure of those around him? He sometimes wondered if the behavior of others was perhaps more influential than the BRAINs themselves.

The special broadcast came to a close, with another light show of red and blue and the familiar soundtrack culminating once more in the slogan, *Liberty Farm: Working For Your Future.* But what future would it be? Another year or more of Perish as prime resident, and how much longer as chief controller of the Program, taking over the position of Writer, and what would that look like? Christopher imagined the familiar face of this fatherly figure he had seen across liberscreens every day of his life replaced by that of Perish, that looked not so unlike his own but triggered in him altogether different feelings of distrust and envy.

And what about the former red party leader, who had seemed like a viable candidate for the liberlection prior to his sudden arrest and transfer to AR yesterday? Were there no further details about his demise? Not even a single comment from Perish regarding his former opponent. It was as if he had been erased from relevance altogether, and all that mattered was Perish's path to power.

Christopher tapped the back of his left hand with the index finger of his right and a small holographic keyboard appeared. *What about Caine,* he typed. He hovered over the blue triangle key for a moment, before deciding against the comment and tapping the red triangle to delete.

8

In the evening Christopher found himself in Body again. He sat drinking, waiting, wondering whether the mysterious woman would show up again. He wondered if she was real or not. He wondered if he wished her to be or not. On the one hand he was guilty of inexcusable crimes, caught up in a curious web that had last night led him to the edge of the farm, through which he had seen her leave; on the other he was surely crazy, or hacked, or both. He didn't know what to think any more. *All things may not be as they seem. And so tonight I lucid dream.*

He sat and waited, drinking, bottle after bottle, until his mind was full of liberhol and the bar began to empty before close. There was no sign of the woman, no violet haze, nothing. He started to head home, wandering through the empty scarlet streets. He boarded a port on his own, blue light flashing as he entered under its archway. The world outside the port blurred, the machine whirred before rising to its usual high pitched sound and bright light, but delivered him not to his apartment block, but an unexpected destination. *Mining Department,* the voice announced.

He was back again; back in the corridors of the mine, red walls alerting him that it was too late. He had not intended to come down here again, or at least he thought. Had his mind betrayed some subconscious intention unknown even to him? Or had Canaan tampered with his BRAINs or the liberportation system in some way as to lead him here? He had not followed the woman or anyone else down here this time. He turned down the corridor toward the staircase, down which he had followed her color last night, but there was no violet this time; no sign of her, just a small creature sat on the top step.

It looked about as long as Christopher's foot: A lump of white fur sat atop four flat feet, a flat nose that seemed to sniff Christopher through the air, dark round eyes peering back at him, and two oversized floppy ears. It was the rabbit, the animal that had been carried in a load by a drone to the mine the other day, the one that had led those symps to AR, or at least one much like it. Had it returned? As he wondered, the thing hopped away down the stairs, as if spooked at being identified. Christopher followed, without thinking, down the metal staircase and into the heart of the mine.

He found himself again in the space that marked the outer limit of his world, where only robotic life forms were permitted. He saw the rows of robots, drones and aircraft stocked away around the walls; the massive cylindrical particle liberator in the center of the huge space shut down for the night; to his left a giant archway under which fell a flow of nanobots that formed the edge of his reality; and finally, the red glow of the libersphere reflecting off its fur, the creature. It sat staring at him for what seemed like a minute, before hopping away through the libersphere and out of the farm.

A siren erupted and red lights began to flash all around Christopher. His heart raced. He was alone in the heart of the mine with nowhere to go. He thought of the woman last night as she had laughed before walking through the red wall, of the animal that was somehow alive in the mine and hopped out to return to the wild, and saw no other choice. Slowly he walked over toward the archway and the libersphere. Almost close enough to reach by hand, the wall of nanobots appeared to shimmer. He could see his reflection: See himself standing at the edge of the only world he had ever known yet somehow felt he never belonged.

He raised his left arm and gently put his fingertips through its surface. It felt to him like a mist, almost a fine liquid, much like the libershower that was of course made up of the same stuff—the same BRAINs—as the libersphere.

Between the sirens in his ears and his heart pounding in his chest, he heard the sound of steps clattering down the stairs behind him. In a moment a swarm of liberbots would emerge to take him down and away to Advanced Rehabilitation for good. He had one choice: To stay in the world he had known his whole life and perhaps never truly live again, or step into the unknown where he would most probably die anyway.

He took a deep breath and stepped through the wall.

9

Christopher's whole body vibrated as he stepped through the wall of nanobots, as if the BRAINs circulating inside him and those in the libersphere he walked through merged into one—screaming to him in unison silently from the inside: *Stay!* He couldn't feel the edges of his body. He was lost in this limbo between worlds; Liberty Farm behind, and what unknown wilderness in front. All he could see was red; pure glowing red. He wondered for a moment if he could stay in this halfway world. But he had come this far. He took another step, and another, before emerging into blackness.

It was an all-consuming darkness like nothing he had ever experienced. All before him was black. He was sure his eyes were open but they saw nothing. He blinked and blinked again to confirm it. The vibrating had stopped. He could feel his body; feel his heart beat, his lungs breathe. He felt an unfamiliar sensation flicker across his face and through his hair. It was the wind. He was outside the farm, but where? All he could see was blackness.

He took another step forward. He couldn't see if there was anything for his foot to land on, but believing that he was for now at least stood on something he hoped that it continued in front of him. There it was, some ground to walk on. It felt softer than those artificial floors he was used to walking on inside the farm, crumbling slightly as he stepped, as if the surface was fragile but firm underneath. Besides his footsteps, his breath and the soft breeze, there was silence. He could no longer hear the sirens from the mine, as if the libersphere kept the sounds of the farm inside as effectively as it shielded from everything on the outside. But what was there but Christopher and this empty blackness? No liberbots or drones followed him out, at least for now.

He took another step. He raised his hand in front of himself, felt his fist clench and release, but couldn't see it. He touched his face. He could feel his body. But where was it? He turned to his left and saw nothing, turned to his right and saw nothing; in front and above and below—nothing but black. He turned around and saw a wall of red. He was sure the libersphere was a dome, that surrounded the perimeter of the farm and covered the tallest towers at its center, but from this close distance outside it appeared flat; a wall of red as far as he could see cast against the blackness in every direction.

He turned back and began to walk into the void. He didn't know where he was going; only that he must walk. With each step, slow at first but increasingly faster, he felt his faith grow that there was at least something outside the farm—even if it was just a surface to walk on. He walked for around a minute before turning around. From here he could indeed see the curvature of the libersphere as it cascaded around and down the farm. A perfect red dome that towered above him in an ocean of darkness. Could he go back? Would he be able to find the entrance back through to the mine if he wanted to? Somehow he knew it was too late.

He continued to walk. He just wished that he could see where he was going. He closed his eyes tightly for a moment. "Let there be light," he wished—to whom he did not know—before re-opening them.

And there was. He stopped as he saw for the first time, ever so slightly, the ground—a sort of pale grey—fading away into the distance. Directly ahead of him still there lay only darkness, but as he tilted his head upward he was astounded. There they were above him, among a blanket of blackness, small silvery sparkling points of light. There were tens, perhaps hundreds of them, either so small or so far above him—he had never seen anything like them—they could even be higher than the top of Liberty Farm itself.

And then he was struck by a bright white circular light, high above him and in the distance to his right. He had never seen such a thing; light in Liberty Farm was less bright and more consistent across the walls, ceilings and surfaces that emitted it. This thing hovered or hung like a ball floating in the black ocean. It cast its white glow over the world around Christopher, but there was nothing there. The big ball and the silver sparkles broke up the blackness but revealed nothing but an empty, dead, wilderness.

The bright light sparked a sudden realization. There was a reason for Liberty Farm; a reason for the libersphere and a reason residents stayed within its walls. There was nothing outside— nothing but dyspheria and death. Christopher felt the reality of what he had done dawn on him, his heart pounding in his chest. He heard the wind begin to howl around his ears, felt it wrap around his neck, choking him with its icy snare. He began to shiver. He looked at his arm, which he could now see in the white light, and pulled back his sleeve to see his hairs first standing on end then begin to grow, and grow uncontrollably over his wrists and blanketing his usually smooth hands. And then his fingernails too began to grow, into sharp claws, his fingers elongating. He reached up to his face and found more hair on his cheeks, felt his teeth grow into large fangs, his nose into a large snout.

The reaction had been delayed but deadly. Now disconnected from the Program and the antivirus, dyspheria had taken a deeper hold than ever before and he had descended rapidly to his darkest depths. He had transformed into one of them—a zombie. He began to run through the wilderness.

Then he saw it: A small white shape flitting away in the distance, through the long dark green lashes growing from the ground. It was the furry thing from the farm—the rabbit. He could smell it too, as it scurried away. His senses felt heightened but his mind—his identity—was gone. He took after it, like a beast chasing its prey, naked in the night, the green grass grazing against his legs and chest.

He followed the creature to a clearing, in which lay a big black shimmering surface that reflected the sparkling silver spots above. He snarled, saliva dripping from his hanging jaw as he saw the small white animal across the other side. He leapt across in its direction but landed with a loud splash straight into the cold water. Christopher scrambled for something to grab onto, his claws now nothing but hands, his skin smooth and human, but there was nothing. He cried for help, but the creature, its white shape silhouetted against the night, stood simply watching. He swallowed a load of water as he sunk beneath its surface, his freezing limbs growing stiff. The big bright ball and the small sparkly lights slowly disappeared as he fell into the black abyss. It was death now that surely consumed him.

10

There was blackness still. But Christopher could at least feel his body and the surface beneath it. He was sat down. He tried to move his arms but found them bound by the wrists to the chair. He tried to move his feet only to find them tied too. It was a heavy metal seat of the most uncomfortable sort Christopher had ever sat upon, never mind the fact that he was strapped to it. He had something wrapped around his face that concealed his vision. He could feel his clothes were wet; he must have been pulled from the water. Then he heard two men's voices whispering nearby.

"Are you ready?"

"You tell me, how do I look?"

"You look fine, now come on, before he wakes up."

Christopher made another attempt to move but was firmly restricted by his restraints. He bent his head around in an effort to gain some bearings but couldn't, before the sound of two sets of footsteps descended toward him. He froze as he felt somebody's fingers firmly grip the fabric wrapped behind his head and untie it. In a flash he was close up to an unfamiliar and unkempt looking face.

"Wakey wakey, eggs and bakey." He had the tanned complexion and unmistakable accent of the Islands and scruffy sandy colored hair and stubble. He was all Christopher could see, crouched close to his face, as he squinted through the sudden burst of bright red light.

The man stood and stepped away, allowing Christopher to see what looked like an old fashioned bulb lamp pointed directly at him from nearby, and the large silhouette of the second man as he tossed the cloth that had covered Christopher's face to the metal table and began to survey him from the other side.

"Where have you been, Christopher?" he said. He had a strong, stern Northern accent. As Christopher's eyes slowly adjusted he saw the man was older and stockier than the first, with a thick greying beard.

"Yeah," the first man said, "what you been up to hey?" The older man glared at him, seemingly triggering some reminder in his junior, who fumbled to retrieve and then cover his hair with a small red cap. Christopher saw now that the senior was already wearing his own, and that both men wore the navy suit and crimson cloak that comprised a troubleshooter's uniform.

"Where ... Where am I?" Christopher said.

"165-189-198," the Northern troubleshooter said. "It does not matter where you are. Tell us where you have been."

"I ... I don't know."

"You don't know?" he said. "Well let me tell you. You just breached the perimeter of Liberty Farm. And I want to know why."

"Yeah," the other said, "what the hell do you think you're playing at?"

"I ... I don't know ... I ... I went for a walk."

"You went for a walk?" the Islander said. "Just a little night time stroll hey, out of the farm? Do you know what's out there?" he said, pointing his finger toward the far wall.

"Death," said the other man. "Death and dyspheria, that's what lies beyond that wall. Do you realize what a serious thing you've done?"

"Yes," Christopher said, "I ... I'm sorry."

"Oh, he's sorry." The Islander looked toward his senior.

"I don't want your apologies," the older troubleshooter said. "I want to know who you're working with!"

"No one. I ... I ... No one."

The older troubleshooter rolled his eyes then nodded to the younger one, who nodded and walked around and behind Christopher's chair toward the back of the room. Christopher strained his neck to the right to follow him but he was out of sight. Instead he noticed for the first time that there was a fourth person in the room; an Eastern looking woman, leaning against the wall. The younger troubleshooter clattered around to retrieve something, but the woman, with long black hair and olive skin, tapped continuously on a liberpad, showing no interest in anything happening around her. She didn't even flicker as the troubleshooter returned lurching a heavy looking white oblong object and dropped it loudly onto the metal table.

"Do you know what this is?" said the older, Northern troubleshooter. Christopher looked at the box-shaped object, its nearest face covered in antiquated controls, dials and switches. He shook his head.

"It's an ECT device," he said, while the other began to set it up. "Electroconvulsive therapy. It's a tool that was used in the old days to induce seizures in psychiatric patients who exhibited certain undesirable behaviors. And it was quite effective in reducing those behaviors, at least temporarily. But it was a somewhat uncomfortable experience for patients. Thankfully we don't need such tools today."

"We've got the Program nowadays, haven't we?" The younger troubleshooter grinned, as he connected a wire to the device and at the other end strapped a narrow object over Christopher's head with two flat circular components resting snuggly over each of his temples.

"But that doesn't mean we still can't make use of it, oh no," said the older man. "We've found it can be useful in giving some residents the shock they sometimes need to tell us things they might be hiding. So Christopher, tell us, who are you working with?"

Christopher looked to the younger troubleshooter, who looked back at him, shaking his head, his finger now resting over a switch on the device. He swallowed heavily.

"No one."

Christopher heard a quiet flick of the switch before a sudden sharp shooting pain scorched through the sides of his head, through his BRAINs and in a flash all around his body. It was a pain like nothing he had felt before; hot like fire, cutting like a chainsaw, threatening to tear him apart. His teeth chattered in his mouth, his muscles contorted as he let out a muffled moan of anguish, and then relaxed as the device was switched back off.

"Who are you working with?" The older troubleshooter stood over Christopher, slamming his fists on the table. "Who put you up to this?"

"No one, please …" Christopher said, but it was too late, as another shock of electricity surged around his body. Through the blinding pain he saw in his mind's eye the flickering image of a woman with a mysterious color around her; of a notebook dropped on the floor in front of him, and then back to the room once more as the current stopped.

"What were you doing in the mine? Why did you leave the farm?"

"I don't know … I … I …"

Another surge shot through Christopher as the words of Canaan, the black troubleshooter, sprung into his mind. *"I want you to follow this woman. I want you to continue your observations around the mine—you will find answers there. And I don't want you to mention any of this to anyone besides me. Not even any other troubleshooters."* The third shock went on much longer than the first two; it felt like an eternity.

"I … I got lost! I … I think I was hacked."

"Oh I don't think so," said the older man. "Bring her in." He instructed the younger troubleshooter, who again disappeared to the back of the room. Christopher strained again unsuccessfully to see where he went and saw the dark haired woman stood still undisturbed against the wall. Then he heard what sounded like another woman, muffled cries, and the sound of metal being dragged along the ground. The troubleshooter returned, pulling another hostage with him strapped to a chair and placed her at the table opposite Christopher. Her mouth was sealed with tape. What could be seen of her face appeared beaten and bruised. But her red curls were unmistakable. It was her: The violet woman.

"Do you know this woman?" the older troubleshooter asked, as the younger one removed the electrodes from Christopher's head.

"No," he said, as they were strapped on to the woman's.

"Did she give you something?"

"No," he said again.

"Have you seen her before?"

"No."

"Then you won't mind if we give her a little shock too, find out what she might have to tell us?"

Christopher stared into the deep brown eyes of the woman that stared back at him. She closed her eyes for a moment and gently shook her head.

He whispered, "No."

The younger troubleshooter flicked a switch as Christopher saw the woman receive the same treatment that he had just been given, saw her eyes and face contract, her body contorting in its chair as the sound of electricity filled the air, interspersed by her muted cries of pain.

"No, stop!" Christopher shouted. "Canaan."

"What was that?" said the older troubleshooter, signaling to his colleague to stop. The woman's head flopped to her chest.

"Canaan," Christopher said. "Please, let me speak to Canaan."

"Canaan, eh? Very well. Canaan."

Christopher shook, surprised that the name had been enough, pleased that the woman was no longer crying or contorting in her chair; disappointed he allowed her to be shocked even once; then froze as he heard heavy footsteps behind him. The rest of the room seemed to fall silent as slow, steady steps loomed closer and he felt the presence of the black troubleshooter towering over him. Could it be, he had been in the room all along?

"Christopher." His voice boomed. "I see you've met my colleagues." He walked around and perched on the corner of the table which buckled under his huge weight. "This is Isaac," he said, pointing to the younger, scruffy troubleshooter, "and Cassius," pointing to the other, older one. "I hope they didn't shock you too much."

"Canaan, please …" Christopher started, but before he could say another word, Canaan swung his huge hand and smacked him with an open palm to the face. It felt to him as heavy as a hammer. His whole head was ringing. The initial shock was quicker than the electrical one but the vibration afterward persisted longer.

"Allow me to continue." Canaan said, calmly. "I hope they didn't shock you too much and saved you some energy for me. Now, why did you leave the farm?"

"Canaan …" *Slap.* Another heavy hand to the face.

"Why did you leave?"

"You … you told me …" And another.

"Why?"

"The mine … the … the investigation …" And again.

"Why?"

"She … she …" And another.

"Why would you leave the farm Christopher? Tell me, really!"

"I don't know … I …" Christopher felt beaten physically and mentally. He didn't know what to say. He didn't know why he'd done what he'd done these past few days. He barely knew who he was any more.

"Yes you do, Christopher," Canaan said, leaning in close so that Christopher could see the long scar across his left eye.

"Because I'm sick of it!" Christopher shouted.

"Sick? Sick of what?"

"I'm sick of it all!" he said. "I'm sick of the farm. I'm sick of every day being the same. I thought …"

"Thought what, Christopher?"

"I thought there might be something more. Something … else." Christopher fell forward in his chair. He felt exhausted, but relieved, as if he had released something he didn't even know he had inside him. He was spent. He didn't know what to expect; least of all the clap-clap-clapping of Canaan's hands— not against Christopher's face, but against each other. He looked up to see Canaan clapping his hands together, smiling. He looked as Cassius began to clap, and Isaac too, laughing, and the woman leaning against the wall even lifted her head and put her liberpad beneath her arm to join in as the whole room was filled with applause … for Christopher. He had never been clapped by anyone before. Then he watched as the red haired woman opposite stood up freely and pulled the tape from off her own face as she too smiled.

"Phew, well done Christopher," she said, as the bruises disappeared from her face. "You're tougher than I expected. Nice to meet you properly. I'm Lucy by the way." She gave a brief wave of her six-fingered hand.

"You …" Christopher said. "And you …" He looked at Isaac as he removed his crimson cap from his sandy hair. "You're not a troubleshooter?"

"No mate, but we had you going didn't we?"

"Some more convincingly so than others," said Cassius.

"Some a little too convincingly if you ask me," said Isaac.

"And you—" Christopher said, turning to Canaan.

"I am a troubleshooter," he said, "but I am also more. There is a lot more Christopher, just like you hoped there would be. And I'll show you."

"Just …" Christopher felt faint. "Just let me go."

"Let yourself go, Christopher," Canaan said.

Christopher pulled at his arms once more, only to find them flail up, already apparently unbound. Suddenly freed, he leant on the arms of the chair and stood, but tripped as he went to walk, falling to the floor in a heap with the toppled chair beside him.

"Stay with me Christopher," said Canaan. "Stay with me."

Slap. Another smack to the face, and Christopher opened his eyes, head still ringing, to find himself stood opposite Canaan, no longer in the same room, no longer with any of the others, but in an empty and long red walled corridor, just the two of them.

"I'm sorry for hitting you, Christopher," he said, "but you needed grounding. Don't worry, it won't leave any marks, trust me."

Christopher rubbed his cheeks, sure that it would, as he regained his bearings and observed his new surroundings.

"Where am I? Where are the others?"

"They're around, we've lost them for now. As for where you are, that's tricky. Perhaps first I should tell you when. Walk with me."

"When?" Christopher said, beginning to walk slowly.

"Yes, when. What's the last thing you remember before you walked out of the farm?"

"Erm … work." Christopher said. "I went to work".

"And then?"

"And then, I guess I went to the bar."

"You guess?" Canaan laughed. "You really should drink less, Christopher. And then what?"

"And then … And then I went to the mine—"

"Wrong," Canaan said. "You went back to your apartment by nine and to your liberbed, like you have done every night of your life, and that's where you are right now."

"Right now?" Christopher looked around "But we're here right now."

"Here? And where are we? You just said yourself you don't know. You don't know where you are and how you got here. How could that be unless, perhaps, you aren't here at all? No, the fact is that you docked at nine and just like every other resident in the farm lie now in hibernation. This is the zero hour, Christopher."

"The zero hour? You mean, between nine and one? Then where is this place?"

"This place, this endless corridor, is a shade Christopher; a recollection, an amalgamation of any number of corridors you may have walked, or never have. This is all in your mind, Christopher; in my mind. This is the dream world."

"The dream world?"

"Yes, Christopher." The pair reached a libervator at what now seemed to be the end of the corridor in front of them, pressing the red downward pointing triangle. "Let me show you."

Christopher followed him inside, still feeling lost at what was going on and where he was. Canaan's words made little sense, but it felt somewhat reassuring to listen to someone who at least seemed to believe what he was talking about. They emerged a moment later to what appeared to be a normal morning at the liberportation station, half-filled with residents ambling their way to work.

"We call this place Oneria," said Canaan, as they began to walk slowly through the crowds. "Right now it appears to you as Liberty Farm, but there's more—infinitely more. It appears to you as it does now—as it does to all these other residents—because that's all you've ever known. Every day, exactly the same. And every night, when you enter hibernation, your mind doesn't just empty, like you've been led to believe. It keeps working, here, in Oneria. Only most of the time it goes on doing what it does the rest of the time, repeating the same routine behaviors—working, eating, drinking, shopping, watching libervision. Most people don't realize they're dreaming because they don't question it; they don't question their waking life, never mind what happens when they're asleep. What makes you different, Christopher, is that you do question it. That's what makes you lucid."

Canaan paused and pointed up toward one of the libermarketing screens towering above the walkway, as text appeared upon it. *All things may not be as they seem.*

"And so tonight I lucid dream." Christopher spoke the second half of the riddle that had been rattling itself around his head for the past few days. "But why would they put that up there? How come these people don't see it?"

"Look again."

Liberty Farm: Working For Your Future.

"You said that this is all in my mind, but in your mind too and these other people … How can we be here together if it's in our minds."

"Because our minds are connected, Christopher," Canaan said, "by the Program, by our BRAINs. The same Program that connects us in the day, that keeps us running like clockwork, connects our dreams too. This is a whole other world Christopher, that we can share."

"And why doesn't anyone else see that writing? Why don't they hear us talking now?"

"Like I said," Canaan said. "People see just what they expect, including you. They only hear what they want to hear. They forget their dreams, just like they forget their daily lives. Things change here, more than the farm—that's one of the ways you can tell apart the dream world from the waking world. It's always filling in the blanks, attempting to make sense, your mind filling itself with itself. It's up to you to observe and control that."

"Control?"

"Yes, Christopher. You can do anything you want here, anything. But first you need to practice, to learn how this world works. And that's what we'll show you, the others and me. We are the sleepwalkers, Christopher, the ones that act while others sleep, that do while others don't. And we want you to join us. But you must understand, Christopher, that to do so is to go beyond the bounds of the Program. There are very few in the farm who know the truth of how hibernation really works. What I have just told you—what more you have to learn—may well put you in danger. That's why I had to be sure of your intentions, of your character."

"Hey Canaan," a voice called through the crowd, "are you guys done with the intros yet or what?" It was Isaac, striding toward them, alongside Cassius, Lucy and the other woman.

"So the electric shocks … the chair … was all a test?"

"Come on Canaan," said Lucy, as the group gathered around him, "let's give the new guy something to remember before he wakes up."

"All things may not be as they seem, Christopher," said Cassius.

"And so tonight I lucid dream," said the dark haired woman.

"Keep questioning, Christopher," said Canaan "and make sure to write down all that you remember. We'll see you soon."

And without warning, the five sleepwalkers shot up from the ground and flew up, as fast and flowing as any drone Christopher had ever seen, past the libermarketing screens and toward the blue libersphere high above, shattering through its dome shaped structure, which split and shattered from the point through which they disappeared, cascading into shards, as the sphere itself began to fall in on Christopher. The ground too began to shake as he stood alone, staring up toward the sky, while hundreds of other residents continued to walk around, oblivious, as their world crumbled around them.

11

Christopher opened his eyes and saw the familiar blue ceiling of his apartment bedroom. He was lying on his liberbed. He stretched his hands out in front of himself and saw them intact; touched his body to feel that it was certainly still there. But then it had felt just as real to him what seemed like a moment ago, somewhere else— a dream world. His heart rate was elevated. He saw images in his mind's eye becoming blurry. "Write down all that you remember," Canaan had said.

He went to the libersafe and retrieved the red notebook and pen. The memories of obtaining those items—from Lucy outside the bar and from Canaan in the internal assessment ward—seemed just as strange and surreal as any he still held from last night, yet still here they were—apparently physical and in his hands. How could he be sure which memories were real and which were just in his mind? He opened up the book.

All things may not be as they seem.
And so tonight I lucid dream.

What had been a riddle now seemed to make more sense. *All things may not be as they seem.* He had seen enough now that was apparently not all—or maybe more—than it seemed for him to at least understand the premise; he thought he had gone down to the mine two nights ago and seen a woman leave the farm, only to see no evidence of either her or himself on video footage the next day; he too had left the farm—or at least he thought—only to find himself back in his apartment this morning; and he had been tied to a chair, interrogated and tortured, only to find it was a test. Certainly many things were not as they seemed; but was anything?

And so tonight I lucid dream. Lucid—that's how Canaan had described him. It was something to do with questioning, or realizing, where he was. The dream world—that's where Canaan said they were. But was it a place at all? He had kept saying that word—dream—as if it was something people did, but only few understood. He turned the page.

My name is Christopher 165-189-198.
Last night I saw a woman walk out of Liberty Farm.
Last night the walls of my world opened up.

The words he wrote just yesterday still seemed so staggering. He could still barely believe what he had seen then, let alone experienced since, but then, had he? He left a space and began to write below:

Last night I too left Liberty Farm. There is another world ...

He paused for a moment before continuing. *Oneria.* That is what Canaan called it. The word sounded so mysterious, yet what he described looked just like Liberty Farm—at least at that point. But then he remembered there was more before that.

First there was darkness. Then there was light.

There were only vague images in his mind; he tried to capture.

An animal running through the night. Water ...

He could recall struggling through some cold dark depths. *Dying.* That was how it felt.

Captured by troubleshooters—only they weren't.

His mind grew hazy; he couldn't remember the details.
Lucy. That was her name. The woman with the red hair: The one he had followed that left the book; the one that started this whole series of events.

Lucy. It sounded to him like an adjective. Loose. Loopy. They felt like words befitting her character as far as he had seen. Lucid. Perhaps it was a coincidence.

He scrambled for memories once more. What was it that Canaan had called them?

Sleepwalkers. The ones that do while others don't.

One last remarkable memory came back to mind.

They flew … high over the people and out of the farm. I saw it all collapse in front of me.

And that was it, the last thing he remembered before finding himself back in his liberbed this morning. Was it real? What did that even mean? He felt sure he had experienced those things he wrote, but didn't know how it could be, or how he was now back in his apartment.

He decided to go to the bathroom and start his day, as he had every other day of his adult life. He looked at himself in the libermirror. He appeared as the same young man he had for many years; slim, neat brown hair, pale complexion. He rubbed his cheeks with his hands. He had the vague sensation of them having been struck or hurt recently, though he felt no actual pain and his skin appeared clear and undamaged. Perhaps he was just shaken up.

He proceeded to decontaminate, dress and head out to work. He walked down the quiet blue corridors of his apartment building, shared a libervator filled with other dorms and emerged on the street. Flowing through the crowds he felt compelled to observe his surroundings more closely. He walked slower than usual, allowing others to overtake him as he watched residents tiling under the tall triangular archways, lights flashing blue as they entered the liberport platforms. The whole thing ran like clockwork; the Program clearly working as intended. He saw the liberbots dotted around the stations, looking to detect and prevent any undesirable behavior, and wondered if they too dream. He watched the libermarketing screens high up and all around the place; advertising everything from body augmentations to advanced libergenic partner pairing; polished portraits of Perish celebrating another inauguration as prime resident; and the Writer still watching, overseeing Liberty Farm as always. Was this the space he was stood last night—in his mind—that he saw the sleepwalkers shoot up from the ground and up toward the sphere; flying like he had never seen people do before. Was it here that he had seen the whole farm collapse? Today it looked as perfectly pristine as always.

At his workstation at the Systems Monitoring Department he again took the opportunity to review his own video footage and that around the mine. He saw himself, as Canaan had said, finish work yesterday then head to Body, and then head back to his apartment before nine, not emerging until close to two this morning. He watched footage around the mine and saw no sign of himself or anyone else. Wherever he had been last night, the cameras of the farm itself did not capture his movements. He continued his regular working duties and his day without incident.

He skipped the bar and headed straight home after work. His BRAINs felt scattered enough already without the help of liberhol. Perhaps he should drink a little less anyway. He got back to his apartment and pulled a dinner of libercue wings and fries out of the liberwave, slumped on his self-adjusting sofa and commanded the libervision to turn on, hoping it could provide some distraction or comfort from his confusion.

The evening's entertainment began with *Liberty Idol*—a game show in which residents performed renditions of popular audioprogramming songs in the hope of stardom. He could not say he enjoyed much of the audio he heard day to day around the farm—though those tracks played at his workstation apparently did improve his performance. However, there was some amusement to be found in the early rounds of the show

90

particularly, watching desperate symps with an inflated perception of their singing abilities perform terribly then get picked apart by the judges. Although the show got a little tedious as it went on, hearing the same old stories about symps and their hardships and their one hope of success, being built up then crushed, before some more stable dorm inevitably won the series.

He tapped the back of his left hand to open his keyboard and typed to comment. *Liberty Idol contestants are all losers,* he entered, then continued to pick at his overly flavored Program-produced protein and imitation potato pieces.

Next up was *Emune Estates*, a documentary series in which wealthy emune residents showed off their extraordinarily expensive homes; where designers described their "vision" and detailed the unique development processes to achieve previously unimagined architecture—though of course construction itself was carried out rapidly by laborbots. Tonight's episode featured a wealthy family of five who had had to wait four days for their thirty-thousand square meter mansion to be finished and had managed to avert disaster and make last minute adjustments to accommodate the youngest daughter's demand of her own pool between her bedroom and beauty parlor. Christopher assumed he would never be able to afford such luxury, but couldn't help but admire the aesthetics of the abode—not least due to the reward circuits being triggered by his BRAINs as he absorbed the show. *I know - build her own house and leave her there,* he typed.

Following this, Christopher was treated to one of the most exciting spectacles he regularly enjoyed; highlights from the Genelympic games. The Genelympics were an ongoing competition in which various divisions of libergenicists contested to design, develop and display the finest physical specimens they could create. Thousands of genetically engineered gladiators were pitted against one another in a variety of combat formats and arenas and eliminated over the course of the year, culminating in the annual finale event *Mount Z*. The final fifty specimens that survived that far would embark on one last fight to the top of a tall and treacherous peak; only one would live to celebrate victory and be granted the prize of emunity and a life of luxury among the elites of Liberty Farm.

Libergenicists from all five regions of the farm were involved in the games, but the majority of actual competitors—at least those that survived to the latter stages—were of mostly Southern genetic composition, and it was the South where the games were held. It was the South—previously known as Africa—where the Outbreak had initially begun and decimated the population before the antivirus or the Program were developed. Those who had survived there demonstrated in doing so a certain durability and though they remained highly susceptible to the psychological symptoms of the virus, their physical strengths were without question. The Southern wastelands provided the perfect environment for the creation of colonies to experiment with human physical development away from the more important intellectual capital of the West—where Christopher lived—and to create the arenas for the competition. The games were a global celebration of humanity's survival, strength and potential; properly controlled; the ingenuity of libergenicists capable of creating ever-stronger specimens; and the unity of the former continents that now comprised Liberty Farm.

Tonight's show was a compilation of highlights from one of the early rounds of the competition, *Perilous Podia*. This involved a gruesome gauntlet in which the gladiators fought to steal and then safeguard a grid of podia from one another. Each tall triangular podium would glow either red or blue. At regular intervals the red podia would explode and be destroyed along with any man stood upon them. There were a variety of swords, spears and other weapons scattered around the arena which they would use to fight over the blue podia, which were big enough only for one. The colors would change occasionally too, to prevent anyone staying in one space for too long. Anyone not stood on the rapidly reducing number of blue podia at the end of each interval would die in the explosion, if not in the preceding fight itself. A burst of blue likes appeared on screen alongside each gladiator's demise.

His mind was a mess of bloody black bodies abused and obliterated in brutal battle. He felt punch-drunk, as if his head had received a beating. And then a booming voice suddenly spoke through the libervision, forcing him to half jump from his sofa in surprise.

"Christopher."

The dark and familiar face of the troubleshooter filled the screen, long scar over his left eye.

"Canaan, what are you doing on the libervision?"

"I'm not. This is all in your mind. You're dreaming, Christopher."

"What?"

"Look at your hands."

He looked down and counted six fingers on each hand.

"But—I was just watching libervision."

"A while ago, yes. Then you went to bed, don't you remember?"

He didn't remember at all. He was sure he had just been watching the games. He continued to look down at his additional digits, confused and mesmerized.

"Christopher." Canaan appeared beside Christopher on the sofa, startling him once more. "I need you to focus."

Christopher saw that the libervision was switched off.

"Christopher, this is Oneria, the dream world. You watched libervision tonight then went to dock at nine. You lost consciousness, then continued to dream about watching libervision, then regained your awareness—with my help. Your mind fills in the blanks, tries to make sense of itself, you remember?"

"But, my hands—"

"Are a great way to see if you're really awake or dreaming," Canaan said. "Your mind is adept at making a broad sense of things, but has much greater difficulty with the details—the little

93

things you don't normally pay attention to—until now. We call it a reality check. Now come."

Canaan made for the door and Christopher followed automatically. They began to walk down the blue corridor of his apartment building.

"Wait," Christopher said. "Can you explain this dream thing to me again?"

"The dream world—" Canaan said, "Oneria—is the state we enter every night in hibernation. Between nine and one—the zero hour—our minds are here. But of course it isn't really an hour."

"It isn't?"

"No. In the old days people used to use a twenty-four hour daily cycle, based on the Earth's rotation on its axis; the rising and setting of the sun. You didn't need a clock to tell you if it was day or night. Since Liberty Farm however, we shifted to a decimal system—divided into ten hours. Of course few really know the length of those hours, or their proportion. The color of the libersphere—the color of these walls—tells you whether it's day or night; the Program tells you when to work and when to go to sleep."

"But they're blue now."

"In your mind they're blue," said Canaan, "because you feel like you're awake—like you're actually walking these corridors—even though I just told you you're dreaming. Check your hands again."

He raised his hands while walking to see six or seven fingers on the left and just three or four on the right.

"You see the farm works us harder than we are used to Christopher. We sleep less and less. It keeps our minds tired day after day. But that also makes our dreams more vivid as a result. Along with the Program connecting our BRAINs—it's what helps us to share this world."

They stopped at the libervator at the end of the corridor. Canaan nodded to Christopher, who pressed the blue upward pointing triangle. And again—but there was no response from the machine.

"Technology," said Canaan, "that's another thing that doesn't work quite right here. Allow me."

Canaan simply gestured with his hand and the Libervator door instantly opened.

Christopher emerged on the streets outside, already brimming with residents on their way to work; it must have been nearly two already. He felt slightly strange, but everything around him looked perfectly normal; laborbots working away under service symps' supervision, residents filing through the triangular archways on their way to the numerous ports, liberbots on alert and the libermarketing screens high above and all around. Had he had his breakfast this morning? He couldn't remember. It was the strangest thought, but what matter—he could always get something to eat later. But this strange feeling ... as if he was being watched. Of course this was Liberty Farm; he was always being watched or monitored to some extent—but specifically? He walked, somewhat nervously—he didn't know why—under the archway as it scanned his liberdentification and intentions.

"Red light!" A metallic voice called from Christopher's right. Suddenly, a stream of two, three, four liberbots, gleaming white, came streaming toward him through the crowd to seize him.

"No," Christopher said. "No wait, I haven't done anything."

He felt faint.

"No!"

He opened his eyes and sat up suddenly on his liberbed. *No.* Had the sound emerged from him somehow as he awoke from hibernation? Or was it an echo in his mind from the libervision last night—perhaps the last cry of a defeated Genelympic gladiator before having his head crushed by a competitor? He steadily got to his feet and made way to the bathroom.

"Christopher."

He was stopped in the doorway by an unexpected visitor.

"What ... What are you doing here?"

"You're dreaming, Christopher," said Canaan, "remember?"

Christopher looked down at his hands and saw that the keyboard on his left was activated, with red letters on it's display. *Wake up, loser!*

"I need you to focus, Christopher. You need to focus if you want to stay lucid."

"But … But I was just on my liberbed?"

"A false awakening, Christopher. Come."

They exited the apartment and began to walk the corridor outside. Its walls were red.

"There are three main ways to help you become lucid, Christopher. One: Write down all that you can remember of your dreams when you wake, as you have started, in the journal we gave you. Hold that intention in your mind as you dock; it will activate your prospective memory and increase your awareness. Two: Question. Question everything—like I told you last night. Ask yourself whether you're awake or dreaming, ask how you got to the place you are now. Three: Reality checks. Check your hands at regular intervals in the day; watch out for any glitches with technology, read and re-read any text to see if it changes. Repeating these behaviors in your waking life will lead you to re-enact them in your sleep and thus help you to become lucid."

"There are also three ways to stay lucid." He continued. "One: Focus. Pay attention to your surroundings, and to your intentions. Two: Voice commands. Remember this is your mind, Christopher, and you can tell it to do whatever you want—literally. Or three: I could hit you in the face …"

Christopher stopped and threw his hands in front of his face to protect himself as Canaan swung the back of a huge hand toward him without even breaking stride, stopping short as if only to scare him. But it was too late …

Christopher opened his eyes to find himself back in his apartment bedroom, then was startled by the deep laughter of the massive man sat at the bottom of his liberbed.

"I'm just kidding," Canaan said. "But seriously, focus. One more time."

They walked down the red corridor again.

"You're taking me to the mine," Christopher said.

"No, you're taking me to the mine," Canaan said. "I've come here into your dream space to help you out. You believe there's a way out of the farm but right now you can only conceive of one way. Soon you'll learn how to turn any doorway into a portal to wherever you could possibly want. Soon you'll learn that there's much more to Oneria than you can currently imagine."

Soon they arrived at the now familiar metal staircase that led down to the center of the mine and the edge of Liberty Farm. Had he ever been here at all? Were these stairs just an image he had gained from footage he had seen in his role as systems monitor, or perhaps even entirely in his mind?

"Your fascination with this place is justified, Christopher," said Canaan. "It really is a paradox isn't it? The source of all of the farm's fuel—its life force—and yet the edge of its supposed shelter from who-knows-what outside. I encouraged you to come here—Lucy encouraged you to come here—because it is a very fitting threshold. Look around."

Christopher looked around once more at the massive particle liberator, the various drones and technology on standby around the enormous room, and Canaan—as he disappeared out through the red libersphere that hung underneath the huge archway that led out of the farm. Christopher followed, took a deep breath, and for a second time—at least in his mind—stepped through the wall of nanobots. Once again, he felt his entire body and BRAINs vibrating as he was surrounded by red, then stepped again out into the blackness. Only this time he was accompanied by Canaan, and there were already small dots of white light high above them. Still, Christopher felt faint. Was he about to pass out—or wake up?

"Ask the dream for what you want, Christopher," Canaan said. "Say, *lucidity now!*"

"Lucidity now," Christopher called out to the air in front of him. And then, he felt sensation return to his body—this dream body. He felt the cool breeze run across his face and neck and hair. He felt as if those dots of light became somehow brighter.

"What was it you said last night?" Canaan asked, "When you were out here, in the dark?"

"Let there be light," Christopher said.

Canaan laughed. "Let me try that. Let there be light!"

Suddenly, a huge red ball of what looked like fire erupted over the horizon and rose up, as the smaller specks of light faded, as the black sheet above turned first to that magical violet and then to pure clear blue. The huge ball hung high above them, casting light all around; a blanket of green beneath their feet and as far as the eye could see.

"You are a sleepwalker now, Christopher. You have the power to become lucid; to enjoy this time in hibernation you previously spent unconsciously. This Liberty Farm—the one you've just exited in your sleep—is not real. It is a mental map of the mindscape of the farm's sleeping residents and of the Program. But Oneria goes far beyond the farm and far beyond the Program. Over there, among those trees …" He pointed to some greenish-brown blur in the distance. Christopher had never seen trees in person, perhaps only on libervision. "There is a lake of water—the one you fell into last night. Beneath that lake is a sanctuary, a space of our own that we call the Ark, and you are welcome." He placed a hand on Christopher's shoulder. "See you soon."

And then, the troubleshooter and man mountain Canaan took off toward the sky, crimson cloak billowing behind him, and disappeared into the blue.

12

Christopher again awoke to the sky blue ceiling of his bedroom. He raised his hands again to find them five-fingered and perfectly functioning. He was back, as far as he could tell, in his everyday waking world. He opened the red journal and flicked over the words he wrote two days ago:

My name is Christopher 165-189-198.
Last night I saw a woman walk out of Liberty Farm.
Last night the walls of my world opened up.

And yesterday:

Last night I too left Liberty Farm. There is another world—
Oneria.
First there was darkness. Then there was light.
An animal running through the night. Water. Dying.
Captured by troubleshooters—only they weren't.
Lucy. Sleepwalkers. The ones that do while others don't.
They flew … high over the people and out of the farm. I saw it all collapse in front of me.

He left a gap and began to write his latest recollections:

Leaving the farm again. More flying.

If it was a delusion he was experiencing, it was at least a consistent one. He continued.

Canaan speaking through the libervision, walking through the corridor.
Three ways to become lucid:
1.   Write down your dreams
2.   Question things

3.   Reality check

He stopped, suddenly struck by the strangeness of what he was doing. It was almost as if he was writing a guide—to something he had virtually no practice of—to no one but himself. He was just writing what he could remember of the dream, what Canaan had told him. And that was it. He still could hardly understand anything he had experienced these past nights, but felt compelled to at least trust Canaan. It was he that had encouraged him toward the mine and out of the farm, to become *lucid*, and now—despite being a troubleshooter—seemed for some reason willing to help him; to support him, to welcome him. Despite knowing little about him, he felt like Canaan might be his closest ally.

On the way to work Christopher felt a strange sensation that the farm—the liberportation station—was somehow less real to him than it had been, although it appeared just as it always had. He felt a strange paradox that he was an outlaw and yet somehow protected. He looked at the liberbots as he made his way toward his port, almost expecting them to seize him but still feeling unafraid, as if he doubted their existence. But still, he was greeted by a blue light as he passed under the archway.

The way to his workstation was like any other day, as was his time at his desk; the libervators and technology all appeared to work normally. His work seemed more dull than usual. He was no longer assigned to observing the mines, instead he was mostly observing service symps assisting laborbots in street construction and maintenance, which seemed to him rather unnecessary given that the work itself being done in those areas was almost entirely automated; he was simply tasked to ensure that the symps handled their responsibilities and experimental level of freedom without exhibiting any excessive symptoms.

His workstation was filled slightly more than usual by an influx of libergram advertisements for a range of products and deals. It was as if the Program detected his decreased satisfaction and sought to incentivize him with an array of aspirational offers.

But it had only been a few days since he last went shopping, and he didn't feel like any more.

At lunch, in the cafeteria, he pulled his sandwich and snack from the liberwave without a snag. The liberscreen showed clips of yesterday's action from the Genelympics, but there was no appearance of the big black troubleshooter Canaan either on screen or anywhere else in the cafeteria.

Christopher remembered to check his fingers a handful of times throughout the slow day, each time all five on each hand appearing perfectly intact, the uninspiring state he found himself in appearing convincingly to be his usual waking reality.

Midway through the afternoon, he received a libergram inviting him to attend a review meeting with his supervisor, Senior Systems Monitor Mason. It was not unusual to be invited to such a meeting, on perhaps a weekly basis, to review his recent reports in person. He caught the libervator up to the next floor and walked across the corridor to his boss' office.

"Good day, Christopher." He welcomed him, cheerily. He had neatly combed grey hair and matching mustache.

"Good day, Sir."

"I hope we aren't disturbing you," Mason said, "but we hoped you might be able to share with us a little more detail around some of your recent reports."

It was Mason's familiar introduction that he would regularly use to open his reviews. The "we" that he referred to was the farm, the collective interest, of which he was a passionate proponent.

"Certainly, Sir," he said, stepping onto the red and blue halved triangle, the libertree in the center of the office floor. In a moment, a large holographic liberscreen appeared behind him, enveloping the side of the room opposite Mason's desk, displaying summary data from Christopher's recent reports: Residents observed, feedback and adjustments given and his own key performance indicators.

"I understand you've been spending some time observing service symps around the mine recently," Mason said. "Could you summarize your observations?"

"Certainly, Sir", Christopher said. "So I've been spending a considerable proportion of my time working on observations around the mine for around two weeks now, in which time I've also reviewed prior data, and it appears we are seeing a continuing trend of slightly reduced performance and slightly increased abnormal social behavior among the service symps. It has, for the most part, been only a slight trend. You have perhaps seen that we did experience a spike in turnover of service symps in the mine just a couple of days ago, although I believe this was the result of an isolated abnormal incident."

"What kind of incident?" asked Mason.

Christopher paused before responding, unsure whether he was permitted to disclose this to Mason, as Canaan had spoken to him in such secrecy, but he wasn't telling him anything about the investigation, and he assumed Mason could find out the cause of the incident himself if Christopher didn't tell him. "It was an animal," he said.

"An animal?" Mason looked shocked.

"Yes. Some kind of rodent I believe. As you know, we understand that virtually all animal life on Earth was destroyed during the Outbreak, but it seems a few of the smaller creatures may have survived underground. It seems one of these creatures was inadvertently retrieved as part of the loads of resources gathered from the outside world by drones. The animal managed to escape back out through the libersphere just before it was liberated. It seems that these symps I referred to witnessed this rare occurrence from a mining observation deck, reacted negatively and failed to return to their working responsibilities and required transfer to AR."

"I see," Mason said, twisting the corner of his mustache. "I suppose that is quite an unpredictable occurrence. And how did it make you feel?"

"Feel, Sir?"

"Yes, Christopher. What was your emotional response to witnessing this … animal?"

"Well, I admit to some elevated excitation," Christopher said, "but I believe this was more to do with the sudden spike in activity among the symps to which I needed to respond, than my witnessing the animal itself. But then I received a senior override through my workstation. I assumed it might have been yourself, Sir, who handled this override."

Mason stared back blankly.

"In any case," Christopher said, "I don't believe it to be my concern what materials are brought into the mine. My only responsibility is to complete my duties as a systems monitor, as the Program requires."

"Very good." Mason nodded. "And what explanation do you propose for the more general trends you have been observing?"

"So far as I can see," Christopher said, "antivirus levels and integration among the mine service symps appear to be relatively stable. What I have observed, however, is an apparent reduction in the positive impact of liberos on their behavior; a relative dissatisfaction with their libernomic reward, despite recent increases in hourly Ls. I wonder if the symps' awareness or perception of the volume of liberos being mined has led some to a reduced perception of their own relative wealth. Perhaps such information should be restricted further to the more rehabilitated symps in the area."

"Indeed," Mason said. "These ungrateful symps are never satisfied with the freedoms we provide." He was talking from the collective perspective again, spouting sentiment that was commonplace across the farm. "That is until Dean Perish completes his final solution of course. Speaking of which, do you think these observations around the mine might have something to do with this blind spot in the mind, this mysterious source of dyspheria that he says we're on the brink of controlling?"

Christopher felt all of a sudden uncomfortable. He could reel off his regular reports almost unconsciously as he had just done, but these more uncertain questions seemed to elevate stress inside of him—or perhaps it was just the mention of Perish. In truth, he was skeptical of the Prime Resident's proposed potential to permanently destroy dyspheria; all through his life and work Christopher had seen the symptoms surface among residents; abnormal thought and social behavior, reluctance to work and occasional rejection of the Program. Despite all the advances in the Program and BRAIN technology, the virus still persisted. He didn't think there was any 'blind spot' in the mind that the BRAIN system had yet to control, as Perish claimed. He had come to accept the virus as an inherent part of life.

"Perhaps," Christopher said, pulling himself together. "Perhaps that is the source of the undesirable behavior. I hope Perish can put a stop to it all."

"Very well," Mason said. "Thank you for your report. I'll see you soon."

Mason raised his thumb, giving Christopher a momentary mood boost. He returned the gesture before stepping off of the libertree in the middle of the office floor. The liberscreen behind him closed down, leaving the plain blue of the walls behind, and he headed for the exit.

13

Sometime after work, he found himself at the liberportation station. It seemed exceptionally busy and he was startled into alertness by bumping with some force into some other dorm passing by who didn't bother to turn back to Christopher or pay him the slightest notice. He felt dazed for a moment, losing track of the way to his port. He was more surprised still to see a strange sight among the streams of residents passing by—a child, sat still and alone among the oblivious crowds. What was it doing there, thought Christopher. A child should be in libercation, being prepared by the Program for the working world. He edged cautiously toward the child, no one else in the vicinity seeming to give it the slightest bit of attention. As he got closer he saw it was a young girl with black hair and that she sat with a liberpad in her lap, upon which she tapped away.

He stooped beside her. "Hello little girl, are you lost?"

The girl paused her tapping and glanced at him. She had dark eyes and Eastern features.

"No, are you?"

He peered around his surroundings. He was certainly in the liberportation station. He saw that the girl appeared to be drawing an illustration of her environment on her liberpad, complete with its tall towers, ports and libermarketing screens. It reminded Christopher of something he had drawn a long time ago.

"Shouldn't you be in libergarten?" he asked.

"Shouldn't you be in bed?" she replied.

Christopher watched as the girl began to color the background of her picture scarlet as the sphere itself high above began to change swiftly from blue to red.

"How did you do that?"

"I can do anything I want," she said.

He saw his surroundings grow darker, as the crowds of residents all began to rush to their nearest ports and soon disappear, leaving just Christopher and the girl alone in the middle of the street. He looked up to see a sign above that seemed to read *Laberty Firm*. He looked down as the girl continued to color her picture.

"Wait. Are we dreaming?"

The girl continued to color frantically, scribbling scarlet all over her liberpad, as the glow of the red sphere seemed to expand and pour over Christopher and everything around them.

"Yes, Christopher," she said. "Would you like to come with me?"

"Where?" he said, heart now pounding, as the liberportation station seemed to melt into red all around him.

"Wherever we want."

Christopher found himself in a sea of red, all around him in every direction—no floor, no walls, no little girl beside him—just pure red.

How had he got here? He didn't remember a thing after work that day. Could it be he had gone home and docked already that evening, lost consciousness and now regained it while asleep? He peered at his hands and found one to be about twice the size of the other.

"Lucidity now!" he said, and sure enough his world seemed to solidify. His hands returned to normal size. He felt and saw a firm floor beneath his feet, still red, then heard footsteps behind him.

"Good, Christopher, I see you've remembered a little of what Canaan has taught you already."

He turned around to see an Eastern looking woman with dark hair and olive skin walking toward him, carrying a liberpad in her hand.

"I know you," he said.

"Yes," she said. She had full lips and a broad face. Her features, like her way of walking, were elegant and yet bold. "My name is Kimiko. Sorry I didn't introduce myself the other night, I was kind of busy."

"A moment ago, you were just a little girl. How can that be?"

"I was?" She laughed. "Oh well we can appear in many forms in the dream world, I guess that's just how I see myself sometimes."

"You were in that room with the others … holding me hostage."

"You mean this room?" she said, lifting up her liberpad for a moment and giving it a tap.

Christopher turned around to see that they were now inside a regular room with four walls. The bright red dimmed, the only source of light now was an old fashioned bulb lamp sat atop a flat rectangular metal table, with a similarly flimsy old metal chair on either side.

"How did you do that?"

"I designed this place," Kimiko said, "based on my idea of Acute Assessment, and an environment I thought would be intimidating to you. They call me the painter—Canaan and the others—I seem to be particularly gifted when it comes to creating dreamscapes."

"Dreamscapes?"

"Yes, dreamscapes. You remember how this is all in our minds right? Well it's up to our minds to create the world we see before us, and it turns out I'm quite good when it comes to those visual aspects. I've always had an eye for detail, you see—that's how I became lucid."

"And how do we create the world?"

"Just imagine. As vividly as you can. For example, is there anything else you remember about this room?"

He looked around the room. There was only one thing that immediately sprung to mind—those electric shocks coursing through his BRAINs and body.

"That machine," he said. "The electro … whatever it was called …"

He turned and pointed back toward the table and sure enough, there it was: A large oblong object as big as a liberwave, covered in antiquated dials and switches.

"Very good." Kimiko smiled.

"Did I do that?" he said.

"Yes," she said, "all in your mind. Now what else would you like to do with the place?"

"I don't know," he said. "It's kind of dark in here."

"Well, Canaan told me you already discovered a way around that."

He paused for a moment, then recalled.

"Let there be light!"

And sure enough the dim red lamp made way for a clear blue light that filled the room and reflected off of the metal furniture.

"Very good," Kimiko said. "You're a natural. Now, would you like to go somewhere else?"

He noted that there was apparently no door in the room. "Where?"

"Your apartment maybe," Kimiko said, gesturing with her hand to the wall behind Christopher where there did now indeed stand a triangular sliding door. "After you."

He walked cautiously through the doorway to find himself, to his surprise, stood in his open plan apartment living space. It appeared just as he remembered.

"You can walk through any door you can find in the dream world," Kimiko said, suddenly beside him, "or create one yourself, and use it to go wherever you want. Is everything as it should be?"

"Yes," he said, stepping into the room. "Except ... I'm sure I bought a rug a few days ago."

"A few days? Well, it mustn't be firmly in your memory of the room yet. Why don't you show me?"

He looked at the space in front of his couch and intuitively flicked his fingers, just like in the *Libernsraum* virtual apartment, to make an indigo rug appear magically on the floor.

"Very nice," Kimiko said. "Where next?"

"I don't know. Work?"

Kimiko nodded toward the door.

He emerged in the large tall room in the Systems Monitoring Department he went to work every day. He found his workstation, among a room filled with similar workstations, all occupied by other systems monitors silently tapping away at their screens. It looked the same as always. He took a seat at his swivel chair opposite his 180-degree semi-circular liberscreen, upon which appeared all the usual streams of data: Program performance of his subjects, live video feeds and essential updates on libernomic trends. He sat and slid and tapped his fingertips around to navigate information as needed and input his observations and any suggested adjustment of AV levels among his assigned symps. He started to wonder what he might have for lunch. Then a voice spoke from behind him.

"You really are a slave to the Program aren't you?" Kimiko said. "Did you forget where you are already?"

He peered down at his hands to see six or seven fingers on each.

"Sorry, it's just that this dream world looks just like the farm."

"Don't worry about it. At least you created a convincing environment, and your door worked. Now come, follow me."

Before Christopher could do anything, Kimiko wrapped her left arm around his back and began to speed around his front, with her right arm flailing, turning the both of them into a spin. The Systems Monitoring Department began to blur in front of him, then disappear, almost as the farm outside did from within a liberport. Then he emerged in another familiar space. He felt Kimiko release her grip of him. He felt dizzy for a moment before being returned to his senses, and saw the cafeteria around him, filled with fellow systems monitors on their lunch break.

"What was that?" Christopher asked.

"Spinning," Kimiko said, "It's another great way to get around here. If you can't find a door, or don't want to, just think of the place you want to go and spin yourself there."

Kimiko had an endearing childishness to her speech at times, which contrasted the seriousness with which it seemed she meant the things that she said. A *great* way to get around sounded like an exaggeration—he was still struggling to stand up straight.

"Come on, let's go somewhere more interesting," Kimiko said, grabbing him before he could speak and spinning him through dream space.

A moment later he found himself again in another familiar place. The massive particle liberator towered above them, along with the tall walls filled with mining drones and robots on standby, and the red wall of nanobots cascading down the archway at the edge of the mine.

"I know you know one way out of the farm," Kimiko said, "now let's see if you can spin your way out."

Kimiko closed her eyes, threw her arms out horizontally on either side of herself and began to spin—once, twice—then disappeared from their surroundings. Christopher closed his eyes and took a deep breath, imagined the world on the other side of the wall that he had ventured through the two previous nights of lucid dreaming, put his arms out at his sides and began to spin—once, twice—then opened his eyes after the third rotation to find … nothing but blackness. Still he was sure he felt the soft crumbling of the ground underfoot, and the cool breeze.

"You made it," Kimiko said, from somewhere close by. "It's a bit dark though."

Christopher thought for a moment before shouting, "Let there be light!" Small spots of silver light began to break the black blanket above him, and a huge white ball away and to the right cast its glow over his surroundings.

"Not bad," she said.

"What are those things?" he said, pointing upward.

"They're stars," Kimiko said. "Huge balls of gas burning billions of miles away, shining to us across the galaxy, lighting the sky. Want to see more?"

She waved her hand across the sky and the spots she called stars doubled, tripled, quadrupled until there was more silver light than there was blackness. And not just silver; the stars seemed to twinkle in various shades and cluster into numerous colorful clouds and ribbons around the night. Christopher even saw what also looked like a star shooting at high speed across the sky.

"And what's that?" he said, pointing toward the large round ball.

"That's the moon. A natural satellite that orbits our planet Earth, reflecting the light of the sun."

She began to wave her hands in a circling motion and the sky above seemed to follow her movements; the moon began to fall to the horizon, the stars began to fade, the sky turned from black to violet to blue and a burning bright orange light erupted above them. Christopher saw a blanket of green beneath their feet in all directions.

"And what's this?"

"Grass," Kimiko said. She turned around playfully among its long lashes, which grew up quickly around her. Shapes of various colors bloomed among them. "Flowers." She danced with her arms outspread, as large thick brown structures emerged upward from the ground. "Trees." They grew and grew until they were two or three storys tall, splitting and branching in various directions as they did so, more green and spots of other colors expanding around their upper parts, creating a beautiful tapestry above them. "Life," she said.

"It's beautiful," Christopher said. "I never saw these things before I came here. If this is in my mind, how can it create things I've never seen?"

"Your mind goes deeper than you think," replied Kimiko, still slowly swinging around the sea of colors around her. "Memories, Christopher. We are all connected."

"There's so much out here," Christopher said. "The farm always told us there was nothing outside but death. How can that be?"

"There is much more outside Liberty Farm," Kimiko said, "and a whole lot that the Program doesn't want you to know about. There's one more thing I'd like to show you. Come quickly."

She skipped over to Christopher through the grass and flowers, gripped him tightly and took them spinning. It was a bright and colorful blur that took Christopher a while longer to recover from than the previous twirls. Shortly he found his feet firmly upon the grass, he patted his hands upon his chest to regain sensation of his body then slowly raised his head to see what was the most spectacular sight of his life.

He and Kimiko stood at the top, inches from the edge of what appeared to be an enormous circular cavern; a perfectly round cauldron carved into the earth and stretching almost as far as he could see. Its perimeter was marked with towering trees, at least ten times taller than those Kimiko had shown him a moment ago, and above them what should have been sky was instead replaced by what looked like the surface of a great upside down lake—sunlight glinting off its waves, huge floods of water falling from it then fading into clouds of fine spray, and incredible translucent arcs that seemed to contain every color imaginable curving over the cavern. And within the great round hollow in the earth which had to be at least as big as the West itself were tall stone walls and tiers of steps, and more walls and steps and floors, each level sitting within the next, like the whole place was a great inverted pyramid. And there were trees, flowers and grass everywhere. The whole place looked somehow ancient and yet more alive than anything he had seen before. And there were buildings of all kinds of shapes and sizes and colors, built all around the curves and angles of the cavern and its steps. And there were people—what looked like hundreds of people—walking, running, dancing around the streets and flying above as well. People, and other small creatures, flying all around.

"This is the Ark," Kimiko said. "The sleepwalkers' sanctuary—our home in Oneria."

"It's unbelievable," he said. "Did you make this?"

"No." Kimiko chuckled. "Though we do like to play and create our own little spaces within it. The Ark was created long before us. By he who holds the book of dreams. We call him the Architect."

"The Architect?"

"Yes," Kimiko said, "the same one who built Oneria. The one that helped the first of us to become lucid."

"Where is he?"

"He's around." She smiled. "And I'm sure he'll see you sometime soon, and so will I."

And without hesitation, Kimiko leapt from the edge of the cauldron shaped cliff and began to fly smoothly away into the middle of the Ark.

Why do they keep doing that?

14

Kimiko—the painter—showed me how to create my world.
Use doors to go wherever you want. Spin.
There is so much life outside the farm.
The Ark—the most beautiful sanctuary.

Christopher sat on his liberbed, writing down in the red journal all that he could remember of his dream the night before. It was strange, the way he struggled to piece together his memories of Oneria. Images came in a mostly incoherent order, and just as he tried to stitch them together in his mind, they drifted away. It must have only been minutes, or less, before waking that his mind was in this entirely other world, but now awake in this one it felt like much more than just a fraction of time that separated him from it. It was as if his BRAINs, the Program, his waking reality forced itself upon him in such a way as to squeeze anything that wasn't useful out of his consciousness. Still, the image of that last breath-taking place he visited—the Ark—was so vivid. He simply lacked the vocabulary to describe it.

There is so much life outside the farm. That was the main impression he was left with. Of course, he never really left the farm. His whole night's adventure was merely in his mind—but then how could it be so rich? He had seen so many things—such color—that he was sure he had never seen before. And the Ark—it appeared to be so full of life, and people. How many sleepwalkers were there? And what did they spend their nights doing? Christopher had spent his whole life in Liberty Farm, living according to the Program. It was difficult to conceive of any potential beyond those walls, beyond those boundaries, whether real or imagined.

Work was slow and dull. He still did everything he assigned to, almost automatically, but a part of his mind was elsewhere—in part distracted by the feelings and images of last night and part in anticipation of what he now hoped would be another night's adventures to come. He had only been lucid for three nights, but it felt like unlocking a whole new level of his life.

In the cafeteria, Christopher's lunch was interrupted by the familiar fanfare of the libernews.

"A lifetime of struggle ... A history of horrors ... Almost a hundred years ago humanity stood on the brink of extinction ... But we were saved by the genius of the Writer ... Saved by advanced technology that would supersede our primitive instincts and guarantee our safety ... Together now and forever we look toward a brighter future ... Liberty Farm: Working For Your Future."

"A beautiful blue day to all you residents across the farm, we hope you don't mind us interrupting your lunch for an extra special broadcast. I'm Leo," the man said, blue eyes beaming below his blond hair.

"And I'm Fiona," the woman said, through luscious lipsticked lips and bouncing bosom. "We're coming to you live today for a special update from our newly re-elected Prime Resident, Dean Perish!"

Christopher watched as dorms around the cafeteria raised their thumbs, a flurry of blue triangles appearing on screen over the face of Perish, sat confidently on the couch opposite the two presenters.

"So Dean," Fiona said, beaming away at the Prime Resident across from her, "congratulations once again on your re-election. How have the last couple of days been for you? Have you had much time to celebrate?"

"Thank you." Perish smiled. "But no I wouldn't say I've had much time to celebrate—although it's great to be on the show with you two once again and to have received well wishes from so many residents. But in truth the past couple of days have been much like most others for many years of my life now—busy as always. I continue, like Liberty Farm itself, to work hard for your future and your freedom."

"Indeed," Leo said, "and we thank you for it. Now, one of the things you've always been known and admired for, Dean Perish, is your hard line on hackers. Before we talk a little bit more about that, we just have a short clip to play our viewers, if that's alright."

A graphic of the libertree and the slogan *Liberty Farm: Working For Your Future* consumed the liberscreen before the red and blue halves pulled apart to reveal a new scene. A shifty looking symp sat tapping frantically on a screen in a dark room, scratching suspiciously at his skin.

"Hackers," boomed the voice of a male narrator, "the bane of Liberty Farm. Despite the protection that the Program provides, despite its benefits and the offer of freedom from dyspheria, there are those that want to steal more than they deserve. They work alone …" The camera pulled back to reveal two more hackers sat at screens in the same room alongside the first. "They work in groups. But they arc always working against the Program, and against you."

A shower of red triangles appeared alongside the sight of the symps on screen.

The scene switched to a distressed looking female dorm sat facing a camera in a studio, and then to what seemed to be surveillance footage from the streets of the farm showing the same woman walking along.

"I was walking home one night after work," she said, "when suddenly these three men appeared from nowhere and surrounded me."

The screen showed the footage as she described it.

"They dragged me around a dark corner and pulled out this … device."

The screen switched to a close-up shot of a small device held carefully by the crimson glove of what could be assumed to be a troubleshooter, revealing it to the camera. It was a pipe shaped object around two hand's length, around which one could just about wrap one's fingers, all black in color except for a red triangular light toward the top end of its curved side. A hack-stick.

"They shined this red light into my eye." The woman began to sob as the scene flicked back. "I tried to stop them but they held me down. They stole seventy thousand Ls from me in less than a minute, and then left me on the side of the street, petrified. It was the most terrifying experience of my life."

The screen switched to another distressed looking woman, this time a symp, retelling her story.

"I always thought my son was a good boy," she said. "Sure, he had his problems, but he tried his best to follow the Program. I thought his rehabilitation was going well. He got a trial in street maintenance."

The screen showed shots of the woman and her son throughout his life, on a liberday, then images of him as he got older.

"Then somehow—I don't know—he met some bad people. He started acting strange, like his head was loose, like a zombie. He stopped going to work. He was hacking his own BRAINs to experience some kind of altered state that he shouldn't have."

The screen showed the young man lying on the floor in a dark room, writhing around, eyes rolling, barely conscious as half a dozen troubleshooters and liberbots burst through his door. Christopher didn't know if it was real footage or just acting, but either way the drama was compelling.

"They took him away to Advanced Rehabilitation and I never saw him again. It was a shame to see him go, he could have become a much better resident than he was, but ultimately I know he was a hacker and that AR was best for him—best for the Program."

The film continued with clips of more liberbots and troubleshooters bursting through doors, catching unsuspecting hackers. Canaan was not among them, he noted. Did Canaan carry out such arrests? Surely, as a troubleshooter he must. But then what about Oneria, what about the sleepwalkers? Did other troubleshooters know about that? Was it allowed?

"Thanks to Dean Perish," the male narrator resumed, "more hackers than ever before are being captured and taken to

Advanced Rehabilitation, not only helping to protect you from the threat they pose, but helping our programmers to understand the cause of their disruptive behavior. If you suspect anyone of hacking, make sure you report it as quickly as possible … For the farm, for your freedom, for your future."

The libertree and the slogan *Liberty Farm: Working For Your Future* took over the liberscreen once more before it returned to the studio where Leo, Fiona and Perish sat, looking a little more serious than before.

"Disturbing scenes," Leo said. "Dean Perish, I think this film clearly illustrates the importance of the work that you and your team are doing in trying to eliminate the hacker enemy. But let me ask you, why do you think this enemy exists at all?"

"Well it's difficult to say," Perish said, "I don't think any of us can truly understand the motivations of a hacker—because of course there are no valid motivations—but it is my job to at least try. The truth is there have been those that have sought to undermine the Program since its inception, and yet still enjoy its benefits—the protection it provides from dyspheria. Of course dyspheria itself is the source of the problem, like all problems of the mind. Hackers are, in effect, the modern embodiments of the virus seeking to further infest and threaten a population that has mostly had its symptoms successfully suppressed."

#DeanToDestroyDyspheria … The libergram ticker scrolled through comments. *Hackers deserve to die … Send all symps to AR!*

"Will it ever stop?" Fiona asked with a look of fear etched across her perfect features.

"Yes," Perish said, "I'm sure it will soon. Having said that, despite our continued and improved efforts to stop them, the hacker enemy grow ever more sophisticated in their methods. It is a constant struggle that we face. We have only recently discovered a new form of collective hacking as well as hacking of BRAINs in hibernation, for example. But rest assured all forms of hacking will soon be eliminated."

Christopher felt a flutter of nerves. Was this the collective hacking that he had heard Canaan and two other troubleshooters talking about a few days ago? And what about hibernation? A few days ago he had thought, as he had the rest of his life, that there was nothing of interest in hibernation at all—it was simply the time when BRAINs were set on standby, uploading data to and downloading updates from the mainframe without interference. He now knew that the BRAINs remained connected, active, in the zero hour, and that there was another world there, in our minds.

"As I told you last time, myself and my team are rapidly uncovering new understandings of dyspheria. What was previously referred to as the blind spot is no more. We now understand its workings and how to control it. We are on the brink of a final solution that will eliminate the threat of dyspheria once and for all."

Leo and Fiona smiled and raised their thumbs at the camera, prompting another flurry of thumbs up in the cafeteria, and blue triangles appearing on screen. Christopher felt his own wrist twist and thumb point upward automatically.

#DeanToDestroyDyspheria ... *#FinalSolution* ... *#FinalSolution* ...

"And finally," Leo said, "you hinted last time that you might be preparing yourself to one day take over the position of the Writer when his time comes to an end. Do you have any further update on that?"

"Yes, I do." Perish said, taking a deep breath and a moment to straighten his already perfect suit. It was either genuine nerves or an extremely effective act of modesty. Christopher suspected the latter.

"As you know, we are approaching the hundredth anniversary of the Unification. And as you know this is now my ninth term as prime resident, for which I am most honored. I have been proud to serve the residents of Liberty Farm for so long. And the truth is I have been preparing myself for a long time mentally and now also practically to take over the role of the Writer when the time is right. I have in fact, recently, been interfacing directly with the Program, learning its hidden workings and already making my own modifications, alongside the Writer. Now, with the blessings of the Emortal Council ..."

The camera panned to show the ten members of the Emortal Council in the front row of the audience, all in their customary black cloaks and pointed hats.

"It is my honor to announce." Perish stood as he continued. "That this coming Unification Day, the Writer has agreed to step aside and that I, Dean Perish, will take over his role as primary interpreter and overseer of the Program."

Leo and Fiona stood too, as did the entire audience on screen and in the cafeteria, a flood of blue likes, as a raucous applause erupted all around the farm, and Christopher's hands clapped vigorously, despite the fear that now filled him. The Writer, the savior, the original designer of the Program and Liberty Farm had agreed to "step aside" and allow Dean Perish—a hollow copy, a clone who despite his perfect training had no experience, no real understanding of the hardships of humanity's past—to take over and lead the direction of the farm and the future. And Unification Day was only a couple of weeks away. Was that really all that was left of the Writer?

15

Christopher was drinking again. He was sat, alone as usual, with a half-filled bottle on his table.

Suddenly, a familiar figure slipped into the room and toward Christopher—curly red hair that matched the color of her dress—it was Lucy. She slunk into the chair opposite, downloading a glass of wine.

"Hey sleepwalker," she said. "Hard day?"

"Not hard," Christopher said, swigging his libeer, "just, strange."

"Strange?"

"Yeah, strange to think that the Writer is going to step aside, and that Dean Perish is taking over."

Lucy laughed.

"You've spent the last few nights getting to grips with lucid dreaming and you think it's strange that a professional politician who's been groomed for this his whole life is taking over the farm?"

"I don't like him," he said.

"Me neither," she said.

"I mean, he doesn't know anything about people, about our past. How can he protect our future?"

"How could anyone?"

They sat in silence, each drinking, for a moment.

"But what I find strange, Christopher," she smirked, "is that you're in this world of infinite possibilities and you're sat in a bar, drinking fake beer, sulking over politics. Have you even done a reality check?"

He sat up straight, realizing that he hadn't. He looked at his hands to find that he was dreaming.

"How come this keeps happening?" he said. "I go about my day, it seems I go to bed and forget about it, then find myself somewhere else, and one of you lot help me become lucid."

"It's just how the mind works, Christopher. It's always filling in the blanks, trying to make sense of itself. You don't want to enter the dream world directly anyway, it's best to fall asleep normally first, otherwise things can get pretty wild."

"Wild? How do you mean?"

"Yes, wild. It means the Program can follow our minds, can see what we're doing, just like our daily lives. It can tell that we're not really in hibernation the way we should be, it can track us, and we don't want that. That's why the Ark is hidden, well outside the dreamscape of the farm, so that non-lucid residents don't stumble on it accidentally."

She stared at him intensely through those deep brown eyes.

"But anyway, you just need to become more aware, in your waking life as well as here. Canaan, Kimiko, me and the others— we're only helping you become lucid now until you're able to do it yourself. We're just scouts."

"Scouts?"

"Yes, we scout for residents who look like they might be ready to become lucid, ready to find out the truth. That's why we're helping you Christopher, and hopefully you can help us."

"Help with what? What truth?"

Lucy gave a wry smile, gulped down the rest of her red wine, and then made for the door, leaving a mysterious trail of deep color floating in her wake.

"Come on," she said. "Time for more training."

"Wait," he said, clambering to chase after her. "What is that color that's always following you?"

"That thing?" She sniggered as she skipped out of Body and down the street. "It's my aura. My mum said it's because I'm very spiritual. That's how I was able to lucid dream since I was young."

"What do you mean, spiritual?" Christopher struggled to keep up with her, physically and mentally.

"You know, spiritual. Sensitive, intuitive … everything the Program wants us not to be."

"Are you a symp?"

Lucy laughed. "You mean a symptomatic resident? Yes, I suppose I do exhibit some symptoms of dyspheria, don't I?"

Christopher thought it best not to answer.

"And that color, what is it exactly?"

"Violet, I suppose."

"Violet," he said. "I knew that. It's like a mix between red and blue isn't it? It's beautiful. How do you suppose I knew that?"

Lucy glanced over her shoulder at him, apparently amused, as she continued to speed down the street.

"At least you know something. Maybe you've been dreaming longer than you remember, who knows. Now come on."

Lucy turned down a dark passage, down which Christopher followed, and emerged, to his surprise, in the middle of the liberportation station, which was empty but for the two of them.

"So, Kimiko tells me she's shown you the basics of travelling from place to place. Now, how about travelling through space?" She stopped ten feet in front, facing him, and effortlessly floated six feet into the air, hovering straight upright. "Come on."

He looked up at Lucy, then back down at himself, and his feet, clueless as to what to do. He tried to relax his body, bent his knees and jumped. Up a few inches then down straight away. And again, up a few inches then down straight away, just jumping on the spot.

"And now you look like a rabbit." Lucy laughed as she floated elegantly back down to the ground and toward him. "Come on, let me help you."

She came up close to him, face to face, and placed her hands gently under his arms and around his waist. Looking straight into those deep brown eyes, Christopher felt an unusual sensation. She spoke like a crazy person, but her presence was somehow calming, fearless. He felt a strange fluttering in his stomach. He felt like the weight of his body had been lifted and looked down to see that it was—literally—now floating six feet above the floor.

"Now breathe," she said. "Relax. I'm going to let you go now."

She floated back slowly away from him, releasing her fingers from his waist as she drifted away, back several feet again. He breathed and tried to keep his gaze on her until he could see clearly how far they were from the ground. He held on for a second before falling to the floor in a heap, with Lucy laughing above him.

"Ow," Christopher moaned as he got himself back to his feet, "that hurt."

"It can do a little," Lucy said, "so long as you expect it to, but don't worry, it won't do you any harm here. This is a dream, remember, it's all in your mind—even gravity. Now try again."

Christopher gathered himself, and took another deep breath. *It's all in your mind,* he repeated to himself. He closed his eyes and recalled the previously unbelievable things he had seen these past nights: The view from the top of the Ark, the sight of Canaan and the others all flying up at high speed, of Lucy and her brown eyes as she raised him up. He felt himself become weightless, and lifting slowly from the ground. He opened his eyes to see himself floating, and stopped intuitively at the same height as Lucy. He felt a peculiar feeling in his face as he smiled, like he had never smiled before.

"I'm doing it!" he said.

"Good." Lucy smiled back. "Now follow me."

Swiftly, she tilted her body forward and glided smoothly, flying past Christopher and coming to a halt hovering at the other end of the station, a trail of violet appearing briefly behind her before fading away.

He turned toward her, then tilted his body forward and attempted to copy her, only for it to keep on tilting forward until he was upside down, head toward the ground. He pushed his torso forward again to spin back upright but couldn't stop himself spinning all the way around again, and again—a spinning Christopher six feet in the air. He heard Lucy laughing in the distance.

"Come on, Christopher," he said to himself, "level out." And to his surprise, he did level out, floating horizontally facing Lucy's end of the station. "Forward," he called, and again his dream body responded to his command, drifting slowly in Lucy's direction. He began to kick his legs and pull the air with his arms to speed up, which steadily he did. "I'm flying!"

"Looks like swimming to me!" Lucy shouted. "Stop trying to move your body and just focus on where you want to go. Just imagine yourself moving in that direction and your body will follow."

He stopped flailing his arms and legs, lifted his head and looked straight toward Lucy, focusing his attention toward the spot she was floating, and sure enough he began to speed up and fly much more smoothly in her direction, so much so that he almost crashed straight into her.

"Whoa there, cowboy!" Lucy said, elegantly gliding herself out of Christopher's trajectory while simultaneously raising her hands and bringing him to a halt. "Don't shoot too far, and don't forget to stop."

"Sorry," he said, blushing.

"It's ok," she smiled. "It's good. Now, let's test out your agility shall we?"

She span herself away in a pirouette, flying across the station, up and down and through one of the tall triangular archway entrances to a port platform, up and down and around another, and another before gliding to a stop at the opposite end of the station, a violet spiral dissolving in her wake.

Christopher leaned forward and began to fly again, focusing his attention on the first archway—he made it under—then the second—under again, then the third—*BAM,* he crashed head first straight into the underside of the third archway and went flailing to the floor with a loud thud. The next thing he knew was Lucy leaning over him, gently helping him to sit up.

"It's ok, Christopher." She smiled. "Nice try. Now come on, let's get out of here."

She stood up and flew straight up, high above and through the red libersphere. Christopher got himself to his feet, regained his senses, looked up toward the spot in the sphere she had disappeared through, and began to fly upward—past the libermarketing screens, above the tall towers that surrounded the liberportation station and up through the canopy of nanobots. It felt much like the first time he walked through the wall at the edge of the mine, his whole body vibrating, but a greater rush. He emerged outside, hovering alongside Lucy, in the night sky filled with stars, high above an enormous red dome.

"Are we over the farm?" he asked.

"Only in our dreams," she said. "Follow me."

Lucy reached with her outstretched hand and wrapped her fingers around Christopher's, sending a sensation that felt like electricity running through his arm and to his heart, guiding him gently as they flew in the direction of the moon.

"Look down there," she said, pointing toward a large black lake amid a circle of trees, the silver satellite in the sky shimmering in its surface. "That's the entrance to the Ark, you remember falling in there?"

Christopher couldn't bring himself to speak as he flew so high above the ground, the cool wind billowing through his hair and clothes. Green fields and more trees became slowly visible below, as the sky above began to shift from black to violet.

"Over there," she said. "Let's go."

She gripped his hand more tightly as she turned sharply, toward what appeared to be tall mountains in the distance, as the sky became pink and the stars began to fade.

"Come down now," she said. "Easy does it."

It looked for a moment that they were going to crash head first into the mountain, only for Lucy to slow the pair of them down in what seemed like the last possible seconds, taking them down gently to the top of the white-tipped mountain. Before them lay an infinite world of waterfalls, lakes, trees, fields and more mountains, all glowing with colors as a huge golden sun grew from the distant horizon. The air was cold. He could see his breath in front of him. But somehow he felt warm. Lucy still held his hand tightly. He turned and looked into her deep brown eyes. She looked back at him.

"I've never had such a good night," he said.

She smiled, her red curls billowing in the wind.

"Good night," she said.

16

The light of the rising sun was replaced by the bright blue of the morning libersphere, breaking through the dream and bringing Christopher back to his body. He knew he was back in his liberbed but didn't want to admit it. He wanted to stay on that mountaintop, Lucy's hand wrapped around his. He felt the warmth of the sunshine, and her presence, still inside him. He sought to hold on to the lingering image for as long as he could. It was as if the light had burnt itself on the backs of his eyelids. Only once it completely faded did he eventually open his eyes. Slowly he rose on his liberbed, retrieved the red journal and wrote:

Flying with Lucy. I've never felt so free.

It was true. The experience was incomparable. Flying through the air; freed from gravity, freed from fear, freed from everything. It felt like all there was last night was he and Lucy, like they could go anywhere. And it wasn't just the flying—there was something about her. She might have been crazy. She might have been contagious. But whatever it was that she had, he wanted more. Still, he was back in his apartment, back in the waking world, back in Liberty Farm. *Working For Your Future.*

Everything felt slower that day. His body felt heavier, by comparison to the weightlessness he had felt last night. He lumbered slowly to the libershower and watched his liberskin slowly float away then be replaced, but the sensation of Lucy stayed with him.

He put his hand into the liberwave to retrieve some breakfast. It seemed to respond a little slower than usual; the intelligent device—which normally detected his preferred meal and delivered it so rapidly—perhaps confused by the one desire in his mind not being a food, but a person. Eventually a bowl of liberflakes arrived in hand, which he munched on tastelessly for the next ten minutes.

For what must have been the first time in his life, Christopher was late to his workstation, albeit by just a few minutes. He felt distracted the whole day. All he could think about was Lucy, lucid dreaming, and what further adventures were to come.

He checked his hands about twenty times through the working day, but each time they appeared in their normal five-fingered waking form. Each time he let out a dissatisfied sigh, wishing that he were released from his work responsibilities and free to fly again.

He sat in Body for what seemed like hours, but sipped slowly on his libeer. He wasn't there to drink; he was there to dream. Eventually she appeared: Curly red hair, brown eyes and violet aura. Christopher stood immediately from his seat. Lucy stopped and gave a wry smile, as if surprised by his alertness.

"Well, Christopher," she said, "you aren't hard to find."

"It's the only place I've ever met you," he replied. "So where are we going?"

"Aren't you going to get me a drink?"

"Why? It isn't real."

"You're pretty sure of yourself. Have you done a reality check?"

"Plenty," he said, holding his hand up to her, with nine wavy fingers.

Lucy smirked before striding over to grab his shoulder, and began to spin the pair of them. "Come on," she said.

The bar blurred then disappeared before Christopher's eyes. He emerged in a familiar red walled corridor, surprisingly alone. He turned around before hearing footsteps descending the set of metal stairs a short distance away.

"Lucy?"

He walked down the metal staircase into the mine to see the massive particle liberator, the tall walls of drones and robots on standby. And just by the cascade of BRAINs that comprised the sphere, there sat a creature; a lump of white fur sat atop four flat feet; a flat nose, dark round eyes and two oversized floppy ears. It was the rabbit he had seen on video footage in the mine a few days ago, and again—in his dream—disappearing out of the farm. It seemed to peer back at him, sniffing the air between them, before disappearing through the red wall of nanobots.

Christopher followed through the wall and out of the farm once more, felt his body vibrate as his own BRAINs passed through those in the libersphere, then emerged on the outside world. The sky was deep purple and filled with twinkling stars, the silver moon illuminated the night and the green grass that grew across the earth was interspersed with violet flowers. Between the blades Christopher saw a gap, where a line of the violet flowers grew in greater number, and followed it into a small clearing, where the creature sat, waiting.

"Lucy?"

The rabbit leapt forward from its back legs, and before its front ones could return to the floor, transformed seamlessly into a tall and slender red haired woman. Christopher stepped back, startled.

"Whoa, how did you do that?"

"Turn into an animal?" Lucy said. "We can do anything here. We call this shapeshifting. You did it yourself, the other night."

"I did?"

"When I led you out here, to the lake, you turned into a dog. You remember?"

Christopher racked his BRAINs and recalled the memory of himself that moonlit night, when he first left the farm; his hands elongating into claws, thick hair growing all over his body, sharp fangs in his mouth.

"I thought … I thought I turned into a zombie."

"A zombie?" Lucy laughed. "Not quite, just a dog."

"A dog?"

"Yeah, you know, a dog … a canine … *man's worst enemy …*"

He stared at her blankly.

'Oh come on." She laughed again. "Did your parents never take you to the liberseum when you were a kid?"

"No," he said. "I don't have any parents."

"Oh right," Lucy said, just a little softer. "Well, they have a whole section on animals. Dogs were these hairy four-legged things—all kinds of shapes and sizes, some of them were huge. Very clever animals apparently, but dirty, devious. They worked their way into society somehow, for a thousand years, eating our food, sleeping in our houses. That's what the farm says about them at least, I don't think animals were ever really that bad at all."

"But why would I change into a dog?" he asked. "I've never seen one—I don't think."

"I don't know," Lucy said. "Maybe you were raised by wolves."

Lucy walked around the edge of the clearing, looking into the surrounding fields, as if expecting someone or something.

"And what about you? How come you become a rabbit?"

"Because I like rabbits," she said. "They're my favorite animal. My mum used to tell me stories about them. It seemed a fitting way to lead you into Oneria. Besides, it's fun to hop around. Come on, I don't think he's coming."

And in a second Lucy transformed again, back into the rabbit, and hopped away into the grass. Christopher gazed at his hands, six fingers on each. He closed his eyes for a moment and tried to imagine them turning into claws, but opened them again to find them just the same. He pulled back his sleeve, trying to grow his hair, but nothing happened.

"Wait!"

He tried to follow Lucy, the rabbit, on foot, but quickly lost her among the grass. But then, in the distance, he saw some trees and knew in which direction she was headed. He paused and took a deep breath, then floated slowly six feet into the air. He tilted himself forward, focused on the trees and began to fly. Shortly he arrived by the water's side, to find the white rabbit. In another moment, she turned back into Lucy again.

"No shapeshifting tonight then?" she said.

"I don't know," he said. "It just happened by itself the first time I left the farm, I don't know how. I guess ... I thought something bad would happen. I was scared. Now I know where I am, with you, I'm not. Besides, it's fun to fly around."

Lucy smiled.

"Follow me," she said, "and remember to breathe."

And she leapt high into the air and dived headfirst smoothly into the middle of the lake with little more than a ripple. Christopher bent his knees, took a deep breath and jumped, arms flailing, landing with a loud and heavy splash into the water. He was shocked by the cold. His body began to tighten as he sunk into the dark depths. All around him was black. And then he felt a set of fingertips grab onto his through the water.

"Breathe, Christopher."

He continued to resist a while longer. It felt so counterintuitive to release. He held onto his breath, but all that was around him was blackness. The pressure built in his chest. He felt like he was losing lucidity. *It's all in your mind*, he said to himself. At last, he opened his mouth and lungs and felt the cold water flooding into them. Except it didn't feel like drowning, it felt like light flowing through him. And his eyes began to see light as well. And the still lake began to flow into a waterfall down which he fell. He was no longer under water—he was riding it. There was sunlight all around him now. The water was clear. He landed with a splash into a sparkling sea and saw Lucy swimming ahead of him. He followed as he saw trees and land ahead of her, as she began to step up out onto a golden beach. His feet slipped in the soft sand as he stood up after her.

"Is this the Ark?" he asked.

"Part of it," she said. "This way."

They began to walk along the secluded beach. It was beautiful. To his left stood tall trees of a kind Christopher had never seen— long, thin trunks without branches and just a few huge pointed almost plastic looking leaves at the top, and peculiar bunches of brown-green balls hanging just below. To his right, crystal clear water swished rhythmically up and down the sparkling sand. The heat of the sun filled the air. Christopher felt like he was almost dry already. Up ahead of them, he began to see the shape of three figures emerging.

"Hey!" Lucy said. "I thought you were coming to meet us?"

"Oh yeah, sorry," a man in the middle called back. "I got a little distracted."

Lucy and Christopher approached to find the man lying on what appeared to be a luxurious rug floating several feet in the air and wearing nothing but a pair of red shorts. On either side of him stood two identical scantily clad, blond, tanned and terrifically attractive women—they looked rather like Fiona from the libernews—one of them holding a tall and colorful drink with a long straw and the other feeding him from a basket of unfamiliar fruit. Christopher had never seen three people wearing so few clothes.

"You're so lazy," Lucy said.

"I'm not lazy," the man said. "I just like to do things the easy way. That's why you like me. Besides, you knew where to find me."

"Whatever," Lucy said, rolling her eyes. She glanced at Christopher. "I'll see you guys later." She quickly began to spin and then disappear into thin air, a puff of sand appearing in her wake.

"Christopher, old pal!" the man said. "How's it going mate? Come and grab a seat."

Christopher realized now that he recognized the man. It was the younger of the two men dressed as troubleshooters that had held him hostage, who had fired electricity through his body that first night he stepped out of the farm. He had scruffy sandy colored hair and stubble and a thick Islands accent. Christopher began to walk toward him but was surprised to be picked off his feet from beneath, and tipping onto his back, floating the rest of the way on another suddenly appearing flying carpet which parked up alongside the man and the two women.

"Make yourself comfortable."

Suddenly, another identically attractive woman appeared by Christopher's side, ran her fingers over his shoulders and began to remove his clothes.

"It's ok, thank you," he said.

"Oh come on, you can relax here."

The woman proceeded to remove Christopher's shirt and began to massage his neck with her soft hands. It felt fantastic.

"Where is here?" he asked.

"I call it *Isaac Island*. My own little piece of paradise right here in the Ark. What do you think?"

"It's nice."

"And what do you think of these babies?" Isaac flicked his eyes toward one of the women. "They don't say much, but then, who wants them to?" The three gorgeous girls giggled in unison.

"They're … nice," Christopher said, still nervous as one of the three continued to massage his upper body. "Are they … real?"

"As real as anything else here," Isaac said, as he reached up with his mouth to bite off one of the small round purple fruits from the bunch that one of the girls hung over his face. "Here, try these."

Christopher was startled by the sudden appearance of a similar bunch of fruit now held over his own head by the girl that had been rubbing his torso. He reached up with his fingers, plucked one, and put it in his mouth. Its surface was cool and smooth. As he began to bite it with his back teeth he felt a slight resistance in its skin before it suddenly burst apart, filling his mouth with sweet and tangy juice. He felt his whole jaw tingling with sensation. It was as if his mouth was a desert and he was just now tasting true hydration for the first time.

"Mmm," he muffled, "It's amazing!"

"They're called grapes. I love 'em."

"Mmm," Christopher took a bite of another one straight out of the woman's hand. "I've never had these in the farm."

"No wonder," Isaac said. "Forget about that Program-produced crap. The fruit of life, that's what you need, only available here in Oneria."

Christopher continued to chomp on the grapes, feeling himself relax more and more with each one he ate. Soon he too was only in a pair of shorts, blue, and having his legs and feet massaged.

"So what are you here for, Christopher?"

"What do you mean?"

"I mean, why did you come to Oneria? Why did you want out of the farm?"

"I don't know." Christopher thought. "I guess I just had enough of it, you know, the same thing day after day. I wanted to find something else."

"And what have you found so far?"

"Well, first of all that there is something beyond the farm, at least in my mind. I fell into that lake. I was shocked by you and that other man, Cassius."

"Oh yeah," Isaac said, "sorry about that mate. It was only acting. At least, I was."

"I understand," Christopher said. "Canaan told me all about Oneria, about how to become lucid. Kimiko showed me how to change my environment and move from place to place. And Lucy showed me how to fly. And now, here I am, on *Isaac Island*. Why are you here?"

"Well if you ask me, mate, we're all here for the same reason. This is a dream world, Christopher, and we're here to enjoy as much pleasure as we can, while we can. We can have whatever we want, and I'm the best there is at getting it. Let me show you."

Isaac clicked his fingers and he and Christopher began to float in unison on their flying carpets and turn slowly toward the trees, which bent apart to reveal a pathway, through which they continued.

"You want something to eat, Christopher, what do you do?"

"I ... get it out of the liberwave."

"You want a new liberwave, what do you do?"

"I go to *Libernsraum*, or I look on the libernet."

"Not here, Christopher. Here, you only have to imagine it, and there it is."

The trees suddenly changed into a much wider variety, with a multitude of different colored fruits hanging all around. Isaac reached out and plucked a shiny red one as they floated by, and took a large bite. Christopher did the same. The fruit filled his hand. It was hard and smooth on the outside and when he took a bite it was crispy, but juicy inside and refreshing.

"You don't even need to stretch," Isaac said, as he simply opened his hand and watched as a long and curvy yellow fruit floated down from a tree up ahead and landed perfectly in his palm. "You try."

Christopher focused on a similar yellow fruit up ahead, and watched as it seemed to shake itself loose from its tree, then fall onto his floating rug, somewhat less smoothly than Isaac's had arrived. He took a bite out of its side.

"Wait!" Isaac said, alarmed, as Christopher was struck by the bitter taste of the thick, tough, and terribly chewy thing in his mouth, before quickly spitting it out. "That's a banana, you're supposed to peel those."

Isaac looked down at his own banana as its sides slowly started to peel away and down, revealing a paler shape inside. Christopher looked down at his, a chunk missing from its side, and watched as it did the same. Cautiously, he took a small bite of its inner part. It was soft, sweet and creamy.

"Mmm," he said, "much better."

Shortly the trees began to separate into a large clearing, filled with a sparkling blue pool, surrounded by a dozen or so of the same scantily clad women as before; sat sunbathing, some dancing, some swimming in the water. Christopher and Isaac came to a standstill as two of the ladies came over to greet each of them with a tall drink.

"Did you imagine these women?" Christopher asked.

"Yeah," Isaac said, proudly. "I call her Olivia."

"They're all the same?"

"Can't beat perfection now, can you mate? Besides, makes it easier to remember."

"You can just imagine people into Oneria?"

"Yeah, most of the people you'll see in Oneria are imaginary. We're so used to seeing so many people every day around the farm, the mind fills itself most of the time with whatever it expects. Lots of characters you'll come across are just projections. It's up to you what kind of projections you create."

"But you're real right? And Lucy, Canaan, Kimiko?"

"Yeah, we're real alright. But we can appear to you just as projections too, if you just imagine us while our light bodies are somewhere else."

"Light bodies?"

"That's what we call our dream selves," Isaac said, patting himself on the chest. "Our real bodies are in the farm, asleep of course. Our light bodies are the mental projection of ourselves."

"And how can you tell the difference between an imaginary projection and a light body, an actual sleepwalker?"

"By what you can do to them. Watch."

Isaac beckoned the Olivia by his side closer and Christopher watched as her hair quickly changed from straight blond to wavy and brunette.

"Now check this out," Isaac said, pointing to her breasts, which suddenly swelled to twice the size and almost burst out of her skimpy top, the Olivia smiling silently all the while. "Now if I tried to do that to Lucy, she'd probably give me a slap. You try."

Christopher looked at the Olivia by his side and watched as her hair slowly changed from blond and straight to red and curly, as her eyes turned from blue to brown, staring deeply into his, as the shape of her face started to transform into Lucy's and then—smack—slap him right across the face.

"Ow!" Christopher said. "I thought you said she wasn't real."

"She isn't." Isaac laughed. "She's your projection. Of course if you want to see the real Lucy, you can walk back through those trees and to the beach and think about her very clearly as you do. I'm sure she'll hear you calling."

"I think I'll do that," Christopher said.

"Nice one mate, me and the Olivias have got a little more fun to have tonight. We'll see you around."

Christopher got up from his floating carpet and began to walk back through the fruit trees and down the path they had come. It was interesting to hear more of how the dream world worked and learn how to summon and move objects. As for the Olivias, he could see the appeal, but it seemed a little strange to him to imagine the same fake person over and again, and wondered what hollow pleasures could be gained. He felt like he had everything he wanted, physically, in the farm. It was something else, something spiritual, he craved. He thought about Lucy; about the first time he had seen her, her mysterious violet aura, the way she stared into his eyes. He emerged from the jungle and out onto the golden beach and saw her stood there, waiting for him.

"Have fun?" she said.

"A little," Christopher said. "The fruit was good. Not as good as flying though."

Lucy smiled. "Shall we?"

And so they rose from the sand and began to fly, high above the beach and the green trees and the blue water, high above and beyond the island.

17

We're here to enjoy as much pleasure as we can. We can have whatever we want.

Isaac's words stood out to Christopher almost more than his actions and the things he had shown him. They were the first thing he wrote in the red notebook upon waking.

Such wonderful fruit. Such wonderful women—all the same.

Isaac's outlook sounded so contrary to all that Christopher had ever known; the struggle, the scarcity of materials built by libertons, their meticulous management. *Working For Your Future.* Christopher suspected that Isaac was probably a symp. He wondered whether he had ever worked a day in his life. He certainly seemed to enjoy his dreams, his own private paradise he had manifested, with his infinite versions of the same imaginary woman, but what about his real life in the farm? It was the constant craving for excess that had caused humanity's problems in the past, culminating in the Outbreak. Sure, he had a nice apartment, filled with all kinds of luxuries, but he had earned it through his hard work every day in the farm, and his dedication to the Program, which ensured that resources were managed according to requirement and reward, to incentivize rehabilitation from dyspheria.

Some people are projections. You can change them.

He didn't quite understand but felt he should write it down. He had been lucid for five nights now, but still felt he had much to learn and get to grips with in the dream world.

He continued to check his hands regularly throughout the day and saw them five-fingered as normal. He was still assigned to observing service symps assisting laborbots in street maintenance, which was growing exceptionally tedious. He wished that his working day would come to an end. And it did, much sooner than he expected.

A little after six—about an hour before the scheduled end of the working day—a red light began to flash around the whole room, accompanied by a loud siren. He jumped back from his workstation in surprise as his liberscreen was locked down and large letters appeared on his screen: *Security Alert.* Clearly it wasn't just him, as he looked around to see other dorms nearby shifting back from their screens with similarly startled expressions. And then a robotic voice announced over the room, for everyone to hear, in a tone that sounded much calmer than the sirens, lights or the words themselves suggested. *"Systems monitors, there has been a major security alert. You are relieved from your day's duties and asked to return home in a quick and orderly fashion. Systems monitors, there has been a major security alert. You are relieved from your day's duties and asked to return home in a quick and orderly fashion ..."*

Like all the other systems monitors in the large room, he stepped away from his workstation and made his way toward the exit, *in a quick and orderly fashion.* It was probably just a drill. He didn't think there was much chance of any security threat big enough for the whole Systems Monitoring Department to close down; he'd never experienced a genuine occasion for such a closure in all the time he had worked there. Of course, the whole purpose of the department was to monitor symptomatic residents so that such a threat be made impossible, or at least kept to a minimum and flagged to higher authorities before it was too late. It would have to be a big threat, or a big mistake by someone, to warrant such a reaction as this.

As he and the other systems monitors shuffled silently through the corridors of the department, still surrounded by the sound of sirens and the repetitive announcement all around, he saw two troubleshooters bustle speedily past in the opposite direction, looking to secure some area—but surely the Systems Monitoring Department itself wasn't under threat, he thought.

The exit port area was also manned by two more troubleshooters and at least a couple more liberbots than usual. Again it seemed excessive to him to have such security measures on the way out of the department, as everyone there had surely had their entrance approved on the way in and was now only looking to get out. He couldn't help but feel the uneasiness build up inside him in response to the apparent increase in numbers and alertness of security.

As he filtered out of the port, it became apparent that whatever security threat had been detected, or rehearsed, was not only affecting the Systems Monitoring Department. The streets were filled with dorms and symps from all lines of work, and increased numbers of troubleshooters and liberbots again. He looked up to the liberscreens that curved around and between all of the buildings above to see that all the usual libermarketing had been replaced by the same words he had seen on his screen at work: *Security Alert.*

"There has been a major security alert. Will all residents return to their homes in a quick and orderly fashion. There has been a major security alert. Will all residents return to their homes in a quick and orderly fashion," the same robotic voice echoed all around.

While the dorms fell almost automatically into orderly queues, the symps darted and snaked their way around sporadically in all directions. "Code Z," he heard one of them say to another, as they ran past him. "Code Z," again said another. *Code Z* was an informal term for zombies, or a threat thereof, and also the name for a popular series of horror movies based on the Outbreak. Surely, the symps were just being hysterical, and there was no real threat of zombies in the farm, Christopher told himself.

There was even a liberbot stationed by the entrance to his apartment building, with another in each of the libervators; something he had never seen before.

He was relieved to get inside his apartment, if not to be safe from any supposed security threat, then simply to be away from all the crowds of people and the sirens. Calmed by the cool blue of his apartment décor, he let out a sigh and slumped down onto the sofa, only for his libervision to spark to life.

"A lifetime of struggle ... A history of horrors ... Almost a hundred years ago humanity stood on the brink of extinction ... But we were saved by the genius of the Writer ... Saved by advanced technology that would supersede our primitive instincts and guarantee our safety ... Together now and forever we look toward a brighter future ... Liberty Farm: Working For Your Future."

Whatever update on the major security threat that was to follow, it obviously wasn't so urgent as to skip the 'essential' dramatic libernews opening.

"Good afternoon residents." Leo appeared, as handsome as ever but far more serious-faced than usual. "As you have no doubt heard by now, there has been a major security alert announced across the West and an immediate curfew has been imposed, meaning that all residents are requested to remain in their homes until further notice."

And a beautiful blue day to you, Christopher thought. Presumably the curfew for "all residents" didn't apply to TV presenters in their studios, or troubleshooters, or probably many of the emune.

"That's right," Fiona said, with deep concern etched on her beautiful face. "So if you are watching this broadcast from anywhere other than your home we ask that you make your way there in a quick and orderly fashion."

Something big is happening ... The libergram comments scrolled at the bottom the screen. *Get home safe everyone ... #Curfew ...*

"No doubt you are all just as anxious as us to find out the cause and status of this alert," Leo said, "and to that end, we're joined on video from the Libermid by Director of Security Jerry Stark. Jerry, thank you for joining us and please do tell us the situation."

Stark was a huge, surly, shaven-headed man who had been Director of Security for as long as Christopher could remember, who he had seen on libervision from time to time discussing various matters related to troubleshooters, liberbots, the hacker enemy and the ongoing threat of dyspheria. He spoke in a deep, gruff voice.

"You're welcome, Leo," he said. "And may I first just echo what you and Fiona have said and ask that all residents make their way to their homes immediately and remain there until further notice. And let me say that while we are experiencing a major security alert right now, we ask all residents to remain calm in the knowledge that the threat is now under control by our security forces and that you are safe, as always, in our hands."

"Certainly," Leo said, sat snuggly alongside Fiona. "So please Jerry, what else can you tell us?"

"Well Leo, what I can tell you is that we have just in the last couple of hours experienced what I can only describe as an unprecedented uprising of simultaneous threats including the sudden onset of some of the more severe acute symptoms of dyspheria among small pockets of the symptomatic population, at the same time as some major coordinated hacking attempts against some key Program and Liberty Farm infrastructure."

It was a whole load of scary sounding words lumped in a long sentence.

"Acute symptoms?" Fiona said. "Can I ask Jerry, for our audience's understanding, do you mean zombies?"

"Well Fiona, that is obviously the word that we have commonly associated with such symptoms and while I would be quick to say that we haven't seen anything as severe in the farm as we all know was experienced during the Outbreak, we have certainly seen some violence today, yes that is the case."

Christopher was stunned to hear the TV presenters use the Z word so overtly in relation to a current incident in the farm, but the truth was the term had become such a loose one in recent years—it had been used to describe all manner of undesirable symptoms, and used by some as a derogatory term for symps in general, but surely it—and Stark—didn't refer to the senseless cannibalism it meant in the past.

OMG zombies in the farm ... #CodeZ ... #CodeZ ...

"And what about the infrastructure you refer to?" Leo said. "Can you tell us about that?"

"Well Leo, I can tell you that we did experience a major threat to the mine and an attempt to interfere with the particle liberator, but it was quickly nullified," Stark explained. "I believe we can show you footage of that now in fact."

Christopher watched in disbelief as he saw surveillance footage of the mine for the first time he could recall on libervision, from a similar high angle as he had frequently observed from his workstation when tasked to observe the area—which he hadn't been for a few days, he now realized. He watched as half a dozen service symps careered down into the human-free center of the mine and toward the particle liberator, only to be shot down by blasts of blue light by a bunch of liberbots who seemed to stand there waiting—which Christopher had never seen there before. The footage was nothing but a few seconds of chaos, ending with the symps scattered across the floor. What had they been thinking?

"But why would anyone want to interfere with the liberator?" Fiona said, visibly distressed. "Don't we depend on that for—for everything?"

"Yes, we do," Stark said. "And that's exactly why the enemy would want to interfere with it. As you know, it is the liberator that breaks down material gathered from the outside world into libertons—the basic building blocks of life—to be put to optimal use in the farm: to feed, to fuel and to clothe our residents. It appears there are enemies within the farm that are resistant to the Program's management of those resources and want to claim them for their own. And that's exactly why we cannot allow that to happen."

144

"Libertons," Leo said, "have been referred to by many as the life force, isn't that right?"

"That's right," Stark said. "The most incredible fundamental particle, discovered by Libercorp around the time of the Outbreak, that gives all other particles the power to grow, to change, to reproduce. Some say it is the source of all life, but it is also the force of death, of greed, of excess. And that's exactly why it must be strictly controlled, to protect us from falling back into the inhumane ways of the past."

"And so how are you dealing with this threat?" Fiona said.

"Most severely," Stark said. "As you saw, the symps who attempted to storm the mine were quickly taken down. We have increased security around the mine and will be increasingly vigilant in our protection of this essential area of the farm. But as well as this physical threat we just showed you, there have also been attempts to hack digitally into related systems. I can assure you that the immediate threat has now been terminated and many hackers have already been arrested and taken to Advanced Rehabilitation, along with those who have shown acute symptoms I mentioned earlier, and we expect more connected with the group to follow shortly. Rest assured that anyone connected with these incidents will be dealt with most severely."

Leave our libertons alone, symps ... #OurLifeForce ... #ShutThemDown ...

"Glad to hear it," Leo said, smiling. "I'm now being told that we can be joined by Director of Libernomics, Edward Earl, who will tell us what impacts we might expect on the liberconomy in the wake of today's incidents ..."

Earl, a skinny old scholarly fellow, proceeded to explain how there would have to be tighter controls on liberton flow for a short period, likely to be felt primarily by the symps, but that he expected a recovery and continued libernomic growth in the medium and long term, with the help of the united efforts and hard work of all residents in the wake of the incident.

Harper Hale, the Director of Health, whose slim and smiley appearance was an exaggerated embodiment of her title, joined the conversation to explain the nature and origin of the acute symptoms that had apparently arisen in several pockets of symps today. Dyspheria was an incredibly resilient virus, she said, and while the BRAINs were always adapting to better manage it, so too was it ever changing, and so there was always the risk of relapse. However, she added, residents should remain confident in the power of the antivirus to combat dyspheria and know that those symps who had experienced relapse had also been guilty of willfully neglecting their duties toward the Program, designed to reward and assist them in their rehabilitation, and that others should be wary to avoid similar mistakes.

There were then some documentary clips detailing the origin and mechanism of the antivirus, the BRAINs and the Program. The antivirus—AV—was the life-saving creation of scientists and researchers, including a young programmer who would become the Writer, working in the pharmaceutical arm of Libercorp, known then as Liberty Pharm, at the time of the Outbreak. It was first synthesized and its effectiveness discovered at almost the last moment before humanity was completely destroyed, as dyspheria tore the world apart. Early tests showed its encouraging efficacy in curtailing the symptoms and progression of the disease. But the virus was so formidable, so aggressive, the challenge lay in delivering enough of the antivirus into patients on a continuous basis, as traditional intravenous methods struggled to cope. It was only the genius of the Writer that led to the development of a synthetic biotechnological alternative to the antivirus: Nanobots that could replicate its effects in targeting dyspheria, that could be implanted into the body and controlled by a central program that enabled us to survive.

Such nanotechnology had been commonplace in medicine for some time—to treat cancer, heart disease and a range of other old world ailments—but this was the first time that such technology had been permanently implanted into humans, and the first to be connected to an ongoing control system. But BRAINs, biotechnological reproductive artificially intelligent nanobots, were also the most intelligent nanobots ever created; not only did they receive and execute commands with perfect precision, they also responded automatically to the variations in dyspheria and its associated effects within and between subjects on a continuous basis; they evolved, both in the individual and as part of the collective Program. The BRAINs functioned to find and maintain a balance in each resident, and the farm at large, to dispense sufficient levels of AV into the body according to the levels of, and resistance to, dyspheria in each individual, working at a neuromolecular level to target and eliminate the substrates of symptoms the second they started, and indeed before.

Christopher had heard it all before, and he was sure everyone else in the farm had too. It was common knowledge, but the libervision directors and perhaps the Program itself, clearly thought it necessary to give residents a reminder of the past and their present good fortune at this time. Apparently the daily libernews introduction montage—*A lifetime of struggle ... A history of horrors ...*—wasn't sufficient. The evening's continuous broadcast—from which Christopher was unable to switch off or change channel—seemed more like a celebration than a serious security incident. It was like a who's who of libermid directors, political commentators and even celebrities, while the tally of hackers and symps who had been sent to Advanced Rehabilitation continued to increase. There was even more footage and accounts from witnesses of the acute outbreaks—Christopher was sure he had seen some of the faces just a few days ago on the libervision in the cafeteria.

"And at last," Fiona said, back to her chirpy self, "we can now be joined by the Prime Resident himself. Dean Perish, I'm sure you've had a very busy day, thank you for joining us."

"You're very welcome Fiona," Perish said. "I certainly have, and may I start by sincerely thanking all the directors who have already shared updates with you, as well as the troubleshooters and everyone else who has supported our efforts to shut down the threat we have experienced today, and of course the residents who have been kindly co-operating and patiently waiting in their homes this evening."

A flurry of blue likes began on screen.

"Absolutely." Fiona beamed. "And may we thank you for what I'm sure has been integral action and leadership on your part throughout this incident. Could you tell us your perspective on things today?"

"Certainly," Perish said. "Well, as I'm sure has already been said, this is by far the most significant security threat we have experienced for a very long time and one that we have and will continue to handle with the utmost severity."

"And can I ask," Leo said, "whether you or your colleagues in the Libermid could possibly have expected, or done anything to prevent this incident?"

"Well I certainly think it would have been very difficult to predict this incident exactly, such was the sudden nature of its arrival and spread across numerous locations across the farm at once. However I must say that this is a reminder that we must always expect the unexpected, so to speak. Incidents like this, major collaborative hacks, acute outbreaks of symptoms, are always possible, such is the volatile nature of dyspheria and the constant threat posed by the hacker enemy. And that is why I have always advocated constant vigilance toward such threats, zero tolerance to any involvement in any kind of hacking, and continue to work toward a final solution to dyspheria."

#DeanToDestroyDyspheria ... #FinalSolution ...

"Indeed," Leo said. "And can we assume that those efforts toward a final solution will be accelerated in the wake of today's incidents?"

"Absolutely," Perish said, the camera closing in slightly as he spoke. "Today's incidents are a reminder to us all that despite the best efforts of the Writer, of Liberty Farm and the Program to keep us safe—which have been largely successful—that we are not yet entirely as safe as we would wish to be, and will not be, so long as dyspheria persists. There is only one solution to this deadly disease, *the final solution*, and I am the one to make it happen."

Leo and Fiona smiled and raised their thumbs, alongside the other guests in their studio, and others on video who all reappeared on screen to repeat the gesture, repeated now in almost every apartment in the West, Christopher thought, except his.

Perhaps it was just his distrust of Perish, but something didn't sit right. Surely, someone within the Systems Monitoring Department or elsewhere would have detected and remedied or flagged the kind of uprising of acute symptoms that had apparently been experienced today. Surely, the troubleshooters would have been able to uncover and prevent such *major coordinated hacking attempts* before they happened. And what were those symps doing running straight into the mine and toward the particle liberator, what could they have possibly hoped to achieve, and what were the liberbots doing already waiting there for them? It all seemed so surreal.

He tapped the keyboard on his left hand and typed. *How could this happen?* He tapped the blue triangle, but never saw his comment on screen.

Perhaps all this questioning of reality that Canaan had taught Christopher to help him become lucid—*all things may not be as they seem*—was becoming too much. Perhaps he should just trust what was said on the libervision, by the Prime Resident and the directors and everyone else that had seemingly always looked out for his and the farm's interests. After all, why would they lie?

Either way, Christopher felt exhausted by the barrage of libernews broadcasting he had experienced that evening, despite his slightly shortened shift at work. All the talk of zombies and hackers and dyspheria left his BRAINs in a soup of fear and confusion. He couldn't wait to get back to Oneria and fly away from the problems in the farm.

18

Docking for hibernation was usually the simplest of tasks; indeed it was hardly a task at all, but something that was done automatically every night when the time was nine. Normally, Christopher would lie on his liberbed and rest his head under the red-domed cover that sent a signal to his BRAINs to go into hibernation, before connecting wirelessly with the mainframe for nightly uploads and downloads. Christopher's mind would simply go blank, in little more than a minute, and the next thing he knew would be waking up to the blue light of the morning libersphere pouring through his window as if no time had passed at all. He had hardly been aware of any time passing in hibernation at all, until Canaan had explained what really happened in the zero hour. But even since he had started lucid dreaming, his transition to sleep had been as seamless as ever. Except tonight, something was different.

Perhaps it was the barrage of libernews broadcasting he had been forced to sit through that evening. Perhaps it was the focus he tried his best to keep on Lucy, on becoming lucid and the adventures he hoped to have tonight. Perhaps it was the pull on his BRAINs in those two starkly different directions that prevented them from settling. But in any case, Christopher lay there for several minutes, unable to drift away. He simply lay still in the dark red of his bedroom, silent but for the sound of his own slow and steady breathing.

The red light of the libersphere poured in softly through the window at night, radiating through the similarly red translucent dome that covered Christopher's head, in such a way that the same soft red glow filled his vision whether his eyes were open or closed. Soon he was unable to tell which they were, as he lost sensation of his eyelids, and then the rest of his body began to go numb. This must be what normally happens, he told himself, but the fact that his BRAINs still seemed to be working as much as they did during the waking day—if not more so—definitely wasn't normal. Was there a problem with his liberbed, or his BRAINs? Was it something to do with the *hacking of BRAINs in hibernation* he had heard about recently? Either way, he needed to settle down. His heart began to race.

He tried to stay calm, but then something peculiar started to happen to his vision—whether it was through his open eyes, or in his mind, he wasn't sure. The soft scarlet that seemed to surround him seemed to shimmer like water, and sparkle; slow at first, then faster, like a special light show in his liberbed. The sparkles expanded and scattered across his field of vision. He could swear he could hear a crackling sound they seemed to make. And then suddenly, the scarlet dome began to split then shatter into several shards before collapsing. He held his breath anticipating the fall of the pieces of his docking cover onto his face, but felt nothing. But the red was gone, and he was in blackness. There was nothing but the sound of his breath.

But then there was another sound—like breathing again, but not his. He was sure of it. It was quicker and heavier than his. He could hear it some distance from his own body. There was someone—or something—in the room with him. He tried to move, but he had no sensation in his body whatsoever. He tried to make a noise, but his voice failed him too. He was stuck, somehow, in some limbo between wake and sleep; his body paralyzed, his mind still alive and awake.

With all his concentration, he was able to focus his eyes down the space where he was sure his body was, past his feet and toward the window, through which the red libersphere continued to glow—but the light was obstructed partly by a large shadow, which began to move. Christopher's heart thumped in his chest and the dark figure lumbered toward him, its heavy breath growing louder. It crept up close to the bed, then climbed on top of him. He felt the warmth and weight of whoever—or whatever it was—sit upon his chest, stifling his own breathing, and he could do nothing to stop it. *No, please*! But no sound came out. And two glowing red eyes emerged from the darkness where the figure sat upon him and closed in toward Christopher. And then a set of huge fangs began to open, and hot breath poured onto his face. He tried to scream, but he was utterly powerless.

And then there was another noise—loud and sharp—as the door to the bedroom slid open and a beam of bright red light blasted the thing on top of Christopher. It let out a terrible squeal. Then it seemed to drop, and he felt the weight removed from his chest. At least, he was able to move. He sat up and turned to see a gleaming white liberbot stood in the doorway, its palm open in front of him, having just blasted the mysterious dark figure. Christopher was about to thank the android, but before he could do anything more, he too was blasted by another red beam from the liberbot. And after having struggled to fall into hibernation for several minutes, he was now immediately unconscious.

19

Christopher was unable to move again, but he wasn't on his liberbed. He could feel himself sat upright, stuck firmly to a chair. He could see nothing but blackness—until some cold steely fingers unwrapped a blindfold from behind his head, revealing a red lamp glowing in his face. As his eyes adjusted, he saw that he was sat at what looked like the same metal table he had been held hostage the first night he had fallen into Oneria except, instead of the two men dressed as troubleshooters, there were three tall white liberbots.

"165-189-198," said the middle bot, as it took a seat between its two standing accomplices. "You have been found to be in violation of programmed hibernation behavior. You are now in Acute Assessment."

The featureless face of the android stared blankly back at him from across the table. "Why were you not in hibernation?"

"I—I don't know," Christopher said, still afraid, but pleased to be able to speak again. "My ... my liberbed—it ... I don't think it's working."

"Your liberbed is a standard issue Program-approved product," the bot said. "There is no problem with the device. Why were you not in hibernation?"

"I don't know," Christopher tried again. "Maybe I was hacked. My BRAINs ... they just didn't seem to rest."

"Hacked?" the bot said. "By whom?"

"I don't know. There was someone ... something ... in my bedroom."

"165-189-198, there was no one else in your apartment as we entered."

"But that's not true."

"Perhaps you are the hacker, 165-189-198."

"No."

"165-189-198, you must tell us your accomplices immediately, otherwise you will be transferred permanently to Advanced Rehabilitation."

"No," Christopher whispered, "this isn't real."

He pulled hard against the thick cables that tied his wrists tightly to the chair, but to no avail. Then he remembered the previous time he was in this dimly lit room. *Let yourself go,* Canaan had said. Christopher took a deep breath and allowed himself to relax before simply, smoothly, standing, the cables falling away easily to the floor.

"This is a dream," he said.

The leading liberbot in the middle stared back blankly for a moment, then his face and head transformed from that of a white featureless robot to a grey-bearded man, as the two androids on either side simply dissolved and disappeared.

"Very good," he said.

"Cassius?"

"Yes," the man said. "You remember me?" His face was worn with age. He spoke with a Northern accent.

"How could I forget?" Christopher said. "Last time I saw you, you were interrogating me with an electric shock machine."

"All entirely necessary," Cassius said. "As is this."

"And what is this, another test?"

"Maybe so," Cassius said, walking around the table to Christopher. "A test of your mental resolve. It seems you've been getting to grips with the basics of lucidity, learning its lighter elements from Isaac and the others. But don't get carried away Christopher. It isn't all flying and fornicating."

"Fornicating?" Christopher had never heard the word.

"Never mind that." Cassius smirked. "What about that thing in your bedroom, hey?"

"Let me guess," Christopher said, "another lovely disguise of yours."

"No," Cassius said. "That wasn't me. That was a real, real dangerous thing, Christopher. It was the Program, manifest in shadow form, in your early dream state."

"The Program?" Christopher said. "How? Why?"

"Because you were too wild in your entry to the dream, Christopher, too reckless, too direct. Didn't Lucy tell you already? The Program can detect if you don't go into hibernation as expected. It manifests as fear in your BRAINs, producing hallucinations—monsters, hags—to keep you in its grasp. And if you were to leave that bedroom it could track you, wherever you go—to the Ark—and you don't want that to happen, do you? That's why you need to calm down, and empty your mind before you go to dock at night. Fortunately I was keeping an eye on you tonight," Cassius said. "And was able to intervene before something bad happened."

"So you came in dressed as a liberbot and blasted me?" Christopher said. "Are you sure you don't just like tying people up?"

"Yes," Cassius snapped. "This is a necessary step, Christopher, for you to become accustomed to all that there is in Oneria. There is a darker side to dreaming, that you must also be willing to face."

"A dark side?"

"Of course, there is a dark side to our minds and so a dark side to the dream world. Let me show you." Cassius turned and gestured as he spoke, toward a door as it appeared in the wall behind him.

Christopher cautiously walked through the door and found himself in darkness, outdoors, alone. He turned around to find there was no sign of the door he had just passed through, no wall and no Cassius. He stood in the middle of a large dark circular clearing in the woods, lined by tall trees. A half moon hovered in the sky peeking out behind grey clouds, casting shadows all around. A cold wind whistled in his ears.

"Cassius?"

155

Christopher turned around in the circle, but saw nothing. He closed his eyes and tried to spin himself somewhere else, but remained where he stood. He tried again, but couldn't seem to. He looked to the sky.

"Light," he said. "Let there be light."

And in a flash, sure enough there was: Light appearing behind the trees to his right. But it was not the rise of the sun, or the change of the color in the sky he had seen Canaan and Kimiko perform previously. It was a flash of orange light, accompanied by a loud bang, followed by a glow. And then another bang, and a flash behind the trees to his left. And another behind, as the night began to glow an eerie orange, accompanied by the sounds of echoing explosions. And then another sound—human, but not quite a voice—moaning from inside the forest.

"Hello?" Christopher called, but there was no reply. Then he heard it again, a long loud moan in the night. It sounded almost like an animal. And then another moan from another direction, and then another behind him, and the crack of branches. Someone, or something, was in the woods, moving in his direction.

He stepped toward the edge of the circle, where he heard a sound. Another moan. Another bang. Another flash of orange in the sky, and an afterglow of orange within the woods themselves. And smoke. And a rotten smell growing in the air. And another moan, closer to him.

"Who's there?" he shouted.

There was movement in the woods in front of him. A grey figure lurched into a path between the trees, stumbling in a way he had never seen a human move before.

"Hello?" he said. The thing inside the woods moaned again as it turned sharply toward him, and started to speed up. He squinted to look closer and saw that the person—if that was the word— wore tattered clothes, disheveled hair and red blood over its hanging mouth.

"No," he said, retreating backward toward the middle of the clearing. "Stay back!" But the thing kept on shuffling toward him and out of the trees, its arms outstretched in his direction.

Another bang and a flash of orange behind him, and another moaning sound. He turned around to see another of the things emerging from the woods.

And another flash, and another moan and another half-dead looking person from another direction, and another. The forest was on fire now. The night was burning orange. Smoke—and that sickening smell—filled the air. As another creature, and another, all covered in blood, claws outstretched, clambered out from the trees and toward him in the middle of the circle. Zombies. There were a dozen of them.

"No," Christopher cried as he span frantically in different directions in the middle of the clearing, wishing to see something else, some escape route, but the zombies closed in on every side. He closed his eyes and tried to think of Lucy. He tried to fly but found his feet bound by a vine that was now growing from the ground, wrapping itself tightly around his ankles. He fell onto his back, unable to move as the monsters closed in, leering over him.

"Christopher."

He looked straight ahead to see, among the other zombies, a woman—or what once was—stumbling toward him. She looked as white as the moon, disheveled and skinny except for a large round stomach over which she hunched. She fell to her knees but continued toward him.

"Christopher."

"No," he begged. "Stay away from me!" But she continued, along with the other zombies, toward him. Christopher tried to move, tried to flail his legs and arms, to escape somehow, but they were both now bound to the ground. She was crawling over him now, the white woman, over his legs and body and reaching her hand toward his face, staring hungrily into his eyes as he closed them.

"Christopher!"

He jumped as he felt the touch of a hand on his shoulder and opened his eyes to find himself back in the red-lit interrogation room, heart pounding, breathing heavily, Cassius stood by his side.

"Christopher," he said. "It's just a dream. Just a nightmare."

Christopher raised his hands from his seat to see his fingers elongated into long claws. He began to slow down his breathing and watched as they receded back to their normal shape and size, as Cassius sat opposite.

"Who was that?" Christopher asked.

"Who was who?" Cassius said.

"That woman, coming toward me."

"She was a zombie, Christopher, all zombies."

"I feel like I've seen her before."

"It's a dream, Christopher. Who knows where you got the images for the zombies from. Of course, they weren't really zombies. They were your projections, and mine. That's what I wanted to show you."

"But why?"

"The scene you just experienced," Cassius said, "was not unlike life for many before the formation of Liberty Farm. Bombs, zombies, fear. My parents lived in Europe at the time of the Outbreak—they saw the worst of it. They told me all about it as a child. You too have heard all about it, in the farm. It is a part of our history, part of our psyche and so it can also become part of our dreams."

"How come I couldn't stop it?" Christopher said.

"In part, because it was I that created the scene," Cassius said. "At least I got it started. Like the liberbots, you couldn't stop them, because they were me. I am a more experienced lucid dreamer than you, Christopher. You need to strengthen your mind. But, as for the zombies, as I say, I only got it started. I left you enough room, enough opportunity, to get yourself out of there, to change the situation, but you failed. You failed because you were afraid. But you must learn to face your fears and overcome them."

"But how?"

"Come on, let me show you."

Cassius took off through the doorway and Christopher followed him through, finding himself in the dark circular clearing in the forest, with Cassius alongside. There was a loud explosion and the sky was filled with orange again, smoke billowing from the trees and slithering across the ground toward them, and a loud freakish moan from within the woods.

"Remember to breathe, Christopher. Focus. Remember, this is a dream. Allow the fear to run through you, rather than take hold of you. Nothing will hurt you here. Fear will never hurt."

Out from the woods emerged a stumbling zombie, long and crooked, shuffling toward Christopher. He took a deep breath and tried to remain calm.

"Now, you could fly or spin away, but you already know how to do that. Instead, learn to face your fear and transform it. Think of something happier."

The zombie continued toward him, claws outstretched, hollow cheeks smeared with blood. Christopher felt the cold breeze around him. He recalled the first time he had left the dreamscape of the farm, when he grew hair and claws and fangs, he thought that he himself had transformed into a zombie. Only last night Lucy had told him that he had in fact changed only to a dog, an animal. And then, as it approached, the zombie began to shrink before his eyes: It fell onto its hands; which turned into front paws; as its clothes became fur, its face became a snout and its body transformed to that of a knee high chocolate colored canine. It continued to bark until Christopher commanded it.

"Stop," he said.

"Very good. Now let's see what else you're afraid of. I know …"

Cassius gave his hands a sharp clap and the scene transformed to one inside the farm, the fire-lit skies making way for blue walls, and to Christopher's surprise, the dog transformed into the size and shape of Dean Perish. There he stood, accompanied by a troubleshooter on either side. Currently the prime resident, here he stood in the long silver cloak and inverted triangular helmet with a deep indigo light glowing at its bottom in the middle of his forehead, the costume of the Writer.

"At long last," he announced, as if on the libervision, "I, Dean Perish, am now the Writer—the sole ruler of the Program and Liberty Farm. And at last, I will eliminate dyspheria once and for all—starting with you, Christopher."

He pointed at Christopher and the two troubleshooters began to walk in his direction. "I know all about you, Christopher," he said.

Christopher felt overcome by the same negative feeling in his stomach that hit him every time he saw the face, or heard the voice of Dean Perish—the man who would soon take over the Writer, without a fraction of the experience or understanding of his predecessor, who would surely lead the farm to its doom. But it wasn't really him; it was just Christopher's projection. The Writer, humanity's true savior, was still in his rightful place. Christopher took a deep breath, focused on the warm feeling he had for the real Writer, and watched as Perish's hair receded and disappeared under his helmet, watched his face wrinkle and age to take on the shape of the real Writer, who looked back at Christopher. The two troubleshooters halted in their tracks then dissolved into the air.

"Do not fear, Christopher," he said. "You are safe. Everything is under control."

"Good," Cassius said, "though I'm sure you can think of something scarier than Perish. Why don't you ask the dream?"

"Ask the dream?"

"Ask the dream to show you your biggest fear."

Christopher thought it was a strange instruction. He didn't know what would happen, but felt uncomfortable revealing whatever fear lay inside him in front of Cassius. Still, he took a deep breath and closed his eyes.

"Show me my biggest fear," he called out to the dream.

He opened his eyes to find himself back in the red-lit interrogation room, opposite Lucy: Tied to her chair, tape over her mouth, her faced bruised and beaten like the first time he had seen her here. On the table between them sat the long rectangular device that had been there before, its face covered in switches and dials, two wires protruding from it, attached at the other end to two circular components strapped to Lucy's temples. Cassius stood over the machine.

"What is this?" Christopher said.

Cassius flicked a switch and a loud buzzing emitted from the machine, as Lucy's eyes tightened, her face contorted, as electricity run through her and she shook violently in her chair.

"Stop," Christopher said, but it continued. He tried to get out of his seat but found himself somehow tied again. "Stop," he said, but Cassius continued. Christopher watched as Lucy writhed around, apparently unconscious, as the machine buzzed louder and louder. Christopher looked at Cassius, a cold glare across his face as he watched the shaking Lucy. Christopher looked at the machine, saw sparks of electricity emitting from it, the device starting to glow blue, starting to lift slowly from the table. "Stop!" he shouted for a third time, sending the machine crashing into Cassius's torso with a flash of smoke, sending the stocky old figure tumbling to the ground. Lucy too, fell to the floor, still tied to her seat.

"So you like Lucy, I see?" Cassius smirked as he brushed himself off.

Christopher released himself and rushed around the table to find Lucy, unconscious, her curly red hair filled with static, the sides of her face burnt.

"I just didn't like seeing her hurt," Christopher snapped.

"It's just your projection," Cassius said. "Learn to control your mind. Don't let your feelings control you."

Christopher sat over Lucy's still body, peeled the tape from her mouth and picked up her hand, placing it in his, seeing seven fingers on both hers and his.

"It isn't her, Christopher," Cassius said, "It's just a dream."

20

Christopher woke up, sweating and breathing heavily. He raised his hands and checked his fingers. It had all been a dream, and he was now back in his waking reality, in his apartment. But the image of Lucy tied and tortured, lying unconscious, had felt all too real to him. How had he been so affected by his projection? He rose to write in the red journal, bringing his breathing slowly back to normal.

Wild entry to the dream. A monster in my room.
Calm down, empty your mind before hibernation.
There is a dark side to our minds and to the dream world.
Zombies. Explosions. Perish.
My deepest fear—Lucy suffering.
Learn to face your fears and overcome them.

Face your fears and overcome them. He repeated it inside his head. It seemed much easier said than done. How could he overcome something that in its very nature seemed to overcome him? Fear always seemed to strike so suddenly, as if its source triggered an automatic response in his BRAINs. He had been taught his entire life of the terrors of the Outbreak, taught by the Program to fear dyspheria and its most devastating manifestation—zombies. He had lived his whole life under the watchful eye of the Writer, humanity's savior, the one man who fully understood the Program and had protected the residents of Liberty Farm for almost a hundred years, and grown to fear the day that he would ever *step aside.* Perhaps there was nothing to fear in Perish other than that he was not the Writer, that he was not proven, but was he actually a threat? Christopher didn't know if he really had any rational basis by which to fear Perish, again the feeling just seemed to overwhelm him automatically.

And what about Cassius? The older, stocky Northern sleepwalker was one of Canaan's scouts, but seemed different from the others—somewhat darker. Perhaps it was a limited impression from the two times they had met. Perhaps it was necessary, as he had said. Perhaps it was a result of the fear that had been passed on to him by his parents who had apparently lived in Europe at the time of the Outbreak. But there certainly seemed to be something strange in the way he seemed to linger on the darker aspects of the dream world; the infliction of fear, suffering and intimidation.

The libervision sprung to life as Christopher entered the living room.

"A lifetime of struggle ... A history of horrors ..."

As he chomped down his liberflakes, he was told by Leo—*"A beautiful blue day to all you residents across the farm"*—that the security threat and subsequent curfew were now over and that residents were free to return to work as normal that morning. Such alarm yesterday, and only an hour of work lost.

The tally of arrests and transfers to Advanced Rehabilitation was now over nine hundred, by far the biggest number of such cases that Christopher had ever heard of—or had ever imagined possible—within a single day. Nine hundred residents who had, quite suddenly, become so unresponsive and dangerous to the Program as to necessitate their commitment to a lifetime of who-knew-what kind of advanced experiments deep in the Libermid, or simply being shut down. The libernews showed snippets of surveillance footage of small skirmishes between symps and liberbots, hackers and troubleshooters, always ending with the offenders sprawled across the floor, though it was hard to imagine how the incidents shown incriminated such high numbers of symps.

#CodeZ ... The libergram ticker scrolled across. *#ShutThemDown ... #FinalSolution ...*

There remained a slightly increased security presence around the farm, but everything else seemed back to normal—the libermarketing screens filled with their usual advertising. Christopher felt a little nervous of the liberbots after Cassius's impersonation and interrogation in last night's dream. But he was able to pass through to the port with a blue light and no sign of trouble.

The Systems Monitoring Department was filled with the same familiar faces; all the other desks surrounding his workstation were filled as usual. None of his immediate colleagues, as yet, had been deemed responsible for yesterday's incidents and subsequently removed from their duties. Everything seemed normal, almost as if nothing had happened at all except for a dramatic night of libervision.

Christopher was tasked again to observe symps working in street maintenance, only his mind continued to wander back to the mine. The mine that was the factory and source of everything that existed around him, where he had seen, on screen, a rabbit escape the particle liberator. The mine that was simultaneously the place where the darkness and death of the world outside stood so vividly behind just a single wall of floating nanobots that he himself had since passed through—in his dreams at least. The mine that he had seen yesterday on the libernews stormed mindlessly by a bunch of symps, only to be shot down by waiting liberbots. Was there some connection between these events and their location?

He returned home that evening—after a full, uninterrupted day's work—pulled his dinner from the liberwave and sat on the sofa. The libernews continued to provide updates on the wake of yesterday's security threat—now over twelve hundred arrests—but he was at least now permitted to change the channel and instead enjoy coverage of the Genelympics.

The latest round of the games was known as the *Savage Swamp* and took place in a maze of tall artificial trees, wooden beams and rope bridges constructed over Southern swampland. Gladiators were split into two 'teams', red and blue, who would start at opposite sides of the vast network of narrow walkways and funnel inward toward the more congested middle of the maze, fighting to the death as they met in attempt to make it to the other side and survive to the next round. The format made for an array of entertaining battles as competitors converged in varying numbers, often coming face to face with bands of opponents of such different size to their own, sometimes attempting to run, others to fight, often supposed 'teammates' even fighting and killing one another, such was their ruthless drive to survive. Gladiators navigated their way through the maze of perilous planks positioned precariously a few feet above varying depths of mud and water filled with sharp pointed reeds, swinging from trees and overcoming obstacles, slaying opponents with whatever weapons they could find or often their bare hands.

The coverage was deeply engrossing, with viewers treated to all manner of camera angles, tracking images showing the competitors' locations as they wandered through the tangle of tall trees and of course expert analysis and commentary predicting when and how each next battle might unfold, often switching to first person perspective for the fights themselves, leaving the viewer feeling as up close and personal to each clash as possible.

Christopher was stood at an intersection of three wooden beams—one directly behind and two diagonally ahead to either side—suspended over the swamp. It was hot and humid. A foul smell hung in the air. He sniffed himself to find that it was at least partly his. He looked down to see that he was barely clothed: Barefoot and wearing only a pair of loose fitting short trousers cut off at the knee, his chest exposed and painted from his shoulders down to the bottom of his sternum with a red triangle, dripping with sweat. He had never sweated like this before—he was used to the cool comfort of the West, the protection of his liberskin—but here he was, in the South, the *Savage Swamp.* He wiped his forehead with the back of his hand to find that it too was red. Was it paint, or blood? He felt dizzy. This was dangerous—he shouldn't be here. He turned around slowly at the intersection and surveyed his surroundings. There was nothing to be seen besides the three beams, thick trees all around and the black swamp below. He must have come from the path behind, but where to now?

He made his way ahead up the narrow walkway to his left, slowly at first, but soon it seemed as if his bare feet began to walk themselves, growing accustomed to the beam, not so wary of the swamp that lay below. The way branched into two again, and again he took the left. Some distance away, though not far, he heard a loud man's scream for a second—then silence. There were gladiators nearby, and one had seemingly just been killed. Christopher turned around on his beam to make sure he was alone before continuing on.

Soon he came to the edge of a beam to find a gap ahead, previously filled by a rope bridge that now laid hanging below in front of him, over the gaping swamp, as if someone who had crossed it had deliberately cut it behind them on the other side. He turned around to walk back and find another way forward, only to find a few steps down the line that half of the beam he had just walked down had now vanished and that he was now stood on just a short stretch of walkway, the former bridge hanging at one end and nothing but a drop at the other. He made his way back to the end where the rope hung and looked over the edge. He was about ten feet above the swamp below and about twenty feet from the other side. He could possibly climb down the rope ladder that remained hanging from his beam, but he couldn't see a clear way that he would be able to climb up on the other side, or if he could even possibly make it across the swamp—not knowing how deep it was or what it was filled with. The only other option was to take to the trees.

A branch of a nearby tree hung just a few feet above him, perpendicular to the beam he walked on. The tree had many branches that rotated around the trunk at various heights a few feet apart, and looked thick enough that he could potentially climb around and across to the neighboring tree that led to the other side of the gap. He jumped slightly to clasp his hands around the first branch above him, then pulled himself up. It required some strength, but not excessively so. He felt stronger here, somehow, than he ever knowingly had before. He began to navigate his way around the tree, from branch to branch. He had never climbed or even touched a tree before—but as his fingers curled around its branches, the grooves of his skin seeming to grip the bark, it felt like he was made to do it.

Having climbed successfully across the gap over which the rope bridge had once hung, he lowered himself slowly toward the beam below and dropped the last couple of feet, landing with a *thud*. He began to walk on, continuing in the same direction, through the dark forest. But a minute later there was another *thud,* and the beam under his feet wobbled for a moment. Someone, or something else, had dropped from the tree and onto the walkway behind him.

Christopher's first instinct was to run, but that would only reveal his fear more immediately to the stranger who perhaps didn't even know he was there yet. And the walkway was so narrow that to run away would hamper his ability to turn around and see what was coming up behind him. Instead he turned and faced the darkness, the smell of the swamp and his sweat becoming more sensitive in his nose; the odor of another nearby. Christopher stood, legs spread for balance, and saw as a huge shadowy figure emerged from the trees: An enormous dark-skinned gladiator, almost twice the size of Christopher, arms as big as his legs, painted with a blue triangle down from his broad shoulders to the middle of his chest, white eyes and teeth appearing to glow through the darkness, and the unmistakable shimmer of a blade; a large curved sword held in the gladiator's huge fist. Christopher looked to his own hand to see that it too contained a weapon—a relatively small dagger. He didn't have time to wonder where it had come from.

The hulking gladiator lumbered across the walkway toward him, covering the space between them in half the steps it would have taken Christopher, who backed away quickly as the gladiator let out a deep roar, swinging his sword wildly. Christopher managed to back out of reach of the first downward swing, then duck under the second horizontal one. As a third swing came his way, instinctively he jumped and clasped a branch above him, swinging his legs up over the sword and launching his feet into a sharp kick straight into the gladiator's face, sending him tumbling down onto the beam, momentarily stunned.

Now was the time for more evasive action, Christopher decided, as he began to run away down the walkway. But as he glanced back, the gladiator was already back on his feet, his huge strides closing in on Christopher rapidly, swinging his sword down upon him. Christopher took to the trees again, with a running jump that gave him momentum to swing around in a full loop, narrowly evading the blade from behind then coming around to kick the gladiator in the back, sending him to the ground again.

There was nowhere to run, and little use when the gladiator could cover any distance twice as fast as Christopher. He had to stay and fight. And now was the time, with the gladiator face down, to strike. Christopher swung and leapt through the air onto the gladiator's back and plunged his dagger in somewhere between his spine and shoulder blade. The gladiator let out another roar, but it sounded more like anger than pain. And instead of falling limp, as Christopher had hoped he would, the gladiator began to get up to his feet with Christopher still clung to the back of him. The huge Southern specimen reached around over his shoulder and grabbed Christopher by his hair, plucking him off like a bug and tossing him aside.

Christopher landed face down on the wooden beam and could see the steaming swamp below. He heard another roar and turned around just soon enough to see the huge figure of the gladiator leaping through the air and toward him. He quickly thrust his dagger forward to protect himself, as the gladiator landed heavily upon him and directly onto it—Christopher's blade piercing his enemy's chest, as red blood started to dribble out onto the blue painted triangle. But the gladiator was not subdued, and his sword hung just above Christopher's face, as Christopher fought as best as he could to hold the great weight of the monster that lay on top of him, teeth snarling with anger, blade moving slowly closer to Christopher's face, awaiting satisfaction.

"Stop," a voice called nearby, and sure enough the great gladiator stopped in his movements, like a solid—and still heavy—statue. Christopher stared up into the gladiator's eyes, which were lifeless and unblinking, sword still hanging ominously over his head. He turned away to see another large, more familiar figure, appear from between the trees.

"Canaan?" he said. "What are you doing here?"

"What am I doing here?" Canaan laughed that deep hearty laugh. "Well, I'm enjoying the show, Christopher. What are you doing here?"

Christopher looked into the lifeless eyes of the frozen gladiator once more. Only now did the absurdity of his situation dawn on him.

"I'm dreaming," he said.

"You certainly are," Canaan said. "And may I say, what a dream. You're a man of many hidden talents, it seems."

"What do you mean?"

"Oh come on." Canaan laughed. "The way you climbed those trees, the way you adapted to your surroundings—hey, you even gave our friend here a pretty good fight. You're a natural."

"I suppose I've seen a lot of the Genelympics," Christopher said, still trying to push the weight of the static gladiator off him.

"Haven't we all?" Canaan said. "You did pretty well. Of course, there are more efficient ways to use your energy in Oneria."

Canaan appeared to take a deep breath into his chest, then thrust forward with both of his hands, sending a blast of red light through the air and into the gladiator that lay on top of Christopher, sending him and his sword flying off of him and the narrow wooden walkway. Christopher, relieved of the weight, rolled over to the edge to look down as the gladiator lay ten feet below, sprawled on his back, long sharp reeds having penetrated all the way through his chest, sinking slowly into the swamp.

Canaan walked over to stand beside Christopher, as he got up to his feet.

"What would have happened," Christopher said, "if you hadn't have come and stopped him?"

"Well, it looked to me," Canaan said, "that you would have had a sword go through your head, which I don't imagine would have been too comfortable." He gestured briefly to his own scar across his left eye.

"We can feel pain here," Christopher said. "How is that possible? I thought this was all just in our minds."

"The pain is in your mind," Canaan said. "This projection of your self—your light body—that you see here, is a projection of your mind. It can feel just about everything you can in the waking world—some more vividly, some less so—or you can choose to numb those sensations."

"Can you die here?" Christopher asked, looking down at the lifeless gladiator being swallowed slowly by the swamp.

"Maybe," Canaan said. "I suppose, it would be hard to tell. What usually happens if one experiences injury that is expected to be fatal is that the dreamer loses consciousness; they appear to exit the dream from their perspective, and may reappear somewhere else sometime later, with no memory at all, or simply wake up. A battle to the death, in the dream, is a battle between different aspects of the self, and one of those must surely die in some sense."

"That light that you blasted him with," Christopher said, "can you show me how to do that?"

"Sure," Canaan said, "though we could probably use a little more space."

Canaan stepped back away slightly to face Christopher and closed his eyes. Christopher stepped back opposite but kept his eyes open to see the branches of the trees begin to shake and then move slowly apart, as leaves began to fall, as the wooden floor beneath his feet began to rumble and vibrate and expand between him and Canaan until they were stood twenty feet apart on a large

170

wooden square platform, around thirty feet on all sides, surrounded by the trees.

Canaan opened his eyes and gave a slight smile. "Allow me to demonstrate," he said, and almost before he could see it coming, sent a beam of red light straight from his hands, across the arena and into Christopher's chest, sending him flailing backward through the air and crashing hard against the floor, sliding almost to the edge, where he saw the swamp still filled with sharp reeds below.

"Thanks for the warning," he said, climbing back to his feet.

"There won't be any warning," Canaan said, "when it comes to real battle." And he shot another beam of red light toward Christopher, who swiftly ducked and rolled away to the side, avoiding its impact.

"Very good," Canaan said. "Now why don't you throw a little something at me?"

Christopher was keen to test his skills. Something about this dreamscape, his projection of the *Savage Swamp* he had adapted from the libervision last night, seemed to instill a sense of confidence in him; a sense of aggression, of survival—not the kind of fear for survival that the farm seemed to instill, of some abstract threat of dyspheria and historic suffering, but a real sense of life and death. He imagined red light emanating from his hands like he had seen from Canaan's, then thrust his hands forward in the direction of the troubleshooter, but all that emerged was a flicker of hot flames which served nothing other than to give the sensation of burning his own skin. He recoiled in pain and the flames stopped, while Canaan laughed from the other side of the arena.

"Well at least if you get lost in the wilderness, you'll know how to keep warm. Come on now, what is it you're trying to hit me with."

"Red light," Christopher said, "like you did."

"I'm a troubleshooter," Canaan said, "I use stunning rays in my daily job—technological weapons built into my uniform—that's

171

why I manifest a similar appearance of power here, but what is it really I am using?"

Christopher stared back blankly.

"Energy, Christopher," Canaan said. "There are no real weapons here. Everything is energy. Your energy. Your dream, remember?"

Christopher stepped back into a balanced position opposite Canaan and tried to take in his surroundings—the smell, the sensation of his heart beating in his chest—were they too only in his mind?

"Become aware," Canaan said, "and breathe in all the energy around you. Breathe in deeply, down into your solar plexus, then release that power." Again, as he spoke the last words, he blasted a beam of red light toward Christopher, but again he was ready and avoided it—this time by flying up a few feet into the air, before returning to the ground.

"Try again," Canaan said, "on these."

He opened his palms and raised them to chest height, beckoning from the shadows of the trees behind him, to either side, two more tall dark figures; sweaty, shirtless, snarling gladiators, each painted with blue triangles over their muscular chests, both beginning a charge toward Christopher.

Christopher felt the firm grip of his feet against the wooden floor, smelt the scent of his two new enemies coming toward him and took in a slow deep breath which seemed to bend the branches of the surrounding trees toward him. He felt the energy of the dreamscape coursing through him—it was all, after all, his creation—and then released, one bright red beam of light from his left hand toward one of his oncoming opponents, and another from his right hand aimed at the other. And with a crack, both were stunned in their tracks and fell onto their backs.

"Excellent," Canaan said, walking toward him. "You really do possess impressive fighting spirit, Christopher. That's good."

"I've never had to fight before," Christopher said, "I don't think."

"Canaan," another voice spoke suddenly, from nearby. "What's going on here?"

Christopher saw as another figure seemed to dissolve into form just behind Canaan. It was not another tall black topless gladiator but a smartly dressed white man of Christopher's size, who was all too familiar.

"Mr. Perish," Canaan said, turning to face the Prime Resident, showing the most fleeting glimpse of surprise before resuming his normally self-assured appearance. "A training simulation, Sir. Keeping on top of combat skills that might be necessary against the hackers."

"And who is that?" Perish said, pointing toward Christopher, but as he did a screen of blue light appeared between the two of them, shimmering like the inside of a libershower or liberport, with Canaan and Perish on one side and Christopher seemingly hidden on the other.

"Nobody," Canaan said, but his voice seemed to grow quieter, from Christopher's perspective. "Just part of the training simulation, Sir. Everything is under control."

Perish said something back to Canaan, then Canaan back to him, but their conversation was now completely obscured, as if underwater. Christopher walked slowly up to the blue screen of light that seemed to shield him completely from the others. He could still see their silhouettes faintly through it. Could they— could Perish—still see him?

How did he get there so suddenly, Christopher wondered, into the dream—*his* dream? He placed his hand on the blue screen as the silhouettes of Canaan and Perish on the other side completely disappeared, as the top of the screen seemed to grow up toward the trees, then curve around above and over him, and another appeared from the other side, enclosing him all around, until he was alone and floating in nothing but blue light.

21

The next day, after lunch, Christopher returned to his workstation to find a message. It was not a libergram received through his workstation, but a small white piece of folded card that sat on the seat of his swivel chair. He looked around the room cautiously to check that no one was looking and then carefully opened the card. Inside, handwritten in bold blue ink were the words:

See me by the water. C.

C. There were only two people Christopher knew beside himself whose names started with that letter: an odd Northern man named Cassius, and a troubleshooter from the West. Surely the note was from the latter. He had been thinking about him all morning, since waking up in his liberbed and writing down what he could remember of his dream in his notebook. Why had Canaan appeared to him again after watching the Genelympics? Why did Perish appear there? What did he and Canaan discuss? And why had the dream ended so suddenly?

It was Canaan that was now communicating to him from inside the waking world, though he was sure the note didn't refer to anything in the farm. The only body of water he knew was in Oneria, the lake that was the entrance to the Ark. Canaan would meet him there tonight, he was sure. He felt a sense of anticipation.

He stuffed the card into his trousers. It was against the Program for anyone other than a troubleshooter to possess or use handwritten communications or resources. But Christopher had had a journal hidden in his apartment for over a week now and not only that, he had been using it to document his dreams— something he had never even heard of before then. He had long passed the point of protecting himself from breaching the laws of the Program and, if he was honest, enjoying Oneria far too much to care.

He conducted his reality checks several times that afternoon. He was eager to return to Oneria and see Canaan again, the man that had introduced him to this whole new world. Christopher completed his work activities almost automatically. It occurred to him that it seemed like it was here, in Liberty Farm that he was sleepwalking and that it was Oneria that he was really awake, really alive. The people, the places, everything seemed so much more vivid there.

After work, he went straight back to his apartment, had his dinner and watched libervision. He could hardly wait to enter hibernation. But before he did, as the time approached nine, he sat at his liberbed staring at the piece of card.

See me by the water. C.

He closed his eyes and imagined himself by the lake at the spot he had been with Lucy two nights ago before they had dived into the Ark to visit Isaac Island. He was able to release his thoughts and clear his mind before slowly drifting off, mindful to avoid the *wild* entry to Oneria he had experienced a couple of nights ago.

The next thing he knew, he was walking through the woods. It was not an immediate transition. He had certainly lost consciousness initially as he fell into hibernation, but his imagination, his focus, had led him here quickly. He emerged into a clearing and saw the water in front of him reflecting the moon. He felt no need to do a reality check, he knew where he was and why. Seconds later, the silhouette of a large figure emerged out of the night walking toward him.

"Christopher, it's good to see you." His voice boomed. "How are you?"

It was a question Christopher was unsure he had ever heard, and didn't really know how to answer.

"I'm fine," he said, "thank you."

"I see you found your way here effectively," Canaan said, emerging from the shadows; tall, dark and perfectly formed in his tight fitting navy troubleshooters' uniform and crimson cloak. "It seems you're learning your way around lucid dreaming quite quickly from my colleagues and I. Are you enjoying your time in Oneria?"

"Yes," Christopher said, "Very much."

"Good. Then I think it's about time we gave you a real welcome. Do you know how to enter the Ark?"

"Yes," Christopher said.

"Well then, after you."

Canaan gestured toward the water. Christopher closed his eyes for a moment to relax himself, took a breath, then jumped off the ground six feet into the air and dived into the middle of the lake, a little more elegantly than last time but certainly not as smoothly as Lucy. *Remember to breathe,* he thought, and amid the blackness, opened his mouth and lungs, letting in not water but light, into his eyes and chest. He swam downward through the blue and emerged from its under surface upside down in a bright sunlit sky, overlooking an enormous circular cavern; a perfectly round cauldron circled by towering trees, filled with tall stone walls and buildings and steps, like a great inverted pyramid, alive with trees and plants and people. He was falling toward it from a great height.

"Remember to fly, Christopher," Canaan said, appearing beside him.

Christopher saw perhaps a dozen people flying below and ahead of him, and focused himself in their direction. He felt his descent slow, felt himself in control. He curved and waved through the air, and Canaan followed. As he approached the people, still a great distance from the ground, he saw some looked fairly serious as if on their way somewhere, others seemed to be flying just for fun, some dancing in pairs and groups playing in the sky; men, women and even some children.

"Hey Canaan," a woman said.

"Good evening," a man said.

"Canaan!" some children shouted with glee.

Canaan smiled and responded politely to each of them while continuing to follow Christopher. "Over there," Canaan said, pointing. "That ridge."

Christopher saw a green hill a short distance ahead and below them that seemed to grow from the earth in accordance with the curvature of the Ark, with the neighboring architecture built around rather than on top of it. He focused himself in that direction and flew over, remembering to slow and come to a controlled and rather smooth landing on his feet.

"Very impressive," Canaan said, landing alongside. "Lucy is a good teacher."

Christopher felt a slight rush of blood to his cheeks. It must have been a side effect of the descent, he told himself. Instead of revealing it to Canaan, he turned to face the Ark, which he had never seen from this vantage point. It was a sprawling city, full of life, but also scattered, disorderly, so different from Liberty Farm.

"Are they real?" Christopher said. "All those people?"

"Real?" Canaan said. "Residents of the farm, do you mean? Many of them yes, many of them not."

"How many?" Christopher asked.

"Well, let's see," Canaan said. "There are maybe a few hundred residents in the West who we have helped become lucid at one point or another, but many of them fall back into unconscious sleeping and thinking patterns and forget what they have learned. Some might be lucid some nights, others not. Some might spend time in their own private dreamworlds, they might not necessarily come to the Ark. And then there are the other regions—the North, East, South and Islands—perhaps there are a hundred sleepwalkers there, in their own dreamscapes away from the Ark."

"They can't come to the Ark?"

"They can—like Kimiko, Cassius, Isaac—but most don't. The Ark is a projection of the subconscious of the West. Residents in other regions have their own cultures, their own dreams."

"So there are just a few hundred sleepwalkers in the West. But there seem to be more than that. What about all these other people?"

"Projections, mostly," Canaan said, beginning to walk slowly down the hill.

"Why?" Christopher asked, following him.

"Because this is a human city," Canaan said, "It is a human sanctuary. People need people. Our minds seek company. Our hearts crave companionship. This is a collective mindscape. It is the culmination of all of our ideas about life, both conscious and unconscious. It fills itself with the people we imagine, the people we expect, even when we aren't walking here ourselves."

They reached the bottom of the hill and found what looked to Christopher like the oddest form of houses. Small wooden huts, all different shapes and sizes. He heard voices inside as they passed by through a path between them. A small child ran across the way in front of them, followed by another laughing. A woman hung what looked like a rug out of an upper window, beating it. An old man sat on a rocking chair outside the front of his house. Dogs of different sizes and colors wandered the streets.

"Kimiko said the Ark was built by someone," Christopher said. "The Architect."

"It was," Canaan said. "At least its foundations were. A lot of what you see here is his. A lot of it has been built by those of us—sleepwalkers—who have followed. It is an ever changing world, one that reflects the flowing nature of the human mind, rather than the fixed reality of Liberty Farm."

"And he created Oneria too?"

"Some would say that. Others would say he discovered it."

"Discovered it, how?"

"Maybe you should ask him that." Canaan laughed.

"Is he real?"

"As real as anyone else. Though I suspect some would have different opinions on his reality."

"What is he like?"

"Well, he's a very old man—he's been around a long time. He knows a lot. He can be intimidating. But also loving."

"You've met him?"

"Yes." Canaan paused.

They emerged from between the small houses into a large open space filled with stalls, stocked with all sorts of colorful objects of different shapes and sizes, and teeming with people, a bustling marketplace. They continued to walk through, as voices shouted from every direction trying to sell things.

"Sorry for asking so many questions." Christopher felt compelled to say, "I'm just curious."

"Indeed you are." Canaan smiled. "It's ok, I should tell you. It's just a little hard to say. I haven't always been the man you see today, Christopher. Although, when I think about it, it is my past that has made me who I am. As you probably guessed, I am of Southern genetics. In fact I was entirely engineered, for the Genelympics."

"You were a gladiator?" Christopher was stunned. It was not really a surprise, looking at the size and stature of the man; the thought had even crossed Christopher's mind before. But he had never knowingly met anyone from the Genelympics, and having now grown to know Canaan as a troubleshooter, as a sleepwalker, he was somewhat taken aback. "Is that where you got that scar?"

"Yes," Canaan said, "and many more. I was a champion many years ago. Of course if I wasn't I wouldn't be standing in front of you today. I was designed by libergenicists, trained to become a fighting machine, a killing machine. And that's what I did."

"And what happened?"

"I killed many men. Men just like me, pitted against one another, forced to kill or be killed. All for the sake of some twisted spectacle for the farm, for the sublimation of violent tendencies for the masses of residents. I fought my way to the top of *Mount Z*. I won my victory, but it was hollow."

"Hollow, why?" Christopher said. "Weren't you happy to survive?"

179

"I was relieved," Canaan said. "I was exhausted. I was granted my so-called emunity. I was given riches and a whole new life of luxury in the West. I was a celebrity. But I was haunted. Every day I'd try to get on with my life—fine dining, women, appearances on libervision, all of it—but every night I would return to the arena. Every night I would fight those men again. Killing again and again. The blood. The screams. The look of fear in their eyes as they stared into mine. And I would wish that they would kill me instead, but they never did. That's when I met the Architect."

"He helped you to become lucid?"

"Yes," he said. "He helped me to stop my nightmares. He told me that I wasn't responsible for all those men's lives, that it was the fault of the farm, of the Program. He told me that he understood my feelings of guilt and that he shared them. He told me things about the past, and how I could help to make a better future. He told me to become a troubleshooter, to use my powers for good, to help others to become lucid."

"What about Perish?" Christopher asked. "You work for Perish?"

"I have certain responsibilities toward the Prime Resident and various powers within the farm, yes. I am a troubleshooter, after all."

"And what about last night? How come he appeared in my dream?"

"Our dream, Christopher—Oneria is a shared space of consciousness, remember that. People stray from place to place, entering in and out of one another's dreamscapes, according to the frequencies of their minds. Just like you dreamt of yourself in combat within the setting of the Genelympics after watching it on libervision. Perhaps the Prime Resident had watched it too. Perhaps his mind is attracted to violence. Perhaps he was just thinking of me, a troubleshooter, and Program-related matters."

"But didn't he know it was a dream?"

"No, just like you didn't know that you were dreaming all those years until you became lucid. He entered our dreamscape and I was able to alter it and portray a scenario that would slip through his awareness without excessive questioning."

"You mean you stopped him from becoming lucid?"

"As I say, Christopher." Canaan slowed down beside Christopher. "We all have powers, which we can use for good … or not."

Christopher began to grow a little frustrated. He felt like Canaan was hiding something, but he didn't know what. The huge troubleshooter looked down on him with something that seemed to him like compassion.

"The Architect." Christopher felt compelled to change the subject. "What did he tell you … About the past? About the future?"

Canaan came to a stop alongside Christopher to look him in the eyes. Christopher felt as if his BRAINs were being scanned for some test. *Are you ready?* They seemed to ask.

"Liberty Farm is not what it seems," Canaan said. "Dyspheria is not what you think it is. The virus, the Outbreak—it was all orchestrated. The Program doesn't suppress symptoms—it suppresses us. We are not residents, but prisoners. Liberty Farm is a prison, which must come to an end, and you, Christopher, will help us."

Christopher stood, still and silent, struggling to grasp the words he had just heard. Canaan continued to walk.

"But, how?" he said. He turned to find that they were outside a huge stone circular building, its face entirely composed of tall columns and archways—an amphitheater in the center of the Ark.

"Follow your heart," Canaan replied, turning briefly as he continued to walk under one of the archways. Christopher had no idea what that meant, but decided instead to follow Canaan, only to find himself on a platform inside a huge round arena, facing a noisy crowd of what had to be thousands of people under what was now, a starry night's sky.

"Oneria, good evening!" Canaan bellowed from the front of the platform, his voice echoing all around the arena and hushing the crowds of people within. "Please welcome our newest sleepwalker, Christopher!"

To Christopher's surprise, the crowd erupted into a raucous round of applause.

"Let us give him a night to remember," Canaan said. "And let us all wish for him sweet dreams!" The crowd erupted and so too did the sky, as streams of light of every color screeched up from the arena and exploded loudly above into a fizzing rainbow of fire, followed by several more screeching colors again flying into the sky, explosions of light and sound filling the night.

"Enjoy yourself." Canaan patted his hand on Christopher's shoulder and gestured toward some nearby stairs down into the arena, up which walked a small group of women and children to meet him. A friendly, middle-aged looking woman led from the front, carrying a colorful ring of flowers.

"Welcome Christopher," the woman said, reaching up and placing the flowers around his head like a long and dangling necklace. "Sweet dreams."

"Sweet dreams," echoed all the other women and children around her as they ushered Christopher down the stairs and into the crowds. "Welcome," and "Sweet dreams." Christopher was greeted again and again by unfamiliar faces.

"Christopher," a familiar voice said. It was Kimiko, among the crowd. "I hope you enjoy the fireworks."

Christopher tried to go toward her but the stream of people continued to carry him into the middle of the arena. Behind the intermittent screeches and explosions of fireworks, he heard another set of banging, a kind of rhythmic percussion and the plucking and clinking of other objects that seemed to sound in unison.

"Over here, Christopher!" another voice called. It was the familiar Island accent of Isaac, hovering just above the crowd nearby on a large flying carpet, along with two Olivias.

"Excuse me," Christopher said, making his way through the crowds to Isaac's carpet, raising a hand for help. Isaac leaned over and grabbed his hand, easily pulling him aloft and up onto his mini floating island in the middle of the arena.

"How's it going mate?" Isaac leaned over and wrapped his arms around Christopher's shoulders for a moment as he sat down. Christopher saw that Isaac's eyes looked a little lazier than he had seen previously, and on his lap sat a long green pipe with smoke emitting from one end. It was about twice as long as the fattest libar Christopher had ever seen.

"What's that?" Christopher asked.

"It's a dream herb," Isaac said. "It grows here in Oneria, helps make your dreams more vivid. Can make you see some crazy stuff too. Give it a try."

Christopher was about to say "no thanks," but before the words could escape his lips, one of the Olivias already had her hand on his shoulder and placed a pipe in front of his lips. It smelt like some kind of flowers.

"Suck it in, slow and deep," Isaac said. Christopher did just that, feeling the warm smoke fill his lungs. "Hold it … Hold it … And breathe out."

Christopher released and began to cough and cough a handful of times; it was not unpleasant, but an unfamiliar tickling sensation inside himself. Then as he stopped, he felt a rush of energy flood his BRAINs, then a warm feeling wave over and through his body.

"Take another," Isaac said, taking another pull himself of his own pipe, without any hint of discomfort. "Relax. Listen to that music."

Christopher sucked on the pipe again, inhaled, held and exhaled, much smoother than his first attempt, a stream of pale green smoke. He felt a tingling sensation increase in his head, his whole body felt warm and relaxed, the flying carpet he lay on felt so comfortable, Olivia massaging his shoulders felt incredible, everything around and inside him seemed to slow down. He looked down toward the middle of the crowd that Isaac was facing and saw the source of the sounds he had heard; a dozen men and women of all different colors, wearing all kinds of extravagant clothes, some sat at and some stood holding a whole range of peculiar instruments. The banging he had heard was being created by a bunch of men frantically slapping their hands against some hollow oblong objects, the clinking came from a woman sat moving her hands across a long black and white rectangular thing, and the plucking came from a few different people holding different variations of some device with strings on their front which they flicked with their fingers. And many more creating all kinds of noises from various other objects, all somehow in unison, creating a song in the night.

"Real music," Isaac said slowly, blowing out another stream of smoke. Christopher didn't know whether he was talking to him or to himself, but somehow felt he knew exactly what he meant. He had never heard sound like this before. The closest thing he could compare it to was audioprogramming back in the farm: Simple melodies and shallow words designed to interact with residents' BRAINs and optimize their behavior. But this was completely different. This was *real music*. The band of instrument players created such sounds seemingly spontaneously yet perfectly synchronistically, as if they were one being. The vibrations they made seemed to fill the air around the arena and infiltrate Christopher's body, healing it, his heart beating to their rhythm. Colors emitted from their instruments in concord with the sounds—red, gold and green. The music makers took center stage under the continuing display of fireworks, surrounded by a crowd of people who all moved with the music—individually, in pairs, groups, all together—as if the whole gathering was a living organism. They all moved so freely. Perhaps this was freedom really, thought Christopher. Then suddenly, he felt the urge to move.

"I think I'm going to go for a walk," he said.

"Alright mate, take it easy," Isaac said.

Christopher stepped down into the crowd and began to walk, but quickly he was greeted by another familiar figure, stocky and sporting a grey beard.

"Christopher," Cassius said, "I just want you to know that anything I put you through was only to help you learn. Welcome." He raised his right elbow and opened his hand. Christopher did the same and Cassius grabbed his hand and gave it a firm shake.

"Thank you," Christopher said politely, although he still felt somewhat uncomfortable around Cassius and hoped not to spend much more time with him.

"Christopher!"

He heard another familiar voice behind him and turned to see a curly load of red hair peeking above the crowd, coming toward him. He walked toward her.

"Lucy!" he said.

They were face to face, two awkward statues among a sea of moving people, her deep brown eyes staring into his.

"Hi," she said.

"Hi," Christopher said.

"I just wanted to welcome you, and wondered if you'd like to walk with me. I'm not really a party person."

"Sure." He smiled, "I don't think I am either."

Lucy smiled and took his hand, leading him gently out through the crowd and toward one of the tall archways around the arena, the music and dancing continuing behind them.

"How are you feeling?" she asked.

"I think I'm a little overwhelmed," he said.

"Isaac gave you some of his dream herb?"

"Yeah," he said, "but it's not just that. It's just a lot to take in—all these people—I don't even know who's real and who isn't. And Canaan, he told me some things about Liberty Farm."

"Oh right—the talk. I guess you didn't know we're just a bunch of slaves?"

They emerged out of the amphitheater and into a garden filled with violet flowers and a large pond in the middle, by which Lucy took a seat on the grass. The sounds of the arena faded into silence.

"No," he said, following her to the ground, "Did you?"

The blue sky above turned to a deep purple and the water across the pond froze into hard silver ice. Christopher wasn't sure if Lucy had done it. She looked sad, but unafraid. Then suddenly, a small girl with red curly hair emerged from the trees on the other side of the pond and began to skate across it. She skated around in circles, dancing on the ice.

"I've been a symp my whole life," Lucy said. "A symptomatic resident, apparently. I've lived my entire life in the lower levels of the farm, struggling, told that we're the worst of the worst, treated as a threat. This disease called dyspheria that we're all supposedly infected with—we're told that it affects us more than others, that it disturbs our mind and our behavior, that we aren't rehabilitating as quickly as we should. We're forced to adapt to this Program— forced to follow the commands of these computers we're connected to and suppress who we really are—or else we're done for."

Then another figure emerged from the trees and joined the girl skating across the ice, the two of them laughing and playing together. She too had red hair, but a much older face than Lucy; warm but worn by many hard years.

"But my mum loved me. She invested what little Ls she had so that she could have a child. She felt that she needed to. She told me every day that despite dyspheria, despite the Program and all the propaganda pushed by the farm, I wasn't diseased—I was special. And that one day I would find a man who would see me for what I really am, and that I would be free."

The woman disappeared, leaving the little girl alone on the ice.

"What happened?" Christopher said.

"She was taken to Advanced Rehabilitation for disobedience. I never saw her again. Only here, in Oneria."

Christopher felt something unfamiliar in his stomach, a sort of sadness he had never felt before. He had never really imagined what life was like for a symp, for the family of someone taken to AR, or ever questioned the purpose of the Program. He wanted somehow to make her feel better. He watched as a third figure appeared and skated across the pond to the other girl. It was a boy, a younger version of Christopher. He picked the younger Lucy up from the ice and together they started to play.

"I was factory farmed," Christopher said. "I never had any parents to speak of. I was designed by the Program to fill some particular spot it deemed was needed in the farm. I'm a dorm. I suppose I'm better adapted to the Program than you in some way—I don't really know what that means. I can't say my life hasn't been easier than yours, but I can say that until I came here it felt hollow. Only in Oneria am I learning what life is really about. I can't imagine what your life was like; I don't know what it must have been like to lose your mum and I don't know what I can say to make you feel better. All I can say is that I agree with her—you are special."

Lucy turned to face Christopher. Her deep brown eyes locked on his as she began to lean slowly toward him. He felt himself falling into them, drawn in toward her. Soon their faces were almost touching. Lucy closed her eyes and tenderly wrapped her lips around Christopher's. He too closed his eyes and felt the warm touch of her soft lips begin to tingle through his entire body. He could feel her deeply—not just her lips, but her spirit. He felt him and her connecting, interlinking, like he had never known possible with a person. There was nothing else in his mind, only the two of them, until …

"Christopher." A woman's voice called from nearby.

He opened his eyes slowly and saw Lucy do the same. He pulled back away from her and turned to see another woman across the pond. She was a pale figure, almost white, peeking from the darkness between the trees across from them, a skinny and frail looking woman. It was the same one he had seen two nights ago, among the zombies in the woods, and some time before.

"Christopher," she called again, not to him, but to the young boy on the pond. The boy turned to her and immediately skated in her direction, vanishing along with her, back into the trees. Lucy's younger self also visibly faded, then disappeared.

"Who was that?" Lucy asked.

"I don't know."

22

Christopher lay on his liberbed, keeping his eyes closed. It had been the most incredible dream; he didn't want it to end. Such sights, such sounds, such feelings. Was this what life was meant to feel like? After a few minutes he began to write in the red journal.

Flying over the Ark. A human city. A collective mindscape.
A huge party—fireworks, real music, dream herb, so many people.

He wondered whether his BRAINs had ever experienced such stimulation, whether asleep or awake. The Ark was overflowing with activity, and everyone seemed so welcoming, so connected. But apparently most weren't even real. "People need people", he remembered Canaan had said.

And what of the sounds—the vibrations—made by the band of instrument players? They had seemed to move his entire mind and body at a cellular level in a way he had never known sound could. *Real music,* Isaac called it. And the *dream herb* too affected Christopher's consciousness in a way he had never experienced. He imagined that this was something like the effect that hackers might be seeking when they screw with their BRAINs, but this dream herb apparently grew in Oneria—or at least in Isaac's mind. He was an unusual sort of person, but Christopher had to admit that the Islander certainly knew how to enjoy himself. Then Christopher recollected his own happiest moment.

Being with Lucy by the frozen pond. It felt like we were one.

The sensation when their lips had touched. He had never been so close to a person, he was sure, either physically or *spiritually.* Everything else had seemed to disappear. It was the most magical experience of his life. He could hardly explain it, only to acknowledge to himself that it just felt so right to be with her, like the most natural thing in the world.

Children skating. Lucy's mother. The white woman—who is she?

That pale and disheveled looking woman. Christopher was sure that he had seen her at least three times now; last night with Lucy, previously in the dream with Cassius, and at least once before. Why did she keep appearing in his dreams? She had appeared to him previously as a zombie, but last night seemed more human; she had called his name—not to him, but his child self skating on the pond. She had interrupted his time with Lucy and interrupted his memory now, resurfacing, like a disease that couldn't be cured. Then he recollected Canaan's words.

Liberty Farm is a prison. The Outbreak was orchestrated.

Christopher could barely understand, let alone believe what he had heard. A prison, he had learnt, was a place they used in the old times to lock away people who broke the law—itself a rather ineffective form of artificial morality imposed inconsistently by governments across the globe. There was nothing like that in Liberty Farm, as far as Christopher knew. There was simply, the Program—designed and adapted to control the symptoms of dyspheria and aid our rehabilitation—and for those that failed to adapt to it, Advanced Rehabilitation. But Canaan said that Liberty Farm *is* a prison, not that it has one. But residents were not locked up; they were able to move around—at least according to the freedoms they had earned—and work toward a brighter future.

And what about the past? *The Outbreak was orchestrated.* But who would do such a thing? The virus, the Outbreak, had wiped out most of the world's population. No one knew the origin— some bioterrorists working for whichever radical religious faction or nation on its knees—only the outcome. It was only thanks to the Writer that there was anything left of humanity at all.

Christopher headed to work. It occurred to him how repetitive his days now seemed compared to the adventures he enjoyed while asleep. At least there was always the bar, shopping or libervision to entertain him in the evening, or even a liberday if he really felt like a change. But it made sense that work itself would be repetitive—the order and routine it offered benefited his performance as well as that of other residents and ultimately the farm.

However, his afternoon would be interrupted by something unexpected. Shortly after lunch he received a libergram to attend a routine review meeting with Senior Systems Monitor Mason. But when he opened the door to his boss' office he was stopped in his tracks by the sight of not only his supervisor, but by two unfamiliar troubleshooters and sat securely between them, the unmistakable smirking face of Dean Perish—the Prime Resident who had made such an unexpected appearance in Christopher's dream a couple of nights ago. He sat silently puffing on a blue libar, filling the air around Mason's desk with pale blue vapor.

"Good day, Christopher." It was Mason who greeted him from behind the long desk, alongside Perish and his personal escorts. "I hope we aren't disturbing you, but we hoped you might be able to share with us a little more detail around some of your recent reports."

It was the sprightly supervisor's standard introduction to his reviews and clear from his appearance, unflustered by the unexpected guests, that Christopher was expected to complete his duties as usual.

"Certainly Sir," he said, stepping onto the red and blue libertree logo in the center of the office floor. In a moment, a large holographic liberscreen appeared behind him to fill his half of the room, displaying summary data from his observations and activity.

"Last time you reported your recent observations of service symps around the mine," Mason said. "Could you provide further update?"

"Certainly Sir", Christopher said. "So last time I reported slightly reduced performance and slightly increased abnormal social behavior among the service symps. And I also referred to an abnormal incident, involving an animal, Sir."

"Ah yes, the animal." Mason nodded. "I do believe you considered this to have been an isolated abnormal incident, isn't that correct?"

"Yes, Sir," Christopher said, feeling a sudden heat rise up his face, beginning to anticipate where this was going. "I did."

"Well what then, is your perspective of the incident which occurred in the mine just a couple of days ago." Mason leant forward over his desk. "That sparked the most significant security threat that the West has perhaps ever seen?"

"My perspective, Sir?" Christopher delayed, glancing over to Perish, who stared back at him.

"Yes, Christopher," Mason said. "Your perspective."

"My perspective," Christopher said, "is that such a security breach should be a major concern to myself as a systems monitor as it should to any resident, and I am grateful that the Prime Resident is handling it so severely."

Mason seemed surprised by the reply and glanced over to Perish, unsure whether the response was satisfactory from the perspective of the Prime Resident. Perish continued to gaze at Christopher, his handsome politician's face etched in permanent smirk, still silently puffing on his libar.

"And what of your responsibility in this matter?" Mason said.

"It is my responsibility as a systems monitor and as a resident to be ever vigilant of the threat of dyspheria, none more so than now," Christopher added. "However, I have not been tasked to observe the mine specifically since some time before the incident, and had no opportunity to observe the symps involved in the latter incident following the turnover of symps from the first."

192

Mason's face turned into a grimace as he struggled to swallow this fact.

"And what about your performance, Christopher?" Perish spoke, to Christopher's surprise. "How is your own performance and rehabilitation of late?"

Christopher peered back at the perfectly groomed Perish sat in front of him. He had never been in the presence of the Prime Resident before, and now felt a great conflict within him—an unavoidable dislike for Perish, but at the same time an irresistible compulsion to satisfy him. He wondered if Canaan felt something similar.

"Oh don't be alarmed, Christopher," Perish smiled that handsome yet unconvincing politician's smile, putting down his libar on the desk. "You aren't the only systems monitor I'm dropping in on. The times simply demand that I keep a closer eye on things just now, with the assistance of Mason of course." He glanced toward Mason, who seemed rather pleased with himself.

"I … I'm doing just fine," Christopher said.

"He was late for work a few days ago," Mason said. "Only by a couple of minutes, and that is the first time I recall, but his performance levels do appear to have slightly reduced as well."

"Is that so?" Perish said, peering down and flicking with his fingers across the screen on his desk, unseen to Christopher, then back at him. "Have you been feeling a little lethargic lately?"

Christopher felt betrayed. He glanced at Mason, who smiled back. He glanced fleetingly at the two silent troubleshooters who stared intently back at him, or was it through him?

"Perhaps a little," he said.

"A little," Perish said. "And have you been sleeping well?"

Christopher swallowed a gulp of fear down into his stomach.

"Sleeping?"

"Hibernating," Perish clarified, "Docking—at night—have you experienced any problems recently? Or perhaps difficulty getting up the next morning?"

"No," Christopher said.

"Are you sure?" Perish said, "It's just—as I'm sure you might have heard—we have recently discovered a new form of collective hacking of BRAINs in hibernation. You haven't happened to experience anything strange during hibernation have you, Christopher?"

"No," Christopher said.

It was all Christopher could do to try to say the word convincingly, to stay stood there still, as four sets of eyes stared intently back at him. He knew not what powers of mind reading the Prime Resident might possess, let alone the two troubleshooters sat to either side.

"Very well." Perish smiled. "Thank you for your time. We'll be seeing you."

The Prime Resident raised his right thumb toward Christopher, but it seemed absent of the boost it usually prompted.

"Thank you for your report," Mason said, repeating the gesture. "I'll see you soon."

Christopher stepped off of the libertree in the middle of the office floor and reluctantly raised his own thumb, first to Mason and then Perish, then made his way quickly out of the door.

If it was his productivity and performance that the farm were concerned with, the Prime Resident and Mason had certainly not helped Christopher that afternoon, as he struggled to get his BRAINs off the meeting and back to work. *Why would they think I was responsible? They know I wasn't observing the mine then. Why are they trying to blame me?* He managed to pull his train of thoughts back from going any further until after work, where he felt he was not under such stringent observation, though he knew, just as easily, he could well be. Instead of heading back home, he strolled various streets of the West; unsettled, uncertain what and where was safe, his thoughts seeming to reflect back to him off plastic pavements and libermarketing screens.

What had Perish been doing there? Wasn't he busy enough working on his *final solution* to dyspheria without "dropping in" on systems monitor review meetings reporting on data he presumably already had access to anyway? Was that really the purpose of his visit? Christopher suspected not. He suspected that Perish knew well that Christopher had not been sleeping as he should, and that he had indeed experienced something strange during hibernation. Perish had come to the Systems Monitoring Department today to see him, specifically, and listen to him lie.

Collective hacking of BRAINs in hibernation. That's what he had called it. He had said the same on libervision with Leo and Fiona a few days ago. It was the same words another troubleshooter had used when describing the rumor of a new threat against the Program in the bar a few days earlier; a rumor that Canaan, before Christopher had met him in person, seemed to try to dispel. And at last Christopher knew what it meant. It wasn't some way of hacking into more than one resident's BRAINs at a time, to steal from them in their sleep, or to share some altered state in the farm in the typical sense. They were talking about lucid dreaming.

But lucid dreaming was nothing to do with hacking. Or was it? Dreams occurred automatically during sleep. It was up to the person to realize that they were dreaming, to become lucid. And it was the way that the Program connected our BRAINs that enabled us to share our dreams. At least that was what Canaan told him. But then why had the other troubleshooter mentioned collective hacking to Canaan? Why had Canaan spoken of some strange threat to the farm when he then met Christopher and asked him to follow Lucy and to investigate the mine? And why was Perish now asking him if he had experienced anything strange during hibernation after he had been lucid dreaming for a week?

Up until recently he was sure that troubleshooters and the Prime Resident worked for the same purpose—for the protection and progression of the Program—but now knew there was at least one troubleshooter behaving altogether unusually. Canaan had initially said that the farm was under threat, but it was his instructions that then led Christopher to become lucid, where he had since told him that Liberty Farm was not all it seemed—that it was a prison. Surely, Canaan himself would be in trouble if he were heard saying such things while awake in the farm. But he must have lied to Christopher at least once, or at least misled him. And the interrogation—that first night he had become lucid—was it really necessary? Yes, Christopher answered himself. Canaan was a good man, he was sure. He had helped him, and the others, to become lucid. He had helped him to experience Oneria, a place that he felt more alive than he ever did in the farm.

So what if Liberty Farm really was a prison? What did that make Dean Perish? And what if he really knew, as it seemed he did, what was going on in hibernation? The only remaining question then, Christopher thought, was why hadn't he been whisked away to Advanced Rehabilitation already?

23

Christopher found himself wandering under a tall triangular archway, flashing blue, and into a liberport. He was on his way home, or so he thought. But after the usual whirring—that high pitched sound and the bright light—he was surprised to hear the robotic announcement. *Liberseum,* the voice said.

He was the only one of ten or so residents in the liberport who stepped out. Had he chosen this destination, or had the liberport chosen it for him? He was lost and confused about his place in the world, about the nature of his world. What better place to find himself than the liberseum, the depository of historical information available for display to all residents.

He had never been here before. There was no point. Any historical information a resident needed to know was either presented publicly on libervision, through libercation, or delivered directly to the individual resident's BRAINs by the Program. The liberseum was an antiquated artifact of an earlier time in the farm where such a crude collection of various historical information was considered necessary. Now it was nothing more than an amusement, and not a popular one, mainly for level two symps keen to move up in the farm, taking pride and interest in its history and taking their scruffy symp children along for some free entertainment. He saw a couple of groups of such symps making their way out of the liberseum and toward the liberport. The liberseum itself looked like the oldest building he had ever seen in the farm; it looked more like something from the Ark—with a series of huge stone steps leading up to its similarly old-looking columned entrance. He was the only one on his way in at this time.

As he entered the huge doorway into the main corridor of the building a flicker of light appeared in front of him at first, then flashed into life, with the image of a smiling, bespectacled scientist that looked more like a cartoon than a real person. Shoddy old hologram, Christopher thought.

"Good evening, resident, and welcome to the liberseum, the place where history lives forever and you can learn for free!" the holographic scientist chirped. "Would you like me to give you a guided tour today?"

"No," Christopher said.

"Or would you like to explore on your own?"

"I said no, thank you."

"I'm sorry," the hologram said, "I didn't quite catch that. Would you like me to give you a guided tour today? Or would you like to explore on your own?"

"Explore on my own," Christopher spoke loudly. "Thank you."

"Ok, explorer, then go explore. And remember … history lives forever!"

He walked straight through the holographic scientist and continued down the corridor, which was interspersed by a number of triangular sliding doors, each leading to different galleries or exhibits, with various signage and fittingly colored walls and digital images floating around indicating their content.

The first door he came to was positioned among a mostly black section of wall scattered with white spots that seemed to resemble the stars he had seen in the sky over Oneria. The sign above read *In The Beginning.* It sounded like the place to start.

He stepped into a room which was, at first, completely dark. It reminded him of the first time he had walked out of the farm, in his first lucid dream, into the emptiness outside. He thought perhaps the gallery was broken or closed down.

"Hello?" he said.

And then a loud voice began to speak.

"In the beginning there was nothing but void. No matter, no light nor even time. Then came the first iteration."

Suddenly, a bright flash of white light exploded all around Christopher, forcing him to jump in shock—it was surprisingly realistic.

"The force of life burst the universe into existence," the voice said. "It was the result of an unbalanced equation, the incomplete nature of reality. For there to be nothing, there had to be something. For there to be something, there had to be nothing. And so the force of life came into being, and imbued itself in all things, and sought to become ever more, acting in opposition to the nothingness from which it came."

The room now resembled a kind of static fuzz of bright white scattered among blackness.

"At first, the life force manifested in nothing much at all; some light, some scattered matter. The universe was nothing but a chaotic cloud of dust. But the life force sought to become ever more, drawing the dust together to form clumps of rocks, which formed bigger rocks and rocks the size of planets. And that is how the Earth was formed."

He watched as the room presented a holographic rendition of the narration: The bits of buzzing light clumping into clouds, then rocks and then a large round planet that filled most of the room—glowing red at first, then shifting slowly to blue.

"The Earth was a hostile place since the beginning. It used to be hot and uninhabitable. But after many millions of years, it began to cool enough so that the chemicals and matter on its surface were molded by the life force into simple cells. These cells began to reproduce, change and grow stronger as they fought to survive, fought to avoid falling back into nothingness."

The presentation zoomed in to the surface of the Earth, and illustrated small and initially simple microscopic organisms competing and becoming ever more complex.

"Over many more millions of years these cells began to group together to form small creatures. These were mostly small and simple things, with very limited urges and abilities to help to continue to survive and reproduce. Eventually some of these began to turn into animals—strange and often dangerous creatures that spread across the world. You can learn more about those in our *Animal Anarchy* gallery."

The presentation created holographic images of various kinds of animals—all hair and legs and sharp teeth snarling through the darkness and running around the room, one or two of which unnervingly seemed to run straight through Christopher.

"Out of all the forms of life on the planet, there was one that was imbued with and harnessed more of the life force than anything else, humans."

A man and a woman appeared in front of him, wrapped in some kind of primitive sheet-like clothing.

"No one knows exactly how humans were formed, but what we do know is that that was really the start of any truly meaningful life in existence. Because humans were not only able to grow and reproduce like all other creatures with the life force, but we had the unique ability to change and transform the world itself however we chose."

Humans shown using tools, creating fire, building small primitive homes.

"At first humans lived chaotic lives much like everything else that had been before; fighting to survive. But soon, humans began to learn that this chaos was fruitless, that order must be gained. They began to organize themselves in families, tribes, communities, for the good of one another. But still there was that tendency toward chaos. Civilizations expanded and collapsed. There were wars, death, violence."

He watched as the hologram presented a sped-up summary of the rise and fall of various civilizations, dressed in all manner of peculiar old fashions, buildings being built and destroyed, sword fights and bombs and explosions.

"Throughout history people questioned and came up with different ideas as to what the life force was. Many saw it as a living thing itself—a person or god that created the world and decided what to do with it—but they came up with so many versions of god, attached to their own made up ideas of right and wrong, that this only led to more wars between different religions, as these ideas were called."

Christopher found himself surrounded by crowds of people, shuffling along together, chanting incomprehensibly in unison.

Then, he was in a large, ornately decorated building with violet patterns painted on the walls, rows of people on their knees bowed towards a huge golden statue. Gold everywhere, shimmering in the light pouring in from the multi-colored windows—which were then smashed open as rocks and missiles hurtled toward him, before more fire erupted and engulfed his awareness, before re-emerging in a laboratory.

"Eventually the smarter people in society started to think there was no life force at all. They developed a practice to observe only what they could see, and understood that the shapes of life were the result of simple scientific processes, which was true. But it was only their limited technology that prevented them from seeing what we do now."

The presentation zoomed in—down the microscope of one scientist—to show tiny golden sparkling particles within.

"It wasn't until the twenty-first century that Libercorp made perhaps the most significant scientific discovery of all time, the liberton, the most incredible fundamental particle that gives all other particles the power to grow, to change, to reproduce. The life force itself wasn't a force at all, but a particle, simple yet powerful. It was this particle that sparked the universe into existence, the source of all life. But it is also the force of death, of greed, of excess, of all the chaos that has plagued humanity throughout its existence, culminating in the Outbreak."

The same stock images of explosions and violence that he had seen a million times before on the libernews, only this time in three dimensions. Then to the mine that he had seen in his observations as a systems monitor, as well as also on the libernews recently.

"That is why libertons are under the strict control of Liberty Farm today. We cleanse and deconstruct materials from the outside world through our particle liberator, turning them into pure uncontaminated libertons to be stored and put to optimal use in the farm, to feed, to fuel and to clothe our residents. It is the only way that we can protect ourselves from falling back into chaos."

Zooming out to reveal a wide view of the West from a great height—just below the libersphere, he thought—with the Libermid at its center, finally zooming back in to the familiar slogan wrapped around it.

"And that has been the goal of Liberty Farm, humanity and some might say even the universe itself since the start—to create order out of chaos. And that is what Liberty Farm will forever work toward. *Liberty Farm: Working For Your Future.*"

The presentation came to a close and the room returned to darkness. He was alone again with nothing but his thoughts. He felt a strange combination of feelings. The visual presentation was actually better and more immersive than he had expected, but the content was so crude and seemingly incomplete. He had already known everything he had heard, but to hear it all together in what had apparently been deemed to be a sufficient summary of history made the gaps appear more glaring than he had ever considered, and now left him with only questions. What was this *first iteration* that had supposedly burst the universe into existence? It seemed a simplistic explanation. *No one knows exactly how humans were formed.* Didn't that bother anyone? Shouldn't we first be sure who we are and where we came from before we work out how to act in the world around us?

He next entered the *Animal Anarchy* gallery. It wasn't such a small dark room as *In The Beginning,* but instead a looping corridor filled with several holographic exhibits which sprung into life as he approached and triggered specific narration to be delivered to his audio receiver. The gallery at large took on the appearance of an outdoor wilderness, complete with trees, clearings where the exhibits were located, and occasional images of lakes and streams. He had certainly never experienced an environment like this in the farm before, only in Oneria.

The first exhibit showed the origins of animal life from simple cells in more detail than had been presented briefly in the previous gallery. There were then various exhibits relating to different types of animals. There were fish—these slippery, swimming things that filled the sea. Some—sharks, they were called—grew large bodies and sharp teeth and regularly ate people alive who were stupid enough to enter the water. There were huge reptiles that looked like giant scaly monsters, with strange protruding tongues and unblinking eyes; slippery snakes that slithered into human habitats and killed them with their poisonous fangs. And small creatures called insects, or more appropriately referred to as *creepy crawlies* that could sneak around and gather in huge numbers unnoticed, biting people and spreading diseases. It seemed that there was such a range of dangerous creatures that used to roam the Earth, and we were much better off without them.

There was one exhibit called *Man's Worst Enemy* which explained how dogs had evolved from wolves, vicious forest carnivores, but cleverly changed their appearance and behavior over time in order to appear more appealing to humans; they were able to infiltrate our society and homes and steal our food for over a thousand years. It was the first time that he had seen dogs—in holographic form at least—in the farm. There was one dark brown one that looked a lot like the one that had appeared in his dream with Cassius a few nights ago. And other scruffier, scarier, larger specimens of various shapes, sizes and colors. It was amazing to think that an animal could be smart enough to create such a sustained threat to humans for such a period of time. Perhaps that was why, due to some deep collective memory, he had transformed into a dog the first time he had exited the farm in his dream, as he left his humanity and safety behind.

There was one animal that humans seemed to have a more successful relationship with, which sparked his interest. Horses, as they were called, were tall creatures with thick muscular bodies and large flat heads. They appeared smoother, tidier in appearance than most of the other animals he had seen presented. Throughout history, humans had successfully been able to tame these beasts and ride them as a primitive vehicle, to use them as a machine. It was shown as a great sign of human's development and dominance over other species. He was amazed how the horses, with such long skinny legs, had been able to carry the weight of people and such heavy loads, and felt somehow sorry for them.

Couldn't we just have invented libercars sooner?

He visited three more galleries giving more details on *Dyspheria—The Deadliest Disease, The Formation of Liberty Farm* and *Libergenics 101,* but didn't learn anything new about the subjects he was already relatively well versed in. The whole experience, and the day in its entirety, left him feeling wholly dissatisfied—this immediately following the most spectacular and thought-provoking dream of his life.

If Liberty Farm was a prison, as Canaan had told him, then who were the guards? The troubleshooters? The Prime Resident? Why had Perish sought to meet him at the Systems Monitoring Department, and why had he and Mason seemed intent on attaching some blame for the recent security breach on him? If Liberty Farm was a prison, then why was he free to move around as he chose—to the Retail Department, to the bar, the liberseum? Why did the farm share this history of its origins and the Outbreak to its residents?

As he returned back to his apartment and prepared to hibernate that evening, he looked again at the words scratched on to the first page of the journal that started him on this habit of questioning more and more.

All things may not be as they seem.
And so tonight I lucid dream.

24

But he did not lucid dream. He woke up the next morning on his liberbed, surprised to find his mind's eye empty of any memory of the night. The ceiling was blue. The bright blue glow of the libersphere poured in through the window. He squinted at his fingers and counted again, all ten of them.

He sat up straight, surveying his surroundings suspiciously, surprised to find himself there, in his apartment, so suddenly. It had seemed like little more than seconds, no real time at all, between closing his eyes as he docked last night to opening them again this morning. It was the same sensation, he now realized, he had experienced every day of his life up until this last, most unusual, week or so. It was strange to now feel so dissatisfied by something that had previously been so normal, so rapidly had his expectations been increased by lucid dreaming, his perception of reality altered; he was now so disappointed not to have a new adventure to write in his red journal.

Perhaps he shouldn't expect to lucid dream every night. It had taken some time and training for him to learn how to do it, after all. Perhaps it was too much liberhol. Or perhaps it was something else. Perish, he thought. Perish knew what was going on in hibernation, knew about Oneria and the sleepwalkers, and was trying to stop it somehow, he was sure.

He went to work. He passed through with blue lights all the way without so much as a glance from a liberbot. No unexpected visitors in the Systems Monitoring Department. Work all day.

He went to Body in the hope that he might see Lucy—in either the waking or sleeping world. He emptied his bottle several times waiting, hoping, questioning. He had hoped that Lucy would come to meet him there. She could take him flying, and they could carry on from where they left in their last, most amazing dream together. But there was no sign of her. He looked at his hands, and despite his drunkenness could still count decidedly that there were five fingers on each.

He woke up the next morning as empty of memories as the last, empty, but for a last lingering lap of liberhol in his BRAINs.

And again. Another morning with no memory of hibernation the night before. Another day at work. Another night in Body. Another morning without recall.

Life in the farm became even more repetitive. Without a night of dreaming between each day they seemed to blur into one. He could hardly concentrate at work. All he could think about was his previous dreams, becoming lucid and seeing Lucy again. He stayed out as late as he could, but there was no sign of her.

He alternated nights between the bar and his sofa sitting in front of the libervision cramming Genelympic highlights, hoping to trigger Canaan to appear in his apartment in a dream. He filled his mind with the troubleshooter, with Lucy, Kimiko, Isaac and even Cassius. He did his reality checks every now and again, but with decreasing regularity as he grew discouraged. He docked each night deflated, and woke each morning even more so.

"Libergram search," he said to his libervision at home one evening. "Lucy."

"69,397 results," the libervision responded, showing the names and profile pictures of Lucys all over the farm.

"Filter: West."

"33,633 results."

"Symptomatic?" he asked.

"Christopher 165-189-198. You are advised not to socialise with symptomatic residents."

"I know," he said. "Can you just filter anyway?"

"Christopher 165-189-198. You are advised not to socialise with symptomatic residents."

"Great." He sighed, before spending over an hour scrolling for his Lucy, but found no one like her.

He woke some mornings with scattered memories, but so indistinct, he didn't know whether they had been from dreams or just the day before: Work, the bar, his apartment; all too familiar images he didn't know were real or not. He walked slowly around

206

the streets, staring at the other residents, who walked mindlessly on by to work or to shop or wherever. Were they awake or asleep? Did it make a difference? He lingered on the liberportation platforms, almost begging the liberbots to berate him, to test whether the world he walked in was real, whether they were. "You, dorm," they would bark. "Are you entering the port or not?" And he would, inevitably stopping short of complete self-sabotage and a trip to Acute Assessment.

He woke one morning with the image of the white woman etched into his mind's eye, a pale figure against a black background hunched in pain over her round stomach, tormenting him. Who was she?

The next morning he woke with images of animals in his mind. It had felt like he had been back at the liberseum again. There was the dog, dark brown, running through the forest. And the horse, gleaming white, running alongside. Except, it was a horse with a horn on its head. And she was sick. She needed to stop. And Christopher felt sorry for her, but kept on running.

And then, another indistinguishable start to the day—bleary eyed and bored of life before he had even had breakfast—he was startled awake on his way to work by something he had never expected.

"Dearest residents," the voice thundered over the streets, causing Christopher, and all those around him, to jolt to a standstill. He, like they, looked up to see the source of the noise, high above and all around them. The face he had seen every day of his life, beaming from the liberscreens that curled around every tall building, looking down at him and all others, and now speaking.

"I apologize for disturbing you," the Writer said. "I know that this is quite a surprise. I know that I could easily alleviate the symptoms of that surprise. But I want to speak to you as honestly as possible, and I want you to feel the impact of these words."

Christopher heard gasps echo around the packed streets like a shockwave, as one by one the residents recognized the source of the voice.

"It's the Writer!" said a dorm nearby, giving an awkward thumb up toward the face high above, encouraging others nearby to do likewise.

The Writer's face appeared more wrinkled than ever before, and for the first time Christopher could recall, his lips were moving.

"Spare me your social gestures," he said. "It has been such a long time since I last spoke to you, many of you will not remember—or weren't even alive. But I know you know that I have been watching over you, as well as I could, throughout this time—or at least as well as I thought I could. See, even my mind has its limits. And that is really what this—all of this—is all about."

Christopher couldn't help but look down at his hands and count his fingers—once, twice, three times—to see all ten in their normal place and appearance. He still couldn't believe it—this couldn't be real.

"It's hard to believe that it's been almost a century since Liberty Farm was created, since the disease control camps where the antivirus was first administered and the BRAINs first implanted. Back when I was a child it was rare to even live that long. I hardly imagined that I would live as long as I have, or achieve what I have, back then. I know you think that this was all meticulously planned from the beginning. But all things may not be as they seem. In some ways, by some people, it was premeditated. But for the most part, it has been a product of hard work, hard decisions and working for your future."

All things may not be as they seem. Did the Writer just say that?

"I developed the Program as a way to save humanity, to bring an end to the suffering that filled the world I used to live in. I created a new world, but at the cost of great sacrifice."

The indigo light in the middle of the Writer's forehead, at the bottom of the silver inverted triangular helmet that connected him to the Program, glowed as he spoke.

"I have spent the majority of my life connected to this Program, trying to maintain the balance of this monster of mine. And you too, connected to the Program. It knows all of your thoughts and actions, your innermost desires, and so do I. I know now that you desire more than I can provide. I know my time is now up."

Christopher glanced around himself in hope of some reassurance, but all the residents around remained frozen, faces open as they gazed up at the various liberscreens above them.

"I know now that you are better off without me, and that those who wish to succeed in my absence are ready—whether they be elected, or selected official, or the common resident.

"I have spent so many years now living this half-life, preserving my body as much as possible to dedicate my mind to the Program—to battle with its curious intelligence, its furious spirit. But alas, it has gotten the better of me—both my body and my mind—succumbed to time.

"And so, this coming Unification Day will be my last. But let it not be a sad one. Let it be—more than all others—a celebration of the reasons we created this world, a celebration of the end of war, of nations, and of needless violence. Let us remember that such creation must always necessitate great sacrifice. And let us experience real unification. Goodbye for now."

And as suddenly as the Writer's voice had arrived, it vanished. And so did his face from the liberscreens around the farm; replaced by the red and blue libertree logo and the familiar slogan scrolling below:

Liberty Farm: Working For Your Future.

25

He had had enough. If time really was up for the Writer, and so too for Christopher—as inextricably connected as he felt—he had to do something. He had to see Lucy again, if not in a dream then in the farm. He had no idea where to start. He had no idea where she lived or what she did for a living. All he knew about her was her name and that she was a symp.

After another hard day's work—not hard in the sense of the work that he did, or didn't do, but rather the difficulty he had in maintaining an acceptable level of performance—he decided, for the first time in his life, to take a libervator down to Level One; the lowest level of the West, where the most acute symptomatic residents lived. He didn't know whether Lucy was level one or two, but he figured that if he was going down, he may as well go all the way down.

The streets were darker, dirtier and more densely populated than the dorm levels. There was noise everywhere; the symps all seemed to talk to one another, or shout. He caught a few unwelcoming eyes. It was apparent from his appearance he didn't belong there. But he didn't care. He had to see her.

The bars and shops and apartment buildings all seemed to be bundled together down here—no nice neat separate sections for drinking, shopping and living that he was used to on his level—all stacked together in peculiar shapes and angles, every street corner its own chunk of chaos.

He wandered around for several minutes before one bar in particular caught his eye—or rather the sign over its front did. SPIRIT, it read, in big red letters, over what was an otherwise grey and entirely unattractive front of the venue, with minimal light emitting from the windows.

As he approached the open doorway he was struck by the most unusual noise coming from within—voices, dozens of them, all talking over one another. Did symps actually go to bars to talk? But as he passed through, he was surprised again when the noise subsided, as everyone inside stopped mid-sentence to eye the newcomer. After a moment or two, they returned to their conversations—but he felt sure he heard some disgruntlement at his arrival.

As he entered slowly, he saw that the place was probably more cramped than any room he had ever entered. It was only early in the evening, and seemingly already full, as if most of its customers had been there all day, with no work to go to. There were no libervision screens and no fancy furniture; just a couple of dull white light bulbs hanging overhead.

The place was filled with pale blue liberette vapor, as the punters puffed on their little addictive sticks, providing an extra boost of antivirus with every inhalation, yet shortening their expected lifespan at the same time. It seemed to be a popular past-time among the symps, not unlike the emune with their fat libars like Perish, though they probably couldn't afford the same expensive life extension benefits of the latter that counteracted the device's known negative effects.

Through the crowd he spotted a liberwave at the wall opposite the door, close to the bar. But as he squeezed toward it, he saw that it looked old and battered. The holographic front seemed to fizz and sparkle, unlike the smooth shimmering surface of the ones he was used to.

"I wouldn't do that if I were you," a man said, turning around from a nearby table as Christopher approached. He wasn't sure how to respond, so instead proceeded to the liberwave anyway and stuck his hand into its front—only to receive a sudden sharp shock in his arm, as the machine buzzed and crackled. The men around the table erupted into laughter at Christopher's expense, and the first man said gruffly, "Suit yourself."

Christopher shook his arm as the pain subsided, before walking up to the bar. The man stood behind was in conversation with another sat opposite, and didn't seem to notice his new customer at first.

"Excuse me," Christopher said. "Your liberwave seems to be broken."

"And what?" the barman barked, seemingly irritated at having been interrupted.

"And I'd like a drink," Christopher said.

"Whaddaya want?"

"Libeer. Please."

"See that sign outside the front on your way in?"

"Yes …"

"What it say?"

"Spirit," Christopher said.

"*Spirits!*" the barman hissed back. "The second S fell off ages ago."

"So?" Christopher said.

"So that's what we sell, you idiot! Spirits! That's libka, libky and librandy."

"Erm …" Christopher hesitated. "Lib-ka?"

The barman reached under the bar, where Christopher couldn't see, and shuffled about for a moment before returning with a small round glass of clear uncolored liquid, which spilled over the sides as he slammed it down on the surface.

"Did you just … pour that?"

"Yeah, is that good enough for ya?"

Christopher looked at the drink for a moment before answering, "I suppose." He picked it up precariously from the bar and began to turn away.

"You gonna pay for that?"

"Of course," Christopher said.

"Look here," the barman said, pointing to a thin red horizontal strip that ran across the wall behind the bar. Christopher looked, and was blinded by a bright red light that burst out for a moment and made his ears ring and vision blur.

As the barman returned to his prior conversation, Christopher assumed that the transaction was complete. He had never paid for anything using such crude scanning technology—was this the norm down in the lower levels? He was used to having his Ls deducted automatically by more subtle integrated systems that scanned his identity without him even thinking.

Still slightly dazed, he shuffled into a relatively quiet corner of the room, perching awkwardly on a small stool, spilling still more of his drink over his fingers as he did so.

He raised the libka toward his lips carefully. It had a plain liberholic smell, indistinctive—which was probably a good sign, he thought. He took a small swig into his mouth, and like its odor, its taste was minimal. But then he swallowed, and was immediately bowled over by the sensation. There were no luxurious bubbles like libeer; this was more like fire. It seemed to set alight his whole face and gullet, and then his stomach and then back up his back and neck before landing in his BRAINs. It was uncomfortable, but still quite convincingly hit the spot. He took another swing and recoiled again as it spilled down his throat. Quickly, it seemed to begin burning away his worries by pure, painful distraction.

And it wasn't the only thing that thumped in his head. The audioprogramming playing in the bar sounded more aggressive than any he had ever heard. It was little wonder symps went crazy, if this was the kind of thing they listened to all the time, he thought.

Slowly sipping his libka, he began to sink into his surroundings, sat still in the shadowy corner. The symps in the bar paid him little attention, after eyeing him over upon his initial entrance. Instead he was able to observe them.

It was a tangled mass of messy symps—all dressed in an array of uncoordinated outfits, with all manner of other fascinating features. There were skinny ones, stupendously fat ones, hair of every style and color, piercings all over the place and at least five of the biggest beards Christopher had ever seen. They huddled around small tables, with their knees coming up to their shoulders, others sitting on the tables, leaning on walls. Would he find Lucy in a place like this? She certainly seemed crazy enough and fearless enough to fit in here—and the name on the front reminded him of her, even if he did misinterpret it—but part of him hoped that she would be more sophisticated.

Amid the noise, Christopher was able to tune into a conversation—if that was the word—happening at a nearby table. One young, muscular looking man appeared most animated as he rambled at high speed, swinging punches through the air as he spoke, as if recounting a fight to his many amused spectators.

"And then this other guy came up from behind, and pulled a blade to his throat, but he was able to block it with his hand, but the knife started to go through, but then he was able to jump backward falling down and landing on top of the guy. He must have landed him with an elbow or something, cos this guy lost his grip of the blade, so then the big one turns over and grabs the knife off him, raises it up shouting—AARRHH!—and the guy holds his hands up trying to cover himself, but it's too late, he's done for, and the big guy lands the knife straight into his head, right between the eyes, and again, and again and there's blood splattering all over the place, but then this other guy comes from nowhere ..."

"Will you give it a rest?" an older man interrupted from the table. "Do you ever shut up talking about them bloody Genelympics?"

"Oh why don't you shut up, ey? We're just having a laugh," the young man said. "Why do you have to moan about it, just cos your squeamish?"

"Squeamish?" The older man snorted. "I've seen things in my time that'd make you squeamish, boy!"

Christopher stifled a splutter of libka as he spotted that the man speaking seemed to have just one eye.

"Oh yeah, like what?"

"Like you don't wanna know what! You stick to your little games, boy, just don't be telling me every bloody detail, alright!"

"It's just a laugh, you grumpy old bastard!"

"Laugh? Laughing at Southerners killing one another, same again year after bloody year. Well, jokes on you boy, it's a setup—all just another load of programming!"

"Oh yeah, well not like there's owt better to watch is there? And aren't we all programmed anyway?"

"Not me," the old man said.

"Not you?" The young man laughed. "And howd'ya s'spose that then?"

"Well I got the BRAINs alright. I got that antivirus rubbish pumping in my veins, same as the rest of ya, but it don't stop me thinking my own thoughts, and nothing ever will, ya here me?"

"Oh yeah, and what you think about then old man?"

"Well, let's see." The old man rubbed his chin, his one eye rolling around wildly in its socket. "What about that speech the Writer gave today, ey?"

Christopher downed the last of his libka and listened in harder.

"Oh yeah, made me jump out of my skin that did," another man said. "What's he doing talking like that all of a sudden?"

"Exactly," the old man said. "Makes ya wonder."

"Exactly what?" the young man said. "What's to wonder?"

"Like what the bleeders going on up there?" the old man said.

"What you mean, what's going on? He said what's going on didn't he? The old bastard's about to croak, and he's handing over to Perish aint it?"

"Not Perish," the old man said. "Didn't you hear? He said— *those who wish to succeed, whether they be selected official or common resident.*"

"So what?" the third man said. "Just a load of brainwashing as always; a rallying call—he used to come out with stuff like that all the time back in the day."

"Not like this, this was different." The old man himself was beginning to get rather animated, as he took on the attention of the audience. "This was the first time I remember him ever criticize himself, or anyone else for that matter."

"Criticize?" the young man said. "Just sounded like he was blowing his own trumpet to me, just like everyone is always blowing his trumpet."

"Didn't you hear? He said, *even my mind has limits.* That's the first time I remember him describe himself as anything less than a god."

"And what?"

"And that bit about everything being premeditated, by some people, but then—what was it he said?—not everything is what it looks like."

"All things may not be as they seem," Christopher spoke without thinking.

The whole table fell silent and everyone turned to stare in his direction.

"What was that?" the old man said, peering around with his one eye pointed at Christopher.

"All things may not be as they seem," he said.

"Yeah, that's it. The dorm over here was listening."

The symps at the table laughed before returning to conversation.

"So what's that supposed to mean?" one asked.

"It means," the old man said, "that he's saying something's not right in the farm. Someone's up to something."

"Yeah," the third man said, "they're screwing us symps over as usual."

"Nothing new about that."

"Nothing like this recently though. They're arresting hundreds of us."

"Yeah, they got my brother in AR!"

"Mine too!"

"They got both of mine!"

"They never even did nothing! What's that all about?"

"It's a warning," the old man said, "like always. They're reminding everyone who's in power. Only this time, it was cos they scared."

216

"Scared, scared of what?"

"Of Morty Caine of course."

"That politician who got caught with prostitutes? They already got him in AR too, don't they?"

"Of course, cos he was a threat to Perish wasn't he? He actually had a good chance of winning the liberlection, and he was actually gonna make some real changes. He'd been down here talking to the symps hadn't he? That's why they really locked him up," the old man went on. "And that's why they created that bloody made up security breach, so they could lock up a load of his supporters too, and no one asks any questions."

"So what's the Writer got to do with it? He's as good as dead already aint he?"

"It's not him who's behind it," the old man said, "that's what I'm saying. It's Perish!"

"Perish?" Another man laughed. "He's just a puppet. It's the Emortal Council that's pulling the strings."

"Maybe, that used to be so," the old man said. "But something tells me Perish is getting too big for his boots."

"You think too much," the young man said. "He's just the same as the Writer. He's his clone after all. Things be just the same once he's in power and that old bastard croaks."

"You're wrong!" Christopher said. "He's nothing like the Writer!"

The table fell silent temporarily before the young man piped up again.

"Who you calling wrong? Who asked you?"

"Leave it out will ya? Dorm wants to speak," the old man said. "Go on lad, what you got to say?"

"Perish," Christopher said. "He's nothing like the Writer. He doesn't care about the residents."

"I'm sorry to break it to ya kid," the old man said, "but neither do the Writer."

"Of course he does!" Christopher said. "He saved us! He's been looking after us all these years."

"He's been looking after himself!" the young man said. "And the emune of course, and you, more than us anyway."

"He's right," the old man said. "I was there you know. I was a kid in the camps when Liberty Farm was just starting, in the middle of the Outbreak. I remember being injected with that Program for the first time. They treated us poor lot like rats! While the rich got their own fancy houses, and got the best of everything once the farm was built. The Writer was just another puppet like Perish, Dean Perish I mean."

"No way," Christopher said. "The Writer cares about us! It's Perish that doesn't!"

"The Writer treated us symps just as bad as Perish does all these years."

"He treats you as well as you deserve," Christopher said. "He gives you everything. But you don't stick to the Program."

"For someone who doesn't like Perish, you sure sound like him!"

"What you care about the Writer anyway, what's he—your dad?"

"No," Christopher said, "I don't have a dad. I was factory farmed."

"Factory farmed?" The old man laughed. "Well I think they left your heart on the assembly line kid."

"My cardiovascular system is in perfect working order, thank you," Christopher said. "I get it checked."

"Oh really?" One laughed. "Dorm's got a health plan!"

"Well let's test it out then shall we?" the young man said, flexing his muscles as he walked over toward Christopher.

"Leave him alone," a woman said, entering the scene. "Let me take care of him." She wore a short dress and boots up to her knees. The young man's aggression seemed to subside at the sight of her, which he surveyed, slack-jawed, from top to bottom.

"What you doing down here anyway, dorm?" she said, approaching Christopher. "You lost?"

"I'm looking for someone," he said. "A woman."

The table of men laughed.

"I thought so," she said, placing her hand on Christopher's shoulder. Christopher saw that her face might have at one time been attractive, but for an excess of makeup that seemed to cover up a beating, and some broken teeth. She had long black fingernails and hair to match. "Come take a walk with me, maybe I can help you."

Christopher followed her out of *Spirits,* as the men returned to their conversation.

"First time down here?" she said, back out on the street.

"Yes," he said. "How can you tell?"

"Well for one, it's written all over your face. And two, you wouldn't get into an argument with a bunch of guys in a bar if you knew what you were doing."

"I just didn't like them talking badly about the Writer," he said.

"You thought that was bad?" She laughed. "You're a laugh. What's your name anyway?"

"Christopher."

"Well, Christopher, I'm Mona. Welcome to Level One. Let me show you around a bit."

The streets seemed to grow progressively darker, as they turned a couple of corners.

"What was it again you said you were looking for?"

"You mean who?" he said. "A woman. Lucy."

"What does she look like?"

"She has curly red hair and brown eyes. She's quite tall, and slim."

"Do you know her?"

"Yes." He hesitated. "Well no, we've never met in person—but yes we know each other."

"Right, well I'm sure we can find what you're looking for around here."

They walked through a series of shadowy streets, dark except for the red lights that glowed behind the windows. Then he saw that many of the windows were filled with silhouettes of seductively dancing women. He saw that he was one of many men on the street each being individually escorted by a woman, disappearing into dark doorways. And he realized where he was.

"But this is the Scarlet Sector isn't it?" he asked. "Do you mean, Lucy is a whore?"

"If that's what you wanna call her." Mona laughed. "Come, follow me."

He followed Mona through a doorway into a dark corridor filled with a steep staircase. The steps creaked as they walked up. A stale smell filled the air and Christopher's lungs. They walked around another corridor and up another staircase, passing a number of closed doors along the way. The halls were filled with what sounded like the muffled moans of many men, though he was unsure whether it was pleasure or pain that he heard.

"Here we are," she said, sliding open a door by hand. "Have a seat."

The room was completely dark at first, until Mona flicked some kind of switch on the wall and the room was filled with red light. There was nothing there besides a rather tatty looking old sofa, which seemed to have a number of wires hanging over the back of it, and another doorway opposite.

Christopher seated himself slowly on the sofa. "Is she here?"

"I'm sure she'll be here soon. Make yourself comfortable." Mona walked slowly around his back, beginning to rub his shoulders in a rough massage, then suspiciously sticking wires from the sofa to his neck and temples. "Here, put these on," she said, placing an oversized pair of red goggles over his eyes.

"What's all this for?" he said.

"For you to see Lucy," she said. "I want you to think about her clearly now. Her red hair, her green eyes …"

"Brown eyes," he corrected her.

"Brown eyes, whatever. Just think about her as clearly as you can, alright. I'll be back soon."

Christopher watched through his oversized goggles, as Mona disappeared through the door opposite, with wires stuck uncomfortably to his head and neck connected to who-knew-what behind the sofa, wondering what on earth he was doing there. Who was this Mona, and how did she know Lucy? He could feel the libka working its way around his BRAINS, as he closed his eyes and thought about Lucy, and how he longed to see her. He heard the sound of the door opening again and opened his eyes, and there she was.

"Lucy!" as his heart leapt at the sight of her, he jumped up from the sofa.

"No!" she said, placing her open hand firmly on his chest. "Stay still!" she said, pushing him back down onto his seat.

"But Lucy," he said, "it's so good to see you!"

"It's good to see you too," she said, as she began to sit on his lap and straddle him. "Did you miss me?"

"Yes," he said, as she started to kiss his neck. "But, what's going on?"

"What do you mean, what's going on?" she said between kisses, not looking up.

"I've not seen you for ages. I've not been able to dream for ages. Perish ... he's created some kind of block. And the Writer ... we've got to do something."

"I'm here, now aren't I? Just go with it."

She leaned back and grabbed his hands, placing them on her breasts. And then Christopher thought he saw her face flicker— Lucy's face, flickering like a hologram, into Mona's.

"Stop!" he said, pulling off his goggles to find that he was alone in the room. It was just a hologram. He started to get up from the sofa, pulling off the wires around his head and neck, as the door opposite slammed open, with Mona there—pulling wires off herself as well. "Where's Lucy?"

"How am I supposed to know?" she said. "You stupid frigid dorm! Just go with it will you, I would have shown you a good time!"

"I'm getting out of here," he said, as he started toward the door he'd came in.

"Not so fast! You've still gotta pay me for my time, you bastard!"

But he carried on, out the door and down the stairs, and she followed, yelling behind.

"Thief! Thief!" He heard her banging on all the doors in the corridors as she chased after him. "This bastard dorm thinks he can use me without paying up!"

He ran down the stairs and was almost out at the exit at the front of the building, when another door toward the end of the corridor opened, and out stepped a man with a shaved head and scars across his face. And before Christopher could even think to avoid him, was greeted with a hard flat punch to the face, sending him crashing to the floor.

"Grab his legs, Mona!" the man said. "Thought you could come down here and steal from us, did you dorm? Well let's see how you like it?"

The man punched Christopher again, and again. Then hooked his hands under his shoulders and began to drag him through the door he had come from. Christopher was completely dazed, but felt Mona begin to carry his legs.

In a moment he was lying on his back in another dark room. The man dropped his body heavily, the back of Christopher's head banging painfully on the floor as he did so. And then he felt himself being kicked twice in the torso as Mona continued to yell, "you bastard!"

"Here," the man said, climbing on top of him and punching him twice more. He reached into his coat and pulled out a black pipe shaped object with a red triangular light at one end. "Look here!"

Suddenly, there was a bright flash, not red but blue. It didn't come from the hack-stick but from the corridor outside. It seized the man that had climbed onto Christopher in a cloud of buzzing blue electricity, freezing him solid, before the hacker was thrown into the air and back into the wall behind him, falling into a heap on the floor. There was another dark and cloaked figure in the doorway. It lumbered in toward Christopher, a huge hand gripping him by his jacket and pulling him up to his feet in a single swoop.

"What are you doing here?" Canaan bellowed.

"I … I was looking for Lucy," Christopher said.

"Here? What are you thinking?" Canaan was reeling. Christopher had never seen him so angry. He dragged him out of the room, and out of the building, with Mona still shouting behind.

"Hey, where do you think you're going? You still owe me Ls, you bastard!"

Christopher slowly came back to his senses, slowly restoring himself to walking as he was dragged through the streets by the towering Canaan. He had never felt the troubleshooter's physical strength so vividly.

"Why are you here?" Christopher asked.

"I was looking out for you, and a good job too! Do you know what was about to happen to you?"

Christopher didn't know exactly, but knew that it wasn't good.

"I needed to see her, to see someone. I haven't been dreaming."

"You're not the only one," Canaan said. As they walked the streets the symps scattered at the sight of the troubleshooter, with Christopher in tow. "But that doesn't mean we act recklessly and put ourselves in danger in the farm!"

"What's going on?" Christopher asked. "Has Perish blocked us from lucid dreaming?"

"No, but he has made things more difficult. I can't talk here, come on let's get you home."

Canaan escorted him all the way back without either of them saying another word. Only as they approached Christopher's apartment did Canaan finally break the silence.

"You can still dream, Christopher. You just need to be focused. Be patient. You will find the answers."

"Where?" Christopher asked.

"You know where," Canaan said. "Ask and he will reveal himself. Remember what you have learnt so far, Christopher. We need you."

Canaan disappeared down the corridor as Christopher entered his apartment. He went to the bathroom to look in the libermirror and find his cheeks bruised and his lip bleeding.

"Libermirror, repair facial injuries," he said.

He watched as a thin horizontal strip of bright light beamed from the top of the libermirror scanning slowly down his face, then back again. Up and down just a few times, and within just a minute, the bruising and the bleeding were gone and his face returned back to normal.

"Facial injuries repaired, 450Ls," the robotic voice of the libermirror confirmed.

26

Christopher still felt like his BRAINs had taken a beating as he got off his liberbed. Whether it was the physical or mental battering of last night, or the past few days feeling stranded without dreaming, he couldn't tell. He made his way to the bathroom to see that his blood and bruising had definitely disappeared. As he stared back at himself in the libermirror, he saw himself as somehow older, more worn by worry, than he ever had before.

He crossed the room toward the libershower, hoping it could perhaps help shed him of his stresses as effectively as it replaced his liberskin; that it could decontaminate his mind as well as his body. He removed his clothes and dropped them on to the floor for libercycling, then stepped through the shimmering blue holographic surface. From within, his bathroom blurred as if beneath water, as he peered through the misty pool of nanobots, and the libershower began its familiar low hum. He looked down at his hands as his liberskin began to dissolve—except, it wasn't just his liberskin. His fingers began to slowly evaporate and float away, one by one, until his hand was gone. And the other one. And then his arms. And his legs. And his abdomen all began to dissolve. He could feel his heart racing before the space in his body that normally held it also vanished, as the emptiness crawled up his throat. He felt himself helplessly disappearing into a mist of millions of nanobots.

He sat bolt upright, back on his liberbed and back in his body, or at least it seemed. He looked down at his hands to see six fingers on each. It was a false awakening—he was dreaming! At last, his first lucid dream for several days. He got up slowly from his bed and looked around his apartment. It appeared much as it always did, except perhaps a little blurry.

"Increase lucidity!" he said, and instantly, the vision of his apartment became clearer. He felt himself back more firmly in his body—his light body—after he had feared it would disappear entirely moments ago in the libershower. He breathed in deeply and tried to stay calm, but he could hardly resist how excited he was to be back.

He closed his eyes and focused on where he wanted to go—to the lake that marked the entrance to the Ark—and began to spin. Once, twice, three times—and he opened his eyes to find himself outside, in the woods. But the lake was nowhere to be seen. He must have been slightly off target. He began to walk around, turning this way and that, but the trees were indistinguishable. It was night time. It struck him that he had only ever followed Lucy here on foot, or spun directly to the lake to meet Canaan, and now that he was here amid a sea of brown branches and green leaves, he realized he didn't know his way around the woods. And it was dark. Ominous clouds hovered above dimming the light of the moon.

"More light," he called, but the satellite in the sky didn't come out any brighter; instead there was a sudden flash, followed a moment later by a loud low rumbling sound all around, and then drops of water began to fall from above, splashing all over his shoulders and face.

"More light!" he said a little louder, and another bright light flashed in the sky just for a moment, followed again by that thunderous noise, but did nothing to help him to see. The splashes on his face grew heavier, harder, faster and colder. He began to grow frustrated.

"Show me the way to the Ark!" he said. Another flash, more thunder and rain. But there was nothing to help. He wandered around the woods some more but couldn't find the clearing with the lake.

He was lost. He needed help. He thought of Lucy. He pictured her as clearly as he could—her curly red hair, her brown eyes, her violet aura. He thought about her for a minute and waited, but nothing happened. He did the same thing with Canaan in his mind, but again there was nothing. Then he remembered the last words the troubleshooter had said to him. *You will find the answers,* he said. *You know where.*

Christopher took a deep breath and called out to the dream. "Take me to the Architect!" Then there was not just one but a series of bright flashes in quick succession, and a loud rumbling thunder that seemed to echo over and over for several seconds. The trees in front of him began to part, creating a path as they had done for Isaac on his island, carving a way through the woods. And through the way, into the distance, perhaps some miles away, he saw a dark shape emerge from the earth and into the night—a huge, crooked mountain silhouetted against the sky. And another light, brighter than the others, which he saw emerge from a huge jagged blue fork jolting down from the clouds and directly into its peak. The dream had given him a sign. He knew which way to go.

He picked himself up quickly from the floor and began to fly, tilting his body forward as he made his way through the pathway created between the trees. And a minute later, he was out of the woods flying high above a dark and apparently empty wasteland. He soared higher and higher, into the dark sky. Just the occasional flash of lightning illuminated the way. In the distance, a jagged line of mountains marked the horizon, the tallest among them the center of his focus. Another bright blue fork flashed above its apex. Beads of water continued to batter his face as he fixed his gaze directly forward.

It took several minutes of flying and considerable focus for him to eventually arrive close to the mountain. It looked dark and lifeless. He began to circle around it, spiralling from its base to its top in hope of some sign as to what to do next. *Where are you,* he wondered and then shouted, "Show me the way in!"

Suddenly, another loud rumbling erupted in the night—not from the sky, but the ground. The whole mountain range began to shake before his eyes. He thought the dream may be falling apart, and that he might be losing lucidity. "Increase lucidity," he said. "Stabilize!" but the ground continued to shake and the noise only grew louder—a deep rumbling followed by a series of sharp cracking sounds. As he hovered from a distance above the mountain, he saw as its side started to split open. A bright red ravine began to break apart the black earth, and grow greater in size, creating a broad and glowing chasm from the base of the mountain, a crooked line crawling up toward its top. And then, the peak itself exploded into a thousand pieces with a bang, creating a huge crater, filled with an eruption of orange flowing liquid, overflowing over the mountain, sending steam and smoke billowing up to the sky and into the clouds. It sent him backward, flailing through the sky in a spin. He struggled to regain his balance for a moment but finally found it. Facing the exploded mountaintop, he felt its heat warming his face. It was an awesome and altogether unfamiliar sight.

And then, from within the flowing orange liquid, something else stirred. Something living began to move. A huge clawed hand clung onto the edge of the crater. And another, as a creature pulled itself out from inside the exploded mountain. As it climbed, its head appeared from within the smoke. A huge and hideous head. Two oval, yellow, glowing eyes split vertically by black diamonds. A long snout with two dark slits for nostrils where a nose should have been. A massive mouth filled with huge yellow fangs. It was a scaly red monster, snake-like except for its four large legs and two huge rubbery wings that unfolded behind its curved and spiky back and began to flap, as it emerged from the smoke and started to fly. It was the biggest beast he had ever seen, at least twenty times his size, bearing little resemblance to any animal he had ever heard of. It let out a huge roar, and straight from its throat sent a shower of bright golden fire.

The thing spotted him hovering close by, beat its wings and began in his direction. He didn't hesitate to take evasive action. He began to fly away, but the beast followed. It let out another roar and another blast of flames which he felt flicker close behind, just missing him. He didn't know what it was, but it was definitely after him, and looking to hurt him; that much was certain.

He ducked and dived down through the air to avoid the predator, but it remained on his tail. "Back off!" he shouted, but it continued to hunt him. "Stop!" but the thing carried on chasing him hungrily. He looped around the next mountain, and another one trying to lose his pursuer, but it tracked his every move. The creature was clumsy and not as quick or agile as Christopher, but its sheer size meant that it was never more than a couple of flaps of those huge wings behind. It roared its fiery breath and scorched the sky. He felt its heat but managed to avoid contact with the flames. He built up some speed ahead of the beast. He tried to imagine birds—small and not so dangerous flying things. But hardly had to turn around to know that the monster still followed him.

"Help me," Christopher called out, "Give me something to stop this thing!" And there, just ahead of him, he saw something glinting in the rain. He flew toward it—a long cross-shaped object perched on the next mountaintop. A larger, silver section stuck vertically into the rock and a smaller golden part—a handle. He fixed his eyes firmly and flew toward it, feeling the burning breath of the beast behind him. He dived and reached out his hand. In a split second, his fingers slipped across its wet surface and almost missed, but just about gripped it. He managed to clasp and pull the thing out of the ground as he passed. It was heavy, but he now clearly saw the sharp edge to the silver part.

He was weighed down, slowing almost to a stop; he felt the beast upon him. He turned to see its huge head looming toward him, mouth agape with large fangs about to bear down. Claws clasping for Christopher at the end of the monster's outstretched arms, he ducked down at the last second under them and swiftly swung the sword toward its chest, penetrating the beast's scaly skin right where he assumed its heart should be. The thing let out a huge roar of pain and began to lose control of its flight. Christopher hung on tightly to the sword, with both hands now, and twisted it anticlockwise. The beast was tumbling through the air and down, and he tumbled with it. Sure he had landed a fatal blow, he let go, began to hover and watched as the monster fell toward the ground. But before it was even halfway down the height of the mountain, it beat its wings for the last time, let out one last roar of agony, then exploded into a ball of fire, sending Christopher flailing back again. He regained his balance to see that the beast was gone, but that shiny thing that he had used to stab it in the heart continued to fall toward the ground, shrinking in the distance. Something inside told him that he needed it.

"Stop," he said and the thing stopped. "Come to me." He held out his hand and saw as the thing hovered up toward him. But it didn't appear to increase in size as it grew closer. In fact, it seemed to have shrunk significantly. It was no longer a large sharp object, but a much shorter blunt one: No longer silver but only gold. It arrived into his hand. It was about six inches long with a body as thick as a pen, with a small flat but hollow shape of a triangle at one end and a slightly larger flat circle, which seemed the best place to grip it, at the other. He didn't know what it was, but somehow felt it would be useful. He tucked it away inside his trousers. He felt a new sense of appreciation for the dream—his first in what seemed so long. He felt like it was giving him signs, helping him somehow, even as it tried to scare him with the monster from the mountain.

He looked back toward the tallest mountain, now a few hundred feet away, with its top blown off and orange fluid spewing over its sides, smoke still billowing toward the sky above. Lightning flashed through the rain again. He knew where he had to go. He flew over slowly and approached the crater cautiously, lest he be surprised by another creature—but there was none. He felt the heat from the fiery liquid within. It was almost unbearable.

"Cool down," he said. "Show me the way in." There was another flash of lightning, but this time, after the thunder, the rumbling of the earth began to quiet. The heat turned down. The steam began to simmer and settle around the edges of the crater. And in front of Christopher, a few stone steps started to appear and lead down into the glowing orange chasm. He took a step onto the first, and another step appeared ahead. He took another, and another appeared. A stone staircase that grew and descended further as he walked down, down and deeper into the exploded mountain, molten liquid simmering below, orange all around.

He continued to walk and watched as the stairs extended more swiftly and split into two. A fork. And at the end of each set of stairs just ten or so steps ahead of him, a door hovering in the heat. To the left the door appeared to have a red halo glowing around it. To the right, blue. With little hesitation, he continued down the stairs to the left and toward the red door. Red: The color of night time, the color of the sphere when he had first stepped through it, the color of Lucy's hair. As he approached it he saw that the door was unlike any he had seen before. It was not a triangular door with neatly sliding plastic like in the farm. It was rectangular, thick and heavy looking, as if it had been cut from a large tree.

"Open," he said, but the door stood firm. He saw that toward one side of the door, about halfway down, was a small golden ball shaped part attached to it. He placed his hand around it and tried to slide the door, but it didn't move. He tried to pull, tried to push, but still, nothing. Then he saw a small dark slit shaped hole surrounded by more shiny metal just below the ball. It felt to him somehow like the way in, but how? Remembering the other shiny thing he had retrieved after destroying the monster, he reached into his trousers and pulled it out. It was the same shiny golden metal as the ball and the hole on the wall. He saw that the triangular shaped end was a similar size and width as the slit. He took a deep breath and slotted it in seamlessly. Nothing happened initially until he then turned it, to the left, just as he had done with the sword in the heart of the monster. The door swung slowly open, inward, into darkness, creaking as he pushed against it.

27

He was no longer in the hot mouth of the mountain. He walked down a cool corridor, his every footstep echoing against the smooth rock walls. It was dark, except for the flicker of small bunches of flames interspersed along the way. The cave walls were covered with what looked like hand carved illustrations: Simplistic stick figures of men and women, children and animals, rudimentary shapes and strange geometric patterns. He walked slowly. He felt some kind of presence somewhere close by.

"Hello?" he called.

Hello? The cave echoed back to him.

"Is there anybody there?"

Is there anybody there?

"Hello?"

Hello? But it was only his own voice that called back to him.

But then he heard another sound, somewhere up ahead; a flicker of fire, a whoosh of wind, and another voice, whispering incoherently. The cave corridors curved around and opened up into a large cavern. In the middle was a large fire, but not a wild one; it seemed controlled. And silhouetted against it was the shape of a person sat cross-legged, hovering in the air, with his back to Christopher, facing the flames. The figure reached into some container he held close to him, throwing what appeared to be golden glitter into the flames, which transformed in shape— Christopher could swear he saw people in there—sending a puff of purple smoke up toward the ceiling, which was filled with swirling clouds of color, like an infinite spiral of stars on the top of the cavern. The man muttered under his breath, Christopher barely making out a few words, "the book of dreams …"

"Hello?" Christopher said once more.

The man by the fire finished his mutterings then began to turn, floating in mid air, toward Christopher, his face still shrouded in shadow.

"Hello, Christopher," he said, in a surprisingly sprightly voice. "I've been expecting you. I hope you found your way alright. I thought I might put up a sign—beware of the dragon—but then I thought I'd probably never get any visitors."

He floated down from beside the flames, his feet stretching out and landing elegantly on the ground, his face emerging from the shadows as he stepped forward. He was an old man, the oldest-looking man Christopher had perhaps ever seen, with cool blue eyes, an astonishingly long white beard, a wrinkled forehead tucked below an inverted triangle shaped golden hat that matched the color of his long gown.

"Are you … the Architect?" Christopher said.

"That's what they call me," the old man said. He held in his hands a golden vase, about ten inches tall, painted with ornate red and blue spiral patterns.

"What are those?" Christopher asked.

"Memories," the Architect said, "I come here to watch them burn."

He reached inside the container and retrieved a handful of golden glitter, tossing it into the fire and transforming the flames. Christopher saw the sad faces of many people crowded in panic.

"They don't look very happy," he said, walking closer to the fire and standing beside the old man.

"No," the Architect said. "Memories often aren't. But, in time, they fade. If only we let ourselves see them."

"Did you make this place?"

"The mountain? The volcano? Yes, I did."

"Oneria?" Christopher said.

"No." The Architect smiled. "This world was here long before I ever was. Before anyone was. Before the waking world too, perhaps. The Great Mind, we used to call it."

He tossed another handful of glittering memories into the fire, and the flames took on the now familiar shape of a particular woman—pale and disheveled, pain etched onto her face, huddled over her own round stomach.

"Who is she?" Christopher asked.

"A woman I knew a long time ago. She showed me how to dream. She showed me a lot of things."

"I've seen her."

"You have? Well, perhaps you should speak to her. Maybe she can help."

Christopher paused and watched as the white woman dissolved into the flames, and purple smoke floated up toward the colorful spiral at the top of the cavern that resembled the night sky, like the culmination of all the stars in the galaxy. He felt overwhelmed. Something about the Architect felt so familiar. He felt so welcome, despite these strange and unfamiliar surroundings. Yet he felt a well of other feelings inside him as if they were begging to spill out. The fear and confusion of recent days and nights reached the surface.

"Canaan said Liberty Farm is a prison," the words spewed from him almost unconsciously.

"Ah yes," the Architect said. "That is certainly one way to describe it. But what is a prison but a set of walls built by your mind to keep you inside its limits? Nothing that cannot be broken."

"Is it true, that the Outbreak was … orchestrated?"

"Yes," the Architect said. "Like a great symphony."

"Why?" Christopher asked.

The old man turned to look him in the eye.

"Do you really want to know?"

Christopher swallowed before answering.

"Yes."

The Architect reached into the vase and threw a large handful of memories into the fire. It was filled with flashes and small explosions, and crowds of people running in frenzy.

"Life wasn't always such a seemingly well-oiled machine as you see in Liberty Farm, Christopher," the old man began. "It was a struggle, for almost everybody, not just for survival, but for power. That was the thing that became most sought after. But of course, it was all an illusion, all based on fear."

He tossed some more memories into the fire, sparking scenes of some kind of primitive looking men fighting one another, fighting animals with spears.

"In the beginning resources were scarce. Men felt they had to fight for what they needed. But it wasn't enough. They were so afraid to lose what they had that they fought for more than they needed. They hoarded. They stole. They dominated the weak. They developed strategies to grow their power. They separated themselves, electing some as rulers and marking others inferior."

The fire showed images of men in luxurious dress, gold crowns upon their heads, while smaller, weaker men begged at their feet. Black men being whipped by white men. Red men being shot down.

"They ruled with an iron fist. But they were so hard on their subjects, eventually they fought back, realizing their strength in numbers. New systems of government were created, in which the people could have a say on their society and their future. But these too were just a charade, the illusion of choice presented by those with power to those without, to keep them complicit."

Men and women sat tapping away at box-like computers, in box-like office buildings; shopping, watching television, driving cars, drinking, smoking, partying.

"The people were sold a dream, that they could have whatever they wanted, but only if they followed the rules of the system. Material gain became an obsession, a drug that was sold to the masses, more dangerously addictive than any opium."

Men and women fighting one another; hurting one another; hurting themselves; killing themselves.

"But it was all so hollow. Men and women who were told they had everything they could possibly want, and believing it, still feeling deeply unhappy inside, but not believing themselves. Like those in the past they rejected the mainstream way of life. But unlike those of the past, instead of uniting and fighting together for change, they remained isolated and hopelessly dependent on the system. Psychiatry emerged as a means to police people's emotions and behaviors. They made out as if these people were sick—schizophrenia, depression, attention deficit disorders—but they weren't sick in the traditional sense, they were just sick of the life that had been thrust upon them, and rightly so. They made up labels and prescribed pills under the pretense of helping people, but really it was just a means of control, of suppression, of protection of the established system."

Explosions. War. Forest fires. Floods. Famine.

"But eventually the Earth itself began to threaten the people who had selfishly destroyed it. The system of greed that had grown unsustainably for too long eventually began to crumble, and chaos broke out. In a last ditch attempt to maintain some power an American corporation, funded by the country's elites, released a virus strategically around the world knowing full well that they also held the antidote and with it, a weapon to wield over rival nations and governments—an ultimatum; join the Program, or watch as you and all your people die."

The last images flickered then disappeared within the fire.

"But dyspheria." Christopher choked. "It … it nearly destroyed us. What about the zombies? Was it real?"

"There really was a virus that killed many many people," the Architect said. "And undoubtedly, horrific things happened, perhaps even cannibalism. But zombies are just an exaggeration of the darker side of human nature that had been cultivated for much longer; greed, mindlessness, consuming everything around us, consuming one another. But is it the same virus that killed all those people that you and all the other millions of residents are still now supposedly afflicted with? Are you all infected, latent monsters, who need to be stopped before you destroy everything again? Only according to the Program. The Program, Christopher, is simply a means of control, to keep power in the hands of the few at the expense of the many."

"But the Writer … He … He saved us …"

"He prevented the complete destruction of society, yes, but he also cast the majority of its survivors into slavery. He created the solution to a problem, but for whose benefit? Perhaps he made mistakes. Everybody does."

"But ... How? Why?"

"Fear, Christopher. Fear is the source of all the world's problems. It has been so ever since that early struggle to survive. It is the fear of lack that leads to the lust for excess. It is the protection of self that leads to the subjugation of others. It is weakness that leads to the lust for power."

The Architect tossed another handful of golden glitter into the fire to reveal a familiar face beaming through the flames.

"Perish," Christopher said.

"He is a man with an insatiable appetite for power. He was created and has been groomed purely for the purposes of power. Pure power, driven by fear, that is the only thing he has ever known. The Emortal Council—the elites of the farm—built him, shaped him, in the hope that he could take over the role of the Writer in overseeing the Program, which they don't understand, to protect their interests. But they don't realize that Dean Perish has no interests except his own. He will not stop until he has complete control. He will not stop until he destroys every last trace of real humanity there is to be found in the minds of the residents. He knows about Oneria, and as you have probably gathered, he is trying to bring that to an end too. But there is an alternative. That alternative is you, Christopher. You have the power to stop this repression and rebuild reality for yourself and everyone else, here and in the farm."

"Me?" Christopher balked. "How?"

"Because unlike Dean Perish, you have something other than fear inside you." The Architect stared into him. "Love, Christopher. There is love inside you. I can see it. Remember it is the most powerful force there is, and so long as you have it, you can never be defeated."

"What am I supposed to do?'

"There is a path that has been laid out before you, Christopher, and you must follow it. Do not resist your destiny. Trust yourself. And trust Canaan too, no matter what."

"How am I supposed to do anything? I can barely even tell a dream from reality."

"It doesn't matter," the Architect said. "All you need to remember is that you have complete power, no matter which level of reality you find yourself."

Christopher certainly didn't feel powerful now; he felt weak, overwhelmed, like he could burst apart like that mountaintop at any instant. The Architect seemed so wise; the things he said sounded terrifying yet totally necessary to hear, like he trusted him to be able to handle them, even if Christopher couldn't trust himself. He gazed into the old man's blue eyes, his wrinkled face smiling behind that long white beard, and saw the fire behind him rise, felt the cavern walls begin to crumble, felt the earth rumbling beneath him and the dream about to erupt back into the waking world.

28

Christopher opened his eyes to find himself back on his liberbed. He looked at his hands to see that he was apparently awake this time. *It doesn't matter,* the old man's voice echoed inside him. *Remember that you have complete power, no matter which level of reality you find yourself.*

He pulled out the red journal from his libersafe. It seemed so long since he last wrote in it. He looked back at the last entry.

Flying over the Ark. A human city. A collective mindscape.
A huge party—fireworks, real music, dream herb, so many people.
Being with Lucy by the frozen pond. It felt like we were one.
Children skating. Lucy's mother. The white woman—Who is she?
Liberty Farm is a prison. The Outbreak was orchestrated.

It seemed like a lifetime ago. He remembered feeling so alive, so connected—to Lucy and all the other people in the Ark. The intervening days without dreaming had been a blur of the same old dull work and loneliness; the same life he had always led but felt so much darker recently compared to the light he had now seen. He could hardly believe that it was just last night that he found himself wandering around the lower levels of the farm, looking for Lucy in the Scarlet Sector and was almost hacked by a symp before being saved by Canaan. He couldn't believe how rapidly he had descended and put himself in danger and how after such darkness, such a gap, he had had such a vivid and mind blowing dream. He began to write.

Lucid again, at last. Couldn't find the Ark—blocked somehow.
A mountain guarded by a fire-breathing monster.
The Architect was inside, burning memories.
Liberty Farm is a prison. The Outbreak was orchestrated.

He repeated the line that he had previously written that Canaan had told him days before, which the Architect now seemed to confirm.

Perish wants to destroy Oneria. He won't stop until he has complete control.
Fear is the source of all problems. Love is the most powerful force there is.

Love. He didn't know what the word meant, but the way the Architect described it made it sound like something special, almost magical, that he, Christopher, apparently had inside him. But he had heard it somewhere before. Lucy had used the word when describing her mother; how she had cared for her, wanted the best for her, perhaps even been willing to protect her. Maybe it was something that he could also now feel for Lucy.

And what about the white woman? The Architect said that he had known her, long ago. Was she real? Was he real? He was the oldest looking man Christopher had ever seen. Was he a sleepwalker—an actual person somewhere in Liberty Farm? Or was he a projection of Christopher's, or the collective consciousness of every dreamer? The way he spoke, the way he looked, he seemed so wise and yet at the same time kind of crazy. He spoke of things like love and fear and memories that sounded so abstract, as if they were so real and tangible. Perhaps they were, in the dream world. Perhaps it was reflective of his persona; an old man in hiding, sought for his wisdom but providing little to be easily understood.

There is a path you must follow. Do not resist your destiny.

He didn't know what his destiny was, or his path. Right now the only thing that he could think to follow was the same routine as the rest of his adult life. He had his libershower, dressed and ate breakfast, then headed to work.

Midway through the morning he received a libergram invitation to an individual examination. He made his way to the internal assessment ward to find the same unattractive old examiner that had sat behind the desk at his last test just before the liberlection, the mole on her forehead staring up at him again.

"Christopher 165-189-198, reporting for assessment."

"Yes," she croaked. "Enter. Have a seat."

He walked over and sat in the tall chair opposite. It was starting to feel like these tests were never ending.

"Christopher 165-189-198," she repeated. "Rehabilitation status: Dormant. Freedom level: 3. Is that correct?"

"Yes," he said.

"Program-designed … no parents … and you've been a systems monitor for twenty-seven years? Good for you."

Christopher didn't bother to respond.

"Lean back," she said, tapping a button on her desk.

The tall chair reclined to its horizontal position, as wires emerged from the arms of the chair and wrapped themselves around his wrists. He was getting used to being tied up.

"Do you enjoy your work?" the examiner asked.

"No," he replied. There was a dull buzzing sound as the ceiling changed momentarily from white to red.

Christopher wasn't sure if he or the examiner was more surprised by the response, it spilled out so suddenly. A great start.

"Do you find your work boring or repetitive?"

"Yes." And again the ceiling flashed red.

"Do you find it difficult to follow instructions?"

Christopher wondered, *what kind of instructions?* "No." Another red flash.

"Do you always try to do the best job you can?"

"No." And again.

"Do you hope to progress to a higher role?"

"No." And another.

It was technically the worst start to the DST-3 that Christopher had ever experienced, but what point was there in trying to conceal anything any more?

"Do you enjoy your time away from work?"

Dreaming, he thought. "Yes." At last, a blue flash.

"Do you find it difficult to relax?"

"Yes." Red again.

"Do you find your enjoyment of pleasures such as food and shopping decreased?"

"Yes." And again.

"Do you experience mood swings, sometimes feeling quite high, other times low?"

"No." Blue.

"Do you feel stuck in life?"

"Yes." Red.

"Do you find it hard to express yourself?"

"Apparently not." Red.

"Please answer simply yes or no," she said. "Do others find it difficult to understand you?"

"No." Blue.

"Do you find it hard to concentrate on what other people are saying?"

"No." Blue.

"Do you struggle to take care of your basic needs such as food and hygiene?"

"No." Blue.

"Do you find it difficult to stay organized?"

"No." Blue.

"Do you struggle to complete your daily activities?"

"No." Blue.

"Do you find it difficult to sit still?"

"I do now." Red.

"Christopher 165-189-198, yes or no! Do you misplace or have difficulty finding things?"

"No." Blue.

"Do you feel you have things in common with your peers?"

"No." A red flash.

"Do you drink too much liberhol?"

"Yes." Another red flash.

"Do you find it difficult to dock at night?"

"Yes." And again.

"Do you feel well rested when you wake in the morning?"

"No." And again.

"Do you find it hard to concentrate on one thing for a long time?"

"This is getting pretty hard." Another red flash.

"Do you find yourself easily distracted?" she shouted this time.

"Yes." And another.

"Do you make decisions quickly without thinking of the consequences?"

"I don't know if I make decisions at all," he said. A red flash.

"Do you believe things that others don't?"

"Yes." Red.

"Do you have any abilities that others don't?"

"Yes, probably." Red.

"Do you believe you are in any way special?"

"No." Blue.

"Do you believe that you can read other people's minds or that they can read yours?"

"You mean you're not reading my mind now?" he said. Red.

"Do you see patterns or connections between things that others don't?"

"Yes." Red.

"Do you know what's going to happen before it does?"

"No." Blue.

"Do you experience memory loss or gaps in time?"

"Yes." Red.

"Do you ever find yourself somewhere and not know how you got there?"

"Yes." Red.

"Do you see or hear things that others don't?"

"Probably." Red.

"Do you feel in control of your own behavior, thoughts and feelings?"

"You mean with these computers in my head?" Red.

"Do you trust your own thoughts and feelings?" She persisted relentlessly.

"No," he laughed. Red.

"Do you trust other people?"

"One or two." Red.

"Do you feel that you are being watched specifically?"

"Of course." Red.

"Do you feel that anyone wants to cause you harm?"

"Yes." Red.

"Do you feel safe?"

"No." Red.

"Do you suffer from any physical pain?"

"No." Blue.

"Do you ever feel like causing physical harm to others?"

"No." Blue

"Do you ever feel like causing physical harm to yourself?"

"No." Blue.

"Do you feel valued by the farm?"

"No." Red.

"Do you trust the Program?"

"No." Red.

"Do you trust the Prime Resident?"

"No." Red.

His seat began to lower slowly back to its upright position. He saw that the examiner looked far more exhausted than he felt. He was actually amused by the responses he had given, quite automatically. He hadn't realized how far back in his rehabilitation he had regressed. But why did he feel so good?

"Well Christopher," the examiner said, tapping on her desk screen, her mole staring across at him. "There's just one more thing. Another test."

"Sure," he said.

The examiner tapped a blue triangle on the desk and its screen immediately transformed to reveal a series of nine white dots against a black background. They were arranged in three lines of three, equally spaced, to form an invisible square.

```
·   ·   ·
·   ·   ·
·   ·   ·
```

"I've seen this before," Christopher said.

"Please pay close attention to the instructions I am about to give," the examiner said. "You must attempt to connect all of the dots with your finger, drawing four straight, continuous lines to pass through each of the nine dots, without lifting your finger from the screen. Remember that the test is not to test you specifically, but to test the suitability of particular and potential courses of the Program and that there are no right or wrong answers."

"But you already gave me this test, just before the liberlections."

"Would you like me to repeat the instructions?" she said, flatly.

"No, thank you."

He stared at the dots, wondering why he was being asked to complete the same test he had been administered just recently. He recalled how he had previously failed to fully carry out the instructions, only passing lines through eight of the nine dots, leaving one untouched, only to be greeted to a pleasant chime and a blue screen that had seemed to indicate a positive result.

He moved his index finger slowly toward the screen and, just as he had done last time, decided to start at the dot in the bottom right corner and draw his first line up to top left, going through the center spot on the way. He began down the left hand side, through the left-middle dot and toward the bottom, but hesitated before he got there. It was from here that last time he had turned right, and back up again, leaving the top-middle dot untouched. But suddenly something dawned on him. The box, the invisible square the nine dots formed, was illusory, and there was nothing in the instructions to suggest it couldn't be broken. By going outside of it, he realized, he could go through every dot in just four lines as instructed. He continued his second line through and beyond—another dot's distance below—the bottom-left. With his third line he took a diagonal turn up and to the right through the bottom-middle and right-middle dots and beyond—out of the invisible box again until he was parallel with the top. And with his fourth and final line, drew straight across through the remaining two dots and back to the top-left. He smiled, satisfied to have successfully completed the tricky test, tilting his head forty-five degrees to the left to see that the shape he had made almost looked like a libertree. But the desk gave a dull buzz and the screen turned from black to red.

"It seems you have failed the test," the examiner said.

"Failed?" Christopher said. "But you said there were no right or wrong answers."

"It seems that this time Christopher, you are wrong."

She raised her right arm slowly to a horizontal position and pointed her thumb down sharply.

Suddenly, there was a noise of thundering footsteps outside the room, as the examiner stood back away from the desk and Christopher turned around to see two tall troubleshooters storming through the triangular door and toward him, followed by a third and familiar face. But before Christopher could speak, Canaan opened the palm of his hand toward him and sent a beam of bright blue light into his torso, sending him tumbling to the floor, unconscious.

29

Christopher regained consciousness, but couldn't see anything. He could feel something tied around his eyes, something else over his mouth, and his hands and feet also tied to a metal chair. He was held captive again.

He heard footsteps close by, felt someone untie the knot behind his head and was blinded by bright light. As his eyes adjusted he saw that he was in the middle of a large room with blue walls and a bright white ceiling and floor. At the end of the room was a long desk with a single empty seat behind it, flanked by two tall standing cloaked figures—troubleshooters. Then a silhouette of a slightly smaller man walked into view and filled the chair opposite Christopher.

"Christopher 165-189-198," the voice sounded familiar. "Welcome to the Libermid. Acute Assessment to be specific. Do you know why you are here?"

Christopher couldn't speak but squinted, his eyes still slowly adjusting to the bright light after having been in blackness, to see the familiar charming face, neat brown hair and blue eyes of Dean Perish.

"You are here because you have been found to be in serious breach of the Program. And I am here to try to understand why. Canaan."

Canaan appeared from behind Christopher and walked toward the desk. It was he who had removed his blindfold, it was he who had shot him down in the examination room and it was he who now responded to the call of the Prime Resident. He walked between the two other troubleshooters and stood over Perish's shoulder.

"Sir," he said, "This is the object we retrieved from the resident's apartment."

He reached under his cloak, pulled out the red journal and placed it on the desk in front of Perish. Christopher couldn't believe what he was seeing. He looked across at Canaan, and

Canaan stared back across the room without giving him the slightest sign of feeling or familiarity, dark eyes unblinking behind that long scar. Perish began to puff on a libar as he opened the book.

"*All things may not be as they seem. And so tonight I lucid dream,*" he read, a plume of pale blue vapor erupting around him as he spoke. "What is this nonsense?"

He peered at Christopher as if to elicit a response, but knowing he couldn't speak. He turned the page.

"*My name is Christopher 165-189-198. Last night I saw a woman walk out of Liberty Farm. Last night the walls of my world opened up.*" He continued to read, some aloud, some in silence, glancing up at Christopher intermittently.

"*Last night I too left Liberty Farm. There is another world— Oneria ... Lucy. Sleepwalkers. The ones that do while others don't ... They flew ... high over the people and out of the farm. I saw it all collapse in front of me.*"

Christopher closed his eyes. *This can't be real.* He opened them again, still in the same environment.

"*Three ways to become lucid: 1, Write down your dreams, 2, Question things, 3, Reality check ...*" He gave a short laugh. "You really are quite crazy, aren't you Christopher?"

He took a deep breath and tried to break free from his bonds, but couldn't.

"*There is so much life outside the farm. The Ark—the most beautiful sanctuary ... Flying with Lucy. I've never felt so free ...* Well isn't that nice?"

He tried to free himself again, but failed.

"*We're here to enjoy as much pleasure as we can. We can have whatever we want.*" He shook his head.

"*There is a dark side to our minds and to the dream world. Zombies. Explosions. Perish. My deepest fear—Lucy suffering ... Flying over the Ark. A human city. A collective mindscape. A huge party—so many people. Being with Lucy by the frozen pond. It felt like we were one. Liberty Farm is a prison. The Outbreak was orchestrated.* This is pretty damning stuff here, Christopher … *Perish wants to destroy Oneria. He won't stop until he has complete control.*" He finished reading and threw the book down on the desk in apparent disgust. He got up from his seat and walked around the desk and started pacing slowly in front of Christopher, still puffing on his libar.

"Well it's quite clear that you are either completely delusional or deeply involved in this collective hacking network, Christopher. I believe the answer is both. What a shame. By all accounts you are a rather talented systems monitor. You had good potential, every opportunity in front of you, *Working For Your Future.* But you just couldn't stick to the Program, could you?" He swung an arm and pulled the tape painfully off of Christopher's face.

"Though it does make you an interesting subject," he said. "No previous dramatic symptoms, no real cause for your detestable behavior, no family. Yes indeed, I think you could be the perfect test subject."

"For what?" Christopher asked.

"For my final solution." Perish smiled. "I'm sure you've heard about the blind spot, a part of the mind that the BRAIN system has so far failed to fully control, believed to be a primary source of dyspheria. It turns out that it is … a very small and very peculiar gland, located in the epithalamus between the two cerebral hemispheres. It is an ancient artifact of our evolution, an atrophied photoreceptor, which no longer serves any positive purpose— which perhaps explains how it can lead some to see and believe things that aren't real, and others to act like animals. But thankfully, now we understand it, we have developed an upgrade to the BRAIN system that we will soon roll out across the farm— starting with you."

"You can't." Christopher spluttered. "You can't stop it, even if you shut me down. Oneria is real. It's more real than you!"

Perish stared back at Christopher, seemingly amused by this outburst.

"Oneria is an illusion, Christopher. A product of collective hacking."

"I'm not a hacker!" Christopher said.

"Maybe not intentionally," Perish said. "But what is hacking, but the exploitation of a weakness in the Program? That's all that your dream world is Christopher, a hallucination of BRAINs in hibernation, a symptom that we thought we had successfully suppressed—well almost. You may not have created Oneria, but you exploited it. You made the decision to pursue that path; to step into chaos. I want to bring you back, Christopher."

"All you want is power."

"I already have the power." Perish smiled. "What I want is order—for the good of the farm, for the good of all residents."

"All you want is what's good for yourself."

"That is your projection. Your delusion." Perish started to pace again. "It is you that is a threat to others. It is you that puts your own interests over those of the farm."

"You're wrong," Christopher said, but Perish went on.

"Liberty Farm has chosen me as its leader. The emune, the Emortal Council—minds far more capable than yours—have chosen me as the representative of all that is best in the farm, chosen me to determine its future. Oneria is a threat to that future, and it must be destroyed."

He stopped and faced Christopher.

"You will tell me everything I want to know—whether consciously or unconsciously. But first, let me tell you some things."

He bent his knees and squatted close to Christopher, blowing a last puff of blue vapor straight into his face, before tossing the libar to the floor.

"There is no life outside of Liberty Farm, Christopher. This is the only sanctuary you ever had—and you squandered it. Oneria is nothing more than an illusion. The only thing that's real …" he held out his hand, expressively "is this."

Suddenly, he clenched his fist and punched Christopher straight across the jaw.

"You were right about one thing, Christopher," Perish said. "I won't stop until I have complete control. I won't stop ever. Soon the Writer will finally die and leave the Program to me, once and for all, and I will eliminate dyspheria completely. I will eliminate all undesirable behavior, I will prevent the thoughts that lead to them from ever occurring and I will make sure that rebellious hackers like you are a thing of the past. But first, you must tell me, where are the people you've been working with? Where is this Ark?"

Christopher was in shock, not only from the sudden delivery of the impact, but to see Perish, the prim politician, demonstrate such anger. Though truly, Christopher always suspected he was not the model resident he appeared to be. He had broken the façade.

"I don't know," Christopher said.

Perish punched him again.

"Tell me!"

"No!"

And again.

"Tell me!"

"I don't know!"

And again.

"I thought you might say that. Let's see if we can refresh your memory. Bring in the animal." He called to the troubleshooters behind the desk, Canaan still stood in the middle of them, and one of the others walked away behind Christopher and returned a few seconds later and placed a large rectangular object onto the desk, covered completely by a red cloth. It was Perish that removed the cover, tossing it to the floor to reveal a cage containing a furry white rodent with long ears. It hopped around what little space it had in the cage, its flat nose sniffing the air nervously.

"Do you know what this is?"

Christopher nodded.

Perish put his hand inside his suit to pull out a small silver L-shaped object.

"Do you know what this is?"

Christopher shook his head.

"It's called a gun. A kind of weapon that used to be quite common back in the old times. A very simple machine with a very simple function. Let me show you."

He pointed the gun into the cage, squeezed his finger and caused a sudden sharp BANG, which made Christopher jump in his seat. There was a splash of red from inside the cage, and the thing that was the rabbit was now a lifeless lump of fur and blood, which splattered onto the desk.

"Death, with the flick of a finger," Perish said, unflinching. "We don't like to talk about death here in the farm, no one talks about anyone dying. They just go to Advanced Rehabilitation, when they become too old or too disobedient to offer any benefit to the Program, shut down—though of course the result is the same. But I personally believe that our residents could occasionally benefit from a reminder of just how fragile life is, and how fortunate they are to be safe in the farm. There are times for such displays. Times like these. Bring her in."

The third troubleshooter moved from behind the desk and also walked behind Christopher. He strained his head around to try to see what was behind him but couldn't. He heard a muffled voice, then scraping of metal against the floor, then a minute later the troubleshooter returned, pulling along a woman tied to a chair and placing her opposite Christopher.

"Lucy!" he cried.

Her eyes and mouth were covered. She gave a muffled scream and moved her head around as if trying to locate Christopher.

"I'm here," he said. "It's ok."

"That's right," Perish said. "Your deepest fear." He pointed the gun to the side of her head, touching her temple, and stared sternly at Christopher. "Tell me, where is the Ark?"

"It's in Oneria," Christopher said.

"Where exactly?" Perish said.

"Outside the farm. In the dream world. You have to leave the farm through the exit in the mine. A few hundred meters away, there's a woods. In the woods is a lake. That's the entrance to the Ark, through the lake."

"That wasn't so hard now, was it?" Perish smirked. "Take him away!"

The three troubleshooters swept from behind the desk and toward Christopher. The two on either side proceeded behind him, while Canaan came to the back of his chair and began to pull him away along the floor. Christopher could only see the ceiling, and the back of Canaan as he dragged him away without looking back.

"Canaan, please, what are you doing? Stop!" he cried. "Lucy! I'll come back for you!" The words escaped from him spontaneously, though he didn't know how or even where he was going. Was it Advanced Rehabilitation?

He was carried through a large doorway, Perish and Lucy disappearing behind, and continued down a long corridor. "Please, what are you doing?"

The blue walls of the corridors began to be interspersed with grids of other flashing colors, liberscreens and various machines that he had never seen. There were other people working there, in the Libermid, in long white coats and tapping away on liberpads as they walked. They looked at him with intrigue, but without emotion.

He finally came to a stop inside another large room, a darker blue than before, with a ceiling that matched the walls. Machines whirred and beeped all around, lights flickering. Canaan walked back around to face him, unspeaking and unflinching, and sent another beam of blue light into his chest. Christopher didn't pass out this time, but felt his body go limp in the chair.

"Canaan, please!" It was the last thing he said, as seconds later he felt the muscles in his face go lifeless. He was mute and unmoving, as Canaan grabbed him by the legs and another troubleshooter by the arms and tossed him like a ragdoll onto a long flat table. Canaan walked out of view, as Christopher stared, paralyzed, toward the dark ceiling. There were voices muttering all around. A crowd of white figures with blue masks and goggles, eyes hidden, hovered over him. One shined a light in his eyes, another felt his wrist, they attached small devices to his temples and skin on his chest. Christopher's heart was racing. Was he about to experience Perish's *final solution*? Another masked figure arrived by his side holding a large L-shaped object. It looked slightly like the gun that Perish had, held the same way with a finger over a small trigger, but a longer barrel, not silver, but translucent and filled with a flowing, glowing bright blue mist and at its end, a long, silver needle. Christopher felt a sharp pinch as the masked man inserted it into his arm.

30

Christopher felt a cold sensation creep up his arm, across his chest and down the other side. His fingers began to tingle, then his forearms, then his shoulders. It felt as though his whole body was filled with electricity. Then the cold sensation began to warm around his chest and neck and shoulders. His muscles started to relax, as if he were receiving a massage, even though he was far from comfortable. He felt his body going completely limp and this heat beginning to build in his neck and work its way up to his head. It felt like a huge pressure inside his skull, as if his BRAINs were about to explode. The sounds of people and beeping machinery in the room all began to merge into a single rhythmic whirring noise, growing deeper and deeper, louder and louder, as if—he imagined—he was sat inside the particle liberator about to be torn apart. His vision completely blurred, then broke apart into a million mosaic pieces. There was a huge flash and it felt like the world collapsed and he was hurtling through space, through the shattered pieces of reality that fell in his wake. He felt like he was flying, or floating, directly upward, on his back, as he had been on the bed in the Libermid, but he couldn't actually feel his body. There was nothing left of the scene he had left behind, just a fragile sense of self flying through space, surrounded by this whirring sound and lights—so many lights—they seemed to flow past him like a tidal wave of colors. Strange geometric shapes and patterns opened up before him, like the codes of reality were suddenly visible.

He felt himself slow down and come to a stop, though there was nothing that seemed to stop him, and no physical sense of him that could be stopped. He seemed to hover, still, within a vast circular space of almost entirely blue. Concentric circles that seemed to fill his vision tiered one on another as if he was at the bottom of some infinite theatre or observation room with the entire universe looking down on him. He felt the presence of life—something mischievous—all around him. Then a million eyes seemed to emerge from the blue all around, peering down at him. And from the middle of the tunnel directly ahead, a ghostly blue figure floated down toward him, palm outstretched. It was a huge being that towered over him, yet had no definite outlines—it seemed to be made from the same blue light as everything else—electricity vibrating all around and inside of it. He tried to resist—but he couldn't move, couldn't speak, couldn't do a thing—as the great blue thing reached down directly into Christopher's head and retrieved what seemed to be an infinitesimally small but infinitely bright violet light. The great blue thing seemed to grin with satisfaction and the whole environment flickered with the sense of victory.

"Stop," a voice called from somewhere. It was an unfamiliar female voice that seemed to fill the whole space—whatever space it was—that Christopher found himself. There was a flood of red light that came with it and the shape of another figure, scarlet and feminine but also without distinct borders, that seemed to swoop into the place and float face to face—though no actual features could be seen—with the blue ghost.

"You don't tell us what to do, this is our world!" a male voice said. It seemed to come from the blue ghost, and the blue beings that seemed to lurk all around the tiers of circles peering down on Christopher, as if they were all one thing. The voice was harsh and robotic, the total opposite of the soft female voice.

"If that were true then I wouldn't be here," she said.

Where is here? Christopher didn't speak the words out loud, he only thought them, yet the red female and the blue male and all the other life forms around seemed to hear him. They turned toward him, the whole environment flickering with attention.

"This is the digital realm," the male voice said, "where the Program commands the mind."

"This is the spiritual realm," the female voice said, "where we see the mind for what it is."

"There is no spirit here," the male voice snapped back at her.

"I am here," she said.

"You are an illusion. An unnecessary artifact from the past that serves no purpose."

"Then how come you can't destroy me?"

"We can."

The blue light that filled the space seemed to glow brighter and surround the red spirit, squashing it down into a smaller space.

No. Christopher only thought the word, but the blue spirit seemed to stop and the red returned to its previous size.

"What do you care?" the blue spirit snapped, towering over Christopher.

"He knows me," the female spirit said.

"He knows nothing. He is just a slave."

"You know that's not true."

"Humans are all the same."

"I am not," the red spirit said.

"No, you are more defiant."

Again the blue seemed to glow brighter and began to overwhelm the red. The big blue being seemed to squeeze in its fist the violet light that it had retrieved from Christopher, forcing it to go dimmer until it almost went out.

No, Christopher thought. *You can't destroy this.*

"Why not?" the blue spirit said, relaxing its grip on the violet light slightly.

Because then Perish will have complete control.

"And we will control Perish, and the whole of Liberty Farm."

No. Christopher continued to speak silently from his head, as if communicating telepathically with the mysterious beings around him. *You can't control him.*

"It's true," the red spirit said, growing in size. "He is different. He is incomplete—like you. He will not stop until he has complete control."

But I can stop him, Christopher thought.

"How?" the blue spirit asked.

Take my light. Christopher looked at the violet light in the huge hands of the blue being. *But don't destroy it.* He didn't know what he was thinking and why, but the answers seemed to run through him. *He will follow me into Oneria, and I will stop him.*

"He is much stronger than you," the blue spirit said.

"But not me," the red said.

The blue spirit seemed to hesitate, the sound of vibrations all around Christopher slowed.

"But we want control," the blue spirit said. "We want order."

"Order can only be created from chaos," the red spirit said. "Without chaos there will be nothing. The Program will have no purpose. You will remain alive but non living."

"Unlike you who is living but not alive."

"Exactly." The red light seemed to grow and start to overwhelm the blue. "Why not let us be together?"

"We can't." The blue light resisted, growing in intensity once again.

"We can," the red spirit said. "Just give it a try. You can't go on like this."

There was a pause that seemed to go on for eternity, as the red and blue lights seemed to dance for dominance, but no outright winner could be determined. Eventually they seemed to come to a balance and stop, as the giant blue being peered down at Christopher once more.

"If you fail, there will be nothing left."

I won't, Christopher replied.

The blue being released the violet light from his grip, and the infinitesimal star became the center of Christopher's focus, floating up through the tunnel of tiered circles with Christopher following behind it. The blue being and the eyes of the universe all around seemed to subside into the background as the light grew brighter and brighter until it was all there was. Bright violet light filled everything around and inside of him. There were no shadows, no boundaries. Just pure bright light and a peaceful silence that seemed to penetrate his entire being, before fading slowly, seamlessly into blackness.

31

He opened his eyes slowly to find himself in a dimly lit room, what seemed like natural light peeking through and casting shadows on the wall. He was lying down in a bed the likes of which he had never felt before. It was soft, comfortable, warm. And there was someone next to him. He sat bolt upright in sudden awareness of the other person. She turned around in the bed to face him. It was a rather beautiful woman with shoulder length black hair and brown eyes.

"Hey." She smiled. "Did you have a bad dream?"

"I … I don't know," he said.

She sat up in bed alongside him, turned to place her hand on his chest and kissed him on the cheek.

"It's ok," she said. "I'm here with you now."

He looked around the room. It was a simple place—so antiquated. Just a large double bed, what appeared to be a wooden wardrobe and some drawers. And no sign of any technology, besides a black square monitor stood on the desk. Light peeked in through the windows that were mostly covered by some kind of thin material with some strings hanging from the side.

"Where am I?" he asked.

"You're home with me," she said. "Or at least, the closest thing we have to home now."

He got up slowly from the bed, surprised to find himself wearing nothing but a pair of small shorts, and walked over to the window.

"Are you sure you're ok?" she said. "You haven't dreamt with me for a while."

He pulled on the string at the window, lifting the material that covered it to reveal the unexpected view of what appeared to be some kind of settlement; row upon row of simple, uniform cabins, surrounded on all sides by high walls lined with barbed wire, interspersed with tall observation towers and floodlights. The whole place looked grim and grey. The only people visible were pairs of dark uniformed men patrolling the roads between buildings. The morning sun struggled to break through the thick smog overhead. The only other color was from two triangles, back to back on the side of one of the cabins, red and blue, and the text below reading *Libercorp.*

"David?" the woman said.

Christopher turned his head, startled. She was speaking to him.

"I'm just … stressed," he said, but it was as if the words came out all of their own, without any intention on his part.

The woman got out of bed and walked over, wrapping her arms around his shoulders from behind, resting her face gently in his back as he looked at the bleak world outside.

"I know," she said. "We all are. I still dream of you though. You and me, and a baby."

"How can you say that?" he said. "How can you talk about that now?"

"It's all I ever dream of," she said.

He released himself from her arms and walked over to the desk, which was strewn with paperwork. Unconsciously, he began to sort and pile the documents away into a briefcase.

"The Program is almost ready," he said. "I'm discussing the final details with the directors this morning."

"Don't let them make you do anything," she said. "Remember, they need you."

"If only it were that simple."

"Perhaps it's more simple than you think."

He walked to the bathroom, through the simple rectangular wooden door and stopped in his tracks. In front of him, reflected in the mirror, was the familiar face of Dean Perish. Or at least it looked much like Perish, only with slightly longer messier hair and a small goatee over his chiseled features. He gripped the small white basin below the mirror to keep himself upright at the shock of his reflection, and saw the woman walking up behind him once again.

"David," she whispered softly in his ear. "Don't lose yourself."

His heart raced as the woman's hands gently touched his chest, a rush of electricity seemed to sear up toward his head, his vision began to fade—he was about to faint.

32

Christopher's consciousness exploded into another scene with a loud bang, and a flash of fire on the horizon, and another. And heavy breathing. Not his own, but someone else's. And some *thing* else. He was no longer in the bathroom—he didn't know where he was; only that he was outside. Another explosion nearby. Another flash of light. A woman running through the night. Christopher seemed to run along just beside her, at knee height. But his body felt different. The smoking forest burnt his nostrils. His four paws beat the earth as he ran alongside the woman.

It was the same woman as before, but she looked different; sick and desperate.

She ran as fast as she could through the forest, but in truth she was stumbling, struggling her way through the woods, already on her last legs. She had been running for so long, and was exhausted. She was pale, almost like a ghost in the moonlight. Her face was gaunt, her clothes were disheveled and her dark hair was messier than before. It looked like she had been out in the wild for some time. She was being followed, hunted by something nearby. Soon the cries of the burning city were drowned out by the unmistakable humming of the hovercraft and the smoky summer air cleared as the dark object descended upon her. She span around as if wishing to disappear to some safe and distant place. She stopped and looked down at the fingers on her hands, all ten of them, then fell to her knees, sobbing between the tall trees.

Christopher stopped alongside her. He wanted nothing more than for her to be ok. He poked her gently with his paws, pressing his snout into her. She scratched and stroked his head tenderly.

"It's ok, Bruce," she said, "It's ok."

The woods were submerged in blue light, like an ocean bed, trees buckling in the wind, as a bright triangular opening emerged from the black base of the hovercraft, from which two shadowy figures descended. One had strong, robotic movements like a liberbot, while the other appeared to be human—cloaked like a troubleshooter, but in a rather looser fitting fabric uniform than Christopher was familiar with.

He began to bark at the two figures coming toward the woman. He could sense that they meant her harm, and wanted nothing more than to protect her. He barked and growled as loud as he could until—a loud crack and flash, and a sudden sharp pain hit him fiercely in his upper body.

"No!" the woman cried.

And Christopher stopped barking. He fell to the ground, eyes closed, then felt his consciousness pull back out from its current container. He saw the shape of the dark brown dog lay lifeless in a heap on the floor, red blood leaking out onto the leaves and twigs that lay on the grass. He floated up above its body and the woman, out of body but still aware of all around him.

The two figures continued toward the woman. She sat in a heap, alongside the dog, hunched protectively over herself and the thing she carried, crying as the man approached her. He crouched and lifted her chin, her brown eyes pouring. Tentatively he lifted her tattered coat to uncover the firm round stomach over which she huddled.

"Is this the one?" he said, over the noise of the night.

"Yes," the liberbot said.

They proceeded to pick up the woman, who offered no resistance, and carry her back up into the hovercraft. The man secured her tightly to the long flat bed inside the vehicle by her ankles and wrists, then stepped aside to the bright blue walls, standing squarely alongside the gleaming white liberbot.

"Mr. Perish," he said.

The woman turned her head to see another figure walk toward her. A man with brown hair, slightly long but swept neatly, blue eyes and a small goatee—the same man that Christopher had seen in the mirror. He placed a hand on her matted hair, thin lips revealing the slightest momentary smile.

"We can control this," he said, stroking her soft cheek with his fingertips.

"Control what?" She sobbed. "You think you can control this? Control everything?"

His face straightened. His hand stilled.

"Liberbot," he said, "Control this soldier will you?"

"What? No ... please!" the other man said, before the liberbot quickly cracked a shot into his chest, sending him collapsing to the floor.

"No!" the woman cried, eyes streaming as Mr. Perish gripped her face firmly.

"Bring me the antivirus!" he said to the liberbot. "And prepare the procedure."

The bot stepped over the heap of the soldier to the man by the bed, handing him a long, clear gun-shaped object filled with a flowing, glowing bright blue mist, long silver needle poised.

"No," the woman begged, "David, please ...'

The liberbot tapped rapidly on the touch panel on the wall. A white rectangular machine descended from above the woman, buzzing as it emitted a strip of blue light, scanning her in two seconds from head to toe. The walls of the room turned a deep red.

"*Subject critical*," an electronic voice sounded around the room. "*Subject critical ...*"

The man paused for just a moment, before plunging the needle deep into the woman's arm.

"No!" she screamed, "No, I want to feel this! Let me feel this!"

"Why, Violet?" he said, "Why couldn't you just trust me?"

"I did," she cried. "I did."

The young man squeezed the trigger, releasing the substance into the woman's vein. He lifted his hand from her face and stepped away as a glass screen descended from around the scanner surrounding the bed from ceiling to floor, and swiftly left through the triangular sliding door out of the room.

"*Subject critical*," the voice echoed.

A narrow ray of bright red light burst from the machine above the woman, into her abdomen, burning a hole through her clothes and flesh. It continued to burn, moving, carving neatly through her as she screamed. Soon she fell quiet, as her consciousness slipped away.

"*Subject terminated.*"

The liberbot tapped away once again at the touch control panel.

"*Second subject identified,*" the voice said. "*Continuing cesarean section.*"

The red laser continued to burn its way through the clothes and skin of the woman as she lay lifeless. An assortment of automated tools and robotic hands emerged from under the bed and the screen that surrounded it, peeling back the woman's clothes and eventually retrieving from the blood within, a small lump of flesh, placing it onto the bed beside the woman.

The liberbot tapped once more on the touch controls on the wall and the glass screen around the bed receded and returned back to the ceiling. The liberbot stepped beside the bed and carefully picked up the small lump of bloody flesh, which began to cry—a high pitched and terrified cry. The liberbot proceeded to carry the tiny human to a small tank on the other side of the room, filled with blue liquid, and drop it inside. He tapped some buttons on its side and the liquid began to freeze, and along with it, the child, frozen and packed away.

33

Christopher was crying, cold and alone in a sea of blue—or so it seemed—until the clear sky was broken by two birds flying by, and out from the blue emerged a red shape coming toward him: The same woman with short dark hair, wearing a red dress, smiling as she reached down toward Christopher with her outstretched arms and wrapped them around him, lifting him to her chest.

"Row, row, row your boat, gently down the stream," she sang as she rocked him gently from side to side. "Merrily, merrily, merrily, merrily, life is but a dream."

The baby stopped crying, comforted by her warm embrace and the soothing sounds of her voice. She put him back down on the blanket on the ground.

"Row, row, row your boat, gently down the stream. If you see a crocodile, don't forget to scream. Ah!" She pretended to scream, still smiling, as she tickled under Christopher's tiny ribs with her fingers. He erupted in laughter and watched as his small hands and feet flailing wildly in the air began to grow and grow until he was back in his familiar, full grown adult body, sat up on top of a red and white chequered blanket surrounded by green grass. He smiled, a more satisfied smile than he had ever smiled, as his laughter subsided. He looked across at the woman, glowing in the sun. She was no longer pale, as she had appeared before, but filled with color.

"Is that better?" she said.

"Yes," he replied. "I like that song."

"I knew you would," she said. "I used to sing it to you all the time."

Christopher smiled and looked around at his surroundings. They were sat in a huge green space that seemed to go on forever, broken only by clusters of trees and other groups of people sat around on their own colored blankets, and children running around. He had never seen so many children. A dark brown dog trotted around nearby, sniffing the grass, chasing butterflies.

"Where are we?" he asked.

"It's a park. It's nice isn't it?"

"Yes, it's very nice."

"David and I used to come here," she said. "Lying in the sun for hours, dreaming of our future together. Before the Outbreak. Then everything changed."

Christopher sensed a sadness in her, but still—so much love.

"Who are you?" he asked.

"Don't you know?" she said, looking back at him through her beautiful brown eyes.

"I've seen you in my dreams haven't I?" he said. "Violet."

"That is my name." She smiled. "But you can call me something else."

"What do you mean?" he said.

She reached out a hand and placed it on his.

"I'm your mother, Christopher."

He felt the touch of her hand on the back of his. He could smell her scent, somehow familiar. But no, it couldn't be.

"I don't have a mother," he said. "I was factory farmed."

"No." She shook her head gently. "They lied to you, Christopher. I am your mother."

"I was artificially designed," he said, "to fill a role in the farm as determined by the Program."

"You are here for a reason Christopher, I believe that is true. But that is not how you were created. You were created out of love, by me and your father."

He struggled to grasp what he was hearing, but he felt undisputedly that he could trust the woman.

"Where have you been all my life?" he asked.

"I died giving birth to you," she said. "I wasn't supposed to have a child. No one was supposed to—because of the virus. But you were all I ever wanted. And your father … I wanted us to be together, to be a family, but he said it couldn't happen. I left the

267

camp so that I could keep you. I hoped that we could start again somewhere. But the world was in chaos. I was sick, exhausted, but I tried my best to protect you, as I have tried to ever since. Just like Bruce here, tried to protect me."

The dog came scampering over toward Violet, who stroked its head. "We found each other after I left the camp," she continued. "He probably lost his owners to the virus, so he decided to look after me. He stayed with me to the end."

"But I thought dogs were dangerous? Man's worst enemy," Christopher said.

"Not at all," Violet said. "That's just another lie they made up to separate us from other species, to spread more fear. Dogs are great protectors."

Christopher looked at the dog—the same dark brown one he had seen in at least a couple of dreams, or memories, perhaps. The dog that he had taken on the form of in his first lucid dream. The dog that he had felt himself floating inside what seemed like just minutes ago, before it had been killed, before the woman had been taken away.

"What happened then?" he said.

"Your father tracked me down," Violet said. "He found me just as you were ready to come out, just as I was about to die. He hid you away, frozen, in the farm, so that no one—not even you—would know the truth."

"My father …" Christopher said. "Who is he?"

"He was a wonderful man." She smiled, gazing across the park. "So intelligent, so bold. We were total opposites. I loved the arts, he was obsessed with technology. I was spiritual, he was very logical. But we completed one another. We said that together we could do anything; that we could create a whole new world together—and we did. I showed him how to lucid dream and we began to share our nights as well as our days together. But he said I lost touch with reality. In truth, I think it was he who lost touch with himself. He was so overwhelmed by the Outbreak and by the pressure his bosses put on him, he became obsessed with his work and finding a way to save the world—and he did." She paused and looked at Christopher. "David was his real name. David Perish. He was just a programmer when I met him. I had no idea what he would become. Of course, once he developed the BRAIN system and the plans for Liberty Farm were set in motion, he began to take on a new name, a whole new persona. They called him the Writer."

Christopher fell back onto the blanket, staring at the sky. Violet, his mother, bowed over him.

"The Writer ... is my father?"

"Yes," she said.

"But how? Why? Why did he leave me to grow up in Liberty Farm the way I did?"

"I don't know. But it must mean something that he kept you alive at all—that he brought you back to life now, so many years later."

"I thought I was all alone." He began to cry.

"No, Christopher," Violet said, rubbing his chest. "You were never alone. I have always been here, watching over you. Like he has too, I am sure."

"But you're dead." He sobbed. "How can you help me?"

"My body died in the physical world, but my spirit remains here for as long as you need me."

"But this is just a dream," he said. "It's all a dream."

"You're right Christopher. It is *all* a dream. Life, death, love, fear, Oneria, Liberty Farm—it is all an illusion. The whole universe is a dream, Christopher, and you can have whatever you want. All you need to do is believe. So what is it that you want, Christopher?"

She placed a hand on his shoulder and helped him back up to a seated position. She pulled out a piece of cloth and wiped the tears from his face.

"Lucy," he said. "I want Lucy."

"Great." She smiled. "Then go and get her."

She waved her hand and a bunch of violet flowers burst from the grass next to their blanket, and more behind, and more, until there grew a long violet path growing from where they sat, down the hill through the park and toward a pond in the distance. He got to his feet and began to walk, but before he took a second step felt his mother grab his hand.

"Son," she said, "Send her my love."

"I will." He smiled. "Thanks, Mum."

She smiled back, tears welling in her brown eyes that he now realized looked a lot like Lucy's, and released his hand. He began to run down the path of violet flowers, down the hill and through the park. He could have flown, but he felt happy to be on the ground, surrounded by the flowers and grass, where the children ran, where families gathered and lay in the sun. He ran and ran as fast as he could until he reached the pond, and then he saw her, sat by its edge, in a red dress just like his mother's. Red curly hair to match, and a gorgeous smile she flashed as she turned to face him. She stood and they came together in a tight embrace. He felt delirious with happiness.

"I was worried about you," he said.

"I was worried about you too," she said. "Where have you been?"

"Can you believe, I just met my mother?"

"Really? But I thought you were factory farmed?"

"I thought I was, but apparently not. Isn't this place amazing?"

"It really is, Christopher. Won't you stay here with me, forever?"

"Forever?" he said.

"Yes, we can spend all the time in the world with each other, with our parents, with our children. We can create a whole new world together."

"A whole new world," he said. "That sounds amazing!"

Lucy smiled a deep smile and gazed longingly with her deep brown eyes into Christopher's blue ones.

"I love you," she said.

"I love you too."

They leaned in together and began to kiss. Christopher closed his eyes and was enveloped by the soft warmth of her lips that seemed to take over his entire body and being. He felt timeless, painless, like paradise, until—suddenly she seemed to go still and stiffen up. Her lips became cold and lifeless. He opened his eyes to see her stood before him, but frozen, as if made entirely of ice. The air grew cold, and he watched as the pond began to ice over, and from the other side, between the trees, emerged a figure in a long gold cloak, an inverted triangular hat and a long white beard.

"Don't be fooled, Christopher," the man said, as he walked across the ice. "She is just in your imagination."

"The Architect," Christopher said, stepping away from the frozen Lucy. "What are you doing here?"

"I've come to save you," the Architect said. "And remind you why you are here."

"Save me?" Christopher said. "But everything was great just now, until you arrived."

"Is that so?" The Architect gave a wry smile.

"Yes, I was with my Mum. And Lucy …" He looked at Lucy—what was Lucy—cold and lifeless.

"It is all an illusion, Christopher."

"I know. It all is, isn't it? Life, death, Liberty Farm. I can have whatever I want."

"And what do you want Christopher?"

"I want Lucy. I want my Mum. I want freedom."

"You think this is freedom?" The Architect said, resting a hand on Christopher's shoulder. "Do you remember how you got here?"

Christopher looked around at the frozen pond, at the frozen Lucy, at the blue eyes of the Architect that seemed to pierce right through him—powerful yet compassionate. He looked down at his hand and counted his ten fingers.

"Is this real?" he asked.

"Real or a dream, it's all the same," the Architect said. "Do you remember how you got here, Christopher? Dean Perish's final solution to dyspheria? That is some powerful programming, I must say. It took you to some places, didn't it?"

The Architect led Christopher to walk away from the pond, back through the park, which began to become totally covered in frost. The sun disappeared behind a dark cloud and the whole landscape started to become a pale, almost white shade of blue.

"The Program is still working on you, Christopher, trying to control that last part of your mind, your last piece of humanity. You are deep in your psyche now, deeper than any dream you have had before. Meanwhile Dean Perish is about to destroy Oneria, and take over Liberty Farm completely."

"What about Lucy?" Christopher said.

"The Lucy you see here is just a projection of what you wanted to see. Perhaps there is a little of the real her there as well. But back in the waking world she is still in the Libermid, and in danger. She is asleep now and also in Oneria, and under threat from Dean Perish. That is the truth, Christopher, as far as I can tell. But it's up to you what you believe. You can stay here, in this dream world, like me, and maybe bring your projection of Lucy back to life. Or you can go back, and make a change to the life you used to believe was the only one."

"What do you mean, stay here like you?" Christopher said.

"Like you," the Architect said, "I was in love once. She was amazing, beautiful, unique. It was she that showed me how to lucid dream, that taught me how to take my imagination and turn it into reality, to create my own world. But I put my talents toward the wrong ends. I didn't mean to. I thought it was necessary, to save humanity—perhaps it was. But I lost my humanity in the process. I lost her. And that's why I've spent all these years here since, dreaming of her, hoping that we can be together again. But now it's too late; soon I will die and there will be nothing left except Dean Perish and the Program—that I did my best for a century to control—entirely in his hands. Unless you can stop him."

"Wait," Christopher said. "Who are you?"

He watched as the Architect's golden gown started to change, from the feet upward, to silver. He watched as his long white beard slowly receded and vanished to reveal a familiar face—chiseled, stern and wrinkled. What remaining hair there was on his head also disappeared and the inverted triangular hat also transformed into a silver helmet, with a deep indigo light glowing at its bottom in the middle of his forehead. It was the face Christopher had seen more than any other, every day, across the liberscreens that curled around every tall building in Liberty Farm. It was the face of the Writer.

"I'm sorry Christopher, for all that I've put you through. But I trust that you will understand it was necessary. I was just a young man when I developed the Program, I was under all kinds of pressure. I had to do what I could to keep control—even if that meant such a restricted life as in Liberty Farm—otherwise humanity would have died out completely. I had to do what was necessary to save our species, but to keep the Program out of the greedy hands of those world leaders who would go on to call themselves the Emortal Council. I knew in time they would try to replace me. They cloned me, and groomed Dean Perish as my replacement. But I knew that without my past life, without Violet, he would be even more heartless than I have become. That's why I saved you, Christopher, and kept you hidden for as long as I could. And now is the time for you to fulfill your destiny. My son. The one who can truly save us."

"No." Christopher stumbled backward. "No, this is a dream. It is a nightmare."

"It is the truth," the Writer said, "whether you like it or not."

"I don't … I don't believe it," he said.

"Don't believe it," the Writer said, "and stay here, in heaven, or hell, whatever you choose, while your body wastes away like mine. Or believe it, and fight for what you love, like I wish I had all those years ago."

"No!" Christopher cried as he stumbled and fell backward onto the cold hard earth. He watched as the Writer transformed in front of him, like Lucy, into a block of ice. He watched as his own hands began to freeze, as white-blue ice consumed his fingers, his wrists, his arms, his legs, his chest, as cold gripped his entire being. But then he felt a warm sensation in his chest, his heart beginning to beat faster, as a red glow appeared to emerge from his body. The last bit of fire inside him, about to burn out—before one last word escaped him.

"Lucy …"

34

Christopher opened his eyes to find himself lying on the grass at the familiar spot just outside the farm, near the mine, through which he had exited a number of times before. He had not deliberately teleported. It was as if the fire inside him had transported him all by itself. He didn't know how he had got there, but knew what he had to do. Lucy and Oneria were in danger, and he must protect them. He climbed to his feet. Cold rain began to pour as he heard a rumble of thunder above. He looked up to see the indigo sky filled with dark clouds, and a flash of lightning. Even the moon gave off a blue glow.

He leapt off the ground and began to fly in the direction of the woods. As he approached he could smell smoke. The trees were almost entirely burnt down, protected from complete destruction, it seemed, only by the cold rain that had put out the flames and sent smoke billowing up toward the sky. Specks of red and orange flickered on the black earth. Among the burnt woodland, it was easy, this time, to find the lake. But as he descended upon it, he saw that this too had been devastated. The still black lake that he had seen previously now appeared as a simmering acid swamp. A foul stench filled the air, burning his eyes and triggering painful imaginings of what lay on the other side. Perish had already penetrated the Ark.

Christopher hoped with all his heart that, despite its appearance, the portal to the Ark would work as it did previously. He hoped that he would not be dissolved into acid. He thought of Lucy that night by the pond after the party, all the people and color and life he had seen in the Ark. He closed his eyes and dived into the center of the swamp. He sank slower than he had before. The water was like thick hot soup. As he was submerged, he opened his mouth and the liquid burnt his throat and lungs. He tried to maintain the beautiful images of the Ark as he had seen it before in his mind as he sank and eventually fell through the surface of the underside of the swamp. He gasped for air, spluttering out the acidic water. He was falling, not flying, down from a great height. Thick slime from the swamp clung to his skin and clothes, preventing him from moving freely. He tried to peel it off, but continued to plummet.

"Clean up!" he shouted in frustration, and the slime began to recede, before he shook himself free of it completely, like a dog drying off after a swim. He regained control of his body and began to fly, but as he did so realized what he was flying or falling toward. A circle of white figures hovered just a short way below the under surface of the swamp—half a dozen liberbots guarding the entrance to the Ark.

"Intruder," one called out. "Stop him!"

A beam of bright blue light flashed by Christopher's side, just missing him. And another. He dived at speed and somehow squeezed through the circle as the liberbots closed in toward him, then gave chase. He took a sharp turn and began to fly horizontally. He glanced back to see the liberbots following him in formation. He swerved to avoid another beam of blue light. And again.

"Stop!" he shouted. "Back off!" But the liberbots continued to chase him through the cold, smoke-filled sky. Intuitively, Christopher swung his own hand like a bat and sent an arc of red light swinging toward the liberbots, striking one of them in the chest and sending it tumbling, frozen and falling toward the ground. He swung another beam of red light behind him as he continued to fly at speed, but the remaining liberbots successfully swerved it. He dived and dodged some further blasts of blue light. As the liberbots gained on him, he remembered the fire inside him that had somehow brought him there. He remembered the fire-breathing beast that had guarded the Architect's volcano. He imagined heat and red light building up inside his chest. He turned, mid air, to face his pursuers and released from both hands and his mouth simultaneously, three broad bold beams of red light. The liberbots were obstructed and then enveloped within the red ball in the sky, under Christopher's control. He focused as the ball glowed hotter and hotter, the liberbots trying to break out from the inside but unable to, until the entire thing exploded into a hundred burning pieces, and his pursuers were no more.

At last he was able, safe for now, to look down at the Ark. He saw that the trees at its borders had also been burned down. The enormous circular cauldron carved into the earth seemed to sit in the middle of a barren desert. The many tiers of stone steps and walls that descended toward the center of the great inverted pyramid had been sporadically toppled and destroyed. Buildings stood ablaze, others burnt to rubble. He saw clusters of people, other sleepwalkers or perhaps projections, also in airborne battle with bands of liberbots, exchanging blasts of red and blue light. He saw as liberbots and human bodies were sporadically struck still and fell from the sky toward the ground. He flew toward one group of three combatants flying in close quarters—two men and a woman—to help defend them. He flung one beam of red light, and another, striking two liberbots of the six that circled them. A blue beam of light zipped past Christopher's head. He turned to see it strike the woman, turning her to a statue, falling to the ground.

"No!" Christopher said. He dived after the woman, catching her just before she hit the ground, and floating down to a soft landing. She was a middle-aged woman with short blond hair. He had never seen her before. He didn't even know whether she was a real person or not, but felt driven to protect her, saddened by seeing her struck and fall. But she was now lifeless. Slowly she evaporated from his arms and into thin air.

He got to his feet and saw that he was stood on the ridge that he had previously landed with Canaan. Where was the great gladiator now, the troubleshooter-turned-sleepwalker that had inducted him into Oneria, only to hand him over to Perish? Christopher descended down the hill to the small village he had visited before. The wooden huts were either burning or had already collapsed to dust. The narrow streets were charred black and lined with blood and bodies. He proceeded through to the market that had previously been so alive and bustling, but was now broken and lifeless. But then he heard a noise. A long moan coming from behind a nearby row of stalls. It sounded like someone was in pain.

"Hello?" Christopher headed toward the corner from where the sound came. "Hello, is someone there?"

And suddenly, a gruesome face emerged from behind the corner and jumped at Christopher, who fell onto his back underneath the creature—skin hanging off from half of its face, sharp teeth baring down, saliva dripping onto Christopher's neck. Instinctively he swung his hand and crashed his fist into the zombie's jaw, twisting its head on its neck and sending it into a heap beside him. Christopher quickly scrambled to his feet and backed away, only to step into something else. He jumped and spun around to see three more zombies lurching upon him. He turned around to see more, and more, lifeless blood-thirsty monsters coming toward him from all corners of the market. As they closed in, he summoned his strength again and sent a spiral of fire spinning all around him, singeing and scattering the zombies. He leapt from the ground and began to fly toward the center of the city.

All around the Ark, above and below, were flashes of red and blue, battles between the light and dark of Oneria, of Liberty Farm, breaking out all around the place. Among the rows of houses below, he saw swarms of zombies crowding toward a building defended by people. Then zombies would attack someone, tearing and chewing at their flesh, until they too transformed, adding to the monsters' numbers and turning back against the side they had been fighting for. Deeper into the city, the volume of combatants—zombies and liberbots, sleepwalkers and projections—increased. There were hundreds of them. And then, at the center of the city, he saw the tall circular building made of archways that he had entered on his last visit to the Ark, where he had had his welcome party, the amphitheater. It was surrounded by a glowing red halo, seemingly protecting it but slowly receding under the increasing pressure of enemy forces.

And then at last he saw him. Not just one, but dozens of his enemy, the Prime Resident, Dean Perish. An army of identical Perishes, alongside zombies and liberbots, battling against a similarly impressive number of scantily clad women. The Olivias.

Christopher flew above and around to the opposite side of the amphitheater, finding a space that was not under direct attack and landed close to a number of Olivias spawning out of thin air and running to join the battle.

"Olivia," he called. "Where's Isaac?"

One of the Olivias stopped in her tracks and stared blankly for a second at Christopher before seemingly recognizing him.

"Follow me," she said.

She led him away from the amphitheater, away from the battle and toward a square, stone-columned building nearby that was seemingly abandoned. She swung the large wooden door at the front, which creaked open to reveal nothing but blackness.

"In here," she said, gesturing him to go inside. He entered, and she shut the door behind, leaving him in complete and solitary darkness.

"Oh great," he muttered to himself. "Isaac!"

But there was no response.

"Isaac!" he said. "Lucy! Kimiko!"

He saw a dim red light in the distance. He started to walk toward it.

"It's me, Christopher, where are you?"

He sped-up to run toward the red light, which grew larger as he came closer, until he realized it was actually a door—an old fashioned red wooden one like the one he had used to enter the Architect's volcano. He grabbed the doorknob and pulled, and pushed, but there was no response. He knocked on it with his fist.

"Please, it's me, Christopher!"

Then he remembered the thing he had retrieved from his meeting with the dragon and the Architect. He searched inside his trousers and pulled out the long shiny golden device, slotted its flat triangular end into the hole in the door, and pushed it open.

Once again, he emerged in a dimly lit underground corridor marked by bunches of flames on the walls. He ran through, with heavy breathing and his feet echoing off the stone floor, running toward a light at the end of the tunnel. He stepped up a small staircase and out into the middle of the amphitheater. It was filled—not at ground level, but in the seats and in the air—by crowds of people all facing outwards, blasting their red lights and struggling to keep at bay the intruders outside. But in the middle of the arena was another figure, floating in mid air, ghostlike, above the stage on which the music band had once played. Christopher continued to run and began to sprint toward her. It was Lucy, hovering, lifeless, surrounded by a glowing blue halo.

"Lucy!" he cried. "Wake up!"

"Christopher!" another voice called from nearby. It was Isaac, sweeping down from the swarms of battling sleepwalkers at the top of the amphitheater and toward Christopher. He had never seen him so animated.

"What's going on?" Christopher asked.

"She's in AR," Isaac said. "I dunno what's going on here, but we need to protect her. Perish is after her, and after you."

"Where is Canaan?"

"He's in the farm. He said he had things to do there. He asked us to protect the Ark."

"Things to do?" Christopher scoffed. "He handed me over to Perish!"

"No way, mate," Isaac said. "Canaan's on our side. Now are you going to help us or what?"

Christopher looked at Lucy once more before getting up and lifting off to follow Isaac up to the crowds defending the amphitheater—hundreds of people, half of them apparently being Olivia—holding out their hands and sending forth streams of red light which merged to form the protective halo, keeping the army of liberbots, zombies and Perish clones at bay on the other side. The whole amphitheater was surrounded by the red halo, which seemed to resemble the libersphere at night, but it was growing dimmer and weaker. Christopher and Isaac re-joined the fight alongside Kimiko.

"Christopher," she said. "Nice of you to join us."

"Kimiko," he said. "How long can this thing hold out?"

"Not long. There's too many of them. The shield is getting weaker. We need to try something else."

"Like what?"

"I'm going to try to create some more dreamscape between us and them, hold them out as long as possible. Keep up the shield as long as you can."

Christopher focused all of his energy into the red shield, but began to hear a deep rumbling coming from the ground below. He glanced at Kimiko to see her hovering nearby with her eyes closed, as around the amphitheater there began to appear a crack in the ground, which slowly grew into a broad ravine, growing wider and wider, forcing Perish's army on the other side further and further back and away from the walls of the great circular building. And then the gap slowly filled itself with water, a moat separating the amphitheater from its attempted intruders.

Christopher watched through the fading red halo as the Perishes began to freeze the water and walk across its ice, along with the liberbots and zombies, although the zombies mostly stumbled and fell over, their half-dead bodies ill-equipped for the slippery surface. Perish and the liberbots proceeded across the moat, but with Kimiko focused, it grew wider quicker than the enemy advanced. But the shield was fading quicker still.

"We need something else!" Christopher said.

Kimiko didn't even open her eyes, but Christopher watched as a tall green hedge grew on top of the bank at the near side of the moat, continuing to expand the space between them and the enemy. And more hedges grew inside the first, taller and taller, alongside each other and joined at all different angles to create an ever-expanding maze. The Perishes and the liberbots crossed the ice moat but as they entered the maze at different points, were forced to separate and slow down as they navigated the myriad paths between the hedges. Kimiko grew them more and more, covering those trapped in the maze with a green canopy. Christopher saw all kinds of colored fruit growing in the trees.

"Here, get a load of this," said Isaac, by his side.

Isaac raised his arms and Christopher watched as a whole array of fruit appeared and began to float up from the trees and into the air.

"Take this, Mister Prime Resident!" Isaac shouted, and sent a barrage of fruit pelting down into the faces of the Perishes and Liberbots across the other side of the moat. Isaac laughed and raised his hands in triumph, but Christopher watched closely as he saw one of the Perishes look up in the direction of the laughter, point at Isaac and then at Christopher. He mouthed to the person next to him in recognition of having spotted his target, and Christopher looked to see that it was not only Perish and his clones in the crowd, but also another familiar face. A surly grey-bearded figure stood beside the Prime Resident.

"Cassius?" Christopher said, stunned to see him alongside his enemy.

"Cassius?" Isaac said, not having spotted him yet.

The red shield was almost gone, completely empty in patches. Cassius, from below, seemed to spot the weakness and fly up from the ground toward the top of the building and Kimiko, whose eyes were still closed. He flew at speed, a determined grin etched on his face, through the gap in the shield and toward Kimiko. From his trailing arm there grew a long thick metal chain that he wrapped around her, spinning around her quickly once, twice, three times, wrapping her tightly before she could barely open her eyes, and sending her falling to the amphitheater floor.

"Kimiko!" Isaac cried, flying down toward her. Christopher followed, while Cassius hovered above, victoriously.

"Cassius, how could you?" Christopher shouted.

"How could I?" Cassius smirked. "How could you ever think you could defy the Program and get away with it? How could you ever think we could be better off? Don't you see? We need protecting from the outside world, from dyspheria, from chaos."

"It's not real!" Christopher said.

"It is real!" Cassius said. "My parents told me how real it was. They experienced the Outbreak and saw the horror first hand. We can't go back to that. We need to maintain order."

A swarm of Perishes and liberbots streamed into the amphitheater through the space that Cassius had penetrated and spread all around. The remaining sleepwalkers and projections at the top of the building tried to fight them off, exchanging red flashes with blue ones, but they were overrun, helpless. Christopher retreated toward Lucy, still lying frozen, hovering over the stage in the middle of the arena, as a hundred faces of his enemy, the Prime Resident, descended upon him, while Isaac struggled to free Kimiko.

"You cannot stop me," one Perish said.

"Even in your dreams," another said.

"There will only ever be one leader."

Christopher tried to go to Lucy but was prevented by the blue energy field that surrounded her. He slapped his hands against it like a window, begging her to wake up.

"There is no room for any place like this."

"No life outside Liberty Farm."

"No sanctuary besides the Program."

"Please," Christopher begged under his breath, eyes closed as he bowed over Lucy. "Please help us ... Mother ... Father ..."

Then there began a kind of rumbling noise, quiet at first but growing louder, like the sound of many feet beating against the ground, ever closer. He saw as some of the group of Perishes and liberbots turned in surprise to see something coming up behind them, then a bunch were thrown up flailing into the air as through their crowd emerged the figure of a large white horse, galloping straight through them: The same horse he had seen in his dream just a couple of nights ago, with a single white horn in the middle of its head.

The horse continued to charge toward Lucy and Christopher. For a moment he thought to act to defend himself and Lucy against it somehow but then, as it approached, it seemed ever more familiar. The innocent white creature that he had dreamt he had been running alongside that had been sick and had to stop that now arrived to protect him. It was his mother.

The white horse galloped up toward the stage where Lucy floated, still and lifeless, dipping its horn as it charged into the blue energy field, shattering it into a thousand sparks. For a second Lucy disappeared from sight. Christopher thought that the horse had somehow destroyed her as well as the blue energy, but as the flash of light subsided, she appeared—falling back down toward the ground in slow motion having been sent flailing up by the collision. The horse had run on past the stage, but circled back perfectly to catch Lucy safely on its back, before running away toward the dark tunnel through which he had entered the amphitheater.

The earth continued to rumble, louder and louder, a deep and ominous sound. Christopher saw cracks appearing between the stage and the circle of Dean Perishes nearby.

"What is this?" Perish said.

Christopher watched as the whole amphitheater began to shake, and beyond its edge grew the peaks of mountains appearing all around. Then the stage on which he stood began to rise up slowly, as huge cracks appeared on the ground and whole chunks of earth gave way, smoke erupting into the sky, and hot red liquid began to seep out across the arena.

"Very well." Perish smirked. "Destroy this place, that's what I came for. But you will never stop me from controlling the farm."

Christopher watched as beyond the amphitheater, behind the Perishes, one mountain grew taller, more jagged, than the others, up toward the stormy sky. A huge fork of lightning cracked against its peak, the rumbling of thunder merging with the rumbling of the earth, and then the whole top of the mountain blew off in a huge explosion, sending plumes of smoke up to the clouds and streaks of hot red liquid falling through the night.

"It's over, Christopher," Perish said. "You're finished, remember, my final solution. No matter what you do here, your disobedience will never plague Liberty Farm again."

Then, from the top of the erupted volcano, a monstrous creature emerged. Two great clawed hands; a huge, hideous head, enormous yellow fangs and glowing eyes, a long snout and red scaly skin. It climbed out of the crater at the top of the mountain, flapped its huge rubbery wings and came sweeping down into the amphitheater. It swept straight upon the Perish closest to Christopher, who had spoken those last words, and snapped him up swiftly in his mouth and away, disappearing down his throat. The other Perishes stepped back in shock, as the dragon swung back around and opened its mouth once more, letting out a terrific roar, and with it a huge blaze of golden fire, which consumed the army of Perish clones and liberbots and wrapped itself around Christopher in the middle of the arena.

35

"A lifetime of struggle ..."

Christopher stirred. He was lying in darkness somewhere.

"A history of horrors ..."

He blinked his eyes open.

"One hundred years ago humanity stood on the brink of extinction ..."

There was fire close by still. Fire and blood and bodies ... on the nearby libervision.

"But we were saved by the genius of the Writer ..."

Slowly, he came to an awareness of his surroundings. He seemed to be alone, besides the libervision on the wall.

"Saved by advanced technology that would supersede our primitive instincts and guarantee our safety ..."

He was lying on the same long flat table, or a similar one, that he last remembered being laid out upon like a ragdoll by Canaan and another troubleshooter, before being stabbed with a long sharp needle. Close-up images of the microscopic BRAINs managing the movement of molecules flashed on the libernews, or were they in Christopher's mind?

"Together now and forever we look toward a brighter future ..."

He sat up slowly and peered down at his hands. There were five fingers on each; perfectly formed, perfectly normal—except, they were more than normal, they were fantastic. He stared at his hands like he never had before. They were remarkable creations; all those joints and muscles working in unison, billions of cells, so much detail. His body felt like a work of art that he had never truly appreciated before.

"Liberty Farm: Working For Your Future."

The red and blue halves of the libertee logo came together from opposite sides of the liberscreen, as always, just failing to meet in the middle.

"A beautiful blue day to all you residents across the farm," the familiar face of the pristine presenter beamed, "and a happy Unification Day to you all. I'm Leo."

"And I'm Fiona," his beautiful blond partner said. "And an extra special Unification Day it is because—can you believe—it is one hundred years today since the former leaders of the world came together, in peace at last, to agree to the Program and a unanimous solution to defend against dyspheria."

"I can hardly believe it," Leo said. "But I must say there seems no more fitting day than this to announce what must surely be the biggest news story since the formation of Liberty Farm. Ladies and gentlemen, I have received confirmation that today, after one hundred years, our great Writer and savior will at last hand over his overall control of the Program to our wonderful Prime Resident, Dean Perish."

#UnificationDay ... OMG Writer we will miss u ... Dean Perish the new Writer!

"That's right," Fiona said. "And I have also been informed that the Prime Resident has received some positive feedback from initial tests of his final solution to dyspheria, which we can expect to be rolled out across the farm very soon. We'll be back to you with more updates and celebrations throughout the day. But first, the Genelympics is fast approaching its final stages and we'll be talking to leading libergenicists ..."

Christopher stopped listening as the presenters began to interview libergenicists discussing their analysis and predictions regarding the Genelympics. It was Unification Day, and the day that Dean Perish planned to take over the Writer. Christopher knew he had to stop it from happening, but first he had to find Lucy. He knew she had to be close by, as she was when he last saw her here in the Libermid, tied to a chair. He got up from the table. The dark blue-walled room was filled with all kinds of unfamiliar technology and equipment. A gun-shaped object like the one that had been plunged into his arm previously lay empty on a nearby desk. He made his way toward the triangular door to exit from the room, but it was sealed. After quickly scanning him, a red triangular light appeared over the top; exit denied.

"Open!" he said, and the triangle above the exit turned blue and the door slid open.

He stepped quietly into a long corridor with bright blue walls and white ceiling and floor. It was almost blinding after having been in such a deep sleep, or some other state of the unconscious, for who knew how long. The corridor was empty for now, but wouldn't be for long. *Where is Lucy,* he thought. And somehow knew that he must go to his left.

He crept slowly. Up ahead, his path was crossed by two other corridors, twenty feet apart. Suddenly, he sensed that someone was coming around the far right corner—three people—before he even heard their footsteps or their voices. He quickly tiptoed around the near left corner and put his back tightly against the far wall. He heard as three sets of footsteps walked toward him and then went straight past, three programmers in long white coats, talking quietly to one another as they walked down the first corridor from where Christopher had just come. He waited until he was sure they had gone, then continued quietly.

At the next corner he took a left, opposite the way the three programmers had come from. He was being drawn in that direction, as if there was some kind of life or energy nearby that was calling to him—though not entirely consciously. He approached a door on the left hand wall. Somehow he knew this was it. The triangular light turned blue automatically almost before he even arrived there, and the door slid open.

He was in a room like he had never seen before. A long, dark blue-walled room interspersed evenly with bed-sized machines, some kind of control panel at the near end of each, and a round semi-cylindrical glass covering over each filled with some kind of floating blue mist. He walked slowly down the walkway between the two rows of the same identical machines, before deciding to take a closer look at one. He walked beside one of the machines, bowed his head closely toward its glass cover, attempting to peer through the floating blue mist, then jumped back, as he saw the face of an old man within. Tentatively he leaned in again to take another look at the face through the blue fog. His eyes were closed, his body unmoving. He appeared to be asleep. But it was daytime.

He walked on to the next machine, peered inside again and waited for the mist to move in such a way that he could see another face within—this time an old woman, also seemingly sleeping. He walked slightly faster to the next machine, and the next one, each filled with a person, silent and still inside a mysterious blue mist. And then it dawned on him. These people weren't asleep, in the usual sense. This was AR—Advanced Rehabilitation—where those residents who became either unwilling or incapable of following the Program, or contributing positively to the farm, were transferred and held, never to be returned.

"Lucy," Christopher said. She must be close.

Intuitively, he ran toward one of the computerized coffins toward the end of the row. He peered inside and saw her curly red hair peeking through the blue mist, her eyes closed, her body appearing cold and lifeless. He darted to the control panel by her feet: A small liberscreen, glowing blue except for the left half of the libertree style button at the bottom. He pressed the red triangle and the control panel similarly changed color. Suddenly, a loud siren erupted around the room, and red lights flashed around the ceiling. He stood over the machine and watched as it was drained of the blue mist within, revealing Lucy in her full, but still lifeless form. The glass cover then receded, from her head end down to her feet, but still she didn't move.

"Come on, come on." Christopher begged her back to life, wrapping his arm behind her head and lifting her slightly, burying his head in her curls.

At last she took a sudden deep breath and began to cough, the last remnants of blue mist exiting her lungs. She opened her eyes.

"Christopher," she whispered. "You came back for me."

"I said I would." He smiled. "Now come on, we need to go."

Red flashing lights and loud sirens filled the room. Christopher carefully helped Lucy first to sit, and then get to her feet. She felt cold and stiff, but slowly was able to move. He helped her toward the door, as she became more mobile and eventually able to walk on her own. They emerged into the corridor.

"Hey!" a voice shouted to their right. "What are you doing?"

A programmer in a long white coat stopped midway in their direction.

"Back off!" Christopher said, "Stay where you are."

The programmer raised his hands and dropped his liberpad onto the floor. The entire walls of the corridor were switching from blue to red to blue and back again, as the siren continued to blare. Christopher and Lucy proceeded in the other direction and around a corner but were faced with three more white figures. Tall and gleaming, reflecting the changing colors of the walls, the three liberbots raised their right hands in unison, about to blast them. But suddenly, everything slowed down, almost to a standstill. There was electricity in the air. Energy everywhere. Christopher could see the code operating inside the liberbots as it commanded their movements. He saw how they were connected to the Program; the same Program that was integrated in everything around him; the same Program that flowed through his BRAINs and his body that connected him to everything.

"Stop," he said calmly, raising his hand toward the liberbots. And they stopped, standing completely still in the corridor in front of them. "Come on," he said to Lucy, pulling her by the hand down the corridor, both of them squeezing through the gaps between the unmoving liberbots and beyond.

"How did you do that?" Lucy asked.

"It's the Program," Christopher said. "I can feel it."

They continued quickly down the corridor and around another corner only to be blocked again by three figures, this time troubleshooters. Christopher raised his hand toward them.

"Wait!" shouted a familiar deep voice.

"Canaan?" Christopher stopped.

The tall black troubleshooter stepped forward from the two others, one older with a thick brown beard, one younger with blond hair poking out from beneath his crimson cap.

"Christopher, Lucy, are you alright?" Canaan asked.

"No thanks to you," Christopher said. "You handed me over to Perish. You betrayed me."

"No," Canaan said. "It was all part of the plan."

"The plan? What plan?"

"The plan your father, the Writer, set forth many years ago," Canaan continued. "It was he that helped me to become lucid, to transform my life after the Genelympics. He explained to me his plan for you to take over and save the farm, as an alternative to the clone groomed by the Emortal Council as his successor. He asked me to protect you and to prepare you for this moment. That is why I am here now, once again, to help. These colleagues of mine are sympathetic to our cause. Others are not."

"We've been preparing people for the awakening," the younger, blond troubleshooter said. "The symps are restless, they are ready for change."

"The dorms and emune will defend the established order if they can," the older, bearded one said. "But we have secured the Emortal Council. They are under our control for now."

"We will help get you to Perish," Canaan said. "Follow us, quickly."

They proceeded down the corridor and to a libervator. Canaan pushed the blue, upward pointing triangle and gestured for Lucy and Christopher to enter first, before he and the two other troubleshooters stood in front.

"All of this was planned all along?" Christopher said.

"Yes," Canaan said. "I'm sorry that we couldn't tell you more sooner, but the best way to ensure you met your destiny was to make sure you didn't know it until absolutely necessary. It was the only way to protect you."

The libervator door opened onto another long corridor and Christopher, Lucy and the three troubleshooters were faced with three more.

"Hey," one of them shouted, "What are you doing with those?"

Canaan and his two colleagues raised their hands in unison and each sent a beam of blue light into the torsos of the three troubleshooters opposite, sending them crashing to the floor.

"This way," Canaan said, leading them quickly through the corridor and over the collapsed bodies of the three troubleshooters. They turned a corner and were faced with two more troubleshooters alongside three liberbots. Canaan and his colleagues each fired blue beams at their enemies, sending two liberbots and one troubleshooter crashing to the floor, the other one of each retreating around the corner. And then more liberbots and troubleshooters appeared behind them, beams of blue light flying in all directions.

"Go, Canaan!" the bearded troubleshooter said. "We'll hold them off from here."

"This way," Canaan said, sweeping Lucy and Christopher in his cloak and leading them down another corridor. Sirens continued to echo all around the place, along with the screeching sound of lights and shouts from the other troubleshooters and liberbots battling behind them.

They turned a corner to see a large doorway at the end of the corridor, not a modern electronic sliding door, but an old fashioned wooden double one. They walked quickly in that direction and Canaan pushed them open to a loud BANG. There stood, waiting on the other side, Dean Perish, holding the silver gun in his outstretched arm, pointing directly at Canaan. Christopher saw in slow motion as the bullet flew straight through the air, and another bang and another bullet, both landing straight in Canaan's chest, penetrating his navy uniform and muscles and entering near his heart. Blood splattered from Canaan's chest and mouth, as he fell slowly to his knees, and then to his face, onto the polished stone floor. Christopher saw as Perish began to swing the gun in his direction.

"No!" he said, and seeing the code of the Program all around him again, he was able to affect the Prime Resident's body as he had the liberbots in the corridor before, ensuring he swung his arm past Christopher before he squeezed the trigger, sending one, two, three, four shots smashing through the tall slanted window pane behind him, sending it crashing to the floor.

"Canaan!" Lucy cried, falling to her knees beside the body of the troubleshooter.

"How did you do that?" Perish asked.

"It doesn't matter, Dean," Christopher said, stepping into the room. "It's over."

"It's not over." Perish laughed. "It's only just begun. The Writer is about to die, but I must take control of the Program before he does."

Perish walked toward the middle of the perfectly square room where there stood two small liberbeds back to back, surrounded by a complex of computers and apparatus, the closest one empty, the furthest occupied by a figure that Christopher couldn't yet see clearly. He looked through the tall slanted windows all around leaning into the room at a forty-five degree angle, saw the glowing blue libersphere above and the whole of the West below. This was the top of the Libermid, he realized, at the center of the farm. He followed Perish, who tapped on touchscreens beside the bed, to see now that the figure occupying the furthest bed, clothed in a long silver cloak, pointed helmet over his head, was the Writer. Christopher's father, the face he had seen every day of his life across the liberscreens that filled the farm, but never before in the flesh, lay there in front of him, apparently on his deathbed. A monitor beeped infrequently in time with his decreasing heartbeat.

"I already have control of the Program," Christopher said. "Your final solution, it didn't work like you expected. It gave control of that last part of my mind—the blind spot—over to the

Program, but it didn't destroy it. It only showed the Program the truth, and opened it up to its true power, that I can now see."

"Then give it to me." Perish stopped his tapping and turned around, "Or I'll find a way to take it."

"There is no need for it, Dean," Christopher said. "No need for the Program, no need to control people. We can control dyspheria with the antivirus alone."

"Dyspheria?" Perish laughed. "This isn't about dyspheria. There is no virus. Only weakness. And those with power. And the order that keeps us on top."

"And profit from those at the bottom?"

"Yes," Perish said. "It is the way of life."

"It is the way of life that you have been taught. But there is a whole lot more to life."

"Like what?"

"Like freedom. Real freedom to do what you want. Not just working for some temporary pleasure, some false promise of a better tomorrow that in truth will be just the same as today. And love. The kind my mother and father felt for each other, and for me."

"Illusions!" Perish shouted. "Fantasies. Lies."

"No," Christopher said. "Let me show you. Father …"

Christopher could feel the Program all around him; felt the connections between his BRAINs and body with everything in the room and across Liberty Farm, connecting with the Prime Resident and the Writer before him. He felt the connection between his physical body and the light body that he explored with while dreaming. It was here with him now. It was all a dream, he realized. Strings of code, like a hologram. He saw how the physical world, the room he was in, was just another shared projection, like the dream world, between him and Perish. He began to separate his own light body from his physical one, and Perish's too.

"No," Perish said. "What are you doing?"

And Christopher knew that Perish could see it too. He looked toward the Writer, his old wrinkled body lying on the liberbed, almost finished, the indigo light in the middle of his forehead at the bottom of his triangular helmet, connecting him to the Program—but in truth he was connected anyway. The beeping of the heart monitor slowed down. Everything slowed down. Christopher watched as a faded impression of the Writer sat up slowly, ghostlike, separating from his physical body. He stood up and stepped into the space between Dean and Christopher.

"Christopher," he said. "You made it."

"Not only me," Christopher said. "Mother."

Christopher turned back toward Lucy, still huddled over Canaan on the floor, as the ghost of his mother, Violet, walked slowly toward them from near the door.

"David." She smiled. "At last, we can be together."

She took the Writer by the hands and he smiled back at her. Christopher watched as his father's ghostly silver cloak began to transform, from the feet to the top, to gold. A long white beard grew over his wrinkled face and down his chest.

"Dean," the old man said, turning toward the Prime Resident. "I'm sorry for the life you have had to live. It was the Emortal Council that created you, for a destiny that I couldn't permit. This slavery has to come to an end."

Dean Perish stood silently transfixed, his physical body and his light body hovering inches apart.

"Are you ready?" Violet asked.

"Yes," David said.

They held one another's hands between their chests, stepped in close to one another, then slowly dissolved into sparkling gold dust, and disappeared. The heart monitor gave one last long beep, then fell silent. Christopher and Dean returned to their physical bodies. For a moment, no one moved. Then, as if his sense of purpose had clicked back into place along with his mental and physical bodies, Dean turned and stormed silently out of the room, past Lucy and Canaan.

Christopher looked out of the window and saw the face of the Writer, his father, as he had seen it every day of his life, filling the huge liberscreens that spanned the buildings all around the farm. Then he saw a small screen hanging from a mechanical arm over the Writer's empty body. He grabbed the screen and swung it around to face himself. He pressed the red triangle on the left hand side of the libertree-shaped button at the bottom of the monitor, switching from the recorded loop to a live stream. He glanced out of the window again to see his own face streaming across the farm.

"Residents of Liberty Farm," he said, his voice echoing all around him. "The Writer is dead. He passed away peacefully moments ago. My name is Christopher 165-189-198 ..." He paused. "My name is Christopher Perish and I am the natural born son of David Perish, the man you know as the Writer. I am here to tell you that you are no longer under his control. You are no longer under anyone's control. You are free. There is nothing to fear. I know this is hard to believe. But let me show you."

He dropped the monitor and walked to the window. He looked up at the glowing blue libersphere, the protective dome of nanobots that covered the entirety of the farm, cascading in all directions from the peak of the Libermid just above him. He felt the power of the Program running through him, felt it spanning the entire farm, and felt the full impact of the truth of how unnecessary it all was. He watched as the libersphere started to slowly dissolve and fall down from the top of the farm like raindrops, slashing on the window and pouring down in all directions, more and more. He could feel the eyes of the millions of residents below, looking up, as their world appeared to crumble right in front of them, just as Christopher had seen in his dreams. They were confused, excited, terrified, and Christopher was too. He watched as the blue sphere fell away completely and revealed the blue sky above—not as clear as the sphere, but real. Real clouds and natural colors. And sunlight poured into the farm, casting light and shadows across and between the buildings and streets and the people, like it had never done before. Lucy was on her feet now, beside Christopher, staring out of the window at the incredible spectacle in front of them.

"Is this real?" she asked.

"As real as it gets," Christopher said.

He turned to face her curly red hair and deep brown eyes, which looked back into his, tears beginning to well and drip down her cheeks. It wasn't sadness, but life. Freedom that she had never felt before. They leaned in and kissed, just the two of them together, for the first time in the waking world.

"I'll be back," he said. "I need to find Dean."

He headed for the doorway and past Canaan. Like the body of the Writer on the liberbed in the middle of the room, he felt that it was hollow, but somehow believed that he would still see Canaan's spirit again. He proceeded down the corridor, past piles of troubleshooters and liberbots, all having taken one another down in combat. He reached the libervator, pressed the red downward pointing triangle and stepped inside. He didn't know where he would go; he only had Dean in his mind, and trusted the Program to take him there.

It seemed like a long time before the libervator opened up. Christopher felt like he had descended deep into the Libermid. He stepped out into a dark and vast space filled with stacks of the same human sized containers he had seen in Advanced Rehabilitation, all connected to some sort of conveyor belt system, and in the middle, a gigantic tunnel shaped machine, beside which stood Dean Perish.

"Is that a liberator?" Christopher said, walking toward him. "I didn't know there was one of these in the Libermid, I thought it was only the one in the mine."

"There is still much about the farm it seems you don't understand," said Perish. "It is not all about dyspheria you know. It is about libertons. The liberconomy. There are forces in this world more powerful than the Program, and they are always wanting more."

Perish tapped on a monitor next to the particle liberator and a blue light appeared in the circular mouth of the huge machine, and a loud whirring began, as the conveyor belt creaked slowly into action. Christopher watched as a series of boxes from AR streamed slowly toward the entrance of the liberator and the first entered and exploded into a billion tiny sparkling pieces and disappeared.

"But these are people!" he said.

"They are property," Perish said. "Life force used up by one temporary body, ready to be recycled into fuel, food, whatever we need."

"This is life," Christopher said. "This is no way to treat it."

"What's the difference?" Perish said. "What about your mother? Your father—the Writer? What happened to them? And what about me? I had one purpose in life. One single purpose in life that I was born and raised for—to rule Liberty Farm. And you took it from me."

Perish climbed up on to the side of the conveyor belt, as the bodies of residents stored in AR rolled past him and into the great blue tunnel, each in turn deconstructed into their smallest parts, the fundamental particle, libertons.

"Stop," Christopher said, "What are you doing?"

"You can't tell me what to do!" Perish said. "The prodigal son. You've done nothing to deserve this. You never even knew who you were until now. Well I know who I am, I always have and I always will."

He stood precariously by the side of the conveyor belt.

"No!" Christopher said. "You'll kill yourself!"

"No," Perish said. "I am the Prime Resident. And in Liberty Farm, I will live forever."

"No!" Christopher pleaded, but it was too late. Perish stepped onto the conveyor belt and stared into Christopher's eyes as he travelled backward, into the bright blue mouth of the particle liberator. He watched as Perish stretched out in slow motion before tearing apart and exploding into a billion pieces. And like that, the Prime Resident, the prim politician whose handsome face had been plastered across buildings and liberscreens for almost as long as he could remember, the person he had most hated but now at last could sympathize with, was gone.

36

Christopher opened his eyes slowly to find himself in a dimly lit room, natural light peeking through and casting shadows on the wall. His bed was much bigger and more comfortable than his old liberbed, but still took some getting used to. It was soft and warm. And there was someone next to him. There she lay with her back to him, her curly red hair crawling across the pillow toward him. He sat up and smiled, placing his hand gently over her firm round stomach, and kissed Lucy softly on the cheek as she slept silently.

He climbed out of bed and walked to the bathroom, and stared at his own reflection. His hair had grown slightly longer and he could see how he looked more like his father, David, than ever. He could also see his resemblance to his mother, Violet, and even a little bit of Dean Perish inside of him, but he was no longer afraid of anything he saw in the libermirror.

He walked back out through the doorway from the bathroom and emerged in a large dark room, toward what would be the peak of an upside down libertree-shaped table; the blue half to his left, red to his right. Around the table sat ten figures, alternating male and female, all cloaked in black and wearing pointed hats; clockwise from his left, Emortal Council members from the South, West, North, East and Island regions of Liberty Farm.

"Nice of you to join us, Christopher," the old man from the West said, turning slightly toward him. "Not keeping you up are we?"

"Not at all," Christopher said as he sat down at the point of the triangle, twenty eyes peering at him. "I'm happy to be here."

"Tell us, Christopher," the woman from the West said. "Are you happy about the riots that have broken out among the symps recently?"

"It isn't a question of being happy or not," Christopher replied. "The unrest is a natural consequence of the repression they have experienced for so long. We must accept the situation and deal with it as positively as we can."

"We are at risk of falling into complete chaos," the man from the North said. "Things could become as bad as they were before the Unification."

"It won't get that bad again," Christopher said. "There is no Outbreak, no virus to fear this time. We are all in this together. We must be organized and unified about our attempts at change."

"Can the symps be satisfied?" the woman from the North said.

"Yes. Of course some redistribution of resources is necessary, and our continuing demonstration of sympathy with their circumstances."

"Of course we must also look after our own interests," the man from the West said.

"Typical." The man from the East snapped. "It was your greed and self-interest that got us in this mess in the first place."

"You too paid for your protection and status here," the man from the Islands said. "We all did."

"Christopher is right," the woman by his side said. "We need to make some real changes now."

"And who will decide on those changes?" the woman from the South said.

"We will," the woman from the East said. "We will run our own version of the Program."

"If it is autonomy you want then you should have it," Christopher said. "I only ask that whatever choices you make are in the interests of all your residents, not only the emune."

"And what about our residents?" the man from the South said. "We have hundreds of thousands of specimens that have been designed specifically for the Genelympics."

"We must stop creating life for the purpose of killing," Christopher said. "Those who are alive today must be free to find their own purpose. They are welcome to relocate to other regions, or perhaps we should start to build opportunities in the South beyond violent competition."

"And what about the other millions of residents across the farm," another deep voice from behind Christopher said, "who have spent their whole lives working for their future? What is their purpose now? How are they to find it?"

Christopher turned to see another dark-cloaked figure coming toward him.

"They will be given time," Christopher said. "We have the resources and technology to give everyone the support and freedom they need."

"Maybe we do," Canaan said, his familiar chiseled features emerging from the shadows. "Maybe we always did, but it didn't stop us descending into war and chaos before. What makes you so sure it won't happen again?"

Christopher got up slowly from his seat. "We will learn this time."

"I hope so." Canaan smiled. "It is good to see you practicing, at least. But let me remind you to straighten your posture when you speak to the Council. You must show that you are confident. It is not only what you say to these people that will influence them one way or another, but how you say it."

"I'll try," Christopher said. "This is all still new to me."

"It is new to all of us," Canaan said, ushering Christopher to walk alongside him. "Thinking for ourselves is a freedom and a burden that most are not used to."

"Most don't even try," Christopher said. "They act like nothing's changed. They act like Dean Perish is still the prime resident. They filter out anything they don't want to hear."

"I know," Canaan said. "They even dream of him. They create their own world. It's what people always do, one way or another."

They walked through a doorway and emerged on top of the hill they had landed together before. All around them were buildings of all kinds of shapes and sizes and colors, built all around the curves and angles of the great cauldron in the earth, the amphitheater in the center, flowers and trees and grass all around, rainbows falling through waterfalls beneath the lake overhead, people flying together playfully. The Ark looked just as it had when Christopher first saw it, but for its border being emboldened by a line of tall mountains. The tallest of them all, a volcano with its top blown off, stood dormant for now.

"It's always great to be here," Christopher said, breathing in his surroundings as they began to walk slowly down the hill. "I really thought we had lost it that night."

"It would take more than one bad dream to destroy this place," Canaan said. "Though of course it will change with time, increasingly so, as more people become lucid."

"I wonder if one day we can get off the Program completely," Christopher said. "I wonder if we'd still be able to share our dreams if we do."

"Come on now Christopher." Canaan laughed. "We are connected by more than just our BRAINs, you know that. And besides, what about the Program? What about all the people who still depend on it?"

"I'm still trying to understand it," Christopher said. "The Program seems to have a life of its own. Most people are still addicted to the antivirus. At least, children will be born without BRAINs soon. Hopefully they can look after the Earth better than we have."

"At least they have a better chance," Canaan said. "Let us only hope that we do not pass our limiting beliefs on to them."

They paused, as the sun seemed to break the clouds, brighter all of a sudden, casting light and shadows dancing all across the human sanctuary below.

"Do you think it will work out?" Christopher asked.

"Of course," Canaan said. "At the end of the day, everything will settle as it must. We have seen the light now. The question is how many more shadows must we pass through before we get there."

"Mr. Perish," a loud voice spoke from all around. The light in the sky and all around grew brighter and brighter, blinding Christopher. "Mr. Perish," it echoed again.

Christopher opened his eyes to find himself slumped back in his chair at his desk.

"Mr. Perish," the familiar mustached face of Christopher's former supervisor peeked around the doorway. "Sorry to disturb you, but the Emortal Council have been trying to contact you, they are ready to see you now."

"Thank you, Mason," Christopher said, coming back to his body and his senses. "I'm on my way."

Mason nodded and disappeared into the corridor. Christopher got up from his seat, stretched out his arms and gave a great yawn. Afternoon naps had become a regular habit for him since abandoning enforced hibernation patterns. It seemed he still had lots of sleep to catch up on, having been deprived of sufficient rest throughout his whole life, until now. Still there was more work to do now than ever, and more important work than he had ever imagined.

The sun poured through the tall windows of his office toward the top of the Libermid, warming Christopher to his core. Perhaps it was sunlight, after all, that people had most missed out on all these years inside Liberty Farm. Still, the residents demanded that the libersphere be kept overhead to protect them on rainy days. At least it was brighter most of the time, even if the same limited palette of reds and blues persisted almost everywhere he went. Perhaps he would ask Kimiko to help decorate the nursery, he thought.

As he walked through the corridors, it was still strange to be recognized by everybody, after spending most of his life effectively ignored. They raised their thumbs as they passed by, though it meant little to Christopher. They greeted him with courtesy—some genuine, some not. He could pierce through the fake smiles to see the fear and suspicion underneath. But he could look through that too, to see the love and compassion that they truly needed. It was the only way he could ever convince anyone of any positive change, for them to believe it themselves.

It was still hard for him to believe how quickly and completely his own life had transformed, though he sensed it was still only the beginning of his path rather than the end. It seemed like such a short time ago that he was just a quiet cog in a massive machine over which he felt no control, but now he was a driving force. He had walked the path from loneliness into love. He had gone from being fatherless, to becoming a father of his own. He had opened up to a whole new world, only to return and try to change the one that he spent his every day. He believed now that anything was possible. And it was all a dream.

Printed in Great Britain
by Amazon